Readers love
Pearl Love

The Uncertain Customer

"This was short, passionate and heartwarming…. Just a fast, fun read that will make you feel all warm and fuzzy inside. I loved it!"
—MM Good Book Reviews

"Read this delicious historical novella. It is a delight!"
—Prism Book Alliance

"The story is light, amusing, and very sensual. I recommend it for a quiet afternoon when you want to relax and be carried away to another place and time. Thanks, Pearl, for introducing us to Wilcox and Church."
—Rainbow Book Reviews

'Til Darkness Falls

"A good story with a fascinating plot. I'd recommend this book for fantasy fans and romantics."
—Reviews by Jessewave

Burnt Offerings

"I found myself enjoying very much the relationship of Alen with his mother, so much that, in the end, I was almost in tears."
—Elisa - My Reviews and Ramblings

By PEARL LOVE

Burnt Offerings
Juicy Bits (Dreamspinner Anthology)
Men of Steel (Dreamspinner Anthology)
'Til Darkness Falls
To Be Human
The Uncertain Customer

Published by DREAMSPINNER PRESS
http://www.dreamspinnerpress.com

to be
HUMAN
Pearl Love

Dreamspinner Press

Published by
DREAMSPINNER PRESS

5032 Capital Circle SW, Suite 2, PMB# 279, Tallahassee, FL 32305-7886 USA
http://www.dreamspinnerpress.com/

To Be Human
© 2015 Pearl Love.

Cover Art
© 2015 Paul Richmond.
http://www.paulrichmondstudio.com
Cover content is for illustrative purposes only and any person depicted on the cover is a model.

ISBN: 978-1-63216-302-8
Digital ISBN: 978-1-63216-303-5
Library of Congress Control Number: 2014950607
First Edition January 2015

Printed in the United States of America
∞
This paper meets the requirements of
ANSI/NISO Z39.48-1992 (Permanence of Paper).

To my family, who have always encouraged me to scribble away.

PROLOGUE

MAN LIVES to die. That's what it means to be human.

The quote was from some book on the human condition, one of the many Father Paul had read to me in an attempt to further my education.

So when I kill someone, am I helping him?

No, my boy. Because to take a man's life diminishes your own humanity.

The exchange was engraved in my memory, a moral lesson that would have to guide me now that Father Paul no longer could. A strange pain stabbed through my chest like a knife as my mentor's voice echoed in my head. First the only mother I'd ever known, and now the man who'd whimsically insisted I call him "father." Both were lost to me. For the first time in my life, I experienced the weight of loneliness. But like all such feelings, I perceived it only in the abstract. Father Paul had sacrificed himself for a reason, and my determination to fulfill his dying request vastly outweighed the brief hesitation I felt at the knowledge that I was leaving behind everything I'd ever known. My breath came easily, my heartbeat slow and steady as I ran in the darkness of the moonless night. My footing was sure as I crossed the shifting, windblown soil. After much reflection, I concluded that the ache in my chest was somehow a manifestation of my apparent sadness.

Books are your window onto the world, my boy. In these pages, you can learn about anything you wish to know. There is so much more to this life than what you have been shown. There is an entire world beyond these walls.

I would miss that wisdom, those pearls and nuggets I had always found so invaluable. But as I pushed my body to its limits in an effort to put distance between myself and the compound that housed the Facility, my eyes remained as dry as the desert around me. My perceived anguish grew all the more acute for my inability to express it.

FATHER PAUL hadn't been a priest. In fact, he had often proclaimed that the notion of God simply reflected the primitive nature of the human mind. But to me Father Paul had embodied everything I'd learned of that divine entity: creator, savior, friend. I understood the concept of death. The ability to deal it to others with cold, efficient precision was my very reason for existing. Yet I was finding it hard to reconcile myself to the logical understanding that my mentor was forever lost to me.

Dr. Paul Anderson, the foremost expert on genetic engineering in the country—if not the world—had been the chief architect of the extraordinary genome that made me so much more than human. The elderly scientist had been there from the beginning, watching over the woman who had pushed me into the world, squalling and red-faced like any other infant. But unlike other newborns, I had nearly perfect recall of that seminal event. I remembered Father Paul's smile, the sensation of being held in thin arms against a narrow chest. I'd relaxed at the sound of a new heartbeat booming reassuringly against my tiny head. And I remembered the trembling plea of the woman who, until moments before, had encompassed my entire world.

"I know I'm supposed to be dismissed after fulfilling the terms of my contract, but can't I stay with him?" The exhausted female voice broke into sobs. "He's my baby."

Father Paul sighed. "The colonel won't like it." The scientist looked down at the tiny boy in his arms, and I looked back at him with a focus unheard of in one so young. His demeanor transformed as his grave, scholarly expression gave way to a kindly smile. "But I'll talk to him and see what I can do. After all," he continued, his expression gaining a hint of melancholy, "a child should have a mother."

2

As Father Paul predicted, the colonel was not pleased. He had come to the delivery room to see the fruits of his team's labors, and his presence filled the sterile space like a pending storm ready to be unleashed on the unwary. "I didn't bring that bitch onto this project to coddle it. She's here only because you said growing it in a human womb would make it healthier than using a mechanical incubator."

"A wise precaution given the difficulties we've had until now, wouldn't you say, Colonel?"

Colonel Woodard glared at Father Paul, his ice-blue eyes unnerving in their intensity. "Don't get smart with me, Anderson. We aren't running a birthing center. If this project is to ramp up production to projected targets, you're going to need to figure out a faster method than natural gestation."

Father Paul returned Woodard's angry stare evenly. "As I've been saying for the past five years, quality, not quantity, should be our primary concern."

"If it were up to you," Woodard spat, gritting his teeth, "we wouldn't have anything else to show for our efforts except for this single *thing*." He injected a world of contempt into his description.

"Fortunately for all of us, the Company agrees that caution is warranted given the expense we've incurred. And he's not a 'thing,' Colonel Woodard. He can hear you, so mind what you say."

"Hear me? That *thing* is nothing but a goddamn useless baby."

But Father Paul was right. I not only heard the conversation, I comprehended everything being said about me. Turning my head on an unnaturally sturdy neck toward the newcomer, I committed the man's face to memory, intuitively understanding that this intimidating stranger was to be of some importance in my life. If the colonel had been surprised at discovering he was being studied by a newborn, his expression never revealed it. Woodard was an imposing figure for all he wore only common military fatigues rather than a uniform befitting his rank. As the person in charge of the project overseeing my development, the colonel was as much my progenitor as Father Paul. But where the scientist considered me a miracle to be cherished, Woodard had merely seen me as a tool to be used.

"Please, Colonel, may I hold him?"

Woodard continued to stare at me, ignoring the tired woman lying on the bed in the cold, sterile room while he studied the results of the project he'd been tasked to supervise. Father Paul took a step back, jostling me slightly as the larger man stepped closer to loom over him and the small bundle in his arms.

"You really do understand me, don't you?" The colonel's lips twitched in cold amusement as I stared at him with abnormal directness. "That's good. Now hear this, TM 05637. I own you. Without me, you wouldn't even exist. If you ever disappoint me, I will make you regret this day."

While growing up, I tried to see Woodard in the same paternal light as I did Father Paul, but I never learned to feel anything toward the colonel except a distant wariness. The memory of his threat stayed with me, spurring me during all of the subsequent years of my life.

"We played at being gods, but in the end, we are capable only of cruelty," Father Paul said to me one afternoon, his gaze sad as he examined me following yet another training session.

My body was marred with bruises and cuts from the myriad weapons that had been brought to bear against me, and while I had inflicted far more damage than I received, it had been a fight of many against one. It was my birthday, the last I was to spend at the Facility, but I was afforded no opportunity to celebrate. Every year Father Paul smuggled a piece of cake into the compound for me, and I was looking forward to receiving my treat later that evening after my grueling daily schedule of physical and mental drills was complete. But some undefinable aspect of his demeanor that day told me something was different.

"When I was tasked with creating you, I thought only of the science. I never anticipated all of the torment you would be forced to endure. You were raised to be a killer, but there is deep kindness inside of you. I would never have chosen this life for you had I known just how much I would come to care for you." The touch of Father Paul's wrinkled fingers against my cheek was familiar and reassuring. "I swear to you, my boy, you will be free."

Freedom. I had hardly known what the word meant, but Father Paul had been determined to offer me this gift. If only the cost had not been so high.

4

IT HAD taken Father Paul no more than two weeks to plan our escape after making the decision to see me freed. His preparation had been meticulous. He'd infiltrated the computer system and planted a false schedule that would allow us time to slip away without any of the project overseers noticing their unit was missing until it was hopefully too late. He'd mapped out the best route for us to follow to avoid detection once we were away from the compound. And now Father Paul's extensive knowledge of the Facility allowed us to proceed stealthily through the corridors of the complex, deftly avoiding the omnipresent security cameras and scouting patrols.

"We'll leave through the secondary exit since the main egress point will be too well guarded. Are you nervous, my boy?"

I regarded Father Paul steadily as he looked back at me with gentle brown eyes and a reassuring smile. "Nervous?" As always when Father Paul asked me a question concerning my emotions, I had to think about how to answer. My breathing and pulse were slightly elevated, and I supposed the slight moistness that dampened my palms qualified. "Yes."

He laughed quietly. "That's good. Fear keeps you sharp."

If such was the case, then I must have been terrified. Each second seemed to last an eternity. The monotonous passageways and drab gray walls. The distant sounds of the soldiers performing drills. The groups of civilian Facility personnel going about their business. I had experienced these things a thousand times. But now everything was in razor-sharp focus, a byproduct of my enhanced senses, my training, and the previously unknown emotion Father Paul had given a name. I moved easily in the baggy coveralls he had stolen from the cleaning crew's locker room.

"Easier to mingle and escape detection," he had explained. "Only those directly associated with the project even know you exist, so we'll be fine as long as we avoid any familiar faces."

The one-piece garment fit easily over my customary black unitard and fortunately didn't hinder my movements, though the soft soled Chinese-style slippers I wore concerned me. The shoes were suitable for the laboratory environments I usually frequented, but I knew they weren't the best option for outdoor terrain. I was unsure what to expect and wanted to be ready for any contingency. Although I'd suggested we bring along the most critical of the supplies we would need once we were out on our own, Father Paul had urged caution.

"If it looks like we're going camping, we'll only raise suspicions. We can procure what we need once we're out, except for this." Father Paul had placed a vial full of familiar blue pills in the pocket of the coveralls. "I trust you know not to lose this no matter what."

I'd silently nodded my understanding, knowing that the vial contained the means to my continued survival.

It was late, my internal clock informing me it was slightly past 0100 hours. I scanned the area constantly but detected no imminent threats. After several minutes we approached a door located at the far end of the compound from my quarters. Father Paul pressed his hand against the biometric scanner set into the adjacent wall. It pinged a moment later, the light below the scanner changing from red to green, indicating he had the clearance to proceed. I had never been through that door, and as far as I knew nothing lay beyond it. Nevertheless, I followed obediently as Father Paul passed across the threshold after the door slid open. As he led me from the restricted security area that had been my home since birth into this new, unfamiliar part of the compound, I couldn't help allowing curiosity to distract my attention.

Gone was the gunmetal façade that made the high-security area seem like a featureless maze. The white walls similarly lacked adornment, but they lent this sector the aspect of an office building rather than a military installation. Automatically memorizing the layout as we went, I noticed the activity in this part of the base was less structured than what I was accustomed to. In the restricted section, pairs of guards were assigned regular patrols, and I couldn't go five minutes without seeing a team on a routine sweep. Here, Father Paul and I had walked for nearly twice that long without encountering anyone. Though I kept on alert, I began to relax as we remained alone. My breathing rate had slowed back to normal when Father Paul abruptly stopped and turned to face me.

"Only one last section lies between us and the outside."

My pulse quickened once more in reaction to the tenseness in his voice.

"The guards on the door around the next corner are probably new," Father Paul explained. "Woodard always keeps his seasoned troops for the restricted zone. If they question you, you're my assistant."

He pressed something into my hand, and I looked down, recognizing a security badge that bore my likeness and a name I didn't have time to read before he demanded my attention once again.

"Just act naturally and everything will be fine."

As Father Paul had predicted, when we turned left into the next passage, we came upon a heavy metal door manned by two broad-shouldered figures wearing military fatigues. I followed closely on his heels as he approached the guards with a smile.

"Gentlemen," Father Paul said, showing them his own badge. The taller guard studied the ID carefully, affirming Father Paul's guess that they were new recruits. Paul Anderson had been a fixture at the Facility for nearly twenty-five years, and anyone who'd been there longer than a few months would have immediately known who he was.

"Dr. Anderson, yes, I was briefed about you. You're cleared, sir." The guard deactivated the lock with the push of a button. "And you?" the man asked, holding up his hand to block my path when I tried to follow Father Paul past the guards' station. "Identification."

I held up my fake badge and tensed as the guard scrutinized it closely.

"Stevens," the guard said, glancing over at his partner, "do you know this name? Is it on the cleared list?"

The other guard came over. "No, I don't," he replied after looking at the name on the phony ID. "Maybe he's new too."

"I'm his assistant," I told the man as Father Paul had instructed.

The guard seemed unimpressed and fixed me with a skeptical look. Father Paul stepped closer to me and leveled an annoyed glare at the guard. The bead of sweat I spied on his upper lip was the only indication of his agitation.

"We really are in a hurry, gentlemen," he said in a clipped tone. "I can assure you this young man works for me."

The guard nodded. "Okay, but I still need to call the general to confirm."

Woodard had been promoted to the higher rank several years earlier, but his disdainful attitude toward me hadn't changed since the day of my birth. If the guards alerted the general that his project was in an unauthorized area of the compound, this excursion would be over before it had even begun.

As the shorter guard moved toward the communication panel, Father Paul tensed and shot me an intent glance. Nodding imperceptibly, I fixed my attention on the taller of the pair, waiting for an opening. The soldier closed his eyes for a split second as he succumbed to a sneeze caused by the slight layer of dust that had built up on the floor. Before he could open them again, he was lying unconscious on the floor. The shorter guard looked over at his partner in shock, only to join him courtesy of the quick, surgically precise jab I delivered to his neck.

Father Paul exhaled sharply with relief. "Nice work, my boy," he said, a hint of pride slipping though his urgency. "Now let's go while we still can."

As we passed through the doorway, I allowed myself to truly believe Father Paul's plan might succeed, that we might really make good our escape. I reached into the pocket of my coveralls, reassured as my hand clutched the small vial of blue pills that contained my lifeline to the outside world.

A sensor set high into a corner of the ceiling where the corridor took a sharp turn to the left caught my attention, but it wasn't a camera, so it didn't immediately concern me. Still, something twitched in the back of my mind. I'd decided to mention the device to Father Paul when emergency lights suddenly began to flash in a clash of yellow and red, accompanied by klaxons blaring at a decibel that threatened to overwhelm my sensitive ears.

"Goddamned Woodard," Father Paul murmured.

My enhanced hearing just barely allowed me to make out the muted comment over the din. "What's happening?" I asked.

"He must have had a tracker implanted in you without bothering to inform me. It seems you've reached the end of your tether." Father

Paul didn't appear to be surprised or even really angry. Rather, his expression conveyed his acceptance of the change in the situation as he sent me a resigned glance over his shoulder. "Come, my boy. We have to hurry."

He led me along another series of nondescript corridors, moving at a speed that would be the envy of someone half his age. Reaching under the coverall, I ran my hand over the curve of my shoulder, the nearly imperceptible scar that had resided there since I was a small child suddenly making sense. I didn't recall ever injuring myself in that location, but I'd never thought to question its presence. I must have been unconscious through the implantation procedure, otherwise I'd remember the event like I did everything else that had ever happened to me. Although difficult to feel, I soon located the slight bump that revealed the low-frequency radio transmitter. My sharp ears had adjusted to the blaring of the alarms, and I picked up the sound of pounding boots as security personnel honed in unerringly on our position.

The first group of soldiers to arrive found us in a short hallway not far from the compound's secondary exit point, and maneuvered to trap us in a pincer formation. The three men positioned themselves at opposite ends of the corridor to block our escape, two ahead and one behind.

"Dr. Anderson! TM 05637! Stop where you are and surrender."

The soldiers trained their automatic rifles at me and Father Paul, the barrels pointed unerringly at the most vulnerable parts of our anatomies. I was prepared to give myself up, not wanting to get my creator in trouble, but Father Paul could be stubborn when he got a notion fixed in his head.

He pulled a handgun from somewhere beneath his white lab coat and shot with unexpected accuracy at the guards ahead of us before they could react to the shocking fact that the elderly scientist actually knew how to use a gun. One of the soldiers went down as the bullet pierced his thigh. His partner quickly shook off his astonishment and dove around the corner to avoid any additional fire. I knew the soldiers would prefer to take me alive, since I embodied hundreds of millions of dollars of cutting-edge genetic technology and decades of research. But I was well aware they wouldn't hesitate to stop me before allowing me to escape, no matter the cost. Assessing the threat potential from the rearmost guard, I turned to check the soldier's position, ready to protect Father Paul any way I could.

Seek target.

Reverting to the skills I had spent agonizing years honing to perfection was as natural to me as breathing. In this at least, even the general couldn't find fault. My field of vision broadened, allowing me to view the entire scene as though I were a removed bystander. Simultaneously my focus sharpened, bringing every detail into sharp relief. The soldier Father Paul had wounded raised his rifle, and it took me less than a nanosecond to analyze the weapon's trajectory. He was aiming, not at me, but at Father Paul, apparently planning to take out the immediate threat before concentrating on his ultimate target. The man would never have time to recognize his mistake.

Target acquired.

The team of geneticists, led by Father Paul, had been brilliant in their design. Without conscious thought, my body tensed, excess secretions from my adrenal glands preparing my muscles for exertion. My gaze, enhanced with increased visual acuity, saw the guard's finger tighten on the trigger even in the flickering shadows cast by the flashing lights. My mind, sharpened by a meticulously engineered and cultivated genius-level IQ, raced through a myriad of probabilities as I calculated the likely path of the bullet. Hundreds of hours of drills in biology, physics, ballistics, and military tactics enabled me to easily factor in every variable, from the vibration due to the accelerated rate of the soldier's heartbeat to the tiny discrepancy in his aim caused by the slight flexing of the man's forearm muscles as he fired. Subconsciously running through a multitude of plans and contingencies for taking out the remaining aggressors, I discarded the least plausible until I'd decided on the most effective tactic to both avoid the projectile myself and save Father Paul.

Eliminate.

Before I could execute my precisely constructed strategy, I found myself stumbling backward, away from the slight figure who suddenly jumped in front of me right as the rifle's report echoed off the corridor's metallic walls. Surprise momentarily threw off my reflexes, and all I could do was catch the frail body that flew into me, forced back by the impact of the .223 caliber round.

"Father Paul!"

The sound of my shout rang in my ears as we hit the ground, but even as my conscious mind froze in shock, my body operated on automatic, my actions dictated by the relentless training I'd been made to endure from nearly the moment I learned to walk. The slug's momentum sent us sliding across the polished floor of the sterile corridor, allowing me time to grab the pistol still clutched in Father Paul's hand. I quickly took out the shooter from my reclined position, my aim effortlessly precise. The remaining soldier sealing off the forward position risked a shot from his hiding place and received a bullet in his forehead for his trouble. Over the thud of the man's body falling to the ground, I heard the scuff of a boot behind me and, without looking, raised the semiautomatic over my head and fired with deadly accuracy in the direction of the auditory tell.

The klaxons continued to wail. I knew reinforcements would soon reach us, but I was heedless of the imminent danger as I gathered Father Paul into my arms. I pressed a hand against the gaping hole in his side, trying to staunch the blood pooling beneath us, staining his white coat and my own borrowed coveralls a gruesome red.

"Why?" I asked, my voice high and tight with what I recognized as stress. "I had them." My arms trembled as I struggled to process the unaccustomed, confusing onslaught of emotions assailing me. "Why did you get in the way?"

"B-because I love you." The words bubbled up from Father Paul's lips in a seep of blood, indicating the likelihood of a punctured lung.

"Love?" I knew the definition of the word in the abstract, but its significance escaped me. "What does that mean?" I asked impatiently, my insatiable desire to understand human emotions paling before the seriousness of Father Paul's condition. I didn't need to draw on my extensive medical tuition to appreciate the severity of the trauma he had suffered.

Father Paul's chuckle quickly deteriorated into a wracking cough. "That's something you will have to discover on your own. I pray you do."

The words were barely audible even with my acute hearing. Agony twisted Father Paul's wizened features at the sheer effort it must have taken for him to simply breathe against the tear perforating his lung. Even so, he lifted an unsteady hand toward me, visibly struggling as his life force ebbed. I grabbed it and pressed it against my face, shivering as his cold, blood-slicked fingers caressed my cheek. He pressed a card-sized object into my free hand.

"Now run, my boy. Run!"

I shook my head. "No, I won't leave you!" Denial screamed in my head, drowning out the wail of the alarms. *You knew I could have stopped them*, I wanted to shout. *You know what I'm capable of. You made me!* Before I could speak, Father Paul's hand fell away as his arm dropped heavily to the floor.

What happened next would forever remain a blur in my memory. I suppose my self-preservation instincts kicked in, enjoining me to survive and complete my mission at all costs. After imprinting his cherished features in my memory one last time, I left my creator's body in the sterile hallway. As I passed the soldier Father Paul had shot, I paused to take the knife from the holster at his waist and used it to quickly cut the homing device out of my shoulder. The cold steel sliced into my skin with a burning sting, but the small discomfort was nothing compared to the crushing pain in my chest.

I rammed the butt of the stolen gun down on the tracker in a sharp blow, reducing the device to a mess of broken components. As I scattered the pieces with my slipper, I realized I needed some footwear that wouldn't track the blood I'd just walked through. I tried not to think about the source of the crimson fluid as I appropriated a pair of ill-fitting boots from the dead guard lying closest to the exit. The keycard Father Paul had given me enabled me to slip past the final checkpoints, and I reached my destination without further detection.

Acting on autopilot, I disposed of the blood-splattered coveralls in a trash incinerator located near the exit, taking care to first retrieve Father Paul's precious gift from the pocket. A quick glance revealed the absence of any hostiles, and I sped through the remaining stretch of tunnel leading to the exterior of the compound. Wearing nothing but the stolen boots and the one-piece bodysuit that had been my only clothing for the majority of my life, I vanished into the darkness blanketing a featureless expanse of desiccated grass and heat-baked dirt.

Less conspicuous attire. Money. Food. These were my immediate concerns. It took me less than a minute to cover the half-mile distance to the electrified perimeter fence surrounding the compound. My body rapidly adjusted to the nighttime cold—blood vessels drawing rapidly into my body to conserve heat. In a single jump, I cleared the fence, a rush of adrenal fluid enabling my muscles to perform beyond the peak of normal human agility. I landed nimbly on the far side of the fence and resumed my flight, heading away from the base, which was starting to bustle with signs of increased activity. Floodlights turned on, illuminating the brutal desert landscape. The edge of the beams fell short of me by mere inches as I moved beyond their reach. Pursuit would come swiftly, and I schooled myself to think of nothing but escape.

But my mind refused to stay focused on the task at hand. The unbearable reality of Father Paul's death chased itself around in my head in an endless loop of anguish. My mentor, my guide, my father was gone. My sense of direction and purpose had been taken from me, and for the first time in my life, I felt completely alone.

ONE

DAVID BOPPED his head as he hummed along with the song playing on the radio. He'd found the only noncountry station that existed on this stretch of highway and programmed it on two of his preset stations in case he accidentally deleted it from one of them. One hand was stuck out the window to enjoy the pushback of air at seventy miles per hour while he tapped the beat on his steering wheel with the fingers of the other. As he drove east on US-84, the small town of Clovis, New Mexico rapidly became a speck in his rearview mirror. The day was surprisingly pleasant for early June in the Southwest, the temperature comfortably on the tolerable side of hot. The wind felt wonderful on his scalp as it riffled through his hair, occasionally whipping it across his face and reminding him he needed a haircut. Fluffy clouds floated along in the clear sky, forcing David to squint his eyes against the rays of sunlight that randomly broke through. A brief spate of spring rain had coaxed the local flora out of hibernation, and desert flowers of all varieties provided dots of color on the harsh landscape.

The highway traffic was nonexistent. A quick glance at the radio clock showed he was making good time. David made the drive back and forth to Albuquerque every six months in order to attend a meeting of franchise owners for the general retail store he ran in Lubbock, Texas. It was a five-and-a-half-hour trip one way, but he didn't mind the drive. Plus, he was watching his pennies. The success of his store meant he pulled in a decent salary, but he didn't like to splurge on needless luxuries. The biannual conference had gone well, and he'd made some good contacts with manufacturers and suppliers who were looking to expand their product lines into the growing market of West Texas. But he wasn't much for small talk, and the endless rounds of after-hours socializing had taken their toll on his energy level. He was more than ready to go home and get back to his daily routine.

"David, you're so booooring," an old boyfriend had told him. He couldn't deny the claim, but boring or not, he was content with his drama-free life. He'd left Oklahoma to avoid his father's not-so-silent condemnation once he'd finally confessed to liking boys more than girls. He hadn't been sure about staying in Texas after finishing college, but when he was offered the chance to buy into the franchise, he'd jumped on it. David liked the simple, productive life he'd made for himself, and it didn't particularly bother him that he'd ended up spending much of it alone. The last thing he wanted was anything to disrupt the oasis of calm he'd so painstakingly cultivated around himself.

Keeping a habitual eye out for state troopers as he sped toward the state line, David glanced over at the fries remaining in the greasy bag lying on the passenger's seat. He reached out to snag a few and almost missed the lonely figure standing on the side of the road, arm extended and thumb raised.

"What the hell?"

He told himself not to stop. That would be really stupid. Who in the hell picked up hitchhikers in this day and age? Though he knew it was a bad idea, he slammed on the brakes, his brand-new pads proving up to the task of slowing him to a stop in less than fifty yards. He shook his head, disgusted with himself, as he pulled over onto the shoulder.

You're a sweet boy, David, but it's going to get you into trouble someday.

"Yeah, yeah," he mumbled, annoyed as his mother's oft-repeated words of caution intruded into his thoughts. He looked into his rearview mirror and watched the figure jog toward his car. A guy, his brain identified. A kid, it clarified a moment later. David turned away from the reflection and groaned.

"Shit."

A perky nose thrust through the passenger's side window, and a pair of big brown eyes blinked adorably at him. *Adorably?*

"Hi," the kid said. His voice was throaty and uncertain, caught on the cusp between lingering youth and full manhood.

"Hey," David responded. "You need a lift?" *Stupid question.* He would have been embarrassed, but he forgave himself for the brain glitch as he studied the gorgeous young man standing beside his car.

The kid looked to be about eighteen, no more than nineteen, though the way he was nervously clutching the strap of his small backpack tempted David to revise down his estimate. The kid had neatly trimmed, wavy black hair and was on the short side of tall, his slim, athletic build all too easy to see with the way he was dressed. Cutoff denim shorts rode high on his thighs, and a tight, sleeveless tank top didn't quite meet the waistband of his shorts, revealing a strip of olive-toned skin. He looked Hispanic. Or maybe he was Apache or Navajo, though they didn't usually live this far east.

David wondered if the young man was aware of the provocative image he presented, or if, perhaps, that was the point. *Shit. Is the kid a hooker?* Reassessing his previous opinion from *bad idea* to *fucking bad idea*, David realized he was staring at the gap between the kid's shirt and shorts, hoping to catch another glimpse of that bare midriff. Dragging his gaze upward toward the hopeful face, David tried to distract himself by once again guessing where the kid might hail from. Asian? Mediterranean? None of the kid's features definitively suggested his ancestry. The only thing David was certain of was his initial appraisal. *Adorable.*

"Yes. Where are you headed?" The young man's accent was as nonspecific as the rest of him.

"Lubbock," David answered, mentally kicking himself as he spoke. He didn't need this. The best thing he could do would be to tell the kid, sorry, he couldn't help, and drive off. But his foot stayed stubbornly on the brake when the kid's fluttering lashes—ridiculously long and a half-shade lighter than the hair on his head—temporarily shielded the eyes silently begging him for assistance. The kid braced his hands on top of the car, the move causing his shirt to ride up, finally revealing a flat, toned stomach. David tightened his grip on the steering wheel as he surreptitiously attempted to adjust the suddenly tight fit of his jeans. After clearing his throat, he asked, "Is that where you want to go?"

"Sure," the hitchhiker replied. "If that's where you're headed."

It had been a long time since he'd heard that particular tone in a man's voice, but for a second David could have sworn the kid was flirting with him. His gaze narrowed warily as he studied the kid's face, but he couldn't detect anything but innocence in those guileless eyes. Resigning himself to his idiocy, David raked the fingers of his right hand through his hair in frustration as he hit the switch at his left elbow to unlock the car doors. A shy smile was his reward, and he cursed as his jeans shrank even more in the vicinity of his groin. He moved the fries out of the way as the hitchhiker settled his bare, tanned limbs onto the passenger seat. The kid's legs seemed to go on for miles before ending at a smallish pair of sandaled feet.

"What's your name?" David asked, pointedly ignoring the temptation of those long legs.

There was the slightest beat of hesitation. "Um, Tim."

David glanced at his new companion. "Are you sure?" He laughed, attempting to distract himself from the fact there was a hot guy in his car and it had been way too long since he'd last had sex. Telling himself he'd wanted it that way wasn't helping even a little.

The kid frowned for a moment as though he was unsure of the joke. Suddenly his face cleared and he nodded. "Yes," he said. "Tim Paul."

David hadn't shifted out of Drive, so he only had to lift his foot from the brake pedal to set the car in motion. Glancing over his left shoulder to check for traffic, he angled back onto the road. "Nice name. It's unusual to have two first names, but it's nice." *Well, that sounded dumb*, he groused silently to himself in disgust. "David Conley," he said by way of introduction. Tim reached out and took hold of his right hand, which had been resting on the gearshift, pumping it up and down firmly in a proper, if overly fervent, handshake. A warm tingle seemed to travel up David's arm from the spot where their hands met, and he was alarmingly disappointed when the kid let go. David wrapped both hands tightly around the steering wheel, trying to rid himself of the lingering sensation.

"Thank you," Tim said. "I really appreciate it. I've been walking for hours and didn't think anyone would ever stop."

David blinked, bemused at the deadpan tone, like Tim was giving him a situation report. He had never been particularly talkative himself, but since he was, in effect, the kid's host during the remainder of their trip, he figured he should at least make an effort. "Where are you coming from?" From of the corner of his eye, David saw Tim turn his head to gaze out the side window.

"Out west."

The answer was vague, but David didn't feel he had a right to press, seeing as how they'd just met. "How old are you?" he asked instead, going for a more innocuous, but important, piece of information. Again there was an almost imperceptible pause.

"Nineteen."

Shit. He was a full twelve years older than his passenger. David tried not to think about it, but he couldn't stop his brain from doing the math. He tried to dredge up the fuzzy memories of the prelaw class he'd taken in college, back when he'd entertained delusions of becoming an attorney. Mental exhaustion and financial reality had put an end to those dreams, but he did remember a lecture about statutory rape laws and was mildly relieved when he realized Tim was well over the age of consent in Texas. Not that he was planning to do anything with the kid other than drop him off somewhere in Lubbock.

Liar.

David pointedly ignored his doubting inner voice. He might not end up in jail over this, but the kid was still young and had no business being out hitching rides from strangers. David was just glad he'd found Tim before someone with a lesser sense of ethics picked him up.

Fighting against his natural reticence, he kept the conversation banal, though he tried to work in questions that might lead him to where Tim was really from among mostly one-sided discussions of the weather and the declining state of college basketball. By the time they reached the Texas border, David had learned that Tim had been on the road for a little over a week and had managed to get this far by hitching with a trucker. Some avoidance about the topic led David to the conclusion Tim hadn't been left in middle-of-nowhere New Mexico by choice. The kid didn't seem traumatized, however, so David didn't think—or rather, hoped—he hadn't been assaulted.

"So you're from California?"

David had decided he might as well try the direct approach, but he received only a noncommittal "hmm" for his trouble. Whether he'd guessed right or was way off, Tim apparently wasn't going to be any more forthcoming on the subject. When a growling sound issued from Tim's stomach, David gave up his attempt at playing detective and pulled off the highway at Farwell. He drove to a local diner he'd stopped at on previous trips back from the conference. Although he was more than ready to get home and sleep in his own bed, he couldn't blame the kid for needing food. Who knew when he'd last had a decent meal?

"You'll like this place," he said as he pulled into a parking space in the lot next to the diner. "They serve up the best hamburgers this side of Austin."

Tim got out of the car without comment, and David sighed in mild consternation at his lack of reaction to the prospect of delicious greasy food. What kid his age didn't like hamburgers? David lost track of the idle thought as he followed Tim into the diner, making a conscious effort not to notice the snug fit of the kid's overly short cutoffs. Forcing his gaze to less dangerous territory, he smiled at the familiar woman standing behind the lunch counter.

"Hiya, Mabel."

"David! Good to see you again." He hadn't seen Mabel since last December, but she'd told him once that she prided herself on remembering the name of every repeat customer, no matter how infrequent the visits. She winked at him flirtatiously like she always did, though she was old enough to be his mother. "I see you brought a friend with you?"

He chuckled at her unsubtle nosiness but avoided answering by glancing at his companion. Tim was staring up at the menu board hanging over the counter like it was written in Martian. David was puzzled. There wasn't anything particularly unusual on offer, just the regular fare of burgers, fries, onion rings, and malts.

"See anything you want? How about the number one combo?" he added after half a minute of uncomfortable silence.

Tim batted long eyelashes at him before nodding. "Yes, that's fine." He reached into his pocket and pulled out what amounted to no more than a few dollars and some change. "Is this enough?"

It wasn't, so over the kid's protests, David bought him the hamburger, fries, and drink combo, getting the same thing for himself, though he substituted a lemonade for the soft drink. He led the way over to his favorite booth, which was next to the front window and offered a clear view of the highway. The diner catered to people on the go, and it wasn't long before Mabel was bringing over their order. With a smile and a swish of her broad hips, she left them to their meal. David sipped on his lemonade as he watched Tim inhale his food, starting with the massive burger. He waited until only three fries and bit of soda remained before broaching the subject that had been worrying him for the past two hours.

"Do you have some place to go when we reach Lubbock?" He sighed when Tim merely stared down at the smear of ketchup decorating his nearly empty plate. "Hell, kid. I wouldn't feel right if I simply let you go off without knowing you're okay." Tim refused to look up, but David pressed on, knowing the issue needed to be confronted. "I mean," he continued as sternly as he could, "you should be home with your folks or in school or something, not traipsing across the country by yourself."

"Father Paul is dead."

The sentence was spoken quietly, as though the kid was afraid to say it out loud. David wasn't sure whether this Father Paul was really Tim's parent or a priest, but it was clear the man was someone important to him.

"I'm sorry," he said reflexively. "Um, what about your mom?"

Narrow shoulders answered him with a shrug.

David figured she must be deceased as well, or was otherwise missing in action. Without asking, he guessed there weren't any other relatives waiting in the wings to give the kid a hand. Sympathy filled him at the thought of Tim being all alone in the world. He knew what that was like. When he'd left home for college, his father had told him in no uncertain terms he would have to make his own way from then on. He'd done it, but it hadn't been easy. Feeling the kid's pain made him want to help, but he wasn't convinced he should get any more involved than he already had. David steeled himself to say what he knew he must.

"I know you're technically a grown man and all, but even so, I can't let you wander the streets with nowhere to go. Why don't I take you to a police station when we reach Lubbock? Surely there's someone you can call—"

Tim's reaction was immediate and startling. David left off in midsentence when the kid abruptly jumped to his feet, drawing several stares from the other patrons. He was halfway out of the booth before David's surprise wore off enough for him to grab a thin wrist.

"Hey, hey! Calm down."

David held on until Tim acknowledged him with a gaze darkened by some emotion he struggled to name. He glanced nervously at the other people in the diner, hoping no one thought he was some sort of kidnapper or child molester. While the kid had said he was nineteen, it was unlikely the casual onlooker would place him at much over seventeen. Tim's skimpy outfit called particular attention to the slimness of his frame, and David, who was a slightly overweight six feet, felt like a hulking giant by comparison. A couple of the other patrons stared at him with growing suspicion as he tugged gently at Tim's arm. The kid might have been a buck forty-five soaking wet, but David quickly became aware that his pulling hadn't budged Tim so much as an inch. Confusion brushed over his mind, but he set it aside in the face of the more immediate problem.

"Please, sit down." He didn't let go until Tim relented and was, once again, seated across from him.

"No police. Please. I don't want to go to the police."

Tim spoke in a monotone, but David suspected he was trying desperately to hide his fear. He had no clue why the kid seemed so reluctant to seek help, but his primary concern was making sure he was safe.

You're a sweet boy, David—

"Shut up, Ma," he mumbled beneath his breath. Tim looked at him strangely as if he'd heard the cryptic comment, but David knew he had barely been audible to his own ears. "Look, kid," he pressed, "it really would be the best thing."

A soft dark curl fell against Tim's forehead as he vehemently shook his head, his face a study in obstinacy. David sighed in defeat, recognizing that option was effectively closed.

"Okay, no cops."

Tim instantly relaxed, his body language one of extreme relief as he slumped back onto the cheap faux leather covering the diner's booths.

"So, what do you want to do?" David asked.

Tim gazed up at him from beneath thick black lashes and wetted his dry lips with the tip of his tongue. Whether the look was intended to be so outrageously suggestive, David couldn't be sure, but he groaned silently as his wayward body reacted in a shamefully predictable manner.

"Can't I go home with you?"

Store owner disgraced after dalliance with teenaged runaway. David could see the headline in his mind clear as day. Even though technically the kid was legal, David still felt like a dirty old man when he grew instantly hard at the ostensibly innocent request. He shook his head, determined to kindly but firmly refuse the entreaty, but when hesitant fingers settled lightly on the back of his hand, he felt his resolve vanish faster than a twenty dollar bill in Vegas.

"Shit."

TWO

I GAZED out the car window as we drove through the town. Lubbock, the man had called it. When I was ten years old, the general had demanded I memorize a world map and the entirety of the Encyclopedia Britannica's online version, a feat I had accomplished anew every year since. Trivial facts about the town came to me readily—*population: 225,856; location: lat 33.65N, long 101.82W*—but those bare details didn't capture the locale's most important aspect. This genuinely human city would guide me toward the first step of fulfilling Father Paul's final wish—that I learn to experience life as an ordinary person.

Perhaps someone more accustomed to these environs would have found them dull. There wasn't much to see beyond small isolated retail establishments, sometimes grouped together in what the man called a "strip mall," and the occasional refueling station. However, as we moved beyond the more commercial sectors into a residential area, I paid great attention to the passing scenery as I attempted to memorize as many details as possible.

Recalling my studies on the various types of organized human habitation, I identified the new locale as a neighborhood. People and domesticated animals residing in houses and apartment buildings crammed together in a small area. There were people of all shapes and sizes walking about or riding in cars, but some of them had clearly not attained their full growth. *Children*, I apprehended with something akin to shock. The only child I'd ever known was myself. I was fascinated by the small figures of varying heights as they walked, ran, and otherwise ambulated along narrow sidewalks lined with grass. Some used more efficient modes of transportation, riding upon two-wheeled vehicles or whizzing along with the help of multiwheeled footwear. Among them were several forms of the species *Canis lupus familiaris*.

I wondered if the children understood how lucky they were to live in such close proximity to one another, how fortunate they were not to have grown up as an isolated lab experiment. I had asked Father Paul once, after I'd learned about the concept of "siblings," why I didn't have one. Father Paul had merely smiled at me sadly and said, "Because you're special, my boy." The response had only made me feel more alone.

I jerked slightly as the blare of a horn and a muttered curse interrupted my thoughts.

"Damn kids." The man rolled down his window to shout at the young girl who had run into the street after a ball. "Hey, be careful!" He shook his head. "Always gotta watch where you're driving around here." The man's amused tone belied his feigned annoyance.

Glancing at my companion surreptitiously, I thought back to our first encounter. I understood now that the emotion I'd experienced when the man—David Conley—had stopped for me on the highway was extreme relief. I'd been wary at first, ready to defend myself like I had to against the truck driver who'd demanded I repay the favor of getting a lift with a sexual act. I had considered it, since I was in a hurry, but when the man reached for me I'd broken his thumb by reflex. The trucker had all but tossed me out onto the highway, nursing his injured digit as he leveled vicious but idle threats at the hitchhiker who'd dared fight back. But within moments of approaching David's car, my caution had vanished. The sensations that had filled me when he offered me a ride were very similar to what I'd always felt around Father Paul. Calmness. Safety. Peace. My intuition had inexplicably urged me to recognize David as someone I could trust. Yet my reaction to the man who'd picked me up was different from how I'd responded to my creator in a way I found difficult to categorize.

As it had several times in the past few hours, my gaze wandered over David's thick hair, so dark as to appear brown until the sunlight revealed the gold hidden within the strands. Seemingly on its own, my gaze continued its journey, tracing down the strong column of David's neck and past the impressive broadness of his shoulders. Long practice at sizing up sparring partners enabled me to measure his proportions to within a fraction: height 6.03 feet, weight 190.285 pounds. Yet I was unable to so easily quantify the sum total of the effect he had on me.

Every time I looked into David's deep blue eyes, I felt a strange tightening in my body. My heart rate had increased by 5 percent when our gazes met over the chipped table at the diner in Farwell, and it had fallen only slightly during the remainder of the drive to Lubbock. The efficiency of my breathing had also decreased, my lungs working as though I were engaged in light exercise. My cheeks even felt warmer than normal, indicating that an excess of blood had diverted to that particular region of my face. I couldn't discern the cause of my odd physical response. Maybe it was simply gratitude at being rescued from a difficult situation. Separating the nuances of feelings that comprised a given sentiment had never been easy for me. My discomfort with emotions was probably the only thing about me the general hadn't considered a failure.

However, the basis of David's reaction to me was unmistakable. He had been singularly unsuccessful in hiding that his interest went beyond merely doing a good deed for a stranger in need of help. Whenever my shirt inched up, his gaze tracked unerringly to my bared midriff. His pulse rate had undergone a substantial increase when I'd shaken his hand in thanks. And at the diner, each time I'd wrapped my lips around my straw to take a sip of my drink, I could almost feel the increased thermal output from David's body.

Homosexual: a man who engages in sexual congress with other men. Father Paul had explained to me once, quite reluctantly, that the details of my appearance had been designed not only to enable me to blend in with nearly any population but also to appeal to certain types of men as well as to heterosexual women. I filed the discovery away in the mental file I was compiling about my rescuer.

David seemed to dislike the prospect of silence and kept up a steady flow of chatter as he drove. But since he offered a variety of personal information as he talked, I had no objections to the aimless monologue. David explained that he owned a franchise of an apparently well-known retailer and was in charge of the day-to-day running of his particular store. He also mentioned that he was originally from a town in Oklahoma, though he neglected to offer its name.

"Why did you move to Lubbock?" Direct questions, I'd been told, were often the best way to obtain desired information.

David shifted his shoulders awkwardly. "Just wanted to make a fresh start."

I paused in an attempt to draw David out, but he remained strangely unforthcoming on the subject. Apparently I needed to brush up on my interrogation skills, but my curiosity would have to wait. We had passed the city limits precisely twenty-three minutes prior and were turning onto the street on which David said his home was located. I sat up straighter in anticipation of seeing a real-world, functional dwelling. Before I could inquire about our ETA, I remembered at the last moment to simply ask, "How much farther?"

"About five minutes," David answered with a smile. I'd obviously said something amusing, though I wasn't sure what.

It was actually only three minutes until David turned his car into a space defined by an expanse of pavement demarcated with evenly spaced lines. The lot, which was about half-full of other vehicles, was surrounded on three sides by identical looking buildings. My memory provided the nomenclature for the arrangement—*a subdivision*—but I still found it extremely curious.

"They all look the same. Like barracks."

"You think?" David blinked as he looked around, apparently seeing the familiar sight with new eyes. "Yeah, I guess so. I never thought about it before. These planned residences are pretty common around here." He glanced at me nonchalantly. "How about where you're from?"

"I suppose," I replied, artlessly dodging his clumsy attempt to ferret out information. Neither of us had gotten very far with that subject, though I suspected David's reasons for being evasive weren't nearly as complicated as mine. I was relieved when he let the matter drop as we got out of the car. While he retrieved a small bag from the backseat, I examined the block of housing units. The glare of the setting sun obscured my vision, but my pupils contracted to a diameter normal humans couldn't achieve, allowing me to examine the multiple facades of indistinguishable, white aluminum siding and brick-red trim without discomfort. "These are called town houses, correct?"

"Um, yeah." David frowned at what had apparently been an odd question. I made a note to be more careful with my queries. David's bewilderment lingered on his face as he jerked his chin in the direction of one particular building. "Mine is this way."

I followed David to the dwelling two units to the right of where we'd parked. David went up a short flight of stairs before fumbling with another set of keys he'd pulled from his pocket as his duffle tried to slip off his shoulder. Without asking, I took his bag and reminded myself to return the grateful smile I received. David stepped inside but paused just past the threshold, blocking my way before I could do likewise. He scratched the back of his head and glanced at me over his shoulder. My gaze fixed on the slight flush of color that had appeared along the bridge of his nose. Once again, the efficiency of my breathing mysteriously dipped.

"Sorry about the mess," David mumbled sheepishly before continuing inside. "I wasn't exactly expecting company."

I wasn't sure what he considered a "mess," but from what I could observe, nothing seemed out of order. Rather, it looked like a place where someone lived, and my curiosity peaked as I studied my surroundings. The domicile was not untypical of those I had been shown during my assimilation training. From my vantage point near the front door, I analyzed the position of the off-white partitioning walls and concluded that the rooms had been arranged to make the most of the limited space.

"Thanks," David said as I handed him his bag after dropping my backpack by the door. He placed his bag beside mine before turning back toward the room. "This is the living room." He led me farther into the dwelling, pausing to swipe up a discarded shirt lying on the back of the three-seater sofa. Forming an L with the sofa was a chair upholstered in the same shade of muted brown. A low faux-wood table covered with a couple of magazines and various handheld electronic devices took up the space between them. The sofa faced a moderately large-screen television that hung on the opposite wall of the room.

"The furniture came with the place," David explained. "Nothing fancy, but it's comfortable enough." He stepped over to the table to arrange the magazines into a single pile. "I keep meaning to buy new stuff, but haven't gotten around to it yet." He reached hesitantly for a mug sitting on a coaster but apparently decided not to move it right then. He noticed that I was staring at the TV and waved a hand toward it. "You're more than welcome to watch it whenever you want. Do you have a favorite show? I have no idea what kids your age watch these days."

"No, I don't," I replied, not sure whether David's interest was genuine or simply another attempt to quiz me. The television could prove useful, allowing me the opportunity to keep abreast of news and to expand my knowledge of popular culture. Such intel could be vital in helping me integrate into this new life while I strove to avoid my old one.

"Damn."

The expletive drew my attention, and I saw David had knocked the fortunately empty mug onto the carpeted floor while straightening up the table. I absently watched the way my host's buttocks pressed against the soft denim of his jeans as he bent in order to reach the low surface. My toes, which poked over the edge of my too-small sandals, unaccountably curled into the dark brown pile carpet, and, accustomed to monitoring my body for any indications of stress, I automatically noted the slight increase in my heart rate as well as a strange tightness in the front of my shorts.

"Um, the kitchen is off to your right," David said after he straightened, pointing in the indicated direction. "I don't have a lot of food on hand, but we could stop at the store if you're hungry."

"Thank you, but I'm fine for now," I replied.

Later, I knew I would need to seek out another meal high in vitamin B12 to offset my condition. The hamburger I'd eaten would saturate my system with the nutrient, boosting my encumbered ability to absorb the essential vitamin. But a food-based source like the burger would last me only a few hours at a stretch, requiring a constant intake. I would have to be careful if I wanted to avoid relying too much on the supply of medication Father Paul had slipped me before my escape. It was all I had, and once it was gone, I would follow soon after.

At the Facility, I'd received daily B12 injections in addition to a weekly dose of oral medication to counteract my inability to metabolize the vitamin. But out here, I had only the pills and my knowledge of what foods could best temporarily give me what I needed since I'd been designed to be resistant to over-the-counter supplements. Such was the failsafe the project overseers had insisted be built into my genome. Father Paul had explained that the project coordinators required I be unable to survive on my own for very long, since they deemed me too dangerous to be let off my leash indefinitely. Distracting myself from thoughts of my manufactured disability, I indulged my curiosity by glancing through the open doorway, noting the contents and arrangement of the dwelling's food preparation unit.

The room was half the size of the living area, the walls broken only by the opening to the rest of the house and one other door, which I guessed led outside the residence. The Formica counters were worn, as if they had seen years of use without being replaced, but they and the tiled floor were within an acceptable range of sanitation. The sink was split into two stainless steel basins, one of which was empty, while a small stack of dishes peeked over the lip of the other. The stove was the same color as the countertops except for the speckle of dried stains in various hues, indicating David often fixed his own meals. A low-pitched hum of a compressor announced the presence of a serviceable refrigeration unit sitting catty-corner to the stove.

My interest was in no way feigned. I wasn't accustomed to normal food or how it was prepared. My usual diet consisted of a carefully prepared porridge-like substance designed to provide the optimal combination of calories and nutrients required to sustain me, but that was all. Lunch at the diner had been a revelation, and my tongue was still tingling even so many hours later from the myriad of never-before-encountered flavors and textures. I knew David must have thought me strange, but I'd been overwhelmed by the sheer quantity of choices on the menu. Most of the items I knew only from books, and I'd had no idea where to begin. The prospect of learning to make those delicious foods for myself intrigued me, and I wondered if I could convince David to teach me.

"Will I be sleeping here?" I asked, gesturing toward the living room.

A strained expression unexpectedly crossed David's face before he shook his head. "Uh, no. I have a guest bedroom. Well, sort of." David headed toward the flight of stairs at the far end of the living room. The carpet stretched up the stairs and extended onto the second floor of the dwelling. We emerged into a small hallway bracketed by three doors. The two on the left were open, revealing a room easily identified as a hygiene/biological waste disposal facility and another, which appeared to be filled with a collection of computer equipment.

"Like I said, I have a second bedroom, but I mainly use it as a home office." David maneuvered through the cluttered space, pushing a couple of boxes labeled with images of a laser printer and a fax machine out of his way. Moving to the far wall, he lifted several more boxes—one for a cell phone, some others for a computer monitor and a keyboard tray—off a large object hidden by the empty cardboard containers. "Sorry, again, about all this junk. I have a hard time throwing stuff away." David grunted as he reached for a box that had wedged itself into a corner. "You never know when you might need something."

I listened to David's rambling with only half of my attention as his efforts revealed a bed covered in dusty sheets.

Nothing like curling up in bed with a good book, my boy.

The observation from my mentor popped into my head unbidden, bringing with it a heaviness that made it difficult to breathe. Grief. I could recognize it more easily now. It took some effort, but I managed to banish the unwanted emotion by concentrating on David's struggles to unearth the buried piece of furniture.

"Okay," David huffed, wiping his hands against his jeans. "That should do. I just need to change the sheets and you should be all set—"

I had moved closer to observe David's progress and was mere inches from him when he suddenly turned around to face me. Fascinated, I watched as the blue of his irises disappeared, swallowed by rapidly dilating pupils as our gazes locked. A quick self-assessment revealed that my current posture, standing with my clasped hands behind my back at military rest, had caused my shirt to ride up and pull tight across my chest. David licked his lips, his breathing quickening, and when I noted the hint of color splashed across his cheekbones, a plan began to form in my mind.

An unexpected opportunity had presented itself in the person of David Conley. "That most intimate of human connections," to quote Father Paul, often involved the psychological along with the physical. The lesson had been meant to enhance my infiltration and espionage skills, but to the dismay of certain of my superiors, the underlying subject of human emotion had found in me an eager, if unremarkable, student. David's reaction confirmed my theory about his predilections, and I was aware I could easily use my rescuer's attraction to foster an attachment between us, thus ensuring my own safety. When I entered puberty, my instructors introduced the concept of seduction as a tool I might find useful during a mission, explaining to me the effect a touch, a look, a certain tone of voice could have on another person. Although Father Paul had strenuously objected to the lessons, I'd been made to practice various techniques with both male and female volunteers until I'd gained satisfactory proficiency. It probably wouldn't take much effort on my part to initiate a sexual relationship between us, but would it be fair to deceive someone who'd done nothing but help me?

David suddenly blinked and shook his head, breaking the silent tension between us. Still occupied by my unaccustomed moral dilemma, I could think of nothing to say as he sidled around me and headed toward the hallway, nearly tripping over a box that had toppled from its stack in his haste.

"Uh, so my room is over there." David pointed vaguely toward the door directly across from the guest room. "And you saw the bathroom, right?" He barely paused for my acknowledging nod, the hint of color still visible on his cheeks. "Okay, then. I got up really early this morning to make the drive home, so I'm going to hit the hay. Just knock on the door if you need anything." With that, David disappeared into his room and shut the door behind him with a firm and audible click.

I stood staring at the closed door for a moment but was no more certain about how I should proceed than before David had made good on his escape. "What should I do, Father Paul?" I mused aloud as I headed back downstairs to retrieve my backpack. It held my pills, and I didn't like it to be out of my sight for long. After stashing it safely in my newly assigned quarters, I decided to make use of the sanitation room. Several days' worth of dirt was caked onto my skin, and a shower was an immediate necessity.

I shed my stolen clothes and dropped them carelessly onto the cool, tan-colored floor tiles. I'd come across a convenience store on the outskirts of Fort Sumner, and it had been simple to bypass the rudimentary security system. Once I'd procured some new garments and other essential supplies, I'd buried my one-piece uniform in the dirt behind the store and continued east on foot. I hadn't had a particular destination in mind, only that I wanted to put as much distance between myself and the Facility as possible. Deep down, I knew it was as much the memory of Father Paul's fallen, motionless figure as my reluctance to be captured that had pressed me onward.

A few days on the open road had begun to test even my limits, and after a week, I'd been ready to drop from exhaustion. Without money, food had been harder to find than I'd anticipated, and the elements had taken their toll as I'd trekked through the Southwestern desert. I thought I'd been saved when the trucker picked me up, but the encounter ended after only a few unpleasant hours. David had found me right when I'd started to doubt how much longer I could go on. Our encounter seemed the embodiment of an intriguing concept I'd read about in one of Father Paul's books. Destiny.

The same tan-colored tiles also covered the walls and ceiling, making the room resemble a featureless enclosure that reminded me uncomfortably of the Facility. I studied the room, ignoring the functional items I recognized like the sink, toilet, and tub, and focused instead on the personal objects strewn about. In addition to the toothbrush and paste sitting on the sink, I saw a blade embedded at the end of a vulcanized rubber shaft. A razor for shaving. I'd never had to use one myself, but I remembered the shadow that had darkened David's jaw, and wondered how he would look when he removed the growth of stubble. A lightweight plaid robe hung from a hook on the door, and I leaned forward and rubbed my fingers over the fabric. The scent that wafted up to my nose instantly brought David to mind, and I stared down at my cock inquisitively when it unexpectedly twitched.

Arousal. I'd received extensive lessons in biology and human anatomy so I could better understand the most proficient way to end a target's life, and the instruction had naturally extended to human sexuality. But this was the first time I'd ever experienced any symptoms myself. I knew the signs David had exhibited indicated his attraction to me, but what did my condition mean? Could I be attracted to David in return? I didn't even know whether I was capable of something so profoundly ordinary.

Exhaustion from days of being on the run suddenly caught up with me, and I went through the motions of showering with what remained of my flagging energy. Once I was clean, I returned to my room, passing by my host's as I went. A sound came from David's room, and I paused to stare at his closed door. I waited until I heard it again, and judging that it wasn't an expression of pain, I continued on to my own bed. Fresh linens were sitting on top of the mattress, but I decided the task could wait until morning. Dropping face-first onto the old, dusty sheets, I was asleep in an instant.

SECURITY CAMERA footage of the unit's escape played on the screen as it had on a near endless loop for the past five days. General Woodard watched the film coldly, his gaze revealing nothing as he saw the guards remove the bodies of the slain men from the corridor for the thirty-second time. Despite himself, he was impressed at the ruthless efficiency with which TM 05637 had dispatched three highly trained soldiers in the time it had taken his team to realize the unit was even missing.

"Sentimental old fool."

Woodard's eyes narrowed into slits. He glared at the image of the retreating gurney that wheeled the good doctor away. He had no doubts about who had instigated the breakout. Anderson had always thought too much of his creation. Hell, the man had treated the damn thing like a son. Woodard supposed the scientist's decision to end TM 05637's involvement in the project wasn't all that surprising, despite the fact that the venture was the entire reason the little freak existed in the first place.

"Sir, what are your orders?"

He glanced at the brawny figure standing at attention at his left arm. A forensic team had scoured the evidence collected from the scene as well as the security footage for clues as to where the unit might have gone, but had come up blank. After forcing him to sit on his ass for a week, the tech rats had finally admitted defeat and given him the go-ahead to hunt down the unit. "Now, Sergeant, we find our runaway and retrieve it." He looked back at the screen, his gaze narrowing at the pools of blood that marked where his men had fallen. "By any means necessary."

"That won't be easy." Sergeant Cooper was a veritable bear of a man, a grizzled veteran who had been under his direct command for years. Cooper didn't hold Woodard's rank in any awe and always spoke his mind without concern that he might be second-guessing the chain of command. Despite conventional wisdom, the habit made Woodard consider him an invaluable asset. "Without the tracker, we're searching for a virgin in a brothel." The sergeant walked over to the box sitting on Woodard's desk and peered down at the tiny pile of crushed electronics scattered inside.

Woodard clenched his jaw as he glared at the box. The short-ranged tracker was rudimentary, but the project leaders had been reluctant to use anything more powerful. They'd determined that the risk of employing anything that would allow them to track the unit over a vast distance was too great. Such a method could just as easily be intercepted, enabling their enemies to likewise pinpoint the unit's location while it was on assignment.

"Then we'll have to go about this the old-fashioned way." Woodard turned his back on the screen, flicking off the less interesting footage of the building maintenance techs sanitizing the floor. "Have security contact Fort Meade and put in a request with NSA for surveillance. I want a team in place monitoring satellite data around the clock. They can make up a reason."

"If the unit has reached an urban area, we could try to get access to police security video."

Woodard frowned. "Give the order, but only if the teams can hack the signals remotely. I don't want local law enforcement involved. This project is not supposed to exist, if you recall."

Cooper nodded his understanding.

"Besides," Woodard continued, "we're pretty remote from any decently populated urban centers. TM 05637 might be as close as we'll ever get to Superman, but it has to eat and sleep eventually." He sat back in his chair and steepled his fingers beneath his chin. "We're in the middle of the Western desert. That little defect couldn't have gotten far, not without anything but the clothes on its back. I want eight two-man teams to head out toward the compass points. Maybe we'll get lucky and can avoid involving outsiders." He glanced up at the giant standing patiently beside his desk. "I want it found, Sergeant."

"It might already be dead."

Woodard grunted in acknowledgement of the reference to the unit's built-in flaw, another reason they'd been overly lax in contemplating how to deal with the current situation. Why waste resources on keeping tabs on something that couldn't survive for long on its own? That had, after all, been the entire reason they'd designed the unit with the fatal vulnerability. Still, he refused to contemplate the possibility that the trapdoor had done its job until he saw the unit's body with his own eyes.

"Dead or alive."

Cooper nodded to indicate he understood and departed without another word. Once he was alone, Woodard turned back to his computer, taking a moment to mentally compose the report he needed to deliver. The project might be military, but the Company, a private organization, provided the funding. They would want to know their investment had disappeared.

Annoyed that he had to take time away from his duties for this, Woodard let out a sharp breath of irritation and typed a special code into his computer. A nondescript logo identifying the secretive group popped up for a brief moment before a video feed was established. A face replaced the insignia, and he grimaced when he recognized the woman who had been designated as the Company's liaison for the project.

"General, I read your initial communication regarding the incident. It was regrettably short on details. Care to elaborate?"

Ms. Talbot wasn't particularly young though she wasn't unattractive for a woman of her years. Her upswept brown hair was liberally streaked with gray, and the skin around her eyes and mouth bore the unmistakable signs of aging. But her piercing gaze—her eyes a sickly shade of peridot, so pale they looked almost clear—was as emotionless and direct as ever. He had always found her no-nonsense demeanor preferable to those disgusting toadies who worked for the defense oversight committee on Capitol Hill, but she was the last person he wanted to see right then.

"TM 05637 escaped from the Facility several days ago. We are currently working to recover it."

The woman's expression didn't change save for a slight tightening about her thin lips. "How did it happen?"

"Dr. Anderson assisted the unit in evading capture."

Her austere features sharpened into equal parts anger and disgust. "And where is he now?"

"He has been neutralized," Woodard elaborated with only mild satisfaction. It was a hollow victory compared to what the bastard had accomplished. "I've ordered search teams to be deployed and expect to have the unit back in custody within thirty-six to forty-eight hours."

"What about the tracker?"

Woodard growled under his breath. "The unit located it and removed it."

"Is that so?" She paused for a moment, an unreadable expression passing over her face so quickly he wasn't sure he'd seen it at all. "See that you do find it, General," she said finally. "This project was unofficially authorized by several high-ranking members of the Joint Chiefs, but I seriously doubt they would want the public to know what we've done." Clasping her long-fingered hands, she leaned forward so her dour visage filled the screen. "I don't need to tell you what would happen if the TM unit is allowed to remain at large. Not only to this organization, but to you, personally, General."

"No, ma'am." Woodard forcefully schooled his features into neutrality, knowing it wasn't an idle threat. He continued to stare at the screen even after it went dark, silently cursing the geneticist who had been a pain in his ass from the moment they'd been introduced nearly twenty-five years before. "Sentimental old fool," he repeated, his finger twitching with the desire to shoot the bastard all over again.

THREE

DAVID GROANED as he turned away from the bright light that had slipped past the blinds and was determinedly striking him in the eye. Raising his right hand, he slapped it over his face, attempting to block out the overly eager morning sun.

"Ugh, what the hell?" He opened one eye to glare at the unpleasant stickiness that had glued his middle and ring fingers together. He stared at the substance in confusion for a moment before the memory of the previous day came rushing back. "Fuck," he mumbled, turning his face into his pillow to hide his shame.

Tim, his distressingly young houseguest. Tim and his scandalously miniscule shorts and too-small T-shirt. Tim moaning his name, his beautiful face twisted in ecstasy as David thrust into him over and over....

Sitting up abruptly, he forcibly buried the fantasy deep down in his subconscious, refusing to give in to the enticing images again. He looked down at his hand in disgust, watching the dried, caked mess crack as he spread his fingers. After running away from the kid the night before like his pants had been on fire, he'd made the most of his solitude and pent up frustration. It had either been that or wait for Tim to finish showering so he could make use of the cold water to alleviate his problem. Of course, the mere thought of that lithe body in his shower had only exacerbated the situation. He'd tried to ignore his predicament, even managing to remember his manners and toss some clean sheets on the guest bed for Tim to use, but he'd grown more uncomfortable with every passing second. It had been all too easy for him to imagine the water streaming over the kid's tanned skin in clinging rivulets as it travelled over his chest and flat stomach, only to gather in the nest of soft hair surrounding his....

David groaned as his wayward body began to succumb all over again to his overactive imagination. "Like a freakin' horny teenager," he mumbled. "And speaking of teenagers...." There was no dodging that simple, unavoidable truth. He would just have to keep his damn hands to himself until he figured out what to do with the kid. Scooting off the bed, David looked around for the pajama bottoms he had eschewed in favor of easy access. Spotting them bunched up at the foot of the bed, he donned them clumsily and shuffled toward the closed bedroom door.

Yawning, he opened it with his clean hand while scratching at his bare chest with the unsoiled edge of his right thumb. Soft breathing coming from the opposite room prompted him to glance that way, and his feet stopped moving as he caught sight of bare, olive-toned limbs. Dead to the world, the kid lay on his stomach, his face—pretty even in sleep—angled toward the open door. The dusty old sheets that had covered the bed for the past two years were spread beneath him, and David recognized with the as yet functioning part of his brain that Tim hadn't changed them before falling asleep. The other part of his brain was too busy indulging in the same illicit fantasies that had kept him occupied last night. As he watched, the kid inhaled deeply and flipped over on his back, revealing a slimly muscled chest and ridged stomach. A swimmer's build if ever there was one. Tim wouldn't blow away in a stiff wind, but it probably wouldn't take much to hold him down and kiss that sweet mouth. And down his thoughts continued to go as his gaze slipped farther south until it brushed over the dark thatch of hair starting barely an inch below the jut of the kid's hipbones, which led to....

David shut his eyes and took a deep, unsteady breath as he registered that Tim wasn't wearing a damn thing. *Who in the hell slept naked while staying in a stranger's home?* A nervous laugh forced its way past his lips at the silly, puritanical complaint. Still, he didn't open his eyes again until he was standing in the bathroom with the door closed safely behind him. Glancing askance at the unsubtle tent which had grown in his pajamas, he clenched his jaw in annoyance. He might be a dirty old man, but he obviously wasn't decrepit.

"A cold shower's not going to be enough for you, is it?" David shook his head as he realized he was actually talking to his erection. Rolling his eyes, he turned the shower on, ensuring the water was pleasantly warm. After all, he was likely to be in there for some time.

David was fully dressed and standing in his kitchen when Tim finally made an appearance. The kid's hair was sticking up every which way, and the slightly dazed look in his large brown eyes made him look like a sleepy puppy. David forced himself not to stare at the strip of flesh that flashed from the open placket of his unzipped shorts. *Whoever taught the kid how to dress himself should be fired*, he thought desperately. As he busied himself with breakfast, David had come up with what he hoped was a surefire way to deal with his inappropriate attraction to his unanticipated guest. The crazy mop of hair gave him the perfect opportunity to test his desperate plan. He reached out and roughly tousled the inky-black mess, leaving behind an even more tangled nest that was desperately in need of a comb.

"Morning, sleepyhead." David turned back to the safety of the stove, proud of his cheerful, unaffected tone.

Tim blinked at the friendly assault, but seemed otherwise unaffected by the brotherly treatment. "Good morning." He absently smoothed his hair down with one hand as he sniffed the air. Moving closer until he was standing at David's shoulder, he tiptoed so he could see past him to the skillet that sizzled over a low flame. "Bacon and eggs?"

"Uh, yeah." When he found himself appreciating the hint of clean sweat wafting from Tim's skin, David wondered grumpily why in the hell he felt the need to stand so close. His nascent plan to treat Tim like a kid so he didn't want to screw him was already in imminent danger of failing. Shifting away to regain his personal space, David expertly folded the eggs and pushed the bacon around the pan to keep it from sticking. Satisfied that the food was almost ready, he looked cautiously over his shoulder at his houseguest. "Guess you need some new clothes, huh?"

Tim looked down at himself contemplatively. David grabbed the excuse of pulling a couple of plates from a nearby cabinet to step farther away from the scantily dressed figure. After gathering forks and knives from a drawer, he turned back in time to catch Tim toying with the frayed edge of his cutoffs where it hit the upper part of his inner thigh. A strangled moan tried to escape from David's throat, but he manfully swallowed it back. That didn't stop him from giving Tim a wide berth as he went to place the cutlery and plates on the small table pushed against the wall opposite the stove. The kid followed him to the table, his slender fingers now busily plucking at the undone waistband of his shorts. In his mind's eye, David put two fingers to his head and pulled an imaginary trigger.

"Yes, I suppose so."

It took a minute for David's brain to reengage enough for him to remember what his question had been. Fortunately, Tim sat at the table and scooted his chair forward until he was visible only from his T-shirt-covered stomach upward. As David walked back toward the stove to retrieve the food, he regained hope that he'd be able to get through breakfast without saying anything too asinine.

"I don't have any money, though," Tim added.

"Don't sweat it." David turned off the burner and carried the skillet to the table. He slid half of the eggs and bacon onto the kid's plate before easing the rest onto his own. "Like I mentioned yesterday, I own a retail store here in town. I can use my discount to buy you whatever you need." He went to place the skillet in the sink, and when he turned back, Tim was staring at him with wide eyes.

"I couldn't ask you to do that," Tim said uncertainly.

"It's no trouble." David sat at the table and picked up his fork, giving his full attention to his breakfast in lieu of the pretty face across from him. "My discount is really good, so it won't cost that much to get you a couple of pairs of jeans and a few shirts. Besides," he continued, mumbling around his food, "I can't have you running around dressed like that."

David wasn't sure whether or not Tim heard his last comment, but the kid merely stared at him for another uncomfortable minute before finally tucking into his own food. Within seconds, Tim had polished off the lion's share of the eggs.

"I see you really like eggs," David chuckled.

Tim glanced up sheepishly. "Um, I guess."

"Well, how about some orange juice?" he asked, remembering to offer the kid something to drink. Scooting his chair away from the table, David went to the refrigerator to retrieve the carton decorated with pictures of sliced oranges. Once it was in his hand, though, he could tell from the weight of it that the carton was practically empty. "Hmm, looks like I'm all out." David poured them each a glass of water instead and moved back to the table to hand one of them to the busily chewing Tim. "I'll stop by the store on the way home and get some groceries. Just let me know what you like." He made a mental note to get more eggs, seeing how much the kid had enjoyed them, before the awareness that he was thinking beyond that day brought him up short. "Let me grab my wallet, and then we'll head out, okay?" Not waiting for an acknowledgement, David retreated up to his bedroom to give himself a moment alone without the distraction of all that smooth, tanned skin.

"Dammit, Conley, what are you doing?" David picked up his wallet from the dresser and paused to look at himself in the attached mirror. "You can't let him stay here. That would be a really bad idea." Kicking Tim out onto the street was out of the question, but this situation needed to be resolved and fast. "Another day, maybe two, and that's it. Just until he gets up the courage to call home." David glared at himself sternly, pointing a finger at his reflection for emphasis. "Seriously, no longer than that. No matter how cute he is when he begs."

He sighed, knowing he was very unlikely to follow his own sage advice. While he wasn't sure what the kid's story was, he knew he couldn't leave Tim hanging with nowhere to go. Not if there was some way he could help. "Yeah, yeah, I'm a fucking prince." That was one way to put it. *Pushover* was another, as his father had countered in disgust when his mother had given him her nice guy speech for the umpteenth time.

David left off with the self-lecture and headed back downstairs. When he found Tim waiting for him in the living room, he knew he had to deal first with his most pressing dilemma: the kid's less than stellar dressing habits. He'd hoped Tim would figure out on his own that he needed to make himself decent before they left the house, but no such luck. "Uhh, you might want to button your shorts before we go."

Tim blinked as though David was speaking a foreign language before glancing down at himself. "Oh, sorry," he replied, his nimble fingers deftly fixing the problem.

David spun on his heel and went outside, pausing to lock the front door after Tim had followed. The kid was quiet as they walked to the car, and by the time they were settled inside, he was eager to break the silence. "Did you sleep well?" The question was completely inane, but David was desperate for any topic of conversation. "You weren't too hot?" He figured the warm, late-spring temperature was the reason the kid had decided to sleep commando. If he didn't want to spend every day of his immediate future taking cold showers, it was imperative he address the situation. "You know, if you closed the door to your room, the AC would work better—"

"I'd rather leave it open. The room feels less closed in that way."

"Oh. Yeah, okay." *That was weird*, David thought. His place might be small as town houses went, but it wasn't like the rooms were claustrophobic. Lifting his shoulders in a shrug, he decided to let it go, concentrating instead on pulling out of his parking spot without hitting the idiot in the neighboring spot who'd parked crooked and way too close. He was supposed to be encouraging the kid to move on, and learning more about him wasn't exactly the best way to go about it. Tim seemed fascinated by the passing scenery, which changed from residential to a more urban setting as they headed into the center of town. David didn't know what the kid found so intriguing about his nondescript neighborhood, but he resisted the urge to ask. "So, did you give any more thought to where you want to go when you leave here? Maybe you have some friends nearby you could stay with?"

"No, there's no one."

So much for that, David thought, turning on the radio to fill the silence. If the kid really didn't have any place to go, there wasn't much he could do about it.

About twenty minutes later, he turned the car into a lot fronted by a large marquee that proclaimed "Barry's Bargain Warehouse." "Barry" was one Bartholomew Rappaport, a Dallas native who had come into wealth when surveyors found oil on his family's land in the early 1960s. He had become filthy rich after investing his oil money and opening up a chain of general stores that offered discounted goods to people from Flagstaff, Arizona to Little Rock, Arkansas. This particular location had been owned and managed by a local couple, Frieda and Cyril Wallace, from its opening in 1974 until they'd decided to retire to Palm Beach, Florida two years ago. David had worked for them while he attended undergrad at Texas Tech and had returned as a store manager after graduating with an MBA from UT Austin. When Frieda and Cyril decided it was time to retire and give up the store, they had offered David an opportunity to buy them out at a reasonable price. Knowing just how much business the store pulled in, he'd considered it a safe investment, a conclusion that had been justified after he'd made back his down payment within a year of taking over.

Although the huge, brightly lit building took up over half of the lot, there was plenty of space for parking. Hardly any vehicles were there at that hour, other than his car and a few others he recognized as belonging to several of the first-shift workers. There weren't too many customers so soon after opening, but he knew business would pick up shortly. The name of the store was blazoned across the front of the building, the style and color of the letters matching the glowing sign anchored at the front corner of the parking lot. David noticed that the letter *A* needed a retouch of paint, a hailstorm from a couple of weeks ago having caused some minor damage to the mural. Caught up in a mental review of the minutiae of his to-do list for the day, David was out of his car and halfway to the store before he remembered he wasn't alone. He glanced back toward the young man following him, noting again the engrossed look that dominated the kid's face. David wondered what Tim could possibly find so fascinating about a big-box store, seeing as there had to be hundreds of others just like it. But mostly he tried to figure out how he was going to explain the kid's presence to his staff. As he led Tim through the large glass double doors, a perky voice interrupted his fretting.

"Morning, Mr. Conley. My goodness! Who is this cute little thing?"

David groaned internally before turning to smile at his first-shift assistant manager. Of all the people he hadn't wanted to explain Tim's presence to, she was probably first on the list. She looked like an ad for a Southern stereotype—riotous blonde curls upswept into some improbable construction, overly made-up eyes, bright pink lipstick, and a bosom which strained the buttons on the red vest of her store uniform. The woman might have a heart as big as Texas, but she had a mouth to match. The fact that the boss had walked into the store with a scantily dressed teenager in tow would be common knowledge among the staff—even the ones who weren't there yet—within the hour.

"Good morning, Patricia. Any problems with the opening?"

It was the job of the first shift to prepare the store for the start of its sixteen-hour day. Barry had insisted his establishment be convenient for its patrons, so the BBW was open seven days a week from 7:00 a.m. to 11:00 p.m. David wasn't usually there the whole day, but he liked to make certain it opened on time. His question was the same one he had asked Patricia nearly every day since he'd promoted her eight months ago. She'd proven herself a reliable addition to his management staff, dedicated and meticulous in her duties. Unfortunately, at that moment, with Tim blinking his big eyes in her direction, the store was the last thing she was concerned about.

"What's your name, sweetie?"

"Tim," the kid answered, with only a fraction of the hesitation he'd shown when David had asked him the same question the day before. "Tim Paul."

Hearing the kid's full name again, David reassessed his assumption about the man Tim had called Father Paul. He'd thought Paul was the man's first name, but apparently not. His confusion about the kid's relationship to this Father Paul person was interrupted as Patricia continued to chirp at the newcomer.

"Well, aren't you just the cutest thing! David, where did he come from? I don't remember seein' him around town before. Is he a friend of yours?"

Amazed she got all of that out without taking a breath, David winced as Patricia turned up her drawl to a level she would have criticized in anyone else. But he guessed he couldn't blame her when faced with a gorgeous, brunet Antinous come to life. So what did that make him? Hadrian? He cursed silently, feeling the sudden urge to go back in time and kill his classics professor.

"Tim is a, uh, family friend. He's in town for a while and is staying with me for a bit." David rushed through the explanation, saying the first thing that came to mind and hoping it sounded plausible. "Some bad stuff happened with his folks, you understand, so best to leave it at that."

Patricia was instantly all helpful contrition, clearly embarrassed by her nosiness if her blush was anything to go by. Or maybe she, too, was feeling the effects of Tim's mile-long bare legs flashing at her. Patricia was a divorcée with two children under the age of fifteen she was raising single-handedly, and though sometimes overly friendly, she was usually quite levelheaded. Still, David couldn't fault her for her reaction to Tim. The woman might have nearly twenty-five years on the kid, but she wasn't dead.

"Oh, isn't that a shame?" she gushed. "Well now, honey, Mr. Conley is just about the nicest man livin' on this Earth. So, don't you worry none. I'm sure he'll take real good care of you."

David glanced at Patricia askance, wondering if her double entendre had been intentional. When he saw nothing on her face but a huge smile, he figured he was just being paranoid. He was the only one with his mind in the gutter. Latching onto her actual meaning, he took it as the perfect opportunity to pawn the kid off on her for a while. David desperately needed to put some distance between himself and Tim, even if it was only the length of the store. Maybe then he could figure out how best to humanely send the kid on his way.

"Say, Patricia, I have some paperwork I need to take care of, and Tim here could use some new clothes. Would you mind taking him over to the men's section and helping him pick out some jeans and shirts or something?"

She agreed with a quickness that made him wonder if he needed to mention the kid was only a bit older than her eldest child, but he restrained himself. If Tim wanted to hook up with an older woman, that was his business. David waved them off and beat a hasty retreat to his office, which was situated at the very back of the store. He glanced up at one of the large, convex mirrors hiding the security cameras strategically located throughout the aisles and swallowed when he met the unblinking gaze of the young man who had turned to watch him go.

I WATCHED David walk away, noting that he was moving near the upper limit of his ambulatory speed. David's elevated heart rate indicated his fight-or-flight response had been triggered. A quick

45

survey of the area, however, indicated no apparent threats, leaving me confused by his hurried retreat.

"Sweetie, you comin'?"

Finding no explanation for David's odd behavior, I returned my attention to the woman looking at me expectantly. "Sorry. After you, Miss Patricia." Her age as well as our geographical location prompted me to add the respectful title to her name. The faint hint of color that rose to the woman's hyperadipose cheeks signified I'd been correct to do so.

"Oh, aren't you a doll?" She patted her blonde hair, which was arranged in a manner that appeared structurally implausible, before putting one hand to her face. Her lips were stretched in a wide smile when she replied, "It's just Patricia."

"Patricia—"

"Tipton. Now, why don't you come with me, and we'll get you all fixed up."

Opening a mental file for this new acquaintance, I followed her as she led me toward the far side of the store. I glanced once more in the direction David had disappeared, but the items Patricia and I were passing by soon drew my full attention.

David had called it a retail store, but the moniker seemed an understatement given the sheer variety of items on the shelves. The stacked metal platforms stretched for dozens of yards at broken intervals from the front of the store to the very back. The parallel aisles were overhung with signs designating various goods. *Housewares. Kitchen. Bath. Health. Camping.* I recognized most of them, but a few, such as *Female Sanitary*, left me confused. Were men typically less hygienic than women?

"How long have you been in town? I thought David got back from Albuquerque only yesterday." The woman glanced back at me as she talked, and I wondered how she could walk without looking where she was going.

"Since yesterday," I replied. "It was somewhat short notice, but luckily for me, David agreed to assist me." I hadn't been at all certain David would allow me to remain in his home. He'd seemed leery of the idea for some reason. When David had told Patricia his "family friend" would be "staying with him for a bit," I'd felt a tension leave my body I hadn't even realized I'd been carrying until that moment.

"Mr. Conley is a dear, make no mistake about it. I'm sure he'll take good care of you until your troubles have worked themselves out."

If only my problems were as simple as she likely believed. *Some bad stuff happened with his folks*, David had explained to her. He would probably never know just how close his fabrication had been to the truth.

"Okay, here we are," Patricia said brightly as she stopped before a group of circular racks. "See anything you like?"

We had emerged from the orderly row of aisles into an open area at the far right side of the building that took up nearly a third of the store's square footage. The items in this part of the store were all clothing, everything from outerwear, shirts, and pants, to shoes and undergarments. Since until a few days ago my entire wardrobe had consisted of a unitard that changed only to accommodate my growth, I was at a loss.

"Um," I hemmed before remembering what David had instructed, "a few pairs of jeans and some shirts would be fine."

"You probably don't have much money of your own, huh?" Patricia apparently sensed my hesitation, though the reason she guessed was only partly true. Her expression softened as moisture collected in her eyes. "I think it's very admirable that you don't want to be beholden to Mr. Conley, but sweetie," she said quietly, stepping close to me as if someone else was around to hear us, "there's no need to feel embarrassed about asking for help. So, go on, pick out whatever you want."

As I went to follow her orders, I pondered her misassumption. I knew people used money to buy things, but since my needs had always been provided for, the concept had been merely abstract to me. If I were going to continue living as a regular person, at least for a while, I would need to find some way to obtain funds. Stealing, as I had done to get the clothes I was currently wearing, was not an option. Drawing the notice of the authorities was the last thing I could afford.

Mulling over this new problem, I wandered over to one of the circular racks and idly flipped through the collection of shirts. Whether she found my lack of concentration annoying or simply pitied my obvious indecision, Patricia soon took over, and within thirty minutes, I was outfitted with two new pairs of jeans, five T-shirts, a light jacket, a pair of sneakers, and ten pairs each of socks and something Patricia called "tighty-whities."

"Let's go over to the registers, and I'll ring these up. I'll go ahead and charge it to David's employee account, so we won't need to bother him right now."

Customers had gradually been trickling in while I was being outfitted, and now a steady stream of people moved through the store. I had to keep track of Patricia by the sound of her footsteps, because I couldn't refrain from absorbing as many visual details as I could manage. This was the closest I had ever been to people—besides David—who weren't part of the project team in charge of me. I was fascinated by the variations of bodies and faces, from size to skin tone to nose shape. There had been some distinction among the military and scientific personnel who drifted in and out of my sphere, but nothing like what I was seeing in the limited confines of this store. But mostly I was amazed that these people were looking back at me, not as a specimen to be examined, but with friendly smiles, absent stares, or, in more than one case, noncasual interest.

"Um, excuse me, ma'am, but can you tell me where your floor cleaners are?"

A young woman, likely only a few years older than I was, had stopped in front of Patricia, blocking her path. She pushed something that resembled a cloth-covered wagon, and I saw that the conveyance held a human of extremely tiny proportions. *A baby*, I identified, staring fixedly at the small being while I absently responded to the woman's request.

"Aisle five. Third section from the front. The fourth and fifth shelves. There are nine brands of floor cleaner available."

The young woman blinked at me for a second before smiling and moving off with a nod and a hurried "Thanks!"

I watched her for a moment, interested in how the tone of her voice changed as she leaned over and talked to the small child, before turning back to Patricia, only to find her staring at me with her mouth agape.

"Well, bless me, how did you know all that? We never even went down that aisle!"

After a moment's consideration, I determined a plausible and not untrue explanation. "I have an eidetic... a photographic memory. I glanced down the aisle as we walked past it."

"And remembered that much just from seeing it for, what, a couple of seconds at best?" Patricia shook her head and pressed her hand to her cheek in what I realized was a favorite pose of hers. "That's amazing. With trying to deal with work and the kids and taking night classes sometimes it's all I can do to remember my own name!" She laughed heartily at her own joke, and I was surprised at how pleasant I found the sound. "Boy, I tell you, a skill like that surely would come in handy around here." Her expressive gaze widened suddenly, and I noticed her eyes were an unusual, but not unpleasant, shade of grayish green. "Now, there's an idea. Yes, indeedy, that's perfect!"

"What is?" I asked.

She grinned and shook her head. "Don't want to get ahead of myself." Patricia continued toward the front of the store where ten computers sat beneath a large sign which read "Check-Out." "Let's get this taken care of. Then we'll go and show Mr. Conley what all you got."

She hummed beneath her breath as she walked, and I pegged her mood as happy or perhaps amused. I followed behind her silently, identifying my own attitude as curious as I wondered what she was up to.

"HIRE HIM?" David stared at Patricia as he echoed her.

She had brought Tim to his office less than an hour after he had left them. He'd been hoping for a longer separation, needing some time to wrap his brain around the riddle of what to do with the kid. Patricia's suggestion, delivered with a beaming, self-satisfied grin, was the very opposite of helpful.

"That's right. Tim told me he wants to earn his keep. Isn't that right, sweetie?"

The kid nodded, and David wondered how much of this had truly been his idea.

"And you should have seen the way he helped one of the customers out on the floor. Why, he's better than one of those GPS devices. Told her exactly where to find what she was looking for down to the inch!" Patricia sidled up to Tim and placed a gentle hand on his arm.

David scratched the back of his head. "I don't know." He didn't like this. Having to deal with Tim at home was bad enough, but seeing him every day at work, too? David opened his mouth to say no, but Patricia must have seen the reluctance on his face.

"You know we could always use another set of capable hands around here." She moved away from Tim and leaned close to David as she lowered her voice. "And, honestly, the poor kid could obviously use the pay." Patricia gazed at him intently through her heavily mascaraed eyelashes. "He sure would be a big help, and it would give him some spending money so he doesn't have to keep asking you for handouts."

As much as he wanted to reject her suggestion out of hand, David had to admit it made sense. He made a decent living, but providing for two people on his salary alone would tax his resources in the long term. And he was coming to accept that his association with Tim wouldn't be as short-lived as he might have originally preferred. He glanced over at the kid and sighed in resignation as he met a fathomless gaze studying him in return. While Tim wasn't the most expressive person he'd ever met, he thought he saw hope there. Or maybe it was Tim's full, slightly parted lips, the lower one pouty and begging to be kissed, that made David believe the kid was waiting breathlessly for his answer. He turned his attention back to his computer screen and took a moment to forcibly stop the nascent fantasy growing in his brain.

"Fuck it all," he mumbled.

"What was that?"

"I said, sure," he replied at a normal volume, tossing his manager a careless grin. "That's a fine idea, Patricia." Despite his better judgment, his gaze wandered back toward Tim. The kid's impassive demeanor wasn't giving anything away, but his stare had become more intense, as if he could see every sordid thought going through David's head. David couldn't help but flinch slightly as he felt himself flush with guilt.

"In fact, why don't you get him started right away?" he said in a rush, manhandling his brain out of the gutter. "I need to stay here for a few more hours, and he'll just be bored if he doesn't have anything else to do but hang out." David stood, tripped over the feet of his office chair in his haste, then walked over to his file cabinet. He opened a drawer and withdrew an employment form before swinging back toward the pair waiting in front of his desk. Shoving the form at Patricia, he stepped around them and opened his door with a smile, trying to pretend he wasn't rushing them out. "Go on and take him to the break room. Once he's finished with the forms, you can get him a badge. I'll go ahead and place an order for his store vest." She could take care of the intake process. Anything to get the kid and his overly exposed legs out of his office. The bags holding Tim's new clothes were resting beside his feet. Why the hell hadn't he changed already? Those damn shorts were going to give him a heart attack. David knew he'd need these next few hours to prepare himself to face the consequences of what he'd just agreed to.

Patricia was still gushing out her gratitude when he closed the door behind her and her new trainee. Speaking from a business perspective, he knew she was right. They did need some extra help, and he'd been planning to place an ad on the store's website and in the newspaper later in the week. Hiring Tim solved several problems in one stroke.

"Yeah, I'd like to stroke something all right." David exhaled heavily and braced his hands against his desk, his head hanging between his arms. He closed his eyes as his mother's fondest warning rang in his ears. "No, Ma. I'm pretty certain *sweet* is the last word you'd want to use for me right now."

FOUR

"FOLLOW ME, darlin'," Patricia chirped. "We'll have you set up in no time."

As she led me toward a door at the back of the store opposite from David's office, I contemplated my recent failure. That morning, I'd decided to act on my plan of encouraging David, walking into the kitchen fully aware of how I appeared with my shorts undone and my tight shirt outlining the contours of my body. Direct eye contact. Close body proximity. Limited clothing. I'd done everything I'd learned was within the parameters of seduction, and David had responded to me as expected on a physiological level. Yet he had seemed curiously hesitant to act upon my obvious interest.

His reticence didn't disappoint me completely. A physical connection between us could secure David's loyalty and make a purposeful betrayal less likely should the general and his men ever catch up with me. But how could I press such a connection when I was so acutely aware how it would end? I couldn't stay here forever. Any attachment I fostered between us would inevitably yield to the clock ticking down my continued viability. What would it do to David if we started having sex, and then I suddenly disappeared with no warning or explanation? Before now, the only consideration I'd ever had to give my actions were whether they enabled me to accomplish a given mission. Goals, meaning, ethics... those things had always been decided by those who held my leash. But now I was completely on my own with only the memory of Father Paul to guide me as I weighed my need for security against my growing regard for the man who had saved me.

"Like Mr. Conley said, this is the break room," Patricia said cheerfully, interrupting my fruitless internal debate. "You're welcome to eat in here during your shift, or to come and hang out for a while if the customers get to be too much for you. Some of them can be real gems, if you know what I mean."

I didn't, so I remained silent as I followed her into the room, her frivolous chatter providing a welcome distraction from my uneasy thoughts. The space wasn't very large, but would comfortably accommodate a moderately sized group of people. Two large round tables were set up with five chairs surrounding each of them, and several folding chairs were stacked against the back wall in case they were required. The walls had been painted white, making the small room seem brighter than it otherwise would have. Three bulletin boards were tacked up, their corkboard surfaces nearly obscured by announcements. Some were about upcoming store events and worker schedules, while others gave information about job safety and minimum wage laws.

"Here, let's take a load off while I explain the forms to you."

I joined her at the table closest to the door and angled my chair so I could face her as she settled into the adjacent seat.

"This is the application form," Patricia explained, pushing the indicated sheet of paper toward me. "Even though you already have the job, we'll need to have this in your file. It's just a formality."

I scanned the form as she spoke, noting the various types of information it requested. Since I had already decided on a name and I had an address, those things didn't present a problem. Social security number. That wouldn't be so simple. I had never been assigned one. The intention of my mission controllers had been to create identities for me on an as-needed basis. I was, however, aware most social security numbers had the digits "3" and "5" in them, so I tasked myself with coming up with a convincing random number. If anyone ever ran it, I'd worry about it then.

Patricia watched me in uncharacteristic silence as I filled out the application form. I could almost hear her brain working as she tried to decide whether she believed David's story about where I'd come from so suddenly. "Is this okay?" I asked, sliding the sheet back over to her.

She gave it a quick once-over. "Perfect! All righty, only a few more to go. This one is for your taxes, and then there's the dress code and conduct policy—just need you to review and sign that one—and then the benefits form." She pointed to each form as she described it. "There's a 90-day eligibility waiting period for benefits, but that'll pass before you know it!"

I went to work filling them out, reassured to note I didn't need to make up any new identifying information beyond what I already had. Completing the paperwork occupied barely a fraction of my attention, so I used the time to quiz Patricia about my new employer.

"How long have you known David? I noticed you don't refer to him by his first name."

She chuckled. "Oh, I've known him since I started working here. It's been, what, three years, I think."

I cocked my head to the side, an expression of curiosity I'd often seen from Father Paul, which I'd picked up subconsciously. "That seems long enough to have developed a more intimate level of familiarity."

Patricia's smile dimmed somewhat as she blinked, her forehead wrinkling slightly in a show of mild confusion. The slight blush which suddenly colored her cheeks was more of a mystery. "Um, I don't think intimate is the word I'd use, but if you mean that Mr. Conley and I are friends, then sure. I don't call him David more as a sign of respect than anything. I'm quite a bit older than him, but he's the boss." Her expression cleared as her smile returned. "I don't want any of the other staff here to doubt who's in charge."

"How old is he?" Determining a person's age by examining skin elasticity and level of mobility wasn't an exact science. David's expressiveness had interfered with my ability to accurately assess his wrinkle pattern. I recognized that I'd made a tactical error when Patricia's friendly expression suddenly turned into a slightly suspicious frown.

"I thought you've known him for a long time. Shouldn't you know that already?"

"He's friends with my parents, so I never really asked," I said, thinking fast. "I just realized I didn't know and was curious."

"Ah," Patricia replied slowly, apparently willing to be convinced by my impromptu falsehood. "I guess that makes sense. My boys sure don't know how old my friends are." She chuckled. "Um, David's in his early thirties, I think." Her contemplative expression shifted into certainty as she nodded. "That's right. He turned thirty-one about a month ago. We had a party for him right here in the break room."

I added the age discrepancy between himself and David into my growing store of information about my new employer, wondering if it might have something to do with his seeming reluctance to engage me on a physical level. I'd been taught that the human male was rarely deterred by pricks of conscience when his libido was engaged, but I'd come to suspect that much of what I'd learned from my handlers was not to be fully trusted.

"Mr. Conley's been the owner here for about two years, ever since Mr. and Mrs. Wallace retired and left him in charge. He's been a terrific boss to work for, always ready to lend a hand and make sure everything runs smoothly. And he's been a real angel when I've had to unexpectedly take time off to deal with the kids. It hasn't been easy since I got divorced."

I'd been listening closely as Patricia bounced around from topic to topic, and latched on to her last statement as the opening I'd been looking for. "Maybe that's because he knows what it's like to go through it?"

"Through what? A divorce?" She laughed and shook her head. "Goodness me, I don't know where you got that idea. No, Mr. Conley has never been married. Heck, I don't even think he's seeing anyone. At least, I haven't heard any gossip about him dating, and believe you me, working in a store like this with the number of people who come through here every day, you get to hear everything about everything!"

"My mistake," I mumbled. I looked back down at the code of conduct form, wondering if Father Paul would have been proud of how easily I had extracted the desired information. Although I'd guessed David was gay, I hadn't wanted to assume what that portended regarding his personal life. I entered the data into the part of my memory I'd started referring to as my "David file." His single status was convenient. I didn't want to have to explain my presence in his life to someone who might have some say over whether I got to stay with him or not. I paused slightly as I read a passage concerning a prohibition on coworker relationships, but quickly moved on. My relationship with David—if one could call it that—was strictly out of necessity. There was no question of "romantic involvement," even if I did eventually try and ease my way into his bed at some point.

Sex isn't love, my boy. I sincerely hope that one day you'll learn the difference. I pushed Father Paul's voice to the back of my mind and concentrated on completing the paperwork.

"All finished?" Patricia asked when I passed the last of the forms back to her. "Good!" she added at my nod. "I'll go ahead and get these squared away. Why don't you change into one of your new outfits. Like the dress code says, cutoff shorts aren't allowed… though it's a real shame."

The last was spoken in a low volume, but I had no difficultly hearing her. I glanced over at her and noticed her gaze was directed toward my mostly bare legs. Her cheeks were tinted pink, and the color only deepened when she realized I'd caught her ogling me.

"Where can I change?"

She flung a flustered hand toward the far end of the room. "The staff restroom is back there."

Following the direction of her gesture, I noticed a door that was slightly ajar, revealing a glimpse of a toilet. With a nod of thanks, I gathered up the bag holding my newly purchased clothes and retreated to the designated location. The unit was small but clean, the toilet and sink spotless and free of any odors that might indicate the room's purpose. After closing the door behind me, I proceeded to strip off my tank top and shorts, then removed one of the pairs of jeans and a shirt from the bag. I left the packaged underwear where it was. I wasn't used to wearing undergarments and didn't quite understand their function. The outer attire was more than adequate to the task of covering the parts of my anatomy that might trigger unwanted interest.

Once I was freshly clothed, having completed the ensemble by exchanging my sandals for the sneakers, I paused to look at myself in the mirror. I thought I looked like an average nineteen-year-old, albeit with one very noticeable difference. Every person I had seen and met thus far had one thing I decidedly lacked—the ability to emote. I had learned how to fake a smile, but it always felt strange, as if I were pushing my face into an abnormal position. Back in the lab, I'd never taken the time to examine myself in a mirror, but now that I had the opportunity, I realized my features were devoid of what Father Paul liked to call *character*. If I wanted to fit in, that would need to change. I'd been schooled in reading people's expressions as a useful way to manipulate their actions. Now I applied the skill to myself.

My skin was smooth, lacking the lines I'd noticed on other people's faces, but since I was young, even by normal standards, I guessed that wouldn't be too much of a problem. My genetics had been designed to slow the rate at which I aged compared to the average person. If I were out in the normal world for any significant length of time, the difference might become noticeable, but that was highly unlikely. The unnatural stillness of my face, however, was something I could work on.

It's okay to smile, you know. You're a little boy, not a machine, no matter what that mean man says.

An unbidden memory came to me of a woman with shimmering red hair bouncing me on her knee as she grinned at me. It had been a long time since I'd thought about the woman who had given birth to me, but somehow I had never forgotten her bright smile. As a very young child, the sight of it had made me feel warm in a way that even now I found difficult to articulate. She had disappeared from my life years ago, but my perfect recall of her face provided a viable model for me to use now.

Concentrating, I pulled back my lips from my teeth and studied the result. No, that wasn't right. It looked like I was in pain. Patricia made it seem so easy, her kind smile blooming effortlessly on her matronly features. Trying again, I lifted the corners of my mouth on either side. The insane, clown-faced antagonist in the movie about the comic book vigilante Father Paul had enjoyed watching immediately came to mind. Breaking years' worth of bad habits wouldn't be an easy task. Sighing, I decided to give up for the time being before Patricia came looking for me.

"SO, YOUR stepdad gives you a hard time, huh?"

David followed the sound of Patricia's voice, guessing she was talking to their newest hire. He paused as he neared them, staying out of sight around the corner of the aisle where they were chatting. It sounded like Tim had succumbed to Patricia's Southern charm and was spilling the beans about his mysterious background. It was a topic David was most interested in, so he waited to see if the kid would reveal any more details about himself.

"I guess so. He was always asking me to do things I didn't want to do."

Patricia tittered uncomfortably, and David wondered if Tim's turn of phrase had raised the same doubts in her as were currently flitting through his head.

"What kind of things? You mean like making you clean up your room?" She laughed. "Despite what you and my boys might think, chores really aren't the end of the world."

"No, not chores."

Tim didn't volunteer anything else, but David felt a tight knot form in his stomach. Hell, was the kid's stepfather involved in something illegal? Was that why Tim seemed so leery of David's offer to take him to the police? Or was it something more sinister than that? David shook his head, trying not to jump to conclusions. But if what he was beginning to suspect was true, it was all the more reason to keep his hands to himself.

"Um," Patricia said after an awkward pause, "what about your mom? Won't she wonder where you got off to?"

"I don't have one," Tim replied succinctly.

"Oh, dear, I'm so sorry," Patricia replied, her flustered tone indicating she'd reached the same conclusion David had that Tim's mother must be deceased. "I shouldn't have pried. So, it's just you and your stepdad, huh?"

David was impressed at Patricia's ability to keep up her nosy interrogation even as she apologized for it. As much as he wanted to let her do her thing, since she seemed adept at getting Tim to open up, it was nearly time for the evening shift to begin, meaning she would be off duty soon. He didn't want the kid to have to make nice with the late-shift manager so quickly after having met Patricia. Something told him Tim didn't open up to others easily, and he knew Patricia was the best person to make him feel comfortable. Besides, he was ready to leave, and without him, Tim wouldn't have any way to get back to his place. David continued around the corner and nodded as they caught sight of him, acting like he hadn't been eavesdropping.

"Hey, you two. How are things going?" He snorted in amusement when Patricia beamed at Tim. It looked like the kid had found a mother figure, whether he wanted one or not.

"Great, Mr. Conley! Tim, here, is a natural at retail!"

David was just thinking her smile was a little too bright when the kid interrupted, confirming his suspicions.

"Patricia's statement is not accurate. Certain aspects of this job have proven... challenging."

Even though it was strange, David couldn't help but be charmed by the way Tim spoke so properly, as if he were far older than his years. "Such as?" he asked, resisting the urge to smile at Tim's utterly serious expression. Someone needed to teach this kid how to take a joke.

"Tim is fantastic at stocking and arranging the merchandise on the shelves," Patricia interjected. "He has a, er, what did you call it, Tim? An Egyptian memory?"

"You mean eidetic?" David asked, his brows lifting in surprise as he glanced at Tim.

"Oh, right! Yes, that's it, eidetic. So, it's like, he can tell at a glance when we're getting low on a particular item, and he remembers exactly where it can be found in the stockroom even though I only walked him through there briefly." Patricia clasped her hands together, warming to her new favorite topic. "And you should see how he has rearranged some of the sections! He fixed it so we can put out twice as much merchandise on the shelves as we had before, but everything is as neat as a pin. Plus, I swear he's faster at calculating totals—with tax— than the registers even!"

"Basic spatial allocation and algorithmic computation," Tim said, like it was perfectly normal to use SAT words in everyday conversation.

"Well, that's good, Tim," David replied. "Glad to hear you're adjusting well."

"People are hard, though."

David blinked. "What do you mean?"

"Um, what he means is...."

Patricia paused, as if trying to think of precisely the right words. It wasn't something David had ever seen her do before; usually she went ahead and said whatever was on her mind. Her hesitation made him dread what she had to say.

"Is what?" he prompted.

"Well, Tim's not exactly great with people."

David looked askance at the kid's still, attractive face, then glanced away when he noticed Tim was staring back at him. "Is that so?"

Patricia squeezed her hands together even tighter and wouldn't meet his gaze, preferring to stare down at the floor. He guessed that she wanted to speak to him in private.

"Tim, why don't you go and gather your things so we can head out." The kid continued to look at him like he was trying to read his mind, but after a long moment he complied. David waited until he was out of earshot before turning back to Patricia. "Okay, tell me. What happened? Did he scare a customer or something?"

"Oh, no, nothing like that," she explained in a rush. "Well, not really. It's just that, well, Tim's a great kid and all, but he's a little, um, I don't know, cold, I suppose."

"He's not one for small talk, I grant you, but he's not unfriendly."

"No," Patricia agreed. "Every time anyone asked him a question, he was always quick to provide information. It's more like he lacks that human touch. He's kind of like a computer or something. Loads of information to share, but he's far too direct about it." She sighed, frustrated at her inability to explain her impressions of Tim more clearly. "For instance, Mrs. Appleton came in with her six kids earlier and asked Tim to show her the new twin bed sets we put in the sales paper. He knew exactly which ones she meant, but instead of taking her there, he merely told her. I could see she was so distracted with dealing with the kids that she was only half listening to him. But when I hinted he should accompany her there personally, he just gave her the aisle number and shelf location and then went back to organizing the area he'd been working on. It was like the idea that he should help her directly was a completely foreign concept."

David struggled not to laugh in her face, knowing she wouldn't appreciate it. "More likely he just didn't want to be in the company of Mrs. Appleton and her brood any longer than necessary." He let a grin escape. "Can't say as I blame him." He wrapped an arm around his assistant manager's shoulder and gave her a little hug. "I wouldn't worry about Tim. He sounds like a normal teenage boy to me."

She glared at him, her skepticism written clearly on her face. "I don't know about that," she sniffed. "My boys are never that rude when they come in to help during the holidays."

"That's because they know you'd give them hell about it if they ever were." After a final squeeze, he let her go. "Just turn some of those motherly skills on him, and I'm sure you'll have the kid whipped into shape in no time."

"And it wouldn't kill him to smile every now and again."

"You're not wrong," David said. "But I overheard you talking to him about his stepfather. Sounds like he's had a hard time of it." David shrugged. "Maybe he doesn't have much to smile about."

Patricia's lips thinned in displeasure. "Tim said you were friends with his parents, but I don't know how you could be friends with a man like that."

Family friend. Crap. David scrambled to come up with something to augment his earlier lie. "Um, I knew his real parents. I don't know his stepfather well. I hadn't seen Tim in years and was as surprised as anyone when he called me out of the blue to say he was in town."

"Hmm, I see." Patricia's face transformed as a wicked little smile crossed her lips. "Well, then, you'll just have to do something to cheer him up, won't you?"

Scandalized at her insinuation, David sputtered as he searched for a suitable reply, but she spun around and walked away before he could find one.

"See you tomorrow, Mr. Conley!" she threw over her shoulder, adding a saucy wave.

"Sheesh," he muttered to himself. "Am I that transparent?"

Patricia knew he was gay and, although she was as straitlaced a woman as he had ever met, she'd never given him any reason to worry about what she thought of him because of it. Rather, it seemed she'd found herself a new project. God knew the woman loved to match-make. She'd been with Tim as he filled out his paperwork, so she had to know how much younger the kid was than him. He had no idea why that didn't bother her as much as it did him. Groaning quietly under his breath, he went to find Tim, hoping he could figure out a way to distract Patricia. But first, if they were going to be living together for any length of time, he needed to find a way to check the less than honorable impulses the kid incited in him so effortlessly.

FIVE

DAVID WAS staring at me as we sat at his kitchen table. He was trying to be unobtrusive, so I pretended not to notice while I concentrated on devouring a salmon omelet. He had been surprised by my request for dinner, but he'd made the dish without protest. It was delicious, although I was slightly more interested in the particular nutrients the food provided me than in the excellent flavor.

"I'm impressed by the job you did today."

When I looked up at the observation, David had finally turned his attention to his own dinner.

"Have you ever worked in retail before?"

I shook my head, guessing it might be improper to speak with my mouth full of food. Besides, silence was the easiest way to avoid David's clumsy attempts to glean more information about my past.

He glanced up briefly when I didn't speak, and caught the gesture. "I see," he said.

I was relieved when David resorted to simply eating in lieu of further conversation. The minutes ticked by in relative quiet save for the clicking of forks and knives on the cheap white plates I'd seen for sale at the BBW. The lack of conversation provided me with the opportunity to mull over David's previous comment. Although he had expressed his satisfaction with my work that day, I didn't share the assessment.

Habit had led me to eavesdrop on David's and Patricia's conversation before we'd left the store. *Information is currency*, I'd been taught, and knowledge of a situation could mean the difference between life and death. I hadn't been surprised when I'd heard her opinion of my performance. I could tell the customers I'd interacted with had been less than comfortable in my presence. It frustrated me that I couldn't manage such a seemingly basic thing as talking naturally to people. I'd watched Patricia do so all day as I'd shadowed her, learning my new job. One of my main functions was the ability to blend seamlessly into any situation I encountered, so why was I so bad at it?

"Teaching it how to emote is as pointless as it having emotions in the first place, Anderson," the general observed when he'd caught Father Paul attempting to instruct me on the subject.

"Surely having knowledge of the full range of the human condition will only help him succeed," the scientist scoffed.

Woodard's bark of laughter was full of derision. *"TM 05637 doesn't need to feel to eliminate a target, doctor. What good is a bomb that empathizes with the thing it's supposed to blow up? No,"* he added emphatically, *"I want a weapon that will kill on command without hesitation. I don't particularly care how well it can fake that it gives a damn."*

Now that the skill would have been particularly useful, I regretted even more that Father Paul had not been able to finish giving me that lesson.

"Hey, kid, what's wrong?" David's blue eyes radiated concern as I placed my fork beside my plate. "You look, well, kind of upset."

I looked up sharply at the man seated across the table from me, amazed that someone other than Father Paul had been able to deduce my mood. I knew I didn't telegraph much about myself and was impressed with David's insightfulness. I would have to be careful not to unintentionally give away anything.

"I-I'm not sure I can do the job you've given me. I can't...." I moved my hands to my lap under the table so David couldn't see my fists clench in an uncharacteristic show of vexation. "Like Patricia said, I'm not really good with people."

"Oh, I doubt that's true. She was just being a bit overdramatic." David chuckled, his smile full of encouragement. "Patricia liked you well enough, didn't she? I didn't receive any complaints from any of the customers about you."

His sound of amusement cut off abruptly when I pushed back from the table, my chair scraping loudly across the tiled floor. "It is true. When Patricia talks to customers, they smile and thank her, but when I try to be helpful, they just stare like they don't understand me." I stood up and moved away from the table, taken aback by how much those awkward interactions had bothered me. "I told them what they wanted to know. So, why?" I inhaled deeply, trying to calm the sudden unsteadiness of my breathing. I had never experienced doubt, and I was confused by my reaction. "Why did they hate me?"

"Hey, hey! Now, wait just a minute."

David had been staring at me in shock at my outburst, but now he scrambled up from his chair and moved quickly over to where I stood. His hands fell on my shoulders, and I felt the gentle squeeze they bestowed throughout my entire body. Reassuring warmth spread from the points of contact until I could sense my tense muscles beginning to relax.

"Nobody hates you. How could you think that?" David's throat moved as he swallowed uncertainly. "Is that why you ran away from home? You think your stepfather hates you?"

I was confused by the sudden turn of conversation before realizing that David was still fishing. It wasn't exactly subtle, but the tactic of putting your target off-balance was often effective. I silently commended David for his cleverness.

"No, that's not why." That wasn't entirely true. I was absolutely certain the general hated me, but I decided I should probably give David something. He deserved that much at least. "He was involved in something... had involved me in something... I didn't want to do anymore."

David's thirst for more details was etched on his face, but to his credit he didn't press in the face of my obvious reluctance to talk about it any further. "Okay, fair enough," he replied. "But that doesn't change what I said." After a final squeeze to my shoulders, David moved back until his hips rested against the table. He folded his arms across his chest and looked like he was settling in for a long talk. "I know this can't be easy for you. You're in a new town and living with a practical stranger." David shook his head, seemingly finding it difficult to make sense of our arrangement himself. "It's not surprising that you'd feel unsettled trying to do a new job on top of everything else, but don't sweat it. Just remember our mission statement."

Mission statement. Those words seemed to resonate in my head. My eyes widened as I stared at David, my pulse quickening as I felt I was on the verge of discovering the solution to a troublesome riddle. Why had I been so inept at insinuating myself with strangers when I'd been trained for it nearly my entire life? Because I hadn't been given any specific task to do. No goal to accomplish.

"What is it? What's my mission?"

If David thought my choice of words odd, he didn't mention it. "We're at your service." He smiled. "That's what Mr. Rappaport, the man who started the BBW, demanded of anyone who worked for him. That we help our customers find what they need, when they need it. That we do everything in our power to make their shopping experience as pleasant as possible so they'll always want to give us their business. See? It's not difficult to figure out." David straightened and paused to ruffle my hair before turning to pick up the dirty plates and silverware. His voice drifted back to me as he walked toward the sink. "You'll get the hang of it as you get more comfortable. Just smile and be helpful! That's all there is to it."

I wasn't sure how well I could do the smiling part, but the rest of it didn't sound too hard. I felt reassured by the simple vision David had laid out for me. *Mission: Be Nice.* Yes, I could do this. And while I was at it, I would do my best to be useful so David wouldn't mind if I stayed for a while. I knew it would be better if I left and continued to run as far away from the general and the Facility as I possibly could, but I was reluctant to follow that course, even if it was the most prudent. I tried to tell myself I simply wanted the experience of living as a normal person, which had been Father Paul's ultimate wish for me. But the truth was simply that I didn't want to leave quite yet. I suspected David had more to teach me about being human, and I was determined to be a good student. I stood for a moment watching him do dishes, his hands moving effortlessly through the familiar task. After a moment I became aware that my body temperature had begun to rise as I found myself thinking of what else those hands might be able to do.

"Good night," I said abruptly.

"Going to bed already?" David glanced at the analog clock hanging on the wall. "It's still pretty early."

"I'm kind of tired," I prevaricated. "I'll see you in the morning."

"Okay," David answered. "Night."

I retreated to the bathroom, carelessly dropping my new clothes onto the floor before reaching for the shower controls. As the small room filled with steam, I retrieved the rectangular case I had been carrying in my pocket all day. I opened it and counted the number of small blue pills nestled inside.

"Twenty-five," I said quietly. Enough for six months, longer if I ate properly, and tonight's B12-rich dinner was precisely what I needed. I gazed at my hazy reflection in the mirror as another memory of my mentor surfaced in my thoughts.

"Come here, my boy." Father Paul had waited patiently until I was settled on his lap as we took a break from the head-to-head, first-person shooter video game we had been playing. Our playtime was precious to us both, although Father Paul knew that, at five years old, I was learning skills more lethal than simply killing as many digital zombies as I could hit. My impressive score had filled him with pride and saddened him in equal measure.

"What is it, Father Paul?"

"It's time for your medicine." A hand that was just beginning to show its age held out a familiar blue pill. He suppressed a grin at the sight of my reluctant face.

"But it's yucky." Complain though I might, I had been trained in unquestioning obedience from the moment of my birth. I took it without further protest, though my expression screwed up at the unpleasant taste.

"That's a good boy. I know you don't like it, but you have to promise me you'll take it every week, even if I'm not around."

"But why do I have to take it?" Obedience hadn't stopped my curiosity.

He took a moment to reply, clearly considering how best to explain such an unpleasant subject to a young child whose life literally hung on his answer. "Remember your biology class last week?" He smiled at my nod. "Well, everyone's body needs certain nutrients so it will work properly. That's why we make you eat that nasty porridge." He tickled me under my arms, clearly gratified to hear the utterly normal peals of laughter which resulted from his attack. At that point, the capacity for merriment hadn't been completely beaten out of me. "Well, while most people can get the vitamins they need from what they eat, there is one specific way in which you're different."

My expression drooped in predictable fashion as it did whenever I was told how I was unlike other people. "How?" I asked, my voice small.

"None of its goddamn business. It will know what it needs to know when I want it to."

The recollection of the general's harsh interruption brought me back to the present. Looking at my nearly obscured reflection, I couldn't help but feel some gratitude that Woodard had kept Father Paul from telling me the truth for so long. Even now, I wished I remained ignorant of the fact that my life had an expiration date. Carefully, I took one of the pills and placed it on the tip of my tongue. Sticking it out, I watched until the pill had completely dissolved. *One more week down the hatch.* Father Paul had tried to make a game out of it, and I wondered now how the old man had managed to stay so upbeat knowing what he'd been forced to do to his prized creation.

Stepping into the shower, I closed my eyes and positioned my head beneath the cascade of hot water. My hygiene while at the lab had been sufficient but perfunctory, and I thought I could come to greatly enjoy the luxury of taking my time in the shower. Tomorrow I would face my first full day at my new job, and I would have an opportunity to put my resolve into practice. *Be Nice.* I wondered how David would react to the name of my self-imposed mission. He would probably laugh in that awkward way he did when he was confused about something. Alone like I was at the moment, I could freely admit I very much enjoyed the pleasant sound.

I came to a sudden decision. Doing my job well would make David's life easier, so I would extend my mission parameters to doing whatever I could to please my new employer. I'd felt a sense of accomplishment whenever Father Paul had praised me, and I realized I wanted the same from David. I hadn't been raised to have independent motivations. Acting for another made things easier. David had asked me about my fictional stepfather, but since my only real father figure was gone, I found I needed a replacement. David would do nicely.

If I could give you any advice, my boy, it would be to never lie to yourself, even if you have to lie to everyone else.

I turned my face up to the spray. I'd been on my own for barely a week and already I was forsaking Father Paul's advice. I couldn't say for certain exactly how I thought of the man who had so kindly let me barge into his life, but "father figure?" I didn't think that quite captured it. "Friend?" The term was more accurate, but somehow lacked the proper connotation. A noise caught my attention, and tuning out the white noise of the shower, I identified the sound of footsteps shuffling along the carpeted hallway. When I heard the closing of a door, I knew David had retired to his bedroom for the evening and would mostly likely soon make use of his bed.

As I lathered myself my thoughts idly turned to what I knew about that particular piece of furniture. Most people slept in them. I'd only had a bunk for my own rest cycles, although it had been more akin to a slab of metal with a cushion on it than the comfortable-looking object David had struggled to unearth for me the day before. Sleeping on it the night before had been a revelation. But I also knew from my lessons that beds could be put to a different use that had nothing at all to do with somnolence.

That's not going to cut it, soldier. My grandma can give better head than that!

Even now the mere memory of the general's biting comment made me shiver as violently as when I'd first heard it. My lessons in seduction had eventually taken on a more practical aspect, resulting in my attempting, on that occasion, to perform oral sex on one of the Facility's guards. The soldier had been sitting on a bunk while I'd knelt at his feet. Ignoring the general's railing as best I could, I'd tried to monitor the guard's heavy breathing and occasional grunts to determine which of my maneuvers were successful and which were not.

Thinking about the various sounds the soldier had uttered instantly took me back to the previous evening. I suddenly understood the noises I'd heard coming from David's room. Not groans of pain, but moans of pleasure. David had likely been performing genital manipulation on himself in the privacy of his room. Surprisingly, no unpleasant associations arose to trouble me as I imagined what David had been doing to cause those intriguing noises. Instead, my cock began to swell, reminding me that, in many ways, I was the same physiologically as any other healthy nineteen-year-old male. But though I had performed manual stimulation on other men, I had never done it to myself.

You sure are taking your time in here. Need any help?

I didn't open my eyes, knowing David hadn't really come into the bathroom to check on me. In addition to those objectionable lessons, one of my instructors had required me to watch sexually explicit pictures and videos under the pretext of educating me. Perversely, I drew on the memory of one particular video my trainer had favored as I allowed my hand to slowly wander over my chest.

Maybe. In my mind, my voice held a sort of breathless emotion I knew I could never achieve in reality. I inhaled as my palm grazed over a peaked nipple.

What, you've never taken a shower before? David's laugh was throaty and went straight to the rapidly hardening flesh between my legs. A phantom finger reached out and traced through the beads of water on my chest. My hand followed as the imagined touch travelled down over my belly and then lower still. *Are you dirty? Huh? Tell me, are you a dirty boy?*

I remembered the bad dialogue perfectly, but while the actors' speech had been stilted and dull, the David of my imagination spoke the words with hoarse passion.

Dirty boys need to be washed clean.

I reached one hand for the soap resting in the holder at my shoulder. The other I wrapped around the erect cock that had risen to bob against my stomach. I gasped at that first touch, amazed at how such a simple contact could ignite what seemed like every nerve ending in my body.

"Nngh!"

Did you like that? You like the feel of a man's hand wrapped around your dick, don't you, boy?

"Yessss...." I hadn't meant to speak aloud, but the fantasy had begun to blur with reality. My hands—David's hands—became one and the same. They were strong and confident, caressing my body with soap and palm, knowing exactly how to draw forth more of the helpless noises from my throat.

That's right, baby. Thumb and forefinger curved into a ring, David squeezed my length, moving from the tip of my cock to the base and back again. *Let me hear you. Tell me how you like it.*

"Ahh, faster!"

You want it faster?

"Yes, please!"

As he was in real life, the David of my fantasy was quick to oblige. Tightening the small circle, the fingers were joined by their fellows as David began to work me in earnest. Without conscious intent, my hips began to move in time with the stroking hand. I groaned and fell back against the wall, the cool tile making no impression as it touched my heated skin.

And what about here? This part looks lonely.

As his hand reached the tip of my cock, a clever thumb stroked firmly over the bulbous head.

"Nngh! Wait, don't!"

Uh-uh. You liked that, didn't you? So why would I stop?

Another stroke, another rub, and I begged again for mercy, dropping the soap to better concentrate on what was happening between my thighs. A deep chuckle greeted my pleas as David's thumb and hand continued their combined assault. The wall was the only thing keeping me upright. I spread my feet, bracing them against the sides of the tub in order to give David better access.

That's it, beautiful. Show me everything. Give it all to me.

A gentle touch ghosted over the sac nestled tautly at the base of my cock. I bit my lip to muffle the shout that threatened to burst forth from my throat. My entire body shook as jets of viscous cream shot from my cock. On it went, until I feared I would turn inside out. As suddenly as it had started, my climax ended, and I slumped to the floor of the tub utterly drained.

Good boy.

I felt a hand caress my head, and my eyes flew open. Both of my hands were hanging between my parted knees. I was completely alone. My first time achieving sexual release perhaps should have seemed more momentous, but instead I was consumed by the ache that slowly spread through me, starting in the region of my chest. It wasn't grief, not this time. Loneliness? Was that it? With heavy limbs, I pushed myself to my feet and turned off the cooling water. A quick glance around revealed that the evidence of my self-indulgence had been thoroughly washed down the drain.

Shame. The nature of the emotion came to me suddenly. It filled me, setting my face aflame. How could I have used David in such a disgraceful way, even if it had all been in my mind? True, I was still contemplating whether to offer my body in exchange for David's fidelity, but this was something else altogether.

Disgusted with my sudden inability to control even the most basic of my body's reactions, I replaced the neglected bar of soap and got out of the shower to reach for a towel. After drying off, I wrapped it around my waist and gathered up my clothes. Opening the bathroom door, I listened carefully for signs of life, but David's bedroom door was closed, and darkness filled the narrow sliver of space between it and the carpet. Moving silently, I walked over to the barrier separating me from the unwitting star of my waking dream. Slowly I raised a hand and placed it against the painted wood for a long moment before retreating to my own room.

"SAY THAT again, soldier." Woodard stared at the hapless lieutenant who had come to bring him news on the search effort. His anger was only slightly mollified by the way the young officer flinched at the slight to his rank.

"We struck out with the NSA, sir. They won't assist us with any satellite surveillance without a direct order from DoD."

Woodard slowly put down the pen he'd been using to sign requisition orders. It had been over five days since the unit had escaped, and given its physical stamina and top foot speed, it could be anywhere in a five-hundred-mile radius. He silently cursed at the eggheads who'd insisted starting a manhunt immediately upon the unit's escape had been an unnecessary risk. He'd given in to their request to delay until they'd gathered more information, and as a result they had lost valuable time. Now the unit had an insurmountable head start. Sitting back in his overly stuffed chair, the one luxury he allowed himself, Woodard stared at the man standing at attention before his desk until the lieutenant began to squirm. The young officer barely looked old enough to shave, and the vast difference in their ages made Woodard intensely aware of how long he'd been on this project.

"That is unacceptable, Lieutenant." Standing quickly, Woodard frowned as his subordinate broke his position of attention and stumbled back. The show of cowardice made him want to attack, like a shark that smelled blood in the water. Weakness was the one thing he hated more than incompetence, and it was this idiot's bad luck to possess both. Still, he couldn't place all the blame at the hapless lieutenant's feet. He'd known it would be difficult to gain cooperation from any agency that operated more or less in public view. The secrecy of the TM project was paramount, and as a result, he couldn't go around asking for help outright without giving the game away.

"Yes, sir." The lieutenant's voice cracked slightly. "Perhaps the Company would be willing to place pressure on the NSA?"

"Doubtful," Woodard spat, resisting the urge to harangue the man more stringently. Talbot and her cronies would likely be extremely reluctant to expose their connection with the project even if they somehow had the clout to bring the NSA to heel. Nothing was ever fucking easy, no matter how much he wished it were otherwise. Woodard turned toward the large map of the Southwestern United States tacked up on his wall, as much to give the younger man psychological space as to avoid having to look at him and his ignorant face any longer.

The lieutenant spoke in a rush as he continued his report, as though he wanted to finish and depart Woodard's office as soon as he could. "We have already searched every square inch between here, Clovis, Roswell, and Las Vegas, but we found no trace of the unit. The dry ground has made surface tracking difficult, and TM 05637 did not leave any indications of its presence in any of the rest stops, gas stations, or other locations where it might have been able to sleep and obtain food."

"Of course it wouldn't," Woodard growled. "TM 05637 has been trained to be a shadow. If it doesn't want to be found, it will be damned hard to track down." He spun around and glared at the unfortunate man. "Widen the search. It's been long enough that the unit may have had to seek medical attention by now. Check all hospitals in the search grid for anyone who has checked-in bearing signs of the unit's condition. Go into Texas, into Colorado, Arizona, Utah. Hell, go into Mexico if you have to, Lieutenant, just find it!"

The young officer wisely took the hint and fled. Woodard waited until the door to his office had finished swinging shut before dropping back into his chair and bringing his laptop out of hibernation. He had been typing up a status report on the recovery mission for Talbot and the Company. The lieutenant's interruption had been welcome before he realized he wouldn't have any new information to pass along to the anxious financiers.

"Fuck 'em." After pushing a button to put the laptop to sleep, Woodard sat back in his chair, allowing it to tip back at a reckless angle. Over twenty-five years of his life he'd dedicated to this project, and what did he have to show for it? Rebellion, insubordination, and incompetence. He'd believed in the mission when he'd been a fresh-faced captain, excited to be a part of the unprecedented venture that had been so secret it was only spoken of in soundproof rooms at the Pentagon. And in many ways he still did. The threat of terrorism had only increased in the years since the Reds had ceased being a thorn in the country's side, and this project continued to hold the most promise for attacking the problem at its source. But he was tired of all the bullshit that came with the job.

The Mobile Termination project, reversed and shortened to "TM" because some young wiseass in development had thought it was a clever acronym, was intended to do precisely that: produce highly mobile, utterly lethal, genetically enhanced soldiers. The TM units could be sent anywhere to do anything at any time. They would be bred and raised to exhibit higher than normal athleticism, extraordinary intelligence, and unquestioning loyalty to their handlers. TM 05637 was the prototype, the result of over twenty years of research, false starts, and crushing failures. It had been the first baby to be born alive with the full complement of genetic modifiers the project's architects,

73

Dr. Anderson and Ms. Talbot, had intended the units to possess. The powers that be had been thrilled to learn of TM 05637's successful gestation. The menace posed by the amorphous terrorist groups that threatened the existence of the free world had only grown more real. The TM units were desperately needed, and 05637 was to be the first of many of its kind.

But while its accomplishments on the simulated missions it had been given thus far were more than adequate by the standards of regular soldiers, Woodard had been greatly disappointed with TM 05637's performance. The unit's physical stamina and martial prowess, its ability to figure out solutions to the trickiest of test scenarios—its aptitude in those arenas was unquestioningly superior, but the little prick's attitude left a lot to be desired. TM 05637 hadn't quite reached the level of insubordinate, but it had been obvious the unit's acquiescence to the tasks it was assigned had been grudging at best. The thinly disguised reluctance had pissed him off to no end, and he knew precisely where to lay the blame.

Dr. Paul Anderson. The man was brilliant, no doubt about it. While Talbot and her consortium had come up with the idea for the TM project, Dr. Anderson was solely responsible for bringing it to fruition. His expertise in the field of genetics was unparalleled. He'd navigated his way through the minefield of DNA manipulation with nary a misstep, taking every failed attempt as an opportunity to gain further knowledge, and presenting a solution on the other side that shaved years, if not decades, off the project's timeline. He was a man of science, the purest of the breed, for whom such quaint notions of ethics and conscience rarely entered into his calculations. He enjoyed the pursuit of knowledge for its own sake, and the trail of miscarried fetuses and broken surrogates he and his assistants had left in their wake were simply curiosities to be studied, learned from, and ultimately forgotten.

And then TM 05637 had been born, and suddenly the scientist had become a father. "Father Paul" the unit had called him, and the man had done his utmost to live up to the moniker. Woodard had no idea why Anderson had become so attached to his experiment, but his commitment, his love for the unit was undeniable. If TM 05637 had been defiant, it was because Anderson had persuaded it to be so.

Woodard felt the muscles in his shoulders tighten at the very thought of the man who'd literally given life to the project and then had blithely taken it all away. Forcing himself to relax, Woodard allowed one corner of his mouth to lift in a barely visible smile. Anderson was no longer a factor, and if that fact couldn't cheer him up, even if only a little, nothing could. As he started back in on his report, he felt his mood sour all over again at the thought of the TM project's other figurehead. If Anderson was the program's father, then Talbot was its mother, and the she-bear wouldn't be satisfied until her wayward cub had been found.

"Fuck 'em," Woodard said again in defiance. But when it came right down to it, he was under no delusions about who wore the strap-on in his relationship with Talbot. If someone was going to be screwed over TM 05637's disappearance, it was going to be him, and he'd be damned if he went down without a fight.

SIX

"YES, OKAY. Bring the samples by this Friday afternoon, and I'll take a look. You have a good day too."

David disconnected the call and placed the phone handset on its cradle. Pulling back his shoulders, he cracked his back before glancing at the clock on his desktop computer. Three-thirty. He and Tim had gotten in at eight that morning, and he didn't want to keep the kid working longer than a normal shift his first day. Tim had been quiet at breakfast and on the drive to the store. After their odd exchange the night before, David hadn't been sure what would be a safe topic to break the silence. He did wonder, though, how his newest employee had fared during his first full day of work. He'd been in his office almost from the moment they'd arrived and had spent the entire day talking to prospective vendors. David felt a bit guilty for keeping holed up in his office all this time without once seeing how the kid was doing. Well, now was as good a time as any.

As soon as he walked out into the main area, David half wished he'd stayed behind his closed door. Lucy Danvers, one of his newer employees, was waiting for him with a fretful look on her pixie-shaped face.

"Oh, Mr. Conley, I was just coming to get you." Without warning, she turned and headed toward the front section of the store. Having no other choice, he followed, his concern growing as he noted her hurry.

"What's going on, Lucy?"

"A gentleman came in with his son and has been causing a disturbance. William was trying to calm him down, but I thought I should get you."

David could already hear the irate customer's raised voice, as well as the slow drawl of his second-shift manager, William Hurley. Lucy led him toward the sporting goods department, and as he rounded a corner into the main aisle, he noticed the squabble had drawn an audience. Several employees and not a few customers were watching the train wreck unfolding in front of a shelf of catcher's mitts.

"I told you, you little piece of shit, it's not the glove. You just can't catch worth a damn!"

"Sir, I'm gonna have to ask you to keep your voice down."

"Mind your own goddamn business. This is between me and my son."

David sighed and held up a hand to let Lucy know he'd handle it. An angry brown-haired man was up in William's face, but the manager was smiling at him with the same placidly benign expression he always wore. His sheer unflappability was what made him so effective in his job. A young man wearing a baseball uniform from a local high school was staring down at the floor, his chagrin evident in his beet-red complexion. The resemblance between the two was apparent, and David immediately grasped the nature of the situation. As he approached the three men, something in the corner of his eye caught his attention. He glanced over and frowned as he saw Tim staring fixedly at the belligerent man and the mortified boy, who was probably only a few years younger than him. His slim hands were clenched around the bottom hem of his store vest, his impassive features frozen but somehow clearly conveying his disquiet.

The man turned his back on William and pulled a packaged catcher's mitt off a nearby shelf. "Go on, then." He threw the glove at his son's feet. "Take it and show me that all you need is a new glove. Let's go out into the front lot, and I'll toss you a few." The man stepped into the boy's space and stared at him until the teen met his gaze. Unfortunately for the father, his son was a bit taller than him, lessening his intimidation factor. But the boy still looked plenty frightened as his father grabbed his chin with harsh fingers. "But I swear to God, if you drop even one ball like you did during that game, you little faggot, I'll show you what a bat is good for!"

David had seen and heard enough. "Sir, can I ask you to please step outside?" He glanced around at his employees, and at his pointed stare, they dispersed, taking the other customers with them. He noticed Tim hadn't moved, seeming rooted to the floor, but he needed to deal with this first. "William, I've got this."

"Thank you, Mr. Conley."

The man glared at him, unimpressed. "Who the fuck are you?"

"I own this store, Mr.…?"

"Baker. And I'm a customer, *Mister* Conley. You have no right to throw me out. Not when I'm trying to make a purchase."

David raised his eyebrow at the man. "Are you? Because it looked to me like you were planning to use my merchandise without paying for it."

Baker sputtered at him. "You've got some nerve!"

"And you've got some nerve talking to your son like that in public." David lowered his voice until no one else could hear him. "Now, I know I have no say in how you treat your kid, but I won't have you verbally abusing him in my store. Is that understood?" With a grin plastered on his face, he turned to the mortified high schooler. "Son, we have a generous return policy. You're welcome to purchase any of our gloves, and as long as you keep your receipt and return it within fifteen days, we'll take it back even if it's been used." David placed a friendly hand on the boy's shoulder and glanced down at the insignia on his uniform. "You go to Estanado, huh? I hear they've got quite a good team this year!" David kept up the small talk with the teen as he ushered him and his father to the front. He personally rang up the purchase of the catcher's mitt the asshole had thrown on the floor, bagged it, and handed it to the boy. The young man hadn't stopped blushing, but now he wore a shy smile, which brightened his expression considerably. "Have a good day, and come back anytime."

A round of applause broke out as soon as the father and son disappeared through the front doors. David looked around in surprise and saw not only his staff, but some customers joining in. Tim was standing toward the back of the crowd, and he could almost feel the kid's piercing gaze boring into him.

"Thanks, Mr. Conley." William blocked his view of Tim as he approached with his imperturbable smile firmly in place. "That was kind of a touchy situation."

"No problem, Will. That's what I'm here for." David clapped his manager on the shoulder. "But now, it really is time for me to go. I think I could use a drink after that."

William laughed, and David joined in briefly before turning back to his office. He needed to shut down his computer and grab his things so he could leave. Or rather, so they could leave. David looked around for Tim and headed in his direction when he caught sight of the familiar dark head. Tim hadn't moved from his position at the head of the aisle leading into the sporting goods section.

"Hey, kid, you okay?" David frowned when Tim looked at him with a rather shell-shocked expression. "What's going on in there?" He tapped Tim lightly on the forehead, and incredibly, it seemed to pull the kid back from wherever he had gone.

"Yes. Sorry. It's just...." Tim hesitated and bit his lip. David glanced at the white teeth worrying the soft flesh only for a second before he forcibly dragged his too-interested gaze back up to the kid's uncertain eyes. "I didn't understand why that man was being so mean to his son."

In a flash of insight, David understood what had Tim so bothered. *And I thought I had daddy issues.* Sighing, he placed a hand on Tim's back and urged the kid to go ahead of him into his office. He waited until he had closed the door behind them before nodding at the chair situated in front of his desk.

"Go on, have a seat." He took his own chair while he waited for Tim to comply. The kid watched him without comment as he turned off his computer, the task giving him a moment to think. "So, why was that guy being such a jerk? Well, I guess sometimes boys can have very complicated relationships with their fathers." He glanced over at Tim. "But you know that, right?" A half smile twisted his lips when Tim nodded. "A father will often have a notion of the kind of man he wants his son to be, but unfortunately, what a father wants and what his son wants aren't always the same thing. And when they aren't, I suppose it makes sense that a father can get frustrated." David sat back heavily in his chair, his smile turning rueful. He wasn't referring only about the baseball player and his overly demanding parent. Though he didn't usually like talking about himself, the wide eyes looking at him so expectantly prompted him to open up. "My own dad had those same concerns about me."

"About you?"

David grinned at Tim's disbelieving tone. "Yeah. Believe you me, I didn't exactly leave my dad bursting with pride."

Tim's forehead creased, as if he couldn't make sense of the revelation. "Why not?"

Because he didn't want a homo as a son. David knew he couldn't come right out with that, though, not when he hadn't come clean to his houseguest about that particular tidbit. No use worrying the kid unnecessarily that he might attack him in the middle of the night or something. Clearing his throat, David came up with something equally true.

"My dad wanted me to go into the service and then to med school, just like he had done. Dad was an Army doctor, and after he retired he was the main physician in our town for over twenty years." David laughed without amusement. "You'd think wanting to be an attorney would make any parent proud, but not my dad. 'No son of mine is going to be some sissy lawyer,'" he grumbled, lowering his voice to emulate his father. "Anyway," he continued in his normal tone, "when I insisted I wanted to get a prelaw degree and then to go on to law school, he told me I was a disappointment and that I'd get no help from him." David didn't add that his father had added the *sissy* label only after he'd confessed to liking men. "So I moved to Lubbock and went to Texas Tech. I majored in finance and minored in prelaw, though it turned out not to be as interesting as I thought it would be. But it all worked out in the end. I got a business degree and an MBA, and now I own this store. There's no place else I'd rather be." David noticed Tim was looking at him thoughtfully. "I say all this only to tell you that you have to live your own life. You can't let anyone else live it for you, not even your stepfather. But you seem to have figured that out already, yeah? Otherwise you wouldn't be here."

Tim blinked, as though appreciating the truth of his statement. "I suppose so. But it is... difficult to handle the criticism. Especially when it's from someone important to you."

"Yeah, it is." David stood and leaned on his desk so he could peer down at Tim with a conspiratorial smirk. "Which is why there's only one thing to do when you're feeling down."

"What's that?"

"Eat a mess of barbeque, of course! Tell me, kid, have you ever had genuine Texas beef ribs?"

Tim shook his head, his expression bemused at the abrupt change of subject.

"A travesty we must remedy right away," David announced. He grabbed his wallet and keys and rounded his desk. "Come on, kid. I promise, after you try the ribs at T&B's, you won't even remember your stepfather's name."

Tim shot him a skeptical glance, but David congratulated himself on ridding him of the haunted look he'd worn earlier. David knew he never wanted to see the kid so upset again and marveled at how very badly he was failing at his resolve to keep his emotional distance from this unexpected addition to his life.

Several hours—and far too much food—later, David fell into bed, still chuckling at the memory of Tim encountering his first plate of beef ribs. The kid had been skeptical at first, but as soon as he'd taken a bite, it had been game on. David had never in his life seen bones cleaned so thoroughly or with such gusto. Tim had devoured nearly half a rack before taking a breath, and he wondered where the kid put it all on his slim frame. *Teenage boys*, he mused. At one time, he'd been the same way, active in sports, growing, and eating his parents out of house and home. Now, not so much. Placing a hand over the slight paunch of his overly full stomach, he acknowledged that his metabolism had taken a turn for the worse over the past decade. There was no way he'd be able to keep up with the human vacuum in the next room.

Closing his eyes, he began the process of shutting off his brain for the night. He had a tendency to dwell on the day's events, making it difficult for him to fall asleep on occasion. But this time it wasn't thoughts of work keeping him up. At one point during dinner, Tim's ribs had fought back and left a streak of sauce on his cheek, starting at the corner of his mouth and ending near his right ear. David had determinedly resisted the desire to lick off the tangy smear. Choosing practicality over lust, he'd merely laughed and removed the sauce with one of the wet cloths the restaurant conveniently provided. In return he'd earned one of those shy almost-smiles he was starting to love.

Love? Whoa. David groaned and turned on his side, beating his pillow and his stupidity into submission. No, that wasn't it, because that would be extremely dumb. Tim wouldn't be here forever, and he needed to accept that he was nothing but a stop along the road of the kid's life. That's all he could be, and dammit, that's all he wanted to be. Right?

"Right," he mumbled aloud, wishing he believed that.

He must have fallen asleep eventually, because the clock read past 2:00 a.m. when David realized he was awake. Groggy, it took another minute before he figured out what had disturbed him. He wasn't certain what the sound was at first, but when he heard it again, he was out of his bed before the newest shout from the other bedroom had died. Tim had left his door open, explaining why it had been so easy to hear him. Another yell dispelled the last dregs of slumber, and abandoning caution, David approached the restless figure lying on the bed in the spare room.

"Tim?"

"Ummmph."

"Tim," he said, trying again. "Wake up." He laid a hand on the kid's shoulder and jumped back to avoid the shadow aimed unerringly at his face as Tim sat straight up and took a swing at him.

"Nooo!"

The room was dim, but David grabbed what he thought was a flailing arm. "Tim! Come on, kid. Wake up!"

Whether it was the sound of his voice or the touch of his hand, Tim immediately stilled. David breathed a sigh of relief, grateful that the nightmare had released its grip. Though he couldn't see clearly, he could feel the kid staring at him. The sense of terror radiating from Tim was palpable. Without thinking, David sat on the edge of the bed. He reached out and rested his hand on Tim's head, smoothing the black tangle of hair in a soothing gesture. For a long moment the silence was broken only by the harsh rasps of the kid's breathing, and then Tim suddenly slumped over, his head landing against David's shoulder. Thinking of nothing but comforting the frightened teen, David wrapped his arms around the slight body leaning against him...

And promptly noticed Tim was as naked as the day he was born. The heat of bare skin burned against him, seeping into not only his chest but also his thigh from the slim leg pressed against his. David's heart sank as other parts of him rapidly stood to attention. He thought frantically about how to most quickly extract himself, but the opportunity to do so receded as Tim returned his embrace, settling against him more fully. He could feel the rapid pounding of the kid's heart and figured the bad dream hadn't yet completely left him. His plan for escape thwarted, David latched on to the question foremost in his mind.

"Um, Tim, where are your clothes?"

"I took them off before I went to bed."

Okay. Apparently he needed to be more literal. "I meant, where are your pajamas?"

"Pajamas?"

With his blood rapidly draining elsewhere, David didn't have the brain power to wonder at the kid's genuine confusion. "Yeah, you know, clothes you sleep in. Like I'm wearing." For once, he had worn his top to bed in addition to the bottoms, and he was beyond grateful that he had. One of them naked was more than enough.

"I don't have any."

That was painfully clear. It made sense that the kid hadn't been carrying them with him while on the road. He'd probably just slept in whatever he'd worn that day. But now that he was in a more conventional situation, the lack didn't make sense. *Unless the kid always sleeps naked.* Desperate to avoid the intriguing assumption, David asked the logical follow-up.

"Didn't you buy some yesterday along with your other clothes?"

"You didn't tell me to."

The response should have sounded strange, but somehow it didn't. Even after only a two-day acquaintance, David had come to understand a few things about Tim. He was secretive, he was eager to please, and he was awkward unless given direct instructions. Even with the clothing he did purchase, the kid had followed David's offhand remark of *a couple of pairs of jeans and few shirts* to the letter. He suspected the other items Tim had bought were thanks to Patricia's intervention rather than his own initiative.

"Okay," David sighed. "Tomorrow, we'll get you a few sets." The head against his chest moved in a nod, but the kid didn't otherwise reply. The pace of Tim's heartbeat had begun to slow but was not yet back to normal. David steeled himself to chip away even further at the emotional barrier he'd tried—and failed—to build between them. "Want to talk about it?" After a brief hesitation the kid's face rubbed against his chest in a side-to-side motion. Rather than admit he was grateful for Tim's reticence, David told himself it was his right to have his secrets.

"That's okay." David glanced at the desk clock sitting next to his computer, barely able to read the numbers in the faintly glowing display. "There's a while before we need to get up for work." Slowly, so as not to telegraph any unintended rejection, he moved to extricate himself from Tim's arms. Or at least that's what he meant to do. Instead he found himself unable to move. At first he thought maybe he was simply weak from waking up so quickly, but even after giving himself a second to gather his strength, he found he was unable to stand up. He was beginning to make the connection between his immobility and the slim arms wrapped around his waist when a small voice broke through his bemusement.

"Please stay."

David looked down and caught a glimpse of Tim's dark gaze before the kid buried his face against his shoulder once more. The heat pouring through the fabric of his shirt indicated just how mortified the kid must have felt at making such a childish request. David remembered back to when he'd been Tim's age. Asking for comfort had been lower than cleaning the septic tank on the list of things he wanted to do.

"Sure," he said, before he could think better of it. "Move over a little."

What followed was a complicated dance that ended up with the two of them lying on the narrow bed, the kid trying his best to meld their bodies together while David valiantly attempted to maintain some physical distance between them. The fact that Tim was still very, very naked made it a matter of life and the little death for him. When a warm hand suddenly burrowed under his top, he sucked in his stomach partly in shock and partly in embarrassment at his nascent spare tire. The hand stopped right above his navel, and he forced himself not to read anything into the unexpected grope as Tim began to relax toward sleep.

"Gawd," he whispered, wondering how in the hell he'd gotten into this situation. He might have been the envy of every other gay man in the world right then, but this whole thing was about to drive him insane.

"What?"

Tim shifted as he opened his eyes and peered up into David's face. David shook his head and reached down to pull the covers up over them. The blankets would make him far too warm, but it might encourage the kid to move away to avoid overheating.

"Nothing. Good night."

And just because the universe hated him, the kid spent the remainder of the night snuggled close to his side, completely ruining any chance of him falling asleep. Tomorrow, he swore to himself, he was buying Tim a goddamn pair of pajamas.

SEVEN

"THIS IS the last time I will tolerate your little toy botching one of my training simulations, Doctor." The colonel loomed threateningly over Father Paul as I watched, the rifle I'd used during the simulation clutched in my small hands. The scientist's gaze was trained down toward his clasped hands, his shoulders hunched in a show of contrition. "You promised me perfection, and yet what have you given me? TM 05637 is nothing but an insanely expensive yet useless mess."

"I assure you, Colonel, he is in prime condition."

"That's a load of crap, and you know it. It's supposed to be able to carry out the most difficult missions, but it can't even finish this basic exercise." Woodard stabbed a finger toward the two dummies that were still standing after I'd run the obstacle course. The colonel ignored the ten that lay in bullet-riddled ruins. "Hell, any green cadet still pissing in his pants could do it!" Woodard's jaw was clenched so hard my acute hearing caught the scraping sound of dental enamel grinding together. "Your precious creation is flawed, Doctor. If not, then you tell me why it can't carry out even the simplest task."

"The scenario is hardly simple, Colonel, and he's only seven years old." Father Paul glanced at me worriedly. "Perhaps if we eased him into the more difficult missions—"

"I'm not running a fucking daycare, Doctor! Either it's ready to perform to spec, or I'm ending this project and finding someone who can give me what I want." A long, meaty finger served as a counterpoint to the warning as the colonel jabbed it toward Father

Paul's face. "I won't repeat myself. Fix the problem, or it will be scrapped."

"He simply needs more time."

Woodard walked over to the video screen on the wall and flipped a switch, bringing up an image of a red-headed woman sitting at a small desk in a sparsely decorated room. Father Paul choked off a gasp and glared at the colonel.

"Don't do this."

Woodard's grin was a frightening thing. "Maybe it just needs a little incentive, one I'd be more than happy to provide." He toggled another switch and spoke into the communication relay. "Sergeant Cooper, meet me in Karen's quarters in ten." Woodard stared coldly at me. "Maybe now you'll learn not to fuck with me."

I STACKED another package of infant diapers on the growing pile, taking comfort in the simple physics calculations that governed how high I could go before the tower toppled over. Patricia kept glancing over at me from farther down the aisle as she helped a young couple choose the appropriate formula for their newborn. The child was securely ensconced in a holster strapped to the father's chest and seemed none too happy about the arrangement. The sounds of the infant's fussing distracted both the parents and Patricia, making the exchange take far longer than it should have.

Silently thanking the young child for the reprieve, I doggedly continued the mindless task. Embarrassment had been completely unfamiliar to me until now, and I found I disliked it intensely. I'd awakened that morning huddled against David, not unlike the baby curled up against its father. Only I'd been far more content with my position. Or rather, I had been until I remembered begging like a small child to be rocked to sleep. I'd retreated to the bathroom before David woke up, and when I finally steadied myself enough to return, he had fortunately gone back to his own room. Breakfast that morning had been a perfunctory affair, the awkward silence that stretched between us broken only by the most necessary of exchanges.

The dream continued to nag at me. It hadn't been a nightmare, but rather a memory of the closest I'd ever come to being destroyed for failing to satisfy the general. And the closest I'd ever been to wanting to kill the man with my bare hands. I'd been tasked with running an obstacle course while hitting a certain percentage of the targets, but the weight of the gun and the equipment I'd been required to wear made success difficult. And it hadn't only been my life at stake. What the general called "incentive" had proven effective—within the next two years I'd grown enough so I could easily finish the course with perfect accuracy. But I'd never outgrown the weight of the general's disapproval or my fear of the man who'd, in many ways, been more central to my existence than even Father Paul. Still, I had never dreamed about the incident before last night. Seeing the man yelling at his son yesterday must have been the trigger. Trying to forget had only made me remember the incident with greater clarity, as well as another I wished I could completely erase from my mind.

Trying to put my humiliation, past and present, from my mind, I continued to precisely stack the packages as the young couple finally moved on, two boxes of high-quality formula in tow.

"I think that's more than enough diapers for now. You can store the rest back in the stockroom."

I glanced down at Patricia and, reacting instinctively to the order, descended from the ladder on which I'd been perched. I arranged the remaining dozen or so bags on the cart I'd used to haul them out to the main floor and began to push it to the back of the store. The stockroom was located adjacent to the break room where Patricia had helped me fill out my paperwork. She followed me as I maneuvered the cart through the aisles, and I tensed, guessing she wanted to speak to me. No one else was in the stockroom when we entered. I turned to her expectantly when she closed the door behind us.

"So, what the heck is going on with you and the boss man? You've been talking and walking past each other all day like a couple of wary coyotes." Her eyes widened as some unpleasant thought occurred to her. I felt trapped as she fixed me with a concerned gaze. "Oh my, you boys didn't have a fight, did you?"

"Well, not really—"

Ignoring me in favor of the crisis she'd built up in her head, Patricia's ample chest swelled as she sighed and shook her head in imagined sympathy. "I know you two have only been living together for a short while. You're both young men, and it can't be easy to always be in each other's way. But you're friends, right? Mr. Conley can be the quiet sort—not that you're mister talkative," she mumbled, "but his heart is in the right place. You two just need some time to get used to each other. You'll see. This little tiff will be forgotten lickety-split!"

"We didn't have a fight," I slipped in when she paused to catch her breath. I glanced longingly at the door, wishing I could walk away from this uncomfortable conversation.

"No?" She regarded me with consternation through long dark lashes that belied her blond hair. "Then what on earth is going on? You two haven't said a word to each other since you came in this morning." She huffed, pursing her lips, as if trying to fathom this mystery that had left her out of sorts.

I didn't give any serious thought to asking her to mind her own business, figuring it wouldn't do much good. But explaining the distance that had formed between me and David since that morning would mean revealing more than my shameful behavior. Caution, necessary and learned, prompted me to hold information about myself close, but I couldn't deny the situation with David was wearing on the few emotions I felt able to claim. I stared at Patricia for a long moment as I considered how to safely assuage her curiosity.

"It's my fault."

Patricia's smile was sad. "Oh, honey, I'm sure that's not true." She blinked when I shook my head.

"No, it is. Something happened last night that... made me feel ashamed, and it's made me uncomfortable around David."

Rounded green-gray eyes stared at me in shock. "You mean, what?" She swallowed, transmitting her nervousness. She leaned in so only I could hear her, though no one else was around to listen. "He did something to you?"

Although I couldn't be certain, I thought her tone hinted at something sexual. Or maybe I was simply putting my own spin on her question. Did she think something physical had happened between me and David? Not likely. For a moment after David had gotten into bed with me, I'd considered putting into action my ill-formed plan of seducing him. I'd even gone so far as to touch the bare skin of David's stomach, intending to follow up the motion with something more definitive. But in the end, what I'd wanted most right then was simply the comfort of his arms holding me close. Humiliating as it seemed in the light of day, at the time, I'd felt safer than I ever had in my life as I listened to his heart beating beneath my ear. My sleep last night had been the most restful I ever had. Now, in the cold light of day, I willingly accepted that my idea of forming a physical attachment to David would never happen, not when the very thought made me feel strangely uneasy.

Shaking my head, I leaned back against the stockroom door and crossed my arms. Although I was reluctant to give Patricia any details, I was secretly glad of the opportunity to unload some of my burden. I trained my gaze down at my new athletic shoes, unable to meet her troubled look. "I-I had a nightmare." I drew in a deep breath and released it in a loud rush. "I woke David up, screaming, and he held me until I fell back asleep."

A line creased her forehead as she looked at me in confusion. "What's so wrong with that? Sounds like something Mr. Conley would do." Her expression grew thoughtful. "Or is it the nightmare itself that's making you so skittish? Something you don't want Mr. Conley to know?"

A jolt buzzed through me as my gaze flew up to meet hers. I stared at her in shock, wondering how she'd figured out something I hadn't even hinted at. Patricia's smile was warm, and the sight of it loosened the knot that had been growing in my stomach ever since I'd woken up in David's arms.

"My mother." I blurted out the words as though they had been fighting to escape. A siren of warning rang shrilly in my head, telling me to keep this particular secret firmly under lock and key, but I ignored it. "She's dead."

Patricia's features slid into genuine remorse. "Oh, sweetie, I'm so sorry." She moved toward me, lifting her arms in the unmistakable precursor to a hug. I continued quickly before she could reach me. "She's dead because of me." *I killed her*, I added silently, stopping short of the full truth.

"What do you mean?" Patricia froze and blinked slowly, her voice reedy as she struggled to process what I'd told her.

"Hey! Drop that!"

We both looked toward the closed door at the same time. I opened it an instant later, only to come face-to-face with David, who had his hand extended toward the doorknob as if he'd been about to open it.

"I mean it!"

There wasn't time for me to determine whether David had overheard my confession. The commotion that had drawn Patricia's and my attention interrupted whatever David had been planning to say. I ran past him and headed toward the noise, David and Patricia following close on my heels. We reached the front of the store just in time to see an elderly man who worked part-time at the BBW standing at the front entrance, his face thunderous as he stared outside.

"Rick," David said when he reached the semiretiree. "What's going on?"

"A damn shoplifter." The old man's frustration was palpable. His pale, mottled hand was balled into a fist against his thigh, and his foot twitched as if he was aching to chase the thief. "I think he stole one of the MP3 players we were getting ready to put in the locked display case. The little bastard was so fast he was practically out the door before I even realized what he'd done."

David sighed and patted Rick on the shoulder. "Well, nothing we can do about it now—"

I was streaking to the front entrance before David even finished his sentence. A customer was just coming in, so I didn't have to wait for the doors to open. In an instant I was outside. Running at my top speed in the most logical direction, I was through the parking lot seconds later.

The stress I was placing on my body felt good. My creators had designed me for this very purpose, to accomplish feats of physical ability and stamina no other human on the planet could hope to match. While the chasm between me and normal people often seemed insurmountable, I was currently grateful for the special skills I possessed. Now to put them to good use.

When I reached the sidewalk encircling the parking lot, I glanced around quickly, my superior vision easily discerning the myriad details that defined downtown Lubbock on a warm afternoon. An old woman strolled along with a small dog in tow; a young man was talking loudly on his cell phone as he maneuvered his large truck into the lot by way of the turn-in lane; a jacket fluttered in the breeze stirred up by a figure moving at rapid speed....

I honed in on the runner, tunnel vision filtering out all irrelevant information. The fleeing person was male and young, no older than his early teens. He was small and fast, though not nearly quick enough to outpace me as I gave chase. The boy led me away from the store and on to the next block, heading east along the main street before taking a hard right at the end of the block a quarter mile from the BBW. I copied the turn easily, and as I closed the distance, I noticed the tattered condition of the shoplifter's coat. The boy's thin legs pumped hard, propelling him toward his destination, which was likely simply wherever he could hide from his pursuer.

Two blocks after the turn, a large park came into view off to the left. The shoplifter darted across the street, barely missing being hit by a car, and headed pell-mell toward the grassy expanse. The boy's trajectory was taking him diagonally across the park toward the fence on the far side. Instead of following directly, I continued along until I reached the end of the block. I crossed the road, timing my passing so the drivers headed toward me didn't need to hit their brakes to avoid me. The sidewalk I turned down ran alongside the fence that defined the boundary of the park. I reached the end of the block right as the boy pitched himself over the chain-link barrier only to land directly at my feet. I had him up against the fence, my arm pressed against his neck, before he could even express his shock at being outmaneuvered.

"Hey, man! Get offa me!" Hazel eyes bulged with fear as the boy glared at me.

"Where's the item you took?"

I stared at him coldly, my tone remote, my only interest to retrieve the stolen property. The size difference between us was not insignificant—I was easily five inches taller—but that didn't stop me from taking advantage of it. I rose to my full height, bringing the boy with me until his feet dangled in the air. His face twisted with panic, his struggles growing slowly weaker as the pressure against his neck began to take its toll.

While talking to Patricia, I'd finally grasped that I wanted only one thing from David, his approval. This opportunity had fallen into my lap, and I refused to let it go to waste. Unlike my failure time and again with the general, I would show David I was someone he could depend on, that I was deserving of trust and was worth keeping around.

"Tim! What are you doing? Drop him!"

David's out-of-breath shout snapped me out of the mission focus I'd been in since beginning my pursuit of the shoplifter. Glancing over at the horrified expression on David's sweaty face, I suddenly realized how the scene must appear to him. I had a terrified child trapped in a choke hold, calmly watching as the boy's life slipped away one missed breath at a time. A sensation I had only ever experienced in the presence of the general jolted me, only this time, the person I was afraid of was myself. I dropped the boy to the ground and backed away. I stood aside as David knelt beside the slight figure slumped in a relieved heap on the sidewalk.

"Are you okay, kid?" David asked, his raspy voice full of concern.

David gently patted the boy's light blond hair, his hand seeming larger than normal against the small head. David shot me a disapproving glare, and it hit me like a punch in the gut. I unconsciously placed a hand over my stomach as my insides seemed to twist and bunch upon themselves.

"Hey," David repeated, "are you all right?"

The towheaded boy took rapid, shallow breaths, desperately trying to fill his starved lungs. "Yeah," he answered, looking up past the man kneeling beside him. The fright on his face as he stared at me only made the rioting in my gut worse.

"What's your name, son?"

The boy stared at David uncertainly, carefully scrutinizing his kind, unthreatening expression. "Bobby."

"Well, Bobby, why aren't you in school?"

The boy's expression changed from fear to sullen mutiny. He dropped his gaze to the ground, refusing to acknowledge either of us as he staged a silent protest at being interrogated.

A wry smile twisted David's lips. "Come on," he said, trying a different tact. "Why don't we grab something to eat?"

The boy glanced up, surprised, his gaze following David, who rose to his feet. "You don't want your MP3 player back?"

David's smile grew. "Oh, I do, but that can wait. Right now, it's time for lunch. I missed it earlier, and I don't know about you, but I'm starving." He turned and started back the way he'd come, glancing around when he was several feet away from us. "Well, are you coming?"

I waited until the boy stood and was following David before joining them, painfully aware that David hadn't spoken to me since he'd first caught up with us. I wondered why I was suddenly having so much difficulty breathing.

EIGHT

"HOWDY! Y'ALL go ahead and have a seat, and I'll be right with you."

David smiled at the woman sporting a flashy pink waitress outfit, matching tennis shoes, and a saucy ponytail. Tina had opened the Ice Cream Emporium fifteen years earlier, and her hot fudge sundaes and triple-stacked burgers brought in loyal customers from as far away as Plainview. Taking her suggestion, he led the two brooding teens to a vinyl-covered booth beside one of the front windows. David sat on one side while the boy—Bobby—took the other. Tim wisely sat next to him but perched as far away on the edge of the seat as he could get without falling off. Rather than comment on the awkward arrangement, David angled himself so he could more easily see them both.

Tim might have several years on Bobby, but the sullen expression on his face made him look uncomfortably close in age to the younger boy. It was a reminder David did not need right then, not with him still trying to sort out his feelings after finding Tim apparently trying to choke the boy to death. No matter the spin he wanted to put on it, it was the only logical conclusion. His heart was still pounding, and not merely from trying to keep up with the teens' blazing speed. David couldn't quite wrap his mind around what he'd seen when he'd finally caught up with them. The bloodless terror on Bobby's face and the utter lack of expression on Tim's. He didn't know which had frightened him more. But he could deal with his overzealous employee later. Right now he had more immediate concerns.

"Bobby, are you hungry?" The unconscious spark of interest in the boy's eyes was all the answer David needed. "Go ahead and order anything you want," he said, keeping his tone light. He glanced over at Tim, who was studiously avoiding eye contact with anyone. While he was disturbed over what the kid had done, from the little he could see of Tim's face, he could tell Tim was equally uneasy with his actions. "Tim, what about you?"

"Hamburger."

David found himself trying to suppress a chuckle. The choice was hardly a surprise. The kid ate little else. All that fatty red meat would probably catch up with him someday, but not until they'd reached a future far removed from the here and now.

"Lisa," he called out, "let me get two burger specials and...." Bobby shrugged in response to his raised eyebrow, so he adjusted his order. "Make that three specials. And three chocolate milkshakes." Unlike Tim, he had no excuse for tempting the heart attack gods, but he never could say no to one of Lisa's delectable triple-stacks complete with curly fries drizzled with gravy. "So, Bobby, you never answered my question. Why aren't you in school?"

During the time the boy spent avoiding his question, Lisa brought the shakes, providing Bobby with the additional delay tactic of trying to draw the thick drink through the too-narrow straw. Tim was also having trouble with the frozen concoction, and the way his lips pursed around the straw as his cheeks hollowed out with the effort of sucking was nearly enough to make David forget why they were there.

"Don't wanna go."

Bobby's sudden explanation drew his thoughts back to something more suited to a late afternoon lunch in a place that had been liberally doused in paint as pink as Lisa's outfit. Expecting further explanation, David watched the young teen play with his drink, experimenting with his straw until he managed to make it stand straight up in the lake of frozen chocolate. "Why not?" he prompted when the boy seemed disinclined to elaborate.

Bobby shrugged. "I don't like it."

A broad answer if ever there was one. Sensing he wouldn't get any better, David tried a different tack. "You're how old? Twelve? Thirteen?"

"Thirteen" was the slightly indignant response.

"Then the law says you have to go to school. I'm sure your folks would be upset if they knew you've been ditching." That got a reaction. Bobby looked up and threw him a glare that was one part anger, one part defiant, and all parts sad.

"They don't care. Momma's always workin', and my daddy don't never come home. And when he does, he's drunk."

"Did you run away?"

David was surprised to hear Tim speak but then realized he shouldn't have been. If there was one thing the kid could probably relate to, it was family troubles. He glanced over at Tim and was amazed at the guarded compassion he could see on his normally impassive face. Some of the tension he'd felt since he'd found Tim assaulting Bobby began to dissipate, but he vowed he would bring it up with the kid once they were home alone.

Bobby looked equally shocked that Tim had addressed him. Like a rabbit watching a fox, he kept his attention firmly on Tim as he shook his head. "No. Momma needs me at home. She don't make much money at her job, so I try to help her out."

"And MP3 players are easy to sell, is that it?" David's smile was sorrowful as the situation became clear. Here was a kid, down on his luck, who was simply trying to do right by his mother. Bobby was quickly headed down the wrong path, but being turned in to the police wasn't what he needed. Coming to a decision, David took a moment to tackle his own milkshake before settling back in the booth. "What's your last name, Bobby?"

The boy stared at him, brows as pale as his hair furrowed in confusion. "What difference does that make?" He obviously thought David was fishing for information in order to press charges against him for shoplifting.

David fought back a grin and took another hard-won swig of his shake. "I can't hire you if I don't know your last name."

"Hire me?"

"Hire him?"

Both young men spoke simultaneously, and David found himself caught between matching confused stares of brown and hazel.

"If he's thirteen years old, isn't he too young to work?"

How Tim knew anything about child labor laws, David had no idea, but the kid wasn't wrong. "That's true, but it will be fine so long as he only works for a couple of hours after school. And," he continued, looking squarely at Bobby, "his mother says that it's okay."

A brief look of panic crossed the boy's face, but it quickly disappeared. It didn't take a genius to figure out that, whether it was through the police or from the man he'd robbed, his mother would learn about his attempted theft one way or another. Better it was from the guy who seemed willing to cut him some slack. David silently watched a variety of emotions flicker across the boy's pale face as he weighed the pros and cons of the offer. After a few moments, the expected nod came.

"Good," David said cheerfully. "Glad that's settled." He kept his tone casual, careful not to make a big deal out of it. He'd been a young man himself once, and he was well aware of how fragile the developing male ego could be. "Ah, thanks, Lisa," he said as the woman sashayed over with their food.

"No problem, sugar." She deftly placed three fully loaded plates in front of them. "You let me know if you need anything else."

David barely took the time to nod as he bit into his huge burger. He waited until both teens were engrossed in their own food before he spoke again. "Provided your mother says yes, of course."

Bobby wilted for a moment before resigning himself to his fate. David gave in to the smile that had been threatening for the past few minutes. He was reaching for a curly fry when he felt the weight of an intent stare. Looking over, he met Tim's gaze, and something visceral moved through him at the—dare he call it—hero worship radiating from those beautiful dark eyes.

After their meal was finished, David offered to take Bobby home. The boy was reluctant to accept but eventually gave in to practicality, since he lived a few miles away from the diner. David frowned as he pulled up in front of a somewhat run-down single-level house. The place desperately needed a fresh coat of paint, but at least it wasn't on the verge of falling apart, unlike the rusted-out car sitting in the driveway.

"Fuck."

David looked in his rearview mirror and raised a censuring eyebrow at the young boy sitting in the backseat. "What was that?"

Bobby glanced at him sheepishly. "My mom's home."

"Good," David said with a nod. "Then we can take care of this sooner rather than later."

The three of them got out of the car and walked up to the front door, Bobby dragging behind. David waited until he'd caught up before ringing the doorbell. A frazzled-looking woman answered, her resemblance to Bobby confirming her identity.

"Yes?" She looked over at her son, worry etching even more lines into her careworn face.

"I'm David Conley. Your son had a little incident at my store this afternoon." He explained the situation matter-of-factly, leaving out the part about what had happened after Tim caught the boy. Bobby remained silent the entire time, his gazed fixed on his beat-up athletic shoes. His mother was obviously none too thrilled with what she was hearing.

"Bobby, get in the house," she said, her voice quiet with repressed anger and not a little embarrassment.

"Don't worry about it, Mrs....?" David paused. Bobby still hadn't told him his last name.

"Wood. Grace Wood," she replied.

"Mrs. Wood," he acknowledged respectfully. "Bobby can easily make it up to me by working at my store, Barry's Bargain Warehouse, a few hours after school for a little while. We're located right downtown. It's easy to get there on the Citibus, and I'll make sure he has enough for the fare."

Grace gave him a tired smile. "Thank you, Mr. Conley. I'd appreciate it."

"Please, call me David."

The woman nodded at him before throwing yet another glare at her son's downcast head. "What do you say to the nice man, Bobby?"

"S'rry."

David hid a smile at the garbled reply, knowing it was the best the boy's mother was going to get from him right then. "It's Thursday, so no point in his working tomorrow. I'll see you on Monday, Bobby. After school, three o'clock sharp." He reached out and placed a hand on top of the young teen's bowed head. "Okay?"

"'Kay."

David said good-bye to Bobby and Grace and made his way back to his car with Tim in tow. The kid had remained silent during the meeting with Bobby's mother, his lack of expression not giving a single hint about his thoughts. Moments after the woman closed the front door, however, he spoke up suddenly.

"She has a nearly healed contusion on her left cheek, and her posture indicates she's nursing an injury to her midsection."

The out-of-the-blue remark sparked two simultaneous thoughts. *Damn*, David cursed silently, hating to have the niggling suspicion that had been brewing in the back of his mind corroborated. "How do you know that?" he asked, giving voice to the second.

Tim paused for a moment, a look of uncertainty brushing fleetingly over his face. "I, uh, I took martial arts for a long time. I guess I'm used to seeing people trying to hide injuries."

"Martial arts, huh?" David replied, indulging his greed for more information about Tim. "Like what, karate or something?" Unfortunately they had reached the car, so he was forced to endure a momentary delay as they got in. He hoped Tim didn't use the opportunity to let the subject drop. He started the engine and pulled away from the curb, resisting the urge to prompt the kid to continue. It was obvious Tim was deciding whether or not he should be any more forthcoming, and David didn't want to give him any excuse to remain silent.

"No, not karate exactly. Or at least, not only karate."

David waited patiently for Tim to elaborate. He kept his eyes on the road, trying not to telegraph his interest.

"It was more of a mixed martial art. A combination of wushu and capoeira."

Images of various Hong Kong action movies flitted through David's head, but he didn't pretend to know what the kid meant. "Is that why you were so aggressive with Bobby?"

He instantly regretted the statement as Tim froze in his seat before turning his head away, ostensibly to look out of the window, clearly trying to shield his face from David's gaze. Tim's entire body indicated his disinclination to continue the conversation, but David felt he'd be remiss if he just let it drop. If the kid was going to be staying with him—as seemed ever more likely—it was important that they didn't ignore problems when they cropped up. But he didn't feel confident enough to press the point, so the silence between them lingered until he was turning the car into the parking lot of the subdivision.

"He took something that belonged to you," Tim said softly. "I wanted to get it back."

David inhaled sharply as he caught a hint of something unexpected in the kid's tone. *Concern? Protectiveness?* He supposed it was natural for Tim to feel gratitude to the man who'd literally taken him in off the streets, but this felt like something more, and David didn't feel ready to examine it too closely.

"Well, um, the item Bobby stole wasn't mine exactly." Scolding himself to stop stalling, David steeled himself to address the issue directly. "I appreciate that you were trying to help, but this probably won't be the last shoplifter we'll have to deal with. Bobby wasn't dangerous," he continued, voicing a concern he hadn't even been aware of until the thought occurred to him, "but you couldn't have known that for certain. Next time let's just leave it for the police. Okay?"

Tim turned to look at him, his expression blank, as though the very concept was completely foreign. But after a long moment the kid nodded. "Okay." He looked around as though he'd only then realized where they were. "Why aren't we back at the store? My shift doesn't end for another hour."

"I didn't think you'd be up for finishing out the day." David smiled at the kid's confused look. "Just think of it as a reward for going above and beyond to help keep the inventory safe, although I meant what I said about letting the police handle it the next time we get a shoplifter."

"Understood." Tim opened his door and slid out of the car, pausing as he waited for David to do likewise. "Um, Bobby's coming to the store next week, right?"

David nodded. "Yes. Well, at least I hope he shows up." He had the feeling the boy could use some positive influences in his life, and he hoped hanging around with Patricia and his other employees while earning some pocket change might provide the young teen with a more encouraging outlook.

"I could, um, show him around. If that's all right with you."

Turning away to hide the smile creeping across his lips, David found his house key in the jumble on his key ring and started toward his door. There was no mistaking the yearning in the kid's voice. He wondered how Tim had been raised to have grown up so lonely. "That sounds like a great idea," he threw over his shoulder. "So, now that that's settled, I know we ate only a little while ago, but I'm guessing you'll probably be hungry again soon. Am I right?" David chuckled when Tim nodded in confirmation. "Okay, what do you have a taste for dinner-wise?"

"A cheese omelet."

David took a mental inventory of his fridge and figured Tim must have done a more thorough visual inspection earlier, as he had pegged the one dish David had enough ingredients to cover. "A cheese omelet it is. And tomorrow we should hit the grocery store again so you can help me choose more foods you like."

A careless glance back at Tim revealed an unrestrained smile that nearly took his breath away. Why the kid found the prospect of something as mundane as grocery shopping so appealing, he had no clue. But if that's what it took to coax that expression from the usually reserved teen, then he was more than willing to make a trip to the store a daily occurrence. And although the thought assumed Tim would become a more permanent fixture in his life, David realized the notion didn't bother him in the least.

HIDDEN BY the closed bathroom door, I took out the case that held my chemical lifeline. I had taken one only yesterday, but the physical exertion I'd put myself through earlier that day had depleted my resources, and the nutritious dinner David had so deftly created hadn't been quite enough to replenish them. Since supplements weren't an option, even if I could get them without unavoidably piquing David's curiosity, I was restricted to boosting my B12 reserves with food alone, though it was a less than ideal method of compensating. Reluctantly, I popped one of the pills into my mouth and washed it down with a handful of water.

"One more down," I murmured, and with it the clock began ticking ever louder.

I snapped the case shut and placed it on the sink as I reached for my toothbrush. Before I could retrieve the tube of paste David had left laying haphazardly on the sink's wide ledge, I caught sight of myself in the mirror. Remembering back to when David and I had gotten home, I reached up with my free hand and touched the corner of my mouth. The skin was still tingling from my spontaneous show of emotion.

A smile. A grin. An unprompted expression of joy. When was the last time I'd expressed an emotion so naturally? When I was very young, I had occasionally smiled at Father Paul's teasing, which the man had frequently used to disguise the harshness of my training sessions. But even those fleeting moments had diminished as I'd gotten older, and I'd certainly never done so without purposeful coaxing. And yet, when David had mentioned wanting to select foods with me in mind, practically confirming that he had granted me permission to stay in this house with him indefinitely, I'd done so unbidden. The sense of happiness that had flooded me had been so intense, even I couldn't mistake what it was. I wanted to stay, wanted to live with David for as long as I was allowed to do so, and the diminishing supply of pills was an unpleasant reminder that it wouldn't be very long at all.

Six months, I'd calculated that first night. Although only two days had gone by since then, I felt the passage of time drowning me, as if I were trapped in the hourglass I'd found so fascinating as a child. But unlike the toy, there would be no reset. Once the sand had run out, it would be the end... of everything.

Thinking about the end of my own life made me regret even more how roughly I'd treated Bobby earlier that day. I had been solely focused on my self-appointed mission, thinking of nothing else but retrieving David's stolen property. I understood now that I'd been angry—angry that someone could wrong the man who had given me a home and the new life I'd risked so much to obtain. Perhaps that's why David's disgust that I could so casually threaten a child's life had hurt so badly. David's disappointment, Bobby's terror—I never wanted either to be directed at me again.

I would learn from this. Even I could tell Bobby needed a friend, someone he could depend on to steady him through the rough winds of his struggle to become a man. David had offered him a way to feel self-sufficient without having to resort to petty crime. Maybe I could give Bobby someone to lean on when he needed to. I hadn't imagined those injuries I had noticed on his mother, and although I hadn't told David, I suspected Bobby was nursing some hurts of his own. It made me feel even worse to think that my relentless pursuit had been the cause of the barely noticeable limp the boy had developed after our ragged sprint. If Bobby needed a protector, I was able and, more importantly, willing, to take on the responsibility. I had been trained to kill, not to protect, but I was surprised to discover the instinct to do so came naturally. And in the process, maybe Bobby could help me regain some of the childhood which had been stolen from me.

"Mission accepted."

Smearing the toothpaste on my brush, I applied it vigorously to my teeth, somewhat amused by the way the foam hid the pleased smile that had sprung to my lips.

SERGEANT COOPER was a man who took pride in his work. Whether it was something as routine as leading a security patrol or as focused as neutralizing a dangerous target, he was never anything less than thorough. General Woodard watched with carefully repressed admiration as his second-in-command worked over the prisoner. While the search groups spread out over eastern New Mexico and west Texas, Woodard thought he might try garnering information a little closer to home.

"All right, Sergeant. Let's see if he's ready to talk to us now."

Cooper stopped in midswing and looked at his commanding officer over his broad shoulder. Without a word, he stepped back from the hunched figure who was half kneeling, half lying on the unyielding concrete slab which functioned as the cell's bunk. Woodard moved around Cooper, pointedly ignoring the gleaming red stains on the sergeant's fists. Reaching out, he fisted a hank of greasy, unwashed hair and lifted the prisoner's head until he could peer into the man's abused face. The middle-aged scientist had worked closely with Dr.

Anderson and the TM unit, and Woodard had every reason to think he'd assisted in the escape.

"Where is he? TM 05637 has never been out of the Facility, so it's doubtful he managed all this without help. Did you give him a fallback position in case we were ever compromised? Did he have some sort of escape route planned?" His lips compressed in the wake of the prisoner's continued silence. The man's reluctance was as much due to his being half-unconscious as to defiance. "Answer me! Where would he go?" Woodard dropped the scientist's head when his question earned him nothing but a spray of bloody spittle on his face as the man coughed around his likely broken ribs. "Fuck!" He wiped the offending fluid away with the sleeve of his uniform shirt. Maybe next time he'd tell Cooper not to be quite so diligent in his interrogation technique, no matter how much he enjoyed watching the man work.

"Sir, Ms. Talbot is on the line."

Woodard turned at the sound of a young woman's voice. The lieutenant had striking jet-black hair, stunning green eyes, and the figure of a woman who enjoyed taking care of herself. Many of the male soldiers who were assigned to the Facility had made her the object of their uncouth fawning, but any harassment she endured never lasted past the first time any of them sparred with her. Woodard appreciated her ballsy attitude nearly as much as he admired her competence, and was considering offering her a promotion despite her tender age. It was only this professional fondness that kept him from snapping at her for the inopportune disruption.

"Thank you, Farley."

He glanced at Cooper and gave the man a slight nod before exiting the cell to the renewed sounds of flesh hitting flesh. He doubted the scientist knew anything useful, but he was more than willing to let Cooper exercise some frustration on his behalf. Woodard had just opened the door of his office when the unexpected sight of the woman standing next to his desk brought him up short.

"Ms. Talbot." Woodard paused as she turned to look at him with her characteristic haughtiness. "This is an unexpected surprise. Lieutenant Farley said you were on the vid line."

"Exactly as I told her to." Talbot turned deliberately to face him, her trim figure bespeaking her mental and physical discipline. "A very intelligent young woman. Someone who knows whose orders she should obey."

Woodard ground his teeth as he struggled to keep his expression as blank as hers. "To what do I owe the pleasure?"

"I want my project back where it belongs, General. You told me you would have it within two days, and that time has passed." She sat in his chair, crossing one surprisingly shapely leg over the other. "I do not appreciate being pandered to."

Resentful of being treated like a schoolboy being scolded by his teacher, Woodard carefully cleared his throat. "We have deployed numerous search teams, but the TM unit was trained in the art of evasion and infiltration. Wherever it is, it has managed to blend in well enough to avoid arousing suspicion. If anything, I would say our difficulty in recovering it simply proves how successful we were."

"A pleasant sentiment, General, but the fact remains that millions of dollars of research is running around in the desert while you and your people fumble around like children in the dark. Since it seems you are incapable of finding your ass with both hands, I decided to come here and oversee this operation personally."

Woodard tightened his fist at the insult he ached to throw back at her sagging face. "I hardly think that's necessary," he began more diplomatically.

"The Company disagrees. We want results, and if you are incapable of delivering them, then the board has decided someone else needs to be in charge." She stood abruptly and walked purposefully toward the office door. "Come with me, General. I think there's something you need to see."

Woodard forced himself to hold his tongue as he matched her brisk pace. She'd been with the project since its inception and knew the layout of the base as well as he did. She led him unerringly toward the section that housed the project's research facilities. At first he thought she might want to examine the video of the unit's last training session to see if Anderson had given any hint about what he'd been planning while he watched the unit being put through its paces. But when he realized where they were actually headed, he frowned.

Talbot stopped before a door labeled "Nursery." One of the eggheads' idea of a sick joke, Woodard had always thought. Talbot pressed her hand against the biometric scanner, which immediately bounced a laser over her palm to capture her handprint.

"What are we doing here?" Woodard asked.

In lieu of answering, Talbot sailed through the door the moment it opened into the frigid room beyond. Reluctantly, he followed, unable to stop the shiver that travelled up his spine, both from the temperature and the freak show nature of the brightly lit lab.

"This place gives me the creeps," he grumbled under his breath.

The lab looked like most of the others housed within the base. Its sterile white walls surrounded raised tables laden with projects in various stages of completion and banks of high-tech equipment, most of which Woodard couldn't identify. But the dominant feature was the large metal cylinder situated in the dead center of the room. White smoke drifted away from the metal as the liquid nitrogen within struggled to escape and freeze the air around the tank as it had its macabre contents.

Talbot glanced at him, showing she'd heard him perfectly well. "And why is that, General? After all, this represents the future... of both the project and of your career."

The "Nursery" was, in fact, an incubator. The metal tank held a score of frozen embryos, each bearing the signs of Anderson's tinkering. Woodard let his gaze roam over the half-dozen men and women who were engaged with various tasks, some watching monitors displaying indecipherable medical jargon, while others fiddled with the tank's control, ensuring the optimal environment for the undeveloped beings waiting in stasis within. Woodard could guess why Talbot wanted to have this conversation here, but he refused to let her succeed in her clumsy mind games.

"You know, Talbot, we wouldn't be in this mess if the Company had agreed to finance the gestation of additional units."

She glared at him. "It was Paul's idea—and a good one at that— to ensure TM 05637's viability before impregnating more surrogates with the modified embryos."

"Bullshit. The Company refused to finance more units because you're all a bunch of cheap bastards. Having more units as capable and skilled as TM 05637 would greatly simplify the process of bringing our escapee to heel."

"Perhaps," Talbot replied smoothly. "Or, more likely, you'd have an army of deadly TMs to retrieve instead of just one." Her smile reflected her low estimation of his intelligence. "I'm sure you don't honestly believe that Paul would care less for any other TM unit than he does for his *firstborn*." She pronounced the word with pointed emphasis, betraying her opinion of the doctor's untoward attachment to his project.

He didn't, but he hated to admit she had an excellent point. "What do you suggest I do, then, that I'm not already doing to retrieve TM 05637? NSA shut me down. I don't suppose you'd bother to expend a little of the Company's clout so we can use satellite surveillance."

"Alas, General, I'm certain the board would never approve it. However," she added, "I did enlist one of the clever young hackers in our employ to grant you access to any law enforcement monitoring systems you might wish to utilize."

Woodard ignored her smug look. "That would be helpful," he replied simply.

Talbot nodded. "Good. We're on the same side, General. I hope you remember that. I'm as eager to see this project succeed as you are. Perhaps even more," she added softly, glancing briefly toward the cryogenic tank. "Once we've brought TM 05637 safely home, we can concentrate on the final phases of its development. And if it completes the trials, as I'm sure it will, you'll have your army."

Woodard met her discomfiting gaze, her pale eyes seemingly staring straight through him. "That's all I want. It's what this country needs if it's to survive."

"Then have a seat, General." She pointed to an uncomfortably high lab chair. "We have much to discuss if we are to bring our wayward child home."

Resentment boiled in his brain at her condescending tone, but not so much that he missed her unexpected characterization of TM 05637. Frankly, he was surprised. She had always been as careful as he was not to personify the unit. He repressed a disgusted shudder. TM 05637 might walk like a human and talk like a human, but it wasn't. It would serve them all to remember that if—when—the time came to put it down like the failed lab experiment it was.

NINE

"MR. CONLEY, this little one says he's looking for you."

David looked up at the couple standing in his office doorway, and his lips quirked up in a smile when he saw Bobby standing behind Patricia, fidgeting. The boy had a death grip on his backpack and looked like he'd rather be anywhere else. But he had arrived at the store promptly at three as he'd promised. David rose and moved from behind his desk as he nodded at Patricia.

"Thanks, and let me introduce you to our newest part-timer, Bobby Wood."

"Oh! So this is the boy you were telling me about," she said, tactfully not mentioning his attempted theft. "Well, hello there, Bobby."

He looked up at her, his hazel eyes uncertain, and mumbled, "Hi," in return. David ran his hand over his mouth to cover his grin at the show of adolescent disaffection.

"Patricia, could you ask Tim to come in here? Bobby is going to be his responsibility."

Her face lit up, clearly approving of his plan. "Will do!" she chirped, disappearing in a wave of frothy blonde hair.

"Go on, sit." David gestured to the chair arranged in front of his desk and moved back around to his side to give Bobby some space. The boy's face was a study in boredom as he slouched into the offered seat, but the telltale clench of his fists gave him away. David reached into the bottom drawer and pulled out a few sheets of paper. "You'll need to take these home to your mom to sign. One of them is a parental consent form and the other is a tax form." He often hired part-timers from the local high schools, so he was used to dealing with minors. "You can bring them back to me tomorrow." He paused as Bobby slid the sheets off the desktop and crumpled them before shoving them into his backpack. "I can't let you do any actual work until she signs the consent form, so today I'll just have Tim show you around the store." He and Bobby looked toward the sound of the office door opening. "Speak of the devil," David said with a fond smile.

Tim hovered hesitantly in the doorway, his gaze locked on the boy sitting in the too-large chair. Bobby turned to glance at him, and David watched as some sort of silent communication passed between them. Whatever message had been conveyed, it prompted Tim to fully enter the room. He stopped by the edge of the desk, careful to keep enough distance between himself and Bobby so he wasn't looming over the smaller teen.

"Tim, for today I want you to show Bobby how we stock the shelves and keep track of inventory. That will be your primary responsibility, Bobby, to make sure we always have the proper amount of merchandise available for the customers." He shot the boy a friendly smile. "Sound good?"

A shrug was his answer, along with a quiet "I guess."

"Come on," Tim prompted. Bobby rose from the chair and reluctantly followed him out into the store. David wasn't surprised when Patricia popped her head into his office mere seconds after the two young men had gone.

"Trying to coax our boy out of his shell?"

David shrugged. "Well, they didn't get off on the right foot, so to speak." While he had explained that Tim had captured their shoplifter, he hadn't told her all of the unsettling details. "If they're going to become friends, they need to learn to work together. Hopefully they'll come to trust each other."

"And Tim could use a friend, couldn't he?" She turned sideways in the doorway, resting her back against the jamb as she looked out toward where Tim was walking Bobby down one of the aisles. "Still no word from his dad?"

"Stepdad, and no. I've decided to let him stay with me." David shrugged to ease the sudden tension in his shoulders as he spoke his decision aloud for the first time.

Patricia's incongruously dark eyebrows rose as she looked back at him. "For how long?"

He shrugged. "For as long as he needs to, I guess."

A flash of uncertainty crossed her face before she stepped fully into the office and closed the door behind her. "I wasn't sure how to tell you this, or whether I even should, but…."

"But what?" he prompted after a long pause.

"The other day, Tim told me that his mother is dead and that he had something to do with her death." She paused and drew a deep breath. "You don't think that…."

"That what?" David prompted.

"That he killed her, do you?" Patricia forced out in a rush.

David stared at her, shocked at her gigantic and ridiculous leap in logic. "Killed her? That's insane," he replied firmly, before a niggling of doubt crept into his certainty. "Did he tell you that?"

Patricia shrugged. "Not in so many words. He only said she was dead because of him. But I got the impression something truly awful happened between them. I would have asked him to explain himself, but then Bobby distracted everyone with his theft attempt. I couldn't decide whether I should say anything about it later."

Killed her? The impossible thought echoed in David's head. He was sure Patricia was being truthful about what Tim had told her, but he couldn't imagine Tim could have done such a thing. He'd gathered from the kid's reluctance to talk about her that Tim's mother wasn't in the picture and had even guessed she might be dead. But never in a million years would he have thought Tim had anything to do with her absence.

"Are you going to ask him about it?"

David started as Patricia spoke aloud his primary concern. If Tim was going to keep living with him, then surely it was his right to know the truth about something so important. But did he want to? Maybe Tim had been overly dramatic in saying he was somehow involved in his mother's death, his exaggeration brought on by misplaced guilt of some kind. But David knew the kid wasn't one for melodrama. If he was being completely honest with himself, David had to admit he didn't really know much about his new housemate other than that he could provoke inappropriate thoughts without even trying. Unbidden, the image of Tim choking Bobby against the park fence popped into his head and refused to leave.

"I really need to finish this paperwork before I go home for the day." David knew the change of subject was lame, but he was eager to end the conversation. After having recently decided to allow Tim to stay in his home, he wasn't quite ready to deal with this unforeseen turn of events.

Patricia stared at him for a long time before sighing, her lips pursed with mild disapproval. "Okay, you're the boss."

David didn't look away from the papers on his desk until she had gone, although the words on them weren't making any sense at the moment. Groaning, he closed his eyes and leaned back in his chair. "What in the hell?" he mumbled, wondering how he'd gotten himself into this mess.

Son, you have got to learn how to tell people no.

"Thanks, Ma. Now you tell me."

"WE USE this scanner to track inventory using the bar codes tacked on each shelf beneath the merchandise." I proceeded to demonstrate how to use the device when Bobby looked at me with a confused expression. Knowing experience was usually the best teacher, I held the scanner toward the boy. "Here, take this."

Bobby stared at it like it was an alien weapon. "What do I do with it?"

"You see this tag?" I pointed to one of the stickers printed with a series of vertical lines of varying widths.

"It looks like something at the grocery store."

I nodded. "Yes, it's the same thing. So, all you have to do is hold the scanner up to it like this." I showed him how to point the optical reader at the code. "Then push this button on top, and there. Look at the screen."

Bobby squinted at the tiny display situated at the top of the device. "It says 'Beach Bum Beach Towels' and the number six."

"Right, so there should be six of these towels on the shelf." I counted them quickly. "There are, so you can hit the button on the right beneath the screen, under where it says 'Confirm.'"

"Oh! I get it. If there had been less than six, I would have chosen 'Deny,' right?"

Ignoring the incorrect grammar, I nodded. "Yes, that's correct. Or if there had been more than six." I moved toward the next item on the shelf. "Let's continue, and when you finish this aisle you can go on home."

We didn't find any discrepancies until we reached the boxes labeled "Beach Bum Water Bottle and Fan Combo."

"There's only twelve of them," Bobby noted. "There's supposed to be thirteen."

"It's possible there's an extra one in storage that should have been put out on the shelf but wasn't." I stepped around Bobby and beckoned him to follow with a wave of my hand. "Let's check the stockroom."

The storage area was vast, but the merchandise was arranged as neatly as it was out on the main floor. Signs directed us toward the shelves where the recreational items were kept. Bobby started looking for the missing item before I could ask, darting off between the shelves like he was playing a game of hide and seek.

"Found 'em!"

I caught up in time to see Bobby use the scanner on the bar code below the boxes of unpacked water bottle fans. I found myself smiling at his enthusiasm and wondered at the spontaneous show of emotion, my second time doing so in four days.

"There's supposed to be forty-eight here, and I see four unopened boxes of twelve."

"Okay. Probably means someone stole the missing one off the shelf. A purchase would have been automatically registered. The computer is at the front of the stockroom. Let's go mark it for the store's records—" I'd begun walking back to the main aisle and was halfway to the front before I noticed I wasn't being followed. "Bobby?" Returning to the corridor I'd just vacated, I found him staring listlessly at his beat-up sneakers.

"'M s'rry."

"What?" I asked. Even the years I'd spent learning advanced code decryption weren't up to the task of understanding the muttered statement.

"I said, I'm sorry." Bobby threw me an annoyed look for being dense, but his irritation lasted all of two seconds before it melted back into shame. "I didn't wanna steal the player, but I thought if I had enough money, I could...."

I waited for Bobby to continue, but the silence filled the room as he tried to dig a hole in the concrete floor with the tip of his shoe. "You could what?" I finally asked.

Narrow shoulders shrugged in an attempt at nonchalance. "I could help Momma get away."

"From your father." It wasn't a question, and Bobby shot me a startled look, as if the truth should have been impossible to guess. I thought maybe I'd been too blunt, but after a moment the boy nodded.

"Yeah."

Domestic violence. The phrase wasn't much more than a concept I'd learned along with thousands of others during my comprehensive education, but seeing Bobby's apprehension made it instantly real. A new sentiment entered my awareness. Empathy. Somehow I understood what Bobby was feeling. A hazy vision of a small woman with auburn hair and sad blue eyes rose before my eyes before I managed to lock it away again.

"Maybe," I started hesitantly, "maybe if you tell her that he hurts you too, she'd take you and leave him."

Bobby was shaking his head before I had finished speaking. "Nah, she won't. She's too scared." A twisted grin pulled at the boy's lips, looking completely wrong on his youthful features. "She tried once, you know. When I was, like, four or five. I only sorta remember." Bobby slumped back against the shelving. "Mostly I remember being scared." His face scrunched into something more befitting his age as his hazel eyes brightened suspiciously. "And I remember him hitting her, over and over. And blood, I remember that too."

I felt curiously short of breath and sought in vain for the source of my distress until I suddenly realized my body was reacting to Bobby's pain. "I'm sorry," I whispered, feeling inadequate to the situation. I didn't know the first thing about comforting someone.

Emotions are for pussies. Are you a pussy, boy? The general had said those words to me when I was eight years old. I'd broken my arm during a gymnastics lesson and had the unmitigated gall to cry about it. Consumed by the pain, I hadn't answered the sneering challenge, but it was the last time I'd allowed a tear to betray me.

"It's not your fault," Bobby answered. In the next instant the boy looked up at me, his gaze determined. "But you could help me. You know how to fight, don't you?"

I nodded cautiously, wondering where his was leading to.

"Teach me how to fight."

Reluctance was the one emotion to which I was definitely not a stranger. Even beyond the fear I'd seen in Bobby's eyes when I'd caught him, it was my acute recollection of the disappointment in David's eyes that made me refuse. Shaking my head, I glanced away uncomfortably from Bobby's intense stare.

"I don't think that's a good idea."

"Why not?" Bobby shouted. His hands were balled into fists at his side, and his pitch rose in frustration.

"I...." I paused, trying to decide how much I should reveal. *No, I thought, you're striving to be more open, not less.* I'd promised myself I would protect the younger boy, hadn't I? If I was to accomplish my self-appointed goal, I couldn't afford to close myself off now. "I hurt you before. I should have been more careful." I swallowed down the lump in my throat. "I didn't mean to scare you."

That, of course, was a lie. Frightening Bobby was precisely what I'd intended, but I was too ashamed—another new emotion—to admit my motivation, even to myself. Now, looking down at the scrawny figure, I fully appreciated how fragile Bobby was compared to me. My behavior had been inexcusable, a poor attempt to deal with the embarrassment of my postnightmare breakdown and my growing indecision as to how I felt about David. A small hand touched my arm, and I started, unable to conceal my surprise at the unaccustomed touch.

"You didn't hurt me. Not really." Bobby's smile was self-deprecating. "I was more startled than anything. I still can't believe you caught me." He must have seen the disbelief on my face, because he rambled on, his words tripping over themselves. "I deserved it, though. I shouldn't have stolen the player. Heck, you were right to kick my ass." Bobby rolled his eyes when I continued to stare at him. "Look, I just really want to help out my mom, but I know I'm too weak right now." He sighed heavily in irritation. "So, are you gonna teach me or what?"

"All right." I hadn't been certain how I would answer, but Bobby's candor had convinced me. I did want to help him, if only to allow him to gain some confidence in facing up to the bad hand he'd been dealt.

"Sweet!" Bobby pumped his fist, his small body jogging up and down as he bounced on his toes.

"But we'll have to be careful, and you have to listen to everything I tell you. I don't want you accidentally getting injured." I couldn't be sure if Bobby was nodding in agreement or if his head was simply bobbing from his springy dance of joy.

"I will. I promise!"

I nodded. "Then go on home. We'll start tomorrow after you're done with work. We should be able to use the lot behind the store. I'll borrow some mats from the sports department."

Bobby didn't stop grinning as I walked him to the front entrance. "See ya tomorrow!"

I noticed Patricia look toward us from where she was manning a register, her attention caught by Bobby's perky good-bye. I knew she and David would find out about my promise to Bobby soon enough, and I wasn't certain they would approve. But this was important to my new friend, so I would have to hope they understood. I watched Bobby cross the parking lot and turn up the street. Once the slight figure had disappeared from sight, I spun back toward the interior of the store to finish up my work before it was time to go home. It wasn't until a few minutes later that I realized I was smiling again.

TIM WAS quiet on the ride home and had remained so as David prepared dinner. Not that he'd done much to break the silence. Patricia's revelation from earlier that afternoon had pricked at the back of his mind for the rest of the day. Now that they were alone, he wasn't certain whether he should bring it up or just let it go.

"So, how did you and Bobby do today? Any problems showing him around?"

Tim had been picking at his grilled trout without enthusiasm, but he perked up at the mention of the younger boy's name. David found himself staring slack-jawed as a soft, almost fond expression bloomed across the kid's pretty face.

"No, no problems. Bobby is quite clever. He grasped the steps of the inventory process very quickly."

"That's good," David replied. "I'm glad you two are getting along."

Tim nodded and took another bite of the fish they'd picked up from the market on the way home. David was glad his idea to put the boys together seemed to be bearing fruit. He sincerely hoped the trust he was placing in Bobby wouldn't be abused. The boy's situation was pitiable, but the store had a lot of merchandise small enough to slip into a pocket or a backpack that would fetch a decent price on resell.

"Look," he said hesitantly, "I don't want you to feel like you have to watch him all of the time, but could you keep an eye on Bobby for me? I want to make sure he's not tempted to try and steal anything again."

"He won't."

David raised his eyebrows as Tim gnawed complacently on a piece of bread. "You seem pretty sure of that."

"I am. He only took the MP3 player because he wanted to earn enough money to assist his mother in leaving his father."

Sighing, David put down his fork, his appetite vanishing as he recalled what Tim had said about Grace's injuries. "Right. Well, I guess that makes sense."

"Besides, he promised he wouldn't try again if—"

"If what?" David asked, curious at the abrupt cutoff. He watched as reluctance struggled against the kid's apparently unconscious inclination to answer a direct question. He had noticed that, while Tim might hesitate, he rarely refused anything akin to an order. Had his father or stepfather been military? It was one more question to add to his growing list.

Eventually Tim's desire to obey won out. "Bobby wants me to teach him martial arts."

David remembered all too vividly how small and frightened Bobby had looked as Tim pinned him against the fence. Apprehension burned in his gut. While he didn't think Tim had it in him to be purposefully malicious, he worried the kid could be a bit too single-minded and wasn't always aware of the strength buried in his deceptively slim body. David sat back in his chair, trying to figure out how to express his concern without offending Tim. "I'm not sure if that's a good idea. Bobby is pretty young."

"Most children begin training when they are quite small," Tim countered.

David had seen adorable troops of pint-sized tykes going in and out of the studio a few blocks from the BBW, sporting bright white karate uniforms and even whiter belts. He wondered how old Tim had been when he'd started taking lessons, suspecting he'd been even younger than those little children. For some reason, the thought made him uneasy.

"Okay." He nodded. "I guess that's true. But you'll have to be real patient with him. He's probably a complete novice, so it will likely take a lot of work on your part. Plus—" David took a breath, but plowed onward. "—you need to be very careful not to hurt him." The "again" hung silently in the air between them. David stared in alarm as Tim's olive complexion suddenly grew pale. Tim swallowed convulsively, and David found his gaze drawn to the long line of the kid's throat.

"I-I just want to help him. All he wants to do is protect his mother."

"Tim, what happened to your mom?" The question was out there before David could think to rein it in.

Tim went so still that he briefly resembled a mannequin, inhuman in his frozen perfection. Stillness burst into violent motion, and David found himself gaping at the spot where Tim had been but an instant before, a toppled chair the only betrayal of his presence. He stared in shock for a moment at the tableau of the abandoned meal, but the sound of the front door opening prompted him into a mad scramble. Rushing into the living room, he managed to catch up right as Tim was slipping out into the darkness.

"Tim!" David was afraid the kid would ignore him, but the slight figure came to an abrupt halt immediately beyond the doorway. His heart hammering from more than the sudden exertion, David walked slowly over to Tim and lifted a cautious hand toward his shoulder. It didn't quite make it, hovering in an awkward holding pattern as he tried to judge exactly how welcome the contact would be right then. "I'm sorry," he said instead, letting his hand fall to his side. "I shouldn't have asked. It's not my place—"

"Patricia told you." It wasn't a question.

David nodded before noticing Tim wasn't looking at him. "Yes. She thought I should know, but…." He exhaled heavily. "I really am sorry."

Tim deflated like a balloon, the rigid tension in his body vanishing in an instant. Pointedly avoiding David's gaze, he turned slowly and slunk back into the house, shuffling to the sofa before plopping down gracelessly. David closed the door silently and walked over to the adjacent chair, not wanting Tim to feel crowded.

"That's a very effective interrogation technique, you know."

David sat, his brow furrowing at the offhand comment. "What is?"

"Not talking. It invites the subject being questioned to fill the void." Tim kept his gaze on his hands. They were clasped so tightly David feared they might crush each other. "Patricia didn't lie to you. She told you what I told her."

David interrupted, shaking his head. "All she said is that you seem to think you had something to do with your mother's death."

"I killed her."

"Tim," David said sharply, firm in his refusal to believe the bald statement.

The kid flicked him a dark-eyed glance, his gaze searching David's face quickly but thoroughly. Tim must have seen the rejection David could feel lodged in his gut, because he sighed and fell back against the cushions.

"Maybe I didn't kill her with my own hands, but it's the truth that she's dead because of me." His voice dropped to a whisper. "It's all my fault."

TEN

"WHERE ARE we going?"

"Shh! You have to be quiet, or they'll find us."

My sharp ears picked up nothing but the rasp of her labored breathing. "We're alone."

She glanced down at me, her long auburn hair shining beneath the harsh fluorescent lights. The fright in her eyes showed through her forced smile, and her hand tightened almost painfully around my smaller one. "Okay. Can you run? Can you keep up with me?"

I glanced up at her and responded with a single nod. Without a word, she pulled me along the corridor, moving quickly enough that even I was hard pressed to keep pace with her adult-sized stride. The Facility was a maze, and I had not yet completely mapped the layout, so I had to hope she knew where she was going. My trust seemed well-placed at first. We didn't encounter a single guard until we neared a heavily fortified door, a black sign with the notice "RESTRICTED AREA: SECURITY CHECKPOINT" emblazoned on it in blocky red font. My ears picked up a faint sound, and I pulled anxiously at the woman's hand.

"What is it?" Her tone was strained with urgency. "We're almost there—"

"Stop and let the boy go!"

Spinning around at the familiar voice, I fixed my attention on the man who stood in front of the armed soldiers.

"I said, let him go, Karen."

"That's not my name! My name is—"

"It hardly matters, does it?"

Even at that tender age, I knew the colonel was not a man to be trifled with. I stepped in front of the woman I'd always thought of as mother, even though Father Paul had said she was merely a surrogate. She was sobbing, the hands she'd placed on my narrow shoulders trembling uncontrollably.

"Please, Colonel. Please! He's my baby. Just let me take him and go."

"Out of the question."

"No child should have to grow up in this place!"

Woodard sighed, his expression exuding a sympathy so fake it should have been apparent to anyone. "Karen, you know I can't let him go. But, perhaps...."

"Perhaps, what?" The hope in her voice hurt to hear.

"What do you say I let you spend more time with him? You're right. He's too young to spend all of his time surrounded by nothing but tutors and military personnel. Maybe regular interaction with someone ordinary will help with his emotional development."

I knew it wasn't what she wanted. The tightening of her grasp on my shoulders telegraphed her disappointment, but it was just as apparent she would take what she could get. I feared the colonel was lying. Father Paul had very explicitly warned me never to take the man at his word.

"Mother," I whispered, "be careful."

She lifted one hand from my shoulder to stroke my hair. "It's all right, sweetie. I'll stay here with you, and it will be like we're a family. Okay?"

I nodded, schooling my features to give nothing away. The colonel's victorious smile was smug, but he merely held out a hand and beckoned me forward.

"Come along, TM 05637. It's late, and good little soldiers need their sleep."

The woman whimpered as I moved away from her. "Do you have to call him that?"

Woodard ignored her. She was still in her sleepwear—a nighttime escape had been the extent of her plan. Although her slippers were almost noiseless against the floor, I could hear her following closely behind me. I didn't know how she'd thought we could survive in the desert in nothing but nightclothes, but it was all academic now. I tried not to flinch as the colonel took my arm in a hard grip.

"Shoot her."

The command was thrown calmly over his shoulder as we passed the armed guards. I tried to break away, but for all of my unnatural strength, I was too small and the colonel's hold was too solid. I could do nothing but listen to her surprised cry, the utterance quickly cut off in a hail of semiautomatic rounds.

"Mother!"

"TIM?"

I gasped, the sound of my assumed name dragging me back to the present. Concern was etched into the lines of David's face, and I felt the inexplicable urge to smooth them away with my lips. I looked down, focusing instead on my knees.

"She died trying to protect me." My thoughts felt scattered, and I struggled to edit the truth enough to disguise those facts that needed to remain hidden. "When I was seven, we were held up on the street by a mugger. He was trying to take her purse, and I stupidly tried to stop him." I folded my arms across my chest, clasping an elbow with each hand. "He pointed his gun at me, and she got between us."

David's face crumpled, sympathy radiating from him in waves at the lie. *So this is what guilt feels like*, I mused. Lying might be the most prudent option, but it somehow made me feel worse. I hugged myself tighter.

"Oh, Tim."

I heard David move, but my reaction time was too slow. The cushion beneath me dipped with added weight, and David's arms were around me before I could even think to evade him.

Feelings are useless. Sentiment will only get you killed.

The general had warned me about the dangers of becoming emotionally compromised. This must have been what he meant. It was like the embrace tripped a switch I hadn't known existed. I collapsed against the broad chest that was so temptingly close, my eyes drifting shut as David tentatively stroked my hair.

"I know it probably doesn't mean a lot, but I really am sorry. I'm sure she was glad she was able protect you, but… well, growing up without her couldn't have been easy."

David was right. His platitudes were meaningless, though I didn't doubt his sincerity. The tightness in my chest was almost certainly regret at telling such a blatant lie, no matter the small nugget of truth I'd hidden within it. Besides, I realized I wanted something besides words right then.

"So, your stepdad raised you?" David asked, still trying to suss out my past.

I definitely did not want to think about my "stepfather." I suddenly recalled my abandoned plan of taking advantage of David's attraction for me, but this time it wasn't protection I sought. A slight tilt of my head and my lips were pressed against David's, lightly at first but then with increasing pressure as he stiffened in shock. Committing fully to the tactic, I angled my body so we were pressed somewhat awkwardly against each other side-by-side. I wrapped my arms around David's neck to prevent his nascent struggle to put space between us.

"Tim—"

Weakness detected. Pursue strategic advantage.

David's attempt to speak had given me an opening, and I deftly slipped my tongue between his parted lips. The sound of my name—yet another lie in my growing trail of falsehoods—was muffled against my lips as I raised up and shifted around until my legs straddled David's thighs. Large hands came to rest lightly against my hips, as though uncertain whether they wanted to push me away or hold me in place. A bulge pressed against the growing hardness trapped in my own jeans, informing me that my actions were not wholly unwelcome. But as always, something held David back from taking what he so clearly wanted.

"Tim, wait—" David rasped again my mouth.

I didn't want to wait. I wanted this. Kissing wasn't something I'd been taught, but when I found David's tongue with mine, I instinctively sucked on it to keep him from pulling it away. I knew immediately I'd made precisely the right move. The hands against my hips tightened spastically as an unprompted groan vibrated between us. The tension which had gripped me eased away, only to be replaced by anxiousness of a different kind as David's hands slid up my sides and flattened against my back. He pulled me closer until not even air could come between us.

This was what I'd thought I wanted since first discovering David's sexual proclivities, a way to bind him to me so he would be willing to keep me. But now the meaning of my longing had changed. It wasn't devotion I sought but a deeper connection. Something that would sustain me even after I was once again on my own. Something I could hold on to when my body finally betrayed me and my only companion was the inevitability of death.

"I want you," I whispered, surprised at the breathy need in my voice. David's shirt was suddenly offensive, a barrier between my hands and the skin I wanted so desperately to touch. I took a fistful of cotton-polyester blend and yanked upward, revealing the coveted expanse of pale skin. David's scent intensified as his body temperature increased, overwhelming my enhanced senses and making my head swim. I placed the flats of my palms against David's chest, following the ripple of muscle as he started at the abrupt contact. His flesh was firm and soft at the same time, the physique of a man who rarely overindulged but was unaccustomed to exercise. The hint of vulnerability spiked my lust even higher. I struggled to remember not to press too hard, to not bruise David's more fragile human form when all I wanted to do was hold him so tightly he could never escape. I relinquished the grip of one hand in order to yank my own shirt upward. It bunched underneath my armpits, but removing it completely would have meant breaking the kiss, which I had absolutely no intention of doing.

Chest against chest, I could feel the heat pouring off David, warming me in places I'd never before acknowledged were cold. My hips moved unconsciously, the hardness in my pants rubbing achingly against the matching ridge in his. I still hadn't gotten into the habit of wearing underwear, and the friction of denim against my bare flesh forced a whimper from my throat.

"Holy fuck….," David swore helplessly, breathing another of those throaty groans as he broke the kiss. David tilted his head back and pushed our groins more firmly together.

"Mmmm," I moaned in return. I chased David until our lips were joined together once more. The sound of his need increased my own, and I dug my fingers into his thick hair. Blunt fingers pressed restlessly into my skin, urging me to continue the mindless rocking of my hips. My movements grew more restless as the same urgency I'd experienced while masturbating in the shower to thoughts of David built within me. And yet it was completely different. This was real. Although we were nearly fully clothed, I knew I was on the brink of coming.

"God, Tim—"

Good boy, my mind supplied from the soundtrack of the porn video I'd been forced to watch. But this wasn't the nameless man from the artificial scene. It was David, the savior who had taken me in when I was running for my life, who'd offered me the chance at normalcy I'd so desperately craved. For David, I wanted to be a good boy. I'd do whatever he wanted of me, if only to make him happy.

"Please." I wasn't sure what I was begging for, so I deepened the kiss, letting my body speak for me.

"Wait. Tim… shit. Just, wait a minute."

No, I wanted to cry out. I didn't stop, pretending I hadn't understood. So close, I was so close. I only needed a little bit more, and….

"Tim, stop." Heavy breathing filled the air, ending in a tired sigh as David dropped his head back against the cushion. "We shouldn't do this."

I could have forced him. David wasn't nearly strong enough to resist me, but I let him lift me off his lap and settle me on the cushion at his side. In a daze, I watched silently as he rubbed both of his hands over his face before dragging them upward until they were buried in his dark blond hair. Unsteady fingers left grooves behind when he finally let his hands fall heavily to his thighs.

"I'm sorry." David cut himself off with a dry chuckle and shook his head. "Damn, I keep saying that, don't I?" he mumbled, pointedly not looking anywhere but down at his feet.

"Do you hate me?" Was that me sounding so young and confused? I barely recognized myself, but not even the general had made me feel such a debilitating level of rejection.

David's head shot up at that, his pupils so blown his blue eyes looked almost black. "God, no! I could never hate you." He twisted his body so we were facing each other. "Why would you even think that?"

"You stopped. Why?" I sounded more normal that time, the uncertainty forced beneath a layer of wariness as I tried to make sense of what I had done wrong. If David had felt anything even remotely approaching what I had, how could he have pushed me away so easily? I was burning, helplessly aware of the throbbing pressure between my thighs. Only my ingrained ability to withstand physical distress allowed me to hide my discomfort. Gazing steadily at David, I waited for an explanation.

David closed his eyes, his expression pained as he shook his head. "Fuck if I know."

Not helpful, I thought. I needed information if I was to prevent this from happening again. "I didn't do it right," I said, giving voice to my suspicion. "Is that it?" I leaned forward into David's personal space. "Tell me what you like, and I'll do it."

David's gaze was slightly horrified when he finally looked over at me. "No, Tim. You definitely didn't do anything wrong. It's just...." His pinched expression eased, but the sympathy that replaced it wasn't any more promising. "I know you were just looking for comfort after talking about such an awful memory, and I apologize for letting things get so out of hand. It was wrong of me." David gave me a self-mocking smile. "What can I say? I was weak. You're... you're very beautiful, Tim. I'm sure you know that."

I did, in a way. I was aware my designers had intended for me to be attractive yet nondescript. Perfect for espionage work. But David seemed to mean something beyond pure aesthetics.

"So, you're gay too?"

The question was unexpected, though it probably shouldn't have been. Though not technically incorrect, particularly considering what had just occurred, I wasn't sure whether the designation strictly applied to me. Male or female, I'd been trained to interface with any target as necessary. I hesitated for a moment before ultimately nodding, deciding it would be easier to simply encourage David's assumption.

"Is that one of the reasons you ran away from home?"

I refrained from either affirming or denying the supposition, reluctant to heap yet another falsehood onto the mountain I'd built that night alone. But, of course, David drew his own conclusions from my lack of response, as I'd known he would. He reached out and patted me understandingly on the shoulder.

"Well, you don't have to worry about that with me, as you've probably guessed by now." With a soft laugh, David stood before lifting his arms over his head to stretch, his rumpled shirt riding up and flashing a sliver of pale skin. He remained unaware of my stealthy gaze as I honed in intently on the unintentional tease. "I think we should both get some sleep," David continued. "Patricia has to take her son to the doctor, so I need to open tomorrow. Unless you want to walk all the way downtown, you'll have to ride in with me."

The entire speech had been made without David looking at me for longer than a second. Only the rapid beat of the pulse I could see at his throat offered proof that he wasn't as unaffected as he was pretending to be.

"Good night."

And with that David beat a hasty retreat, leaving me alone on the sofa. The entire interlude had been a revelation. At first I'd thought only to recapture the feeling I'd experienced when David had held me after my nightmare. Now I knew better. I wanted to have sex with him. It was that simple, and despite his continued evasion, I knew David wanted me just as much. Getting past whatever was holding him back wouldn't be easy, but I was accustomed to taking on difficult challenges. I refused to give up, not now that I'd had a taste. I was no longer worried about David throwing me out on the street. He'd made it pretty clear I had a home with him for as long as I needed it. But my lips still tingled from the kisses we'd shared, and my body ached with the need for release. I needed this, I realized. Needed to do more with the time I had left than merely existing.

"Target locked," I whispered before retreating to the bathroom to take care of the demanding problem David had left me with.

"UNIT THREE reporting from grid point six."

Woodard was keenly aware of the woman standing closely over his shoulder as he listened to the voice coming in over a secure line. "Go ahead, Three."

"Sir, we finished the final sweep of Clovis, including a check of the area hospitals. No signs of the unit. Our next search point is Amarillo—"

"Sir, I have a report from the surveillance team."

Woodard turned to find Farley standing in his office doorway. "What is it, Lieutenant?"

She stepped inside and inclined her head respectfully toward Talbot. "Ma'am. Sir," she continued, "the team thinks it may have gotten a possible hit on the unit in—"

"Lubbock," Talbot interrupted, her tone declarative rather than questioning.

Farley stiffened slightly, but her expression didn't convey any surprise. "Yes, ma'am," she confirmed with a nod.

Woodard pursed his lips, annoyed at Talbot's seeming clairvoyance. "Care to share how you figured that out?"

"Lubbock is the only other town of any significant size near this location," Talbot replied. "TM 05637's training will prompt him to seek out someplace he can blend in. A small town where any outsider is a stranger would be an illogical choice, and we already have teams in Santa Fe."

"Have the surveillance team follow up on the lead, Lieutenant," Woodard ordered, determined to wrest back control of his own damn command. He angled himself so his voice would be audible to the person on the other end of the line. "But I want the mobile units to consider their sweeps. I don't want to put all our resources in one basket based on a single unsubstantiated lead. Report daily as ordered. Woodard out."

Farley departed to convey his instruction to the team he'd placed under her command. Woodard glanced up at Talbot as she made a slow, thoughtful circuit of his office, her hands tucked neatly into the small of her ramrod-straight back. His gaze narrowed at her carefully restrained expression. "If I didn't know any better, I'd say you were proud this is the first potential glimpse we've had of the TM unit until now."

Talbot shot him an indecipherable look but didn't pause in her deliberate pacing. "It's been nearly two weeks since it escaped. Between this Facility and the Company, we've made use of every available resource. Yet it continues to elude us." The quirk at the corner of her lips might have been called a smile on anyone else. "I have to commend you, General. The unit's instruction in infiltration and evasion has been most successful."

For some reason he didn't feel like he'd received a compliment. He knew she was as frustrated with TM 05637's continued disappearance as he was. Besides the time and money the Company had invested in the project, the higher-ups were doubtlessly aware that much of the research which had gone into the TM project had not been officially sanctioned by the Congressional oversight committee that was nominally in charge. Not to mention some of the aggressive methods they'd employed to make the unit mission ready could land them in front of the ICC for human rights violations. Except TM 05637 wasn't human, as far as he was concerned, so the squeamish civvies on the Hill could go fuck themselves. If, however, the unit were to be discovered by the wrong people, it was a certainty more than careers would be destroyed in the aftermath.

Woodard placed his fingertips together and touched them absently to his lips as he considered where the unit might be hiding. "TM 05637 would want to stay out of sight as much as possible and keep to itself. It understands surveillance techniques as well as, if not better than, our own personnel. It's probably living on the streets somewhere, but not so as to attract the attention of the authorities." He hummed to himself. "Yeah, my guess would be a homeless shelter. Livable, but completely below the radar."

"You are an idiot, General."

He glared at her, the ticking muscle in his clenched jaw visibly signaling his anger at the insult. "I beg your pardon, Ms. Talbot, but I am still in charge here."

"More's the pity." She halted her pacing and spun sharply on her heel so she could fix her unnerving gaze directly on him. Despite himself, he struggled to hold her unblinking stare. "Think, General. Think about who had the most access to TM 05637 and who helped it escape in the first place."

Not following her point, Woodard's brow furrowed in bewilderment. "You mean Anderson? What about him?" He tried not to feel relieved when she turned away after shooting him a look of subdued disgust.

"The good doctor treated the unit more like a child than a science project. Have you ever considered the reason he helped it escape? It's because he wanted it to have an ordinary life."

"How do you know?"

The costly material of Talbot's dark gray suit bunched as her shoulders lifted on a deep breath. "We were married for over twenty years. Or had you forgotten?"

He had, to be honest. He couldn't imagine anyone taking the ice queen for a wife, let alone the brilliant yet scatterbrained scientist he had been tasked with watching over for so long. He grunted rather than admit to his lapse of memory.

"I know Paul better than anyone," she added, "and I know what motivated him."

Woodard waited, but when she remained silent, he spoke up. "And that is?"

Her light green eyes were hard as she turned to look at him. "Love, General. He loved that genetic freak like it was his own son." Her fingers tightened their grip on each other until her knuckles grew pale. "He would have urged it to try and live as normal a life as it could secure for itself. It has found someone to shelter it, to hide it. You can be certain of that. We specified that its appearance be appealing, and I am well aware you taught it to use that fact to its full advantage. It will attempt to form an attachment with whomever it has enticed to protect it, to ensure that it won't be betrayed."

Woodard felt as much the fool as she had called him. Everything she'd said made complete sense, but it also made the task of recovering the TM unit that much harder. The prospect of possibly having to search every house in Lubbock, Roswell, or any number of other towns in the three-hundred-mile radius of their search parameters, all without attracting inconvenient attention, gave him a headache. And if the unit had gotten as far as Albuquerque....

"Fuck," he breathed, leaning back in his chair.

"Indeed, General. Let's hope the Lubbock lead isn't a dead end, for both our sakes." The click of her heels as she walked out of his office punctuated her parting remark.

ELEVEN

"VENTI BLACK eye!"

"That's mine."

David gave the barista a weak smile, which she barely acknowledged before swinging around to whip out her next beverage order. He stumbled over to the nearest empty table in the coffeehouse he'd escaped to at the earliest opportunity that morning, maneuvering unsteadily around a few Texas Tech students who were taking advantage of the free Wi-Fi. He all but fell into his seat and spent a few minutes staring blearily at his drink while he tried to figure out what the hell had happened to his life.

Two hours of sleep per night—three at the most—over the last few days kept his tired brain from pondering the situation too deeply. All he was really fit for was reliving the tantalizing snippets that had been playing on a loop in his mind ever since Tim's surprise attack several nights before. The taste of Tim's mouth, the feel of that hard young body against his own, the astonishing realization that his desire for his new housemate wasn't one-sided after all.

"Ugh," he groaned, forsaking the liquid consciousness in the poorly insulated paper cup in favor of thunking his head down on the faux wood table.

Tim was gay. Even days later, the revelation continued to amaze him. Honestly, he hadn't seen that one coming. It put everything about their previous interactions in a brand-new light. The way the kid had been a little too willing to show as much skin as he could get away with around him, especially during those first couple of days. The direct, soul searching looks he apparently hadn't misinterpreted as flirting after all. How, after waking from his nightmare, Tim hadn't hesitated to sleep in his arms even though he'd been bare-assed naked.

"I'm such an idiot," he announced to no one in particular.

An older woman, the only noncollege student in the café besides himself, smiled at him uncertainly as he mumbled to himself. He started to return the gesture, but opted instead to take a restorative drink of his espresso-laced coffee. It was more bitter than he usually preferred, but the instant hit of caffeine was just what the doctor ordered. After leaving Tim alone on the sofa—he still wasn't sure how he'd found the fortitude to do that—he'd gone straight to bed. He'd spent that night, and every one since, jerking off like he was a fucking sixteen-year-old. He could still smell the healthy musk rising from Tim's skin, could still feel the press of those firm buttocks against his crotch, shifting around in artless, maddening circles that had threatened to make him come in his damn pants.

It would have been so easy to take what had been offered. He'd been that close to tearing off Tim's jeans and showing him exactly what he wanted to do to that luscious little ass. But he wouldn't ever have been able to look the kid in the eye again, let alone look at himself. As it was, he'd been avoiding Tim as much as he could, given that they lived in the same house and worked together. He took pains not to come downstairs in the morning until the very last minute. At the store he hid in his office all day. And, whenever they were alone, he pointedly maintained an awkward silence between them. He knew he was acting like a coward, but what were his options?

He was convinced he'd done the right thing by turning the kid down as gently as he knew how. Tim might have thought he wanted sex, but the fact that he had been upset enough to let his usual stoicism slip told David just how much his mother's death had affected him. How could it not? If even only half of Tim's story had been true.... David shook his head. He didn't know what he'd have done if he'd seen his own mother killed so tragically. Indulging his lust when the kid was so troubled would have been unforgiveable.

David wondered if he'd guessed right about Tim's stepfather kicking him out after finding out he was gay. If so, it was all the more reason not to take advantage of the situation. He'd been lucky his mother had been willing to put aside her small-town Oklahoma upbringing and accept that her strapping boy was a queer. But, like he'd hinted to Tim, his father hadn't been quite so sanguine about his revelation. If the confrontation that had prompted Tim to leave home had been half as painful as what had transpired between him and his own father, well, he wouldn't wish that on anyone.

He told himself he would be there for Tim for as long as the kid needed him. But if Tim tried again to entice him into something more intimate, well, he was the adult here, and he would fucking act like one. At least taking cold showers once a day would save him a ton of money on hot water. As though sparked by the very thought of bathing in ice-cold water, David was wracked by a sudden fit of coughing.

"Oh, great," he groaned under his breath. "That's just what I need." Taking one more fortifying sip of his espresso, David pushed back from the table. When he stood, he was forced to grab the edge of the table as a wave of dizziness hit him. "No, I do not have time for this." His lungs stubbornly ignored him, hitting him with another bout of wracking spasms.

He had stuff to do and needed to get back to work no matter how crappy he felt. It was probably nothing more than a symptom of his recent sleep deprivation. He simply needed to sort out his conscience and get back into his regular routine. Hiding away from Tim wasn't the answer. His evasiveness was just causing him stress he didn't need. Eventually they would have to face each other and figure out how to go about their relationship. Their very platonic relationship.

"Yeah, right."

"You okay, honey?"

The woman who'd smiled at him earlier was looking at him with concern. *Great, now she thinks I'm crazy.* "Yes, ma'am," he said aloud, tipping her a polite nod. Beating a dignified retreat, David ambled back out into the somewhat painful sunshine. What he wouldn't give for one of those stereotypical Texas ten-gallons right then. He squinted in annoyance at the offending expanse of blue sky as he started toward the parking lot.

He was rounding the corner of the building when he nearly ran into a couple of men who could only be described as suspicious characters. They were dressed casually enough in collared shirts and khakis, even with the matching aviator sunglasses they wore. But something about their bearing screamed they were out of place. Lubbock wasn't some tiny backwater, but neither was it New York City. Unusual folk stood out, and these guys were definitely unusual.

David wasn't a small guy. He was a very respectable six feet and hadn't yet lost the build that had made him a modestly successful halfback in college, though his middle had a bit more girth than it had in his heyday. But the two strangers dwarfed him by inches and dozens of pounds, all of it muscle. They moved like athletes, although something about the way they carried themselves made David think of something far more deadly. Military? One of the men was blond and the other brunet, but they both sported what seemed like military haircuts that had recently started to grow out. Cannon Air Force Base near Clovis wasn't all that far away. He'd done some business with the procurement officer there. He figured he could spot an airman, but these guys didn't look like any he'd ever met.

David hadn't noticed he'd stopped dead on the path leading from the café entrance to the parking lot to stare at the strangers until they had reached the front door. The dark-haired man turned and shot him a mirrored glance before he followed the blond and disappeared inside. David blinked and shook his head, scolding himself in a voice that sounded suspiciously like his mother's to stop being so nosy. She'd always been adamant about how a respectable young man should behave, and gawking at strangers and sleeping with his barely legal housemate were definitely not on the list.

He should probably give his mother a call, he thought idly, promising himself he would do so right after he and Tim finished with dinner that evening. He also swore he would stop acting like a chump where the kid was concerned. The car was stifling, though he'd been in the café only a short time, so he cranked up the AC as soon as he started the engine. Though he felt overheated, he wasn't sweating. Still, the blast of air made him shiver. Ignoring the ominous sign, David pulled out of the lot and headed back toward the BBW and the test of willpower that awaited him there in the form of one nineteen-year-old runaway in tight jeans.

"SO, HOW was your day?"

I was caught off guard as David spoke to me for the first time in nearly three days. I'd been too distracted by the odd physiological signs he was exhibiting to notice he was actually looking directly at me for a change.

"Fine," I replied, watching as a smile stretched the abnormally dry skin of David's face. Although he had been avoiding me, I'd kept a close eye on my elusive quarry, unsuccessfully trying to determine the best way to break the impasse that had arisen between us after my botched seduction attempt.

"Good." David's blue gaze flitted toward me quickly before darting back down to the plate holding his dinner. "That's good." David sighed and tapped his fork against the bargain dinnerware. "Look, kid, about the other night—"

"Are you okay?" David's breathing sounded labored, and I grabbed on to the excuse to stop him from continuing with what he'd been about to say. I didn't want to hear him tell me again that what we'd done was wrong. Besides, my concern wasn't completely feigned. "You look a bit peaked."

David blinked. "Uh, yeah. I'm fine—"

I jumped up from my chair and quickly rounded the table to kneel beside David as a violent bout of coughing interrupted him. "You're not fine," I said tonelessly, completely focused on dealing with whatever was happening. "What's the matter?" Hesitantly, I placed a hand on David's back and waited until the coughing subsided enough for him to talk.

"Nothing." David groaned and braced his head in his hands, his elbows planted on the table. "I'm just coming down with something. Hopefully not the flu."

"The flu?" I echoed. "You mean you're sick."

"Nah, it's probably just a cold."

"Which means you're sick." I was suddenly aware I had no idea how to handle treating someone who was ill as opposed to injured. I'd never been sick a day in my life, and my triage experience went more toward dressing wounds than taking care of someone under the sway of a viral or bacterial attack. "What should I do?" I asked, determined to be helpful.

"Do?" David's laugh morphed into yet another minute of coughing. "Nothing," he gasped, catching his breath. "I'll drink some orange juice and go to bed." He must have seen something in my expression because he smiled and patted my cheek fondly. "Don't worry about me. I'll be as right as rain in the morning."

I didn't know what the weather had to do with anything, but within the next couple of hours, it was apparent David's forecast was less than sunny. I didn't need any instruments to tell me his fever had begun to spike alarmingly. His skin was deeply flushed, and his breathing was even more labored than it had been at dinner.

"You need a doctor," I recommended, hovering in the doorway of David's bedroom, having been drawn there by his incessant hacking. I had never been inside and didn't feel comfortable entering without an invitation.

"No" came the rasping answer. "I just need to get some sleep."

Despite David's attempted reassurance, his condition continued to deteriorate until he was unable to respond when I checked on him again twenty minutes later. Necessity overrode my hesitancy to invade his room, and I headed straight for the phone resting on the table next to the bed. David was sleeping restlessly, and I watched him closely as I dialed a phone number I'd committed to memory from the store's employee records. I'd been trained to be nosy, and right then I was glad for the compulsion to gather information whenever the opportunity arose.

"This is Patricia."

"David is sick. Can you come to his house?"

"Tim?" Her tone relayed her surprise. "Is that you, sugar?"

"Yes."

"He's sick, you say?" she echoed. "What's wrong with him?"

"He's coughing a lot and his skin is flushed. I tried to wake him up just now but couldn't," I added.

She hummed thoughtfully. "Does he have a fever?"

Remembering a lesson concerning how to check body temperature on the fly, I placed a hand against David's forehead. He was burning to the touch. "Yes. It's too high," I said succinctly. "Please, come quickly."

"Okay." She agreed without further questions. "I'll be there in about fifteen minutes."

I waited by David's bedside for Patricia to arrive, feeling useless. Right on time the doorbell rang, and I abandoned my position for the first time since placing the pleading call. I rushed downstairs and opened the front door, revealing a frazzled Patricia.

"Hey, sugar," she said, stepping inside as I moved back to let her enter. Her hair was in a messy ponytail, and her face was devoid of makeup. She was wearing a tracksuit, and a huge bag was slung over her shoulder. "You didn't give me a lot of details, but from what you said, Mr. Conley sounds pretty bad."

"Yes, and I don't know how to help him. Should I get him to a hospital?"

She smiled at me and held up her hand. "Now, hold your horses. I doubt it's quite that serious. Where is he?" She glanced around, noticing David was nowhere in sight. "I can tell you more after I take a look at him."

"Upstairs," I said, turning to lead her without further elaboration. She followed closely on my heels, and I paused to check that David was still sleeping before letting her into his room.

Patricia took one look at him and nodded. "It's the flu. My youngest boy recently got over it. That bug has been going around since spring." She shook her head. "It's a shame Mr. Conley caught it, but that's the way it goes. I just hope I'm not the one who passed it to him," she said with a self-effacing chuckle. She reached into the large bag and pulled out an object enclosed in a long thin plastic box. "Thermometer," she explained. "Let's see how bad off he is. David, honey," she said, opting for a more informal mode of address as she bent over the prone figure. "I need to take your temperature."

She placed a hand on David's head, and I felt something clench hard in my stomach at the sight of her touching him. Shaking off the disconcerting reaction, I went to the other side of the bed so I could see his face. "He's waking up."

With a groan David turned his head and squinted at the woman standing over him. "Patricia?" His voice was hoarse, and the effort of talking made him start coughing again. "What are you doing here?" he gasped.

"Tim called me. He was worried about you and rightly so." Patricia held out the thermometer and stuck it in David's mouth. "Now, let's check that temperature. Tim, honey, can you go and get him a glass of water?"

I did as she instructed, running downstairs to the kitchen for a glass. Now that someone had arrived to take charge, I could appreciate how much the sight of David had affected me. I was breathing rapidly, and my pulse rate had increased in a telltale sign of stress. Patricia had been right. I was worried. Yet another new emotion and one I didn't much like. I was relieved someone was here who seemed to know what she was doing. Careful not to spill the water, I rushed back upstairs in time to see Patricia squinting at the readout on the thermometer.

"101. Hmm, that's not too bad. My son spiked a fever of 103. But then again, kids are funny that way."

I knew the standard temperature for a human male was 98.6 degrees. That David was running over two degrees warmer than the ideal seemed a cause for more concern than Patricia was displaying. But I was forced to bow to her judgment, having no knowledge of my own to go by. "Will he be all right?" I asked, needing verbal reassurance.

"Hmm?" Patricia looked toward me and blinked like she'd forgotten I was there. "Oh, yeah. He'll be fine." She reached in her bag and pulled out a box and a bottle. "Just give him two of the ibuprofen four times a day until his fever is gone. You should wake him up so he can take his first dose after I leave. This," she said holding up the bottle, "is for his cough and congestion. The directions will tell you what you need to know." She smiled at my perplexed expression as she handed the medicine over to me. "Honey, I'm a mother. I keep a pharmacy on me at all times." Laughing, Patricia crooked a finger at me, beckoning me to follow her out of the room.

A glance told me David had fallen back to sleep, so I obeyed without comment until we were back downstairs. "What else do I need to do?" I inquired once we were safely out of earshot of the sleeping man.

"Make sure he drinks plenty of fluids. Water, juice, that sort of thing." She thought for a moment. "Oh, and you'll need to make sure he stays cool. He's going to have chills, but it's important that his fever goes down. The best way is... well, don't worry about that," she went on after a curious pause. "The medicine should do the trick."

"The best way is what?" I pressed. I frowned in bemusement as her cheeks tinged pink.

"Well, I always give my boys sponge baths using cool water. But, like I said, don't worry about it," she added in a rush. "He'll be fine."

The descriptive term was self-explanatory, and I immediately decided I would take her advice. Now I just needed her to depart so I could implement the suggested treatment. "Thank you, Patricia," I said, wishing I could adjust my tone to more adequately express my gratitude. "I don't think we'll be in to work tomorrow."

"Oh, don't worry about that. Just tell Mr. Conley when he wakes up that I hope he feels better soon." Patricia turned and headed toward the door. "And give me a call sometime tomorrow evening to let me know how he's doing."

"I will."

She left with a final wave, and I stood for a moment staring at the closed door. David had made it clear he didn't want to encourage any renewal of our interlude on the couch, but the situation had changed. He was sick and needed assistance. It wouldn't be taking advantage. After all, getting David well as fast as possible was in everyone's best interest. Satisfied at my reasoning, I headed to the kitchen to retrieve a bucket from beneath the sink. Returning upstairs, I adjusted the thermostat to turn up the heat on the second floor level before taking the bucket with me into the bathroom. I sat it in the tub under the running tap, and once it was full of cool water, gathered up a washcloth and headed back to David's bedroom, bucket in hand.

David was still asleep, his mouth open as he struggled to breathe around his congestion. I briefly reconsidered what I was about to do, wondering if it would be taking unforgivable liberties to basically molest a man while he was so impaired. But Patricia had assured me it was an effective treatment to help him get well, so my brief attack of conscience was easily silenced.

I set the bucket on the floor with the towel draped over its lip before easing back the comforter beneath which David was huddling. He was shivering, making me glad I'd thought to turn up the room temperature beforehand. He hadn't buttoned his pajama top—probably hadn't had the energy to do so—making my task easier as I pulled the edges of the shirt apart to reveal his torso. Even without touching him, I could feel the feverish heat radiating up from his body. Picking up the washcloth, I dipped it into the water and knelt on the bed to carefully lay the sopping towel against the exposed patch of overheated skin.

"Wha—" David's blurry blue eyes peeled open, and he stared up at me. His attempt to speak prompted a coughing fit. "What are you doing?" he asked when his cough had quieted down, lifting his head to look down at the towel lying on his chest.

"Giving you a sponge bath?" My answer unintentionally seemed like a question, signaling my uncertainty. "Patricia recommended it."

David blinked, his muzzy brain seeming to take a second to make sense of the explanation. "Oh, okay," he said finally. "Yeah, I remember my mom doing this for me when I got sick as a kid." He laid his head back on his pillow, exhausted by the small exertion. "But you don't have to."

"It's fine." I reached again for the towel and began moving it lightly over David's skin before he could protest further. His breathing was labored, but after a moment, it seemed to even out. A glance at his face revealed he had fallen asleep again. Taking David's abrupt reversion to unconsciousness as a tacit approval, my hesitation vanished as I accepted the rare opportunity I'd been offered to study him with impunity.

I drew the towel slowly up the column of David's neck, soothing away the heat. As I moved the towel lower, I noticed his skin tone was quite a bit lighter than mine. Based on the differences in our complexions, I absently calculated the amount of time David would be able to spend in the sun without damage. As well as being fair, his chest was bare, save for the light sprinkling of slightly darker hair that was scattered between his nipples and trailed down toward his stomach. The strands became plastered against the pale skin as I wetted them. I followed the towel with my bare hand, telling myself that a tactile examination was simply another way of gathering information. David's pink nipples had pebbled reflexively at the coolness of the water, and a smile tugged at my lips as they tickled my palm.

I noticed a dark red mark on the far outside of David's left pectoral, barely peeking out from where his arm lay against his side. The blotch of pigment was smooth to the touch, and I wondered whether he had any other identifying marks. I felt an intense desire to find them all, to chart every inch of his body. But now wasn't the time. Focusing back on the task at hand, I ignored the sudden throbbing in my groin and concentrated on bathing every part of him I could see. Already his breathing seemed easier, and I silently thanked Patricia for her advice.

As I drew the towel low over David's stomach, I met the barrier of his pajama bottoms. I knew from my biology lessons that nearly all of the organs that could be affected by overheating were located in the torso, but that didn't stop me from extending my treatment lower. In the interest of thoroughness, of course. After all, the male genitalia were delicate and prone to damage from heat, which was why the testes were located safely away from the body's heated core. David's fever was conceivably placing his reproductive system at risk of permanent damage.

It made for a convenient excuse, at least.

I decided to go about my task as if I were administering first aid—as impersonally as possible. Ignoring the surprisingly intrusive voice in my head urging me to pull the obfuscating item of clothing down past his hips and take a peek, I contented myself with merely reaching beneath the waistband of the pajama bottoms with the towel. A surreptitious glance toward the head of the bed showed that David remained asleep, though I wasn't sure whether that fact made my actions more or less acceptable. Relaxed as he was, his flesh was quiescent and didn't stir as I caressed his cock and testes with the towel. My hand briefly lost its grip on the cloth and my fingers ghosted over his soft, flaccid length. I told myself it was an accident, but when David suddenly moved his hips, a hoarse groan spilling from his slack lips, I knew I had pressed my luck as far as I dared.

Ignoring the quickened pace of my own breathing, I withdrew my hand from David's pants and stood. I tossed the towel into the bucket and leaned over David to pull the sides of his shirt back together before pulling the comforter up so it covered him from the neck down. Perspiration had beaded on my forehead, and I wondered absently why my body hadn't automatically compensated for the room's increased warmth before noting that my internal temperature had, in fact, far outpaced that of the room. The last time I'd felt like this was after my encounter with David on the couch.

"Interesting," I murmured softly, pondering what other signs of arousal I might manifest if given another chance. I wanted to find out, and I wanted David to be the one to show me. Later, I promised myself. After returning the bucket to the bathroom, I went back to wake David long enough to give him two of the ibuprofen. He barely stayed conscious long enough to swallow. Once that was done, I settled myself on the floor against the wall within view of the bed. Better to be close in case I was needed. Watching David sleep, I felt my body gradually return to its normal parameters. With the image of David's naked chest flitting endlessly through my head, it was a long time before I managed to fall asleep.

THE FIRST thing David noticed was that his eyes were gummed shut. The second was that he was sweating from head to toe. Dealing with the first problem was the easiest, and using the heels of his hands, he rubbed his eyes until he was able to pry them open. Blinking, he looked around the familiar confines of his bedroom. Weak light streamed in through the slats of his blinds, and he guessed it was late in the afternoon. It was the first clear thought he'd had in he didn't know how long. Wondering what time it was, he turned his head toward the clock on his nightstand and started in surprise when he saw the figure sitting hunched against the wall across from his bed.

"Tim?" he croaked. Clearing his parched throat, he tried again. "Hey, kid! What are you doing?"

Tim's eyes popped open, and in an instant he was standing beside the bed. David tried not to sigh in pleasure as Tim rested a cool hand against his forehead.

"Your fever has dropped considerably. Are you feeling better?"

David nodded, careful not to dislodge the hand. "Yeah. What time is it?"

"Seven in the evening. It's Friday."

David stared up at Tim in disbelief. "Friday? I thought it was Wednesday?"

"It was Wednesday when you first fell ill. You've slept on and off for nearly two days." Tim's lips curved up in that lovely shy smile. "You needed the rest."

David sighed. "I guess I did." He pushed himself up to a sitting position, happy to note that his head wasn't spinning and his chest didn't feel as tight as it had the other day. "Have you been sitting there the entire time?" He didn't know how he felt about the kid watching him sleep for so long.

"I wanted to be close in case you needed me."

He didn't want to read too much into that, but David was touched despite himself. He searched for a change of topic before he said something embarrassing. "Um, did Patricia come here, or did I dream that?"

"She came Wednesday night to tell me how to take care of you."

Something else flitted through David's memory, and he forced himself to ask even though he wasn't sure he wanted the answer. "And did I dream that you gave me a sponge bath?" He groaned to himself as Tim shook his head. If he hadn't dreamed it before, he sure as hell would now. What little he did remember of the feel of Tim's hands touching him was enough to make him hard even as tired and hungry as he was.

"Um, is there anything to eat?" he asked, latching on to that last thought.

"I'll go make soup."

Taking advantage of his momentary privacy, David used the bathroom and changed into a pair of dry pajamas. As he stood at the toilet, he pondered briefly how the kid had managed to deal with this necessity while he'd been out of it. Better not to think about it, he decided, firmly shutting the door on any speculation in that direction. Tim didn't look freaked out, so perhaps he had experience taking care of an invalid, although he said he'd needed Patricia's advice. The kid had certainly done a good job of it. The lingering doubts David had been fostering since Tim's violent encounter with Bobby began to fade. If he could trust the kid with himself, then he could trust him not to hurt Bobby. He'd stress to Tim the importance of using caution during the fighting lessons, but he felt even more certain he'd done the right thing by encouraging a relationship between the two young men.

He heard Tim return to his room and headed back out to meet him. Tim had switched on the light to counteract the growing dusk, making it easier for David to navigate back to the bed. He still felt kind of weak, so he was content to sit with his back propped against the headboard while Tim handed him a tray. He took it gratefully, smiling at the bowl of soup, crackers, and glass of orange juice.

"Thanks," he said, starting in with tired gusto. The kid merely nodded and continued to stand at his bedside, watching him eat. It was disconcerting, so David gestured for him to sit. "And thanks for taking such good care of me," he added. "You have some practice at this, I take it."

"Patricia told me what to do."

With his ferreting attempt neatly sidestepped, David decided eating was more important than playing detective. "Well, the sponge bath was definitely a good idea."

"You mentioned your mother used to do that for you when you were young. Are you still close to her?"

David took the non sequitur in stride. He could understand Tim's desire to hear about a normal mother-child relationship given what had happened with his own mother. He nodded while savoring a mouthful of the hearty soup.

"Mmm-hmm," he replied after a moment. "We're pretty close. She's up in Oklahoma, so I don't really see her that often. But we talk pretty regularly on the phone." Which reminded him again that he hadn't spoken to his mother since Tim had come to live with him. It wasn't a conversation he was particularly looking forward to, knowing she probably wouldn't understand why he'd allowed a stranger into his home on what was basically a whim.

"What about your father? You said before that your relationship is… strained."

David didn't like talking about his father, but he figured he owed the kid for being such a capable nursemaid. "Well, like I told you, my dad wanted me to study medicine and go into the Army. When I didn't, he wasn't too thrilled. But I also came out to him and my mom as gay my senior year of high school, which was the last straw. My father wanted to throw me out right then, but Ma convinced him to let me stay until I'd graduated. I'd already decided to go to school here in Lubbock, so he only had to put up with having a gay son under his roof for a couple of months." Shaking his head, David huffed in a humorless laugh. "He made my life hell during those last weeks. You'd think I'd tried to screw a dude right in front of him." He smiled to soften his crudeness. "My mom was the only thing that kept me going until I was able to move out." David glanced over at Tim. "You know, that's the first time I've ever told anyone about that." Tim watched him steadily, and his smile grew more genuine. He could get used to the kid's way of just accepting things without batting an eyelash. Tim's stoic demeanor was calming somehow. "So, what about you? You never did answer me. Did you run away because your stepfather found out that you're gay?"

Tim shook his head. "No. I, um, just wanted a fresh start somewhere away from him." Tim looked thoughtful. "If he had known, I don't know whether I would have survived long enough to get away."

David's stomach twisted. The kid's tone had been even, almost deadpan, but the matter-of-fact conjecture made him want to throw up. Even when things had been at their worst, he'd never been afraid his father would hurt him. The "you're-dead-to-me" treatment had been bad enough.

"Look, we don't need to talk about this right now." David cracked a huge yawn, which was only partly feigned. In an instant the tray had been whisked away, and Tim was holding out the glass of juice and a couple of pills. David recognized the medicine as a popular brand of ibuprofen. "Patricia?" he asked. Tim nodded, and David chuckled, making a mental note to buy his assistant manager a gift for her thoughtfulness. Once he'd swallowed the pills, he scooted back down under his comforter, content from having a full stomach and relieved he was no longer shivering from fever chills.

"Good night," Tim said quietly.

"Night. Oh, and I think I'll be well enough to go to work in the morning." David was reluctant to even think about everything that had probably piled up on his desk after his impromptu two-day absence.

"If you're sure." Tim switched off the light and turned to leave, tray in hand.

David looked over at the kid when he paused at the door. "What is it?" he asked.

Tim glanced back at him, his dark eyes unreadable in the dim light. "I'm glad your father's hatred didn't damage *you*."

As Tim disappeared into the hall, David wondered at the odd emphasis. It made it sound as though the kid hadn't been so lucky. He prayed that wasn't the case. As he drifted to sleep, David realized he would do whatever it took to help Tim overcome the trauma of his mysterious past.

TWELVE

"BOW."

I faced Bobby and demonstrated, bending from the waist at a precise sixty degree angle. The midafternoon sun was warm as it shone down on my back. Bobby had done very well with keeping the store's inventory up-to-date over the past week. As a reward, I'd decided it was a good time to give Bobby his first lesson—some beginning karate drills to provide him with the proper fundamentals.

"What's that for?" Bobby asked.

"It shows proper respect for the art and to your teacher."

"If you say so." He looked skeptical but imitated as best he could.

The back lot of the BBW was covered with grass, which would provide a less dangerous surface as we progressed in our lessons. I could always borrow some exercise mats from the store if we needed them. David had decided not to spend the money necessary to tame the stubby growth, and as a result the ground was slightly uneven. I had offered to help with the upkeep of the lot for David's sake as well as for my own purposes in training Bobby, and David had graciously accepted my offer.

"So what are you gonna teach me first? One of those sweet Jet Li moves?" The grass was still damp from the rain shower that had popped up earlier in the day, and Bobby's bare feet slid over the slick surface as he executed a clumsy imitation of a jump kick. I didn't remark as he struggled to regain his balance after stumbling slightly as he landed.

"We'll start with basic punches. Place your feet shoulder-width apart. Wider." I used my equally bare foot to nudge Bobby's until they were in the proper position.

"This feels weird." The slight whine in Bobby's voice made him sound younger than his thirteen years.

"The stance is to give you stability."

Without warning, I pushed sharply against his shoulders. Bobby windmilled his arms but only shifted a tiny bit.

"Hey!"

"See? You didn't fall over, did you?"

Bobby blinked before looking up at me in wonder. "You're right!"

"Good. So, no more complaining. Just do as I say."

"Whatever." Bobby's tone was grudging, but the smile on his face revealed that he was only teasing. He watched with attentive curiosity as I positioned his arms so his fists were tucked into his sides.

"This is the simplest punching stance." Standing in front of Bobby, I mirrored his posture, angling my body so he could see me from both the front and the side. Pushing my arm out quickly from my waist, I snapped a front punch with my right hand, followed swiftly by my left, then right and left again. I lowered my arms back to the ready position and glanced over at a wide-eyed Bobby. His jaw had dropped slightly and he looked entranced.

"Whoa. You're fast!"

"You try it," I replied, accepting his admiration without comment. My speed was due to my enhanced muscle response, as well as from constant drills and threats about what would happen if my technique wasn't flawless. I hastily banished the unpleasant thought, refusing to let it mar this experience. If I had to find a word to describe this moment with Bobby, teaching him a useful skill in the incongruous setting of the back lot of the BBW, I would choose "enjoyable." Part of it was the knowledge that I was pursuing my self-imposed mission to become Bobby's friend. The other part was the unexpected pleasure I got from simply hanging out with him. I refused to allow any painful recollections to spoil the experience. I'd had my fill of that when I'd spun the tale of my surrogate mother's death for David. Passing on these simple techniques was vastly preferably to wallowing in dark memories.

A few minutes spent observing Bobby's punching form had revealed an easily addressed problem. "Keep your thumb on the outside of your fingers." I took hold of one of his hands and correctly positioned the offending digit. "If you tuck it into your fist like that, it's more likely to get broken."

Bobby's face scrunched in confusion. "But isn't it safer to have it out of the way when you're hitting something?"

I nodded. "Yes, but see?" I turned his hand palm up. "You punch with the flat of your fist, here." I tapped the upper part of Bobby's fingers right below his largest knuckles. "It's best to keep your thumb down here, against the lower part of your fingers, out of the way."

Bobby's face lit up with understanding. "Oh! I get it." He threw another air-punch, his fist perfectly positioned. "Like that?"

"Yes. Very good," I added, figuring Bobby might respond well to the deserved praise. I briefly considered what I should have him do next. "Okay, now let's—"

"Who taught you how to fight? Your dad?"

The question was so unexpected it was a moment before I could think of how to respond. I didn't really have a "father" in the way Bobby was thinking, though I'd always placed Father Paul into that role. Thinking of the other so-called paternal figure in my life, I answered hesitantly, "No. My stepfather."

"He taught you?"

Not exactly, I thought. "He made me learn."

Bobby had been practicing his punches while waiting for me to answer the uncomfortable question, but my strangely worded response made him pause and look up with a confused squint. "What do you mean, he made you?"

"He thought I was weak, so he insisted I take lessons." It was the truth more or less. *Pussy boy!* I could still hear the general's sneering tone as he barked his favorite nickname for the experiment under his command. Not even after I'd successfully completed an exercise that had included fighting and disabling a group of Army Rangers in one-on-six combat had the general stopped using the cruel moniker.

149

"So, you and he had a fight, huh." It wasn't a question. Bobby sounded like he knew what my answer would be.

"What do you mean?" I asked, unwilling to acknowledge how accurate the guess was.

"That's why you left home, right? You and he must have fought, and you kicked his ass. So he threw you out. Or you left, one or the other." Bobby shrugged. "I mean, you're so smart. Like the way you've been helping me study. It took my teacher two days to explain how to do my math homework, and I never got it. But in five minutes you showed me exactly what I was doing wrong. You're probably good at sports too. You sure had no problem catching me that time, and I'm the fastest runner in my school!" Bobby shook his head. "I can't imagine why your stepdad wouldn't be proud of you. So you must have kicked his ass."

My vision blurred, the image of Father Paul's body lying in a dark red pool of his own blood flashing across my mind. I hadn't had to face the general directly, but I certainly wouldn't say I'd won the altercation precipitating my escape. Catching my breath against the flare of pain in my chest, I determinedly blinked the agonizing memory away. The sight of the overgrown, abandoned lot and of Bobby staring up at me with expectant sympathy calmed me, grounding me in the present.

"He wanted me to do things I didn't want to do," I replied simply. "So I left."

"Why didn't you stand up to him and tell him no? I bet you could have made him listen to you."

I recognized the hero worship in Bobby's eyes. It was the same expression I'd caught myself wearing whenever Father Paul had shared something just between us, making me feel valued and special in the midst of a life of constant struggle. Seeing that look on Bobby's face made something bloom warmly in the region of my heart. But I didn't want him to put me on a pedestal when that was the last place I belonged.

"My stepfather was bigger and meaner than me. In the end, it was best to just leave."

"But—"

"Fighting isn't always the answer, Bobby."

He pouted, obviously wanting to argue the point, so I distracted him by getting the lesson back on track. I held my hands in front of me, palms facing out. "Let's work on your accuracy. Try to aim for the very center of my hands."

Bobby stared at me stubbornly for a long moment, but apparently decided to let the matter drop. After a few awkward tries, he got the hang of the technique and the rhythm of the exercise. He improved rapidly over the next half hour, and eventually his punches were landing on the same place on my palms each time. It was slightly past the time when Bobby usually went home when I finally called a halt.

"We'll work on this again the day after tomorrow, and maybe we'll have time to try some kicks as well."

"Awesome!" Bobby raised his hands and foot in a classic crane stance, and I wondered where he'd learned that. "Karate Kid, here I come!" he shouted.

The comment meant nothing to me, so I merely nodded and pretended I understood what he was talking about. Bobby had left his bag inside the store, and I watched as he headed toward the propped-open door that opened onto the back lot. I was curious when he suddenly stopped and spun back toward me, but nothing could have prepared me for the shock of his small body barreling into me, a pair of thin arms wrapping tightly around my waist.

"Thanks, Tim."

In the time it took me to regain my breath, Bobby was gone. I glanced toward the doorway and received a second surprise as I saw David leaning against the doorjamb.

"I-I didn't notice you watching us," I stammered as David abandoned his position and walked out into the lot. The ability to minutely observe and track every aspect of my environment had always been my strong suit, so I was taken aback that I had so completely missed David's presence. Had enjoying my time with Bobby distracted me that much?

"It looked like you two were having fun, so I didn't want to interrupt."

"Oh," I answered in lieu of anything better to say. Ever since I'd nursed David back to health, my thoughts seemed to dwell constantly on how his body had felt under my hands. The sensation joined the phantom tingle of David's strong fingers pressing into my skin as we'd kissed that night on the couch until I was able to think of little else. Forcing my scattered thoughts into some semblance of order, I wondered how long he had been watching me and Bobby and how much of our earlier conversation he had overheard.

"I'm really glad you guys are getting along so well."

The late-afternoon sun was in David's eyes, striking azure sparks that glowed in the orange-tinted light. Entranced by the brilliant display of color, I was reminded of a picture of the Mediterranean Father Paul had shown me once years ago. At the time, I hadn't possessed enough of an individual will to consider that I might want to visit such a place someday. But the image had stuck with me, growing in importance as I began to understand exactly how restricted my life was to be. I'd come to associate the picture and the particular hue of the deep sea with freedom, and now here it was again, serving as a reminder of everything I had gained thanks to Father Paul's sacrifice. I realized after a moment that I was staring and hoped David mistook my ogling for my customary forthright gaze.

"He's a good kid," I replied. "He follows instructions well and performs his assigned tasks proficiently." Even before I fully registered David's slightly bemused expression, I recognized how stilted and unnatural I sounded. I chalked it up to my nervousness at recalling those intense moments of intimacy we had shared. But it had been several weeks since I'd joined the real world, and there was no excuse for my occasional failure to talk like a normal person. Spending more time around Bobby and his childish, casual vocabulary would surely help with that.

"Uh, yeah," David continued. "Well, I was just going to say, you and Bobby have had a difficult time at home, and you both tend to play your cards close to the vest."

I wasn't familiar with the idiom, but I nodded anyway, not wanting to interrupt.

"It's good you guys are hanging out like this, just being regular kids. I know trust is a hard-won commodity in this world, but if the two of you could learn to depend on each other, well, I think it would go a long way to helping you both."

The statement mirrored my own line of thinking. Hadn't I promised myself I would be there for Bobby as his friend, and if necessary, his protector?

"I would very much like to become Bobby's friend, if he'll let me."

David's grin was as bright as the light illuminating his eyes. "Oh, I wouldn't worry about that, if that hug was anything to go by. I'd say Bobby is quite fond of you already. I don't know any thirteen-year-old boy who hands out hugs to just any old person."

I found myself smiling in return as David chuckled, glad to know the unexpected embrace had been a positive thing. I wasn't familiar with the various forms of physical affection beyond what little Father Paul had endeavored to show me under the watchful eye of the general and the other researchers. The memory of the pressure and heat of David's lips against mine flitted back to the forefront of my mind, and I suddenly wondered if the kiss we'd shared had been more than simply a mutual expression of lust. Had David felt the same warmth in his chest I had felt as we'd clung together, every kiss a shared breath, as though we were a single body?

"And you were right," David continued, his gaze growing unexpectedly somber. "The fighting lessons are a good thing. Bobby needs to gain more confidence in himself, especially given the situation with his father. I'm not worried exactly, but—" David lifted a hand to rub awkwardly at the back of his neck. "Just be careful. You're a strong kid—really strong—and sometimes I think maybe you don't know your own strength." He didn't mention what had happened the day we'd met Bobby, but there was no doubt what was prompting the warning. "I know you'd never do anything to him on purpose, but, well, you could really do some damage if you aren't mindful."

"I wouldn't. I won't." I spoke with complete sincerity, never more sure about anything in my life. "I'd never do anything to hurt Bobby. I promise you that." Perhaps it was the unwavering conviction in my tone that relaxed the tension in David's shoulders. Whatever the cause, I was relieved when his smile returned.

"I know. But I'm the adult around here, and it's my job to be a worrywart."

David's laugh hit me with the same force as Bobby's hug had earlier. It made me feel giddy, and I wanted nothing more than to hear it again. The grin which unexpectedly stretched my lips felt surprisingly natural.

"That's okay. Is it time to go home?" I wanted David to myself for the rest of the evening, even if all we did was watch a sports match on television. Not to mention I was starving and needed to replenish my flagging levels of B12. "I could grill the beef liver you bought the other day." Liver wasn't my favorite, but it had one of the highest concentrations of the essential vitamin of any food I knew. I was clearly in need of a good dose, the lack in my system providing an acceptable explanation for why I had failed to notice David's presence earlier. Damage to the nervous system was one of the symptoms of severe vitamin B12 deficiency, and with the trapdoor built into my genetic code, any depletion was—by design—severe. Plus, I'd been enjoying learning how to cook. The offer earned me another one of those addictive laughs.

"You're going to spoil me, kid. Yeah, let's go on home." David turned back toward the store before pausing to glance at me over his shoulder. "Last one to the car has to do the dishes!"

I gaped in amazement as David took off at a run and disappeared through the doorway leading inside. Although I knew my hesitation placed me at a tactical disadvantage, I didn't care. The sight of David sprinting away at such a rapid speed for such a ridiculous reason....

It was funny. And so I laughed. For the first time in my life, I laughed fully and without reservation. I dashed after David, more eager to share my spontaneous outburst of happiness than to overtake him, although I did so easily. I laughed harder after catching a glimpse of Patricia's astonished face as she watched her boss and their newest full-time employee running through the aisles of the store to the front entrance. I passed David and reached the main door before he had covered half the distance. I turned to face him, ignoring the customers who were watching our antics with varying degrees of confusion and amusement. David was a surprisingly graceful runner, and the sight of him approaching me went straight to my libido. The doors opened as I disrupted the beam of the infrared motion detector. David quirked his lips in mock defeat.

"Man, you're fast!" he breathed, his voice ragged from the unaccustomed exertion. His expression changed to an openmouthed gape as he noticed I was nearly in stitches.

"I win." The muscles of my face were aching from the prolonged expression of glee.

David nodded, his wonderment remaining even though his amusement returned. "Yep, you did. Or did you? We're not at the car yet!" He darted around me to fling open one of the manual doors which flanked the automatic ones, and hit the pavement of the parking lot at a dead run.

"You boys stop messing around!"

Patricia was working the closing shift since she'd had to take one of her sons to the doctor that morning for a checkup. Her "annoyed mom" tone prompted me to emit what could only be called a giggle before I exited through the open center doors to resume the chase.

EXHALING SHARPLY in disgust, Woodard threw the latest batch of progress reports onto the already cluttered surface of his desk. Santa Fe, Albuquerque, Amarillo. Hell, he'd even ordered the search to be expanded as far as Colorado Springs and Tucson. Nothing. It was as though TM 05637 had dropped off the face of the goddamned Earth. Though he knew it was futile, he glanced down at the report at the top of the pile for a fourth time. Grid point eight: Lubbock. The search team had reported in as ordered every day for the past month with nothing to show for their efforts.

"Sweep of postal code 79416 complete. No signs of the unit."

In the weeks the team had been in the modest-sized city since one of Farley's surveillance minions had thought he'd identified the unit on a police camera, they had only managed to finish searching two zip code areas. Proceeding code-by-code had been Talbot's idea, and he had to admit, albeit grudgingly, that it was a good plan, since the hospital angle hadn't panned out. The only drawback to such a thorough search pattern was the time it took to complete. He didn't have the manpower to assign more personnel to each city—the disadvantage of having to keep the project secret. Woodard personally cleared any new personnel to ensure that everyone on his staff was completely trustworthy and understood the meaning of discretion. It meant keeping the community of those in the know as tightly knit and limited as possible. The teams were spread thin as it was, and he had to match the number of men to the size of the target. It had been a stretch to spare two teams each for Albuquerque and Tucson, both of which were twice the size of Lubbock. The smaller city had earned only a single two-man team.

Woodard clenched his jaw as he pushed the report to the other side of his desk and sat back in his chair. The only good news was that Talbot was back on the East Coast temporarily to deal with Company business and wasn't due to return for at least another week. Her absence took a great weight off his shoulders, although the relative peace wasn't enough to completely restore his calm. But he had the perfect remedy for the tension stretching along the muscles of his neck, threatening him with his third headache of the day.

The guard outside his door saluted sharply as he stepped out into the hallway. He ignored the man, his thoughts already focused on his destination. The gym the Facility boasted was state-of-the-art and had been put to excellent use conditioning TM 05637 into the perfect fighting machine. The ungrateful little bastard. Although the exercise equipment was the best that taxpayer money could buy, the thoughts of his erstwhile ward had put Woodard in the mood for something a little more fundamental.

Taking the stairs down the two levels that separated the officers' quarters from the common areas to warm up, Woodard reached the gym ready to exorcise his various demons. It took him only a few moments to change into the workout gear he kept stored in his personal locker. The outfit wasn't fancy, just a pair of shorts and a fitted muscle shirt. He didn't want anything that would allow him to be easily grabbed by the man he hoped would oblige him in his pursuit of stress relief.

As Woodard stepped into the open room, the sour odor of sweat and the harsh grunts of exertion melded into a pungent symphony. It was years since he'd been expected to meet the physical requirements of a lower-ranked officer, but he liked to keep in shape, as did the man he spied working over some hapless corporal on the other side of the room. He hadn't had to guess where Cooper would be. Like clockwork, the sergeant could be found every day at that time right where he was, showing some younger grunt precisely why he deserved his reputation as the most feared man on base. The two figures were grappling on top of one of the large mats that covered the floor specifically to accommodate those who wanted to engage in more direct one-on-one face-offs. The space had often been utilized in the TM unit's training, but Woodard didn't let the unpleasant association deter him.

"Sergeant Cooper!"

His voice carried easily across the room, and Cooper looked over at him after neatly pinning his opponent to the ground. The sergeant had the younger man's arm pushed up behind his back nearly to the point of breaking. The corporal's face was red with exertion and pain, and he slapped the mat loudly to signal his tap out. Cooper relented and gave his attention fully to his superior as the corporal beat a hasty retreat.

"Do you want judo today, sir?" he asked as Woodard stepped onto the mat.

"No, nothing so fancy." He didn't have to elaborate. He and the sergeant had worked together for many years, and he swore sometimes Cooper could read his thoughts. Sure enough, Cooper shifted himself into the loose-limbed stance, indicating his readiness to engage in some good old-fashioned street fighting.

The perfect distraction.

No signal was given to begin. There was only the meaty fist Cooper thrust at his head. Woodard ducked quickly, knowing firsthand the power behind that punch. Shifting his momentum, he landed a solid hit to Cooper's midsection, but as expected Cooper barely flinched. At six one, Woodard was no shrinking violet, but the sergeant was six and a half feet of thick muscle. Sparring with him was like fighting a brick wall. *A brick wall that's fast as a motherfucker*, he amended, forced to scramble backward as his opponent came at him with a knee aimed at his chin.

Reversing direction, Woodard moved in close and tried to sweep Cooper's leg, only to be rewarded with an elbow to his lower back. Grunting at the sharp pain, he edged forward and shot his leg out behind him, feeling a spark of satisfaction when he heard the air leave Cooper's lungs as he was nailed directly in the side. Both men spun around and took a moment to assess each other before going in for a second round.

As the minutes passed, Woodard lost himself in the flow of offense and defense. He was dimly aware of the crowd that had gathered to watch the uncommon spectacle of the top brass and his right-hand duking it out among the rank and file. He was tempted to discipline the onlookers for neglecting their own workouts to gawk, but he couldn't begrudge them the chance for some much-needed distraction. Everyone had been on edge in the wake of TM 05637's disappearance, himself included, and Talbot being underfoot had only increased the strain among the Facility personnel. It was like the bitch lived to demean and undermine him with her snide interference.

The very thought of the battle-axe made Woodard itch, and the brief distraction cost him as Cooper landed a right hook across his jaw. The impact exploded through his head, giving new life to the ache that had faded as adrenaline pumped through him. Cursing himself for making such a rookie mistake, he shook his head sharply to regain his equilibrium and raised his right arm just in time to block the second of the one-two punch which would have landed him flat on his back. Stepping to his right, he plowed his left knee into Cooper's gut hard enough that the man grunted, having apparently felt the impact through the thick padding of muscle at his waist. The sergeant caught Woodard's leg and raised his free hand, preparing to land a hammer punch directly on the top of his head. Denying him the opportunity, Woodard grabbed Cooper's meaty shoulders and used the hold for leverage as he hopped forward and jumped up, driving his noncaptive heel into the bigger man's knee. The targeted leg buckled, dumping both of them to the floor as Cooper covered Woodard's hands with his own meaty paws, trapping them there.

The gym was silent while the spectators tried to decide which of the battered men had won. Woodard shook his head, the corner of his lips quirking up in a wry expression which would have been self-deprecating on anyone else. Cooper immediately let him go, understanding the unspoken order that signaled the impromptu match was over.

"Another draw, Sergeant."

"Yes, sir." Cooper got to his feet first and reached down to help Woodard do the same. Woodard glanced around, noting with satisfaction the impressed looks on the faces he swore got younger every day. He hurt all over and his ears were ringing, but at least thoughts of his missing science experiment weren't foremost in his mind right then.

And if that didn't count as a victory, he didn't know what did.

THIRTEEN

"HELLO, DAVY. How are you?"

David winced involuntarily at the nickname, as he'd done ever since first hearing it as a teenager. But the knee-jerk reaction didn't stop the grin that spread across his face at the sound of his mother's voice.

"I'm good, Ma. How about you?"

He hadn't spoken to Suzanna in over two months, since before he'd met Tim. He felt a twinge of guilt at not calling her sooner despite his good intentions to do so. She always sounded so happy to hear from him, as if she was trying to compensate for her husband's distinct lack of enthusiasm when it came to anything that concerned their gay son. Other things had simply gotten in the way. But now he settled back in his office chair, balancing on the back legs in a way he knew she hated, and prepared to rectify his oversight with a nice, long conversation.

"Oh, I'm fine. But I'd be doing even better if you could come and pick me up from the bus station before it gets dark."

"Arrgghh!"

"Davy? Are you all right?"

Only the panicked speed with which he'd caught the edge of his desk with the hand not holding his phone saved him from toppling backward to the floor. "What do you mean, pick you up from the bus station?"

"You know, the Greyhound station over on Crickets. The same place I always wait for you when I come to visit."

David sputtered at her matter-of-fact response. "Yeah, except, usually, I know ahead of time that you're coming!"

A slew of disjointed thoughts chased themselves through his head. Where was she going to sleep since Tim was using the spare bedroom? How would the three of them manage to make do with his one small bathroom? How would his mother, who wasn't overly fond of meat, deal with the fact that he and Tim ate almost nothing but? And of course the big one, what in the world would she think of his living with a kid more than ten years his junior? The deep sigh that poured out from the speaker put the brakes on his wayward brain.

"Hank has been, well, a difficult man to live with lately. All the news about those states allowing gays to marry... let's just say it's got him all in a tizzy."

Only Suzanna could put a soft edge on what was likely a full-fledged homophobic meltdown. David hadn't spoken to his father more than to wish him a happy birthday and a Merry Christmas since the day he'd left home at the age of eighteen. Even so, he was under no illusions as to how his father must have reacted to all of the positive—from his viewpoint, at least—news on the equality front in the past couple of years. Suzanna had called him in exasperated tears after the Supreme Court's decision to kill the Defense of Marriage Act.

"Okay. If I leave now, I can be there in—" He quickly calculated the early rush-hour traffic. "Give me about twenty minutes. We can stop at Orlando's on the way back to the house." A trip to the Italian restaurant had become a tradition whenever his mother came to visit. It had the benefit of being conveniently located between the bus depot and his home on the southwest side of the city. And this time, it had the added benefit of offering a way to delay the unavoidable revelation concerning his living situation.

"Well, I don't know. It was a long trip, and I'm pretty beat."

"Oh, come on." David told himself the eagerness in his voice wasn't at all desperation to put off Suzanna meeting Tim for as long as possible. "We always go to Orlando's when you're here. Honestly, it's the only time I ever manage to get there, and I love their chicken lasagna!" He put just enough little boy pleading into his tone to guarantee she would cave.

"Okay, okay!" she said on a laugh. He knew she was completely aware of his ploy, but it was part of their dynamic that she always let him get away with it anyway. "After eating all of that pasta, I should have no trouble falling asleep, at any rate. Do I need to help you clean out the spare bedroom, or did you actually manage to tidy it up since my last visit?"

David bit his lip as he shut down his computer and grabbed his keys. He considered how to respond without revealing his secret prematurely. As if the thought had conjured him up, Tim chose that moment to stick his head into the office. The kid took in David's urgent posture, the keys in his hand, and his location halfway around his desk with a single sweeping glance. David had discovered Tim always seemed to know what time it was, so he took the kid's swift look toward the clock on the wall as a tacit question.

"Um, Ma, could you hold on a second?" The identification of the person on the other end of the call made Tim's beautiful eyes widen in surprise. David spent a moment being distracted by the pleasant fact that his housemate had become a lot easier to read of late. He could trace the change back to his bout with the flu, and it had only gotten better as Tim interacted with Bobby on a nearly daily basis. Smiling helplessly at the adorable look on the kid's face, David pushed against the screen of his phone to mute it.

"Your mother?"

"Yeah. She's in town for a surprise visit."

For a moment David worried his announcement might cause Tim to experience some traumatic memories. He didn't want Suzanna's presence to make Tim think of his own mother's senseless death. He scrambled to think of how to soften the blow. "Look, kid, if you're not comfortable with her being here—"

Tim scuffed his sneakers on the linoleum. "How should I get home? Or, should I not go there?"

Of course, Tim's concerns were of the more mundane variety. David was constantly impressed at how nothing seemed to faze him. It was a good question, though. David felt bad for not having an immediate answer. But what were his options? Ask the kid to find somewhere else to stay while Suzanna was in town? Not likely.

"I need to pick my mother up from the Greyhound station. We're going out to dinner at her favorite restaurant in town, so we won't be back to the house for a few hours." He smiled reassuringly and moved closer to Tim so he could place his hand on the kid's shoulder in what had become a familiar gesture. "William doesn't live too far from us." David retrieved his wallet from his pocket and pulled out a twenty dollar bill. He had already given Tim his own key to the house, so he didn't need to give up his. "If you don't mind staying an hour late, ask him to give you a ride home and give him this for the extra gas. Go ahead and fix yourself dinner." Among the things he'd learned about Tim was that it was best to give him direct instructions to follow rather than leaving things open for interpretation. Sure enough, the kid relaxed and nodded as he took the money.

"Okay."

Tim stared at him with that direct gaze that never failed to reach straight into his shorts. This time was no exception. David reached up and ruffled Tim's hair until it stood up in childish spikes, but yet again, his attempt to make the kid seem younger and thus less attractive failed miserably. Instead Tim looked like he'd woken up only moments ago and just gotten out of bed.

"We'll see you later," David mumbled, swiftly cutting off any thoughts of Tim and beds. Remembering he had his mother on hold, David took her off mute as he beat a hasty retreat and headed out to the parking lot. "Ma, you still there? Sorry about that."

"That's okay. I know I interrupted you at work."

"It's not a problem." After unlocking and opening his car door, he paused to lean against it before getting inside. "I'm leaving now. See you in a few."

Traffic was about as he'd expected, but he managed to pull up to the bus depot in less time than he'd estimated. Suzanna was familiar with his car, and as he drove up to meet her, she was already walking toward him, waving her hand above her head. Despite his worry at her finding out about Tim and the general inconvenience any surprise guest would cause, his heart lifted at the sight of her. They had always been close, and he deeply regretted that he usually saw her only once or, if they were lucky, twice a year. Her prior trip down to Texas had been nearly a year and a half ago, so their time together as of late had been

163

infrequent in the extreme. She was slowed by the luggage she was pulling behind her, so he managed to park and get out of his car to greet her before she reached the curb. He swung around the front of his car and wrapped her in a bear hug, lifting her off the ground.

"Oh, Davy! Put me down, you goof." The grin that threatened to crack her face belied her words.

"It's good to see you too." He pressed a kiss to her cheek, which was still smooth even though she was well into her fifties. After briefly tightening his embrace, he set her down gently and gazed happily at her. There could be no question that he was her son. Her genes were stamped indelibly in the dark gold of his hair, in the blue of his eyes, and in the way the lines in his face crinkled when he smiled. "I've missed you. I'm glad you came." He reached around her and took the carry-on out of her hand. "A heads up would have been nice, though."

"Now where would be the fun in that?" Her laugh tinkled over the impatient sounds of rush hour. She settled herself in his car and waited while he stowed her suitcase in the trunk before joining her. "So how have you been?"

David glanced over at her with a slight frown. "I already told you. I'm good."

"Mmm-hmm. So you said." Suzanna had settled back in the passenger's seat in a posture he had long associated with the knowledge that he was about to be lectured. He groaned quietly to himself.

"Then why are you asking me again?"

She looked at him pointedly with blue eyes identical to his. "Call it mother's intuition. I just had a feeling something was up with you, and I figured coming to see you was the best way to get some actual answers."

David swallowed, nervous but not really surprised at her statement. She'd always had an uncanny insight into every facet of his life, even after they were no longer living under the same roof. Still, he wished her freakish maternal instinct had taken a vacation for once. "I thought you came because you needed a break from Dad." The attempted deflection was blatantly obvious, but he didn't particularly care. She arched an incredulous eyebrow in his direction but played along, much to his relief.

"Not a break, exactly."

It was his turn to shoot her a disbelieving glance.

"Okay, yes," she admitted. "I needed to get away for a while."

David smiled crookedly. "I know the feeling."

She slapped him gently on his arm. "Don't be cheeky, David. You know I love your father dearly. It's just, well, I don't always see eye to eye with him on social issues."

Aware of her own rural Oklahoma roots, David never ceased to be amazed by his mother's open-mindedness. That being said, he didn't know if there was enough tolerance in the world to allow her to simply accept his current living arrangement. Not that there was anything he could do about it now.

"Dad is who he is. I doubt he'll change at this point." David firmly put his father out of his mind and felt his shoulders relax as he turned to more pleasant topics. "So how was the ride down? I really wish you'd let me send you money for a plane ticket when you want to come for a visit."

"No need for that. You know how I enjoy long road trips."

He scoffed. "In a car, maybe, but on Greyhound? Come on."

"It's only an eight-hour ride. I napped through most of it. Except for this one young woman who…."

David listened fondly as Suzanna told him about the would-be starlet who'd spent an hour and a half singing folk songs accompanied by a battered guitar until she got off in Lawton. The drive from the bus station to the restaurant was short, so even with the late afternoon traffic, it was less than ten minutes before he was pulling in to Orlando's tiny parking lot. He escorted her inside, her hand resting comfortably on his arm. Suzanna closed her eyes and inhaled as the front door closed behind them.

"Mmmm, it smells so good in here." She glanced back at him with a grin. "Thanks, sweetie, for talking me into coming. You're right, I would have been disappointed if I'd missed eating here."

David nudged her gently with his shoulder. "Told ya."

The easy, familiar banter continued until their waitress came to take their orders. The woman had been working at Orlando's for years, and she greeted them with the same bright, friendly smile she always did.

"How y'all doing this evening? I haven't seen you here in a while, ma'am. I hope you're doing all right."

"I'm fine, thanks." Suzanna blinked at the woman in surprise. "I haven't been here in so long. I can't believe you remember me."

"Sure I do! Let's see if I recall correctly." The waitress had retrieved a pencil from the pocket of her apron, and she pointed it at Suzanna. "You're having the tilapia with pesto Alfredo over penne, and you," she continued, turning to David, "will have the chicken lasagna."

Suzanna clapped in delight. "Amazing! That's exactly right."

The woman laughed. "Well, I always remember nice folks like y'all. Sweet tea for both of you?" They nodded, and she tossed them a wink before disappearing to put in their orders.

David and his mother chatted aimlessly while waiting for their food. She got him caught up on the family gossip, mostly about her younger sister, who was recently divorced and on the hunt for her third husband.

"I swear, that girl will never settle down."

David smirked. "I wouldn't say settling down is her problem."

"Hmm, maybe you're right. And speaking of settling down, have you been seeing anyone lately?"

"Wow, that was smooth." David shook his head and took refuge in his sweet tea. How was he supposed to respond? *Gee, Ma, I'm hot for this barely legal hitchhiker I picked up on the highway. Does that count?* He was attempting to come up with an acceptable reply when their waitress brought out their dinner.

"Here ya go. Do y'all need anything else?"

"No," Suzanna answered with a smile. "We're fine for now. Thank you."

David mentally kicked himself for not being able to think of anything that would postpone this conversation. Fortunately, his mother was thoroughly diverted by her perfectly cooked fish. He felt ashamed of himself. Saved by tilapia? That was just sad. And while he didn't want her probing into his love life, or more accurately, his lack thereof, he did have some very important information he needed to share. He'd kicked this particular can down the road far enough. David picked at

166

his lasagna for a moment longer, silencing the last of his jitters before he took a deep breath and made the plunge.

"I should probably tell you something before we get back to the house."

Enjoying her penne, Suzanna didn't look up as she speared another piece with her fork. "What is it?" she asked absently.

"I've got a, uh, a houseguest."

That got her attention. She looked at him questioningly. "A houseguest?"

He swallowed to cure the sudden dryness in his throat. "Well, more like a housemate."

"A guy?"

"Yeah." He feared where she was going with the question.

"So, you mean like a boyfriend?" The disappointment on her face was palpable, confusing him. She'd never had a problem with his preference for guys before, so why did she seem troubled by it now? Not that there was anything for her to actually be upset about. "Why am I only now hearing about him?"

David groaned when he realized she was simply afraid she'd missed out on some momentous development in his life. "No! That's not it," he said, anxious to disabuse her of her misunderstanding. He'd spoken more loudly than he'd intended, and his cheeks reddened as some people at neighboring tables glanced over at him with varying levels of annoyance.

"Then who is he, if he isn't your boyfriend?" Her gaze widened as something disturbing obviously occurred to her. "Oh, Davy, are you having trouble with money? I thought the store was doing well."

"No, no," he interjected quickly, seeking to reassure her while he tried to figure out how this discussion had gone so far off the rails. "He's just some guy I picked up on the way back from New Mexico." He winced at his thoughtless choice of words. *Well, that was less than ideal*, he thought as Susanna stared at him in shock.

"Just some guy? Good Lord, David." She sighed and shook her head. "It's like I've always told you. You're a sweet boy, but—"

"Yeah, I know. I need to learn how to say no to people."

"I mean, honestly, where did you meet this person? You didn't really pick him up off the side of the road, did you?"

David took temporary refuge in his pasta, though it tasted like sawdust in his overly dry mouth. He nodded, adding a meek, "I did."

"David!" Her unoriginality didn't make her rebuke sting any less.

"Look, what's done is done. And honestly, it hasn't worked out too badly. His name is Tim Paul."

Susanna raised an eyebrow. "That's an odd name."

David shrugged. "Yeah, well, it turns out he was having trouble with his old man, so he left home without any place to go. I got him a job at the BBW, and he's been a good employee." He flashed her the toothy grin he'd been using since he was little to get out of trouble. "So, you see? There's nothing to worry about."

His mother raised an eyebrow and glanced to the side, a sure indication she had picked up on something troublesome in his explanation. "Having trouble with his father, you said? Why would he have to leave home because of that? I mean, how old is he?"

Crap. Of course she had noted that little detail. "…teen," he mumbled.

"David, you know I hate it when you do that." Her tone held an edge of maternal scolding that never failed to make him feel like he was five years old. "Try that again."

"He's nineteen."

She stared at him silently for a moment. "Where is he now? At the store?"

David glanced at his watch. "No, he should have already gone home."

Suzanna sputtered. "You mean you let him stay in your house by himself? He could have robbed you blind by now!"

"Ma!" David sat back in his chair and pinned her with a glare. "He's been living with me for well over a month. I think if he'd been planning on doing something, he'd have done it already." Her pinched expression conveyed her displeasure at his tone. He looked away, unable to maintain his defiance in the face of her disapproval. "He's a good kid," he continued in a calmer voice. "I think you'll like him."

"Hmm. We'll see." Suzanna attacked her pasta with her fork like it had personally offended her. "But if he's up to something, I'm not leaving Lubbock until he's out of your hair."

Dinner continued mostly in silence, with only mundane exchanges about how she wanted to spend her time while he was at work to break the quiet. Soon enough he had paid the check and had nothing left to do but let the two most important people in his life meet. David figured Tim would take the introduction as calmly as he did most everything, but he sincerely hoped his mother didn't come off too strong. He knew she was simply being protective of her only child, but he had long suspected Tim had a secret fragility hidden beneath his imperturbable demeanor. Not to mention, he likely wouldn't react well to harsh words from someone's mother.

They didn't speak much on the drive to David's town house. Suzanna was clearly mulling over the mess she thought he'd gotten himself into, while he didn't want to rehash their conversation from dinner. Traffic had all but disappeared, and he was pulling into his parking spot less than fifteen minutes after leaving the restaurant. His mother got out of the car and waited until he'd retrieved her suitcase from the trunk before marching purposefully up to his front door. She tapped her foot impatiently, with her arms crossed over her chest, as she waited for him to lug her bag up the stairs.

"Please, calm down," he begged.

"Open the door, David."

Yikes, he thought. It was never a good thing when she said his name in that particular tone of voice. The last time he'd seen her this mad he was a sophomore in high school and she'd been confronting his phys. ed. teacher, Mr. Eberhart. The man had been a total asshole and had somehow sniffed out that one of his students was a bit light in the loafers. He'd called David "sugar britches" whenever he was in his class, and Suzanna had gotten fed up with her son coming home every day on the verge of tears. She'd gone to see the man one day after David had told her a particularly upsetting story about being made to walk around with his shorts pulled down around his ankles during class. The P.E. teacher had been nearly a foot taller and easily a hundred pounds heavier than Suzanna, but she'd proceeded to give Mr. Eberhart a piece of her mind until he'd sworn he would never bother

her son again. David had transferred out of his class the next day and spent the rest of his sophomore year with the far more pleasant Ms. Englewood. She was the one who had encouraged him to try out for the football team, and he had many fond memories of her.

David glanced at his mother warily as she waited for him to unlock the door. Suzanna wore the very same expression of quiet anger she'd had while putting the fear of motherly rage into Mr. Eberhart. He sighed, figuring there was nothing he could say to defuse her at this point. He'd just have to stand by Tim if, or rather when, she finally laid into him. He opened the door and stood back so she could precede him into the house.

"Where is he?" Suzanna asked, taking in her surroundings as if trying to see if she noticed anything missing.

"Tim?" David called out. He heard a sound from the kitchen. "In there," he said, gesturing toward the room with his chin. Shaking his head, he left her suitcase by the door and trailed behind her as she stomped toward the kitchen with righteous purpose.

When David made it to the kitchen, Tim was looking wide-eyed at Suzanna, holding a fork speared through a hardboiled egg up to his mouth, as though he'd been interrupted right before he could take a bite. He had pushed back his seat from the table at the sound of their entry, the leg of his chair scraping across the tiled floor the source of the noise David heard. The kid was still seated, although his feet were planted to brace him for standing, and he looked uncertain whether or not he should rise to meet the strange woman who was staring daggers at him.

"Ma, this is Tim Paul. Tim, this is my mother, Suzanna Con—"

David stumbled over his tongue as he watched a miracle unfold before his eyes. Tim was staring at his mother like a lost puppy rather than the nearly full-grown man he was. His pink lips were parted like he'd been about to speak but had lost his voice or simply his nerve. His usual impassiveness was nowhere to be seen. Instead, his big brown eyes seemed like they were pleading for something. Reassurance? Approval? David couldn't be sure, but he looked on in astonishment as all of the bluster left his mother in a rush, only to be replaced by an emotion he had only ever seen directed at himself.

"Tim, did you say?" She swept forward and grabbed hold of Tim's hand, pulling him to his feet. "You just call me Suzanna, you hear?"

Tim blinked silently as he was pulled into a hug, his arms hanging uselessly at his sides like he didn't know what to do with them. He looked beseechingly toward David for help or, at the very least, advice on how to respond to the unexpected invasion of his physical and emotional space. Not for the first time, David wondered how often anyone had shown the kid any physical affection. He quickly discarded the intruding memory of them entwined on his couch. That didn't count. But did Tim even remember what it was like to feel a mother's touch? A moment later, he found himself smiling as Tim wrapped his arms tentatively around Suzanna's back and returned her embrace.

FOURTEEN

I COULDN'T help studying the woman while she interrogated me with an adeptness I suspected even the general would find impressive. By now I had solidified my backstory in my mind enough that I could relate my phony upbringing in New Mexico without any telltale hesitation over the particulars. My attention only half-diverted by the effort, I carefully took in all the little details that made up Suzanna Conley.

David's mother. The very thought of her relationship to David put an uncomfortable knot in my stomach. But rather than dwell on the stark memory of Karen's lifeless, blood-covered body, I took in the similarities between the woman and her son. The resemblance was superficial. David was tall and solidly built, while Suzanna was slight and almost frail in her physicality. The strands of her hair had mostly surrendered to gray and bore only a faint hint of the dark blond of her son's.

It was their eyes, I decided, that marked David's similarity to his parent. The woman looked at me with the same intense shade of dark blue and with an identical measure of kindness. But whereas David's gaze often instilled in me thoughts of a more carnal nature, Suzanna's unwavering scrutiny made me feel odd in a different way. I suspected she wanted something from me, though I couldn't imagine what it could be.

"You're about the skinniest thing I've ever seen! Isn't my son feeding you properly?"

Suzanna had made this observation immediately after releasing me from her embrace and right before ordering David to fix me something else to eat. She'd hustled me into the living room and away from David's nervously watchful gaze in order to conduct her questioning. I had to admire her tactics. Removing subjects from their source of comfort was a tried and true way to break them, but being aware of the ploy in no way made me immune to its effects.

"Why my son?" she asked abruptly.

I had been telling Suzanna about my work at the BBW and my burgeoning, sibling-like relationship with Bobby, so the question caught me off guard. "I'm sorry?" I responded, suddenly understanding the proper application of the idiom "a deer in headlights."

Her smile was gentle, but her steady gaze remained disturbingly fixed on me. I resisted the urge to look away, knowing that to do so would somehow betray me.

"David didn't tell me much except that he found you hitchhiking and that you'd run away from home." Her gaze sharpened as she studied me. "You said you were having problems with your stepfather, but you're nineteen. Aren't you a little old to have to sneak away like that?"

My answer came more easily since it was mostly true. "You don't know my stepfather." I took a deep breath and chanced glancing away from her sharp gaze. "He can be... difficult." For some reason, I thought the general might find my description amusing.

"I see. But that doesn't really answer my question," she said. "You could have asked David to drop you off somewhere so you could continue on your way. But instead you invited yourself to stay with him. Why?"

Her expression was full of cautious speculation when I looked back toward her. I wondered how she'd known David wasn't the one who'd first suggested we live together, but I didn't dare insult her by pretending otherwise. Instead I took a moment to seriously consider her question. Yes, I'd needed a place to stay that first night, but I could have easily moved on the next day. Resourcefulness had been drilled into me since I was a child. I could have gone anywhere. Traveling farther east to put as much distance as possible between myself and the Facility would have been the wisest course of action, but I hadn't. On the contrary, I'd put forth a great deal of effort to insinuate myself into David's life, working for him, befriending those he was close to, making myself necessary. And why had I done it? Some vague promise to Father Paul? In retrospect, nothing about my actions truly made any sense.

"He was kind to me when I really needed help," I offered, unsure of what else to say.

Suzanna smiled. "Now that, I believe. But that's not all there is to it, is it?" Her expression, though benign, made it clear she would accept nothing from me but the truth. Full disclosure was, of course, impossible, but I found myself wanting to offer her as much as I could.

"I...." I paused, struggling to find the words to explain without revealing too much. "As you said, my home life was difficult." I looked away from her again, unable to hold her frank gaze as I tried to meld fact and fiction into an acceptable whole. "I never knew my father." True in that I had no clue as to the identity of my biological father, false in that I'd long considered it to be Father Paul. "My mother met my stepfather when I was very young, but she died protecting me from an armed mugger."

As had been her son's, Suzanna's sympathy was immediate. "That's a real shame," she said as she reached out and placed her hand atop one of mine, offering comfort with a light squeeze.

"I think he always resented me for taking her away from him." A blatant lie, but one I could find no way around. I'd wondered occasionally over the years whether the general even remembered the woman who had given her life trying to rescue me from my fate. Lie or not, the memory of her loss twisted my gut as it always did.

Suzanna must have picked up on my discomfort, because her grip on my hand tightened. "I'm sure that's not true."

"Nothing else makes any sense," I countered. "I was seven when she died, and he made my life hell until the day I left." The truth. Every word.

"Oh, honey—" she began.

"You asked me why I stayed with David." I met her gaze, a surge of emotion rising up unexpectedly from somewhere deep inside and nearly taking my breath away. "I just wanted to feel normal. I wanted to be with someone who didn't look at me with hatred, even if it was someone who only felt sorry for me." I hadn't realized how I really felt until I was forced to say it out loud. I'd wanted these last few months of my life to mean something, though I could never tell her that. My thoughts were abruptly derailed as she hugged me again, as natural as breathing.

"Sweetie, my son doesn't feel sorry for you. Trust me on that."

I wasn't sure what she meant, but I couldn't help speculating at her vague words. If David didn't feel sorry for me, then what did he feel? A bewildering need to fully understand his feelings gripped me without warning. Why was possessing that knowledge suddenly so critical I felt my entire life depended on discovering the truth? I was no closer to finding the answer when I noticed Suzanna was smiling at me with a shrewd look on her face.

"It smells like dinner's almost ready. Why don't we go and get some more food into you. David and I will keep you company while you eat."

DAVID LOOKED up from the skillet in his hand as his mother and Tim came back into the kitchen. He wasn't surprised to hear her regaling the kid with embarrassing tales about his growing up years, but he was shocked at the expression of bemused uncertainty on Tim's face. Tim looked a bit shell-shocked, as though he didn't really know what to do with Suzanna. David chuckled quietly, having often felt that way himself.

"Here, kid," he said. "I grilled up a couple of burgers. You can put whatever you want on 'em." He laid out a plate of lettuce and sliced up tomato alongside a bowl of chopped onions. Bottles of ketchup and mustard were already sitting on the table.

"Thank you."

Someone had taught Tim proper etiquette, because he pulled out a chair for Suzanna and waited until she had seated herself before taking his own place at the table. David was impressed, wondering again how strange this must be for the kid. He tried to think about how he'd feel if he had lost his mother in such a heartbreaking manner. He couldn't help but admire how well Tim was dealing with the unexpected reminder of what had been so cruelly taken from him. A lock of dark hair had fallen over the kid's forehead, and without thinking David pushed it back into place with a finger, allowing his touch to linger briefly against Tim's skin. He was rewarded with his favorite smile, which he returned before turning away toward the sink.

As usual, Tim piled his burger high with the fixings before taking a huge bite. David suspected the kid was glad to have an excuse not to talk for a while. He figured Suzanna must still be as full as he was from their dinner at Orlando's, so he joined the pair at the table with nothing but two glasses of water in his hand. After passing one to his mother, his thoughts drifted to how to deal with sleeping arrangements. As usual, Suzanna was one step ahead of him.

"You never answered my question, Davy."

He looked over at her, resisting the automatic urge to ask her not to use the hated nickname in front of Tim. "What question?"

"Do I need to help you clean out the spare bedroom?" Suzanna watched him with a benign smile as his face heated from her insinuation.

David glanced at Tim, but the kid continued to tuck into his burger, unaware of what she was implying. "No, *Mother*." He almost never called her that, but he felt the need to make a point. "I told you Tim has been staying here for more than a month." David took a sip of water, considering the topic closed, but the smile on Suzanna's face merely grew as he tried to ignore her. A knot of foreboding began to solidify in his stomach, and he hoped to God she wouldn't go there.

Of course, she did.

"So? That doesn't mean the spare room is taken, does it?"

Even Tim looked up at that. *Unsubtle,* David griped silently, *thy name is Suzanna.* Or it could have been the sound of him abruptly choking on his water that drew the kid's attention away from his food.

"I've been staying in there," Tim explained matter-of-factly, "but I can sleep on the couch while you're here."

David silently thanked Tim for heading his mother off so effortlessly. The kid had never been the sharpest when it came to reading other people, and for once he was glad Tim was so oblivious.

Seeing her joke had failed to impress at least one of her targets, Suzanna relented, or so he thought. "Thank you, dear. It's very nice of you to give up your room, but you don't have to stay on the couch."

David sighed and slumped into his chair in a way that would have gotten him smacked on the head as a kid. Tim simply blinked at her in mild confusion.

"Then where should I sleep? With you?" He asked the question with such sincerity that the impropriety of the suggestion was easily ignored.

David stood up from the table as his mother's laughter rang against the kitchen walls. He rolled his eyes when she reached out and patted an even more confused-looking Tim on the cheek.

"Oh, you are precious!"

"Ma," David interrupted, "I'll put your suitcase in the spare room. Tim, I'll bring some sheets downstairs for you."

Tim gulped down the last of his burger and was on his feet before David could move. "No need. I'll take care of it." With that he was gone, leaving David alone with his grinning parent.

He glared at her. "What?"

"Sit down. And don't 'what' me. You like him."

David carefully eluded her gaze as he sat, and took a fortifying gulp of water. "Of course I like him. I'm letting him stay in my house, aren't I?"

"No, I mean you *like* like him."

"Oh, for heaven's sake, what are you, in middle school?" He winced as the remark earned him a pinch to his earlobe.

"What are you afraid of? Is it because he's so young?" Suzanna pursed her lips thoughtfully. "I will admit there's quite a gap between you two."

He gave up trying to avoid the conversation, knowing it was pointless when she was so bound and determined to have it. "Well, it certainly doesn't help."

Her gaze radiated approval that he was finally engaging with her on the subject. "He is legal, though. You wouldn't be breaking any laws."

"Ma…." David put a hand to his suddenly throbbing head, trying to remember if he had ever felt more uncomfortable than he did at that moment. He wasn't surprised when he drew a blank. This was easily ten times more mortifying than when she'd handed him a strip of condoms before he'd left to pick up his date for senior prom. To this day he wasn't sure which had been worse, her assumption he'd need them or that she'd known his date was a guy and she'd still thought he might need them.

"I'm being serious, Davy. It's clear as day to me that he's more than just a couch surfer to you. Don't think I missed that little touchy-feely moment between you two earlier, because I didn't. And it's obvious he doesn't think of you merely as his boss."

David felt his eyebrow lift in surprise at her certainty. "What do you mean?" Despite his efforts to remain calm, his heart started beating faster at the memory of his and Tim's ill-advised moment on the couch a few weeks ago. At the time he'd chalked it up to the kid needing to distract himself after recounting the tragic story of his mother's death. He hadn't dared think it meant anything else.

"I mean, when I told him you felt something for him more than pity, the hope that lit up his face almost made me cry." Suzanna's expression softened. "I don't even think he realized it. And it wasn't so different from the look you have on your face right now."

David turned away in an instinctive attempt to hide from her perceptive gaze. "I don't know what you thought you saw, but I'm sure you're wrong. Tim doesn't *like* like me." He glanced toward the sink and moved to gather up the dirty dishes, casting about desperately to change the subject. The sting of a finger flicking at the dead center of his forehead brought him up short. Damn, he'd always hated when she did that.

"Ow," he deadpanned, rubbing at the spot.

"Oh, stop it. That did not hurt." Suzanna's gaze narrowed in disgust. "Quit stalling and answer me. Why are you avoiding this?" Her demeanor shifted from annoyance to despondency so quickly David found himself struggling to keep up. "Son, I'm not getting any younger, and I worry about you being alone down here all by yourself."

He shifted uncomfortably in his chair. "It's not like I'm a hermit. I have plenty of friends—"

"Oh, really? Who? Because I never hear you talking about anyone other than your employees. And you certainly never talk about anyone special." Suzanna placed a hand against his cheek like she'd done to Tim earlier. "I just want you to have someone in your life. Tim is a nice boy."

David snorted. "A couple of hours ago, you were ready to toss him out on his ear."

"Well, I was wrong. He *is* a nice boy, and I know he likes you and you like him. So if it's not his age, then what is it? What's holding you back?"

He leaned away from her hand and scooted his chair away from the table, as if putting physical space between them would help him distance himself from her probing. "I don't know." For once he wasn't merely being evasive. But now that he really thought about it, the actual reason suddenly became clearer. "It's just, it feels like I'd be taking advantage. Not because he's so much younger, but because he's been through so much in his life. I don't know if he told you about what happened to his mother."

She nodded. "He told me."

"And I'm also pretty sure his stepfather abused him, probably for years." She seemed more saddened than shocked by that, and he wondered exactly how much she and Tim had managed to talk about while he'd been banished to the kitchen. "His running away from home after all this time had to be an act of extreme desperation. I think he deserves to have a stable environment after everything he's had to deal with, and he doesn't need me trying to confuse him with something he's not ready for."

"But what if he is ready? What if what he really wants—what he really needs—is to be loved? And not like a child is loved, but like the grown man he is?"

"I—"

"And don't tell me he isn't interested in you because you're both men. I'd guess that's the least of your problems."

David sighed. "No, he's gay. That's one of the reasons he had so much conflict with his stepfather." Empathy shone from Suzanna's face, and he was instantly reminded of the hours he'd spent pouring out his pain to her after the hundreds of fights he'd had with his own father. "I was only going to say I don't want to put any pressure on him."

"He's not a kid, no matter how much you try to convince yourself of that. Don't treat him like one. Let him make his own decisions."

David was saved from replying as Tim came back into the room.

"The room is ready for you, ma'am."

The tension between mother and son disappeared in an instant as David broke out in helpless laughter and Suzanna tried to project disgust through her amusement.

"Oh, for goodness sake," she huffed. "What am I, ninety?"

The perplexed look on Tim's face made David laugh all the harder, even as he suddenly longed to kiss the kid's confusion away. *Damn her*, he thought. Now that his mother had given her blessing in no uncertain terms, he knew he'd have even more trouble reining in his wayward longings.

"All right, all right," he said. "Some of us have to go to work in the morning. Ma, if you want to come downtown with us, we'll be leaving at eight." He leaned over and kissed her on top of her head. "Night." Tim followed him out, leaving Suzanna to finish up in the kitchen in her own time.

Tim paused on his way to the pull-out sofa bed, which he'd made up with his usual military precision. "I like your mother."

David turned back from where he'd started up the stairs and smiled at the unexpected admission. "Good, because she likes you too."

FIFTEEN

"So, I'LL pick you guys up at six, right?"

Suzanna rolled her eyes in exactly the same way I'd seen David do on several occasions since she'd come to stay with us. "Oh, for heaven's sake, David. Like I said, I'll call you when we're ready to go."

I glanced over at Bobby, watching him fidget in the seat next to me while he stared out the window. He was keeping the left side of his face angled away, as he'd been doing since David had picked him up from his house a half hour earlier. He was less successful at hiding the dark marks that stretched across the front of his neck. Respectful of the attempted diversion, I'd put a lid on my growing anger and kept my assessment of Bobby's condition to myself.

We were in the backseat of David's car, about to be dropped off at something Suzanna had called a "county fair." It was my first Saturday off work since I'd started at the BBW, and when David had explained he needed to go in and oversee the arrival of the bimonthly inventory shipment, Suzanna had promptly declared I was hers to do with as she pleased for the entire day. I had mentioned I'd gotten into the habit of hanging out with Bobby even when he didn't have to be at the store, so she'd decided he would simply have to join us.

I knew the definition of the word "fair," but I hadn't had any practical reference to put with the vocabulary. Whatever it was, it was hidden beyond the large wooden fence. All I could make out from this vantage point was the din of many voices and other sounds I couldn't place. A steady parade of people streamed from the parking lot through a large, garishly painted gate. I contemplated how big the space inside must be to accommodate so many bodies.

"Fine." David leaned over and pressed a kiss to his mother's cheek. "You have your cell phone, right?"

Suzanna retrieved it from her purse and waved it in his face. "There, worrywart. Satisfied?" Her teasing won her a wry smile.

"Okay, okay. Go on." David unlocked the car doors with a button at his elbow. Bobby was out in a flash, and I followed to wait with him as Suzanna gathered her purse.

"You know, Davy, you should come back when you're finished at the store. You'll be right on time for dinner. That is, if we leave any food for you." She threw a grin over her shoulder at her son as she got out of the car to join her young escorts.

David laughed. "I might just at that. See you later."

I watched as David pulled away, feeling unexpectedly nervous. David's and my work schedules had always matched before now, and this would be the longest I'd spent away from him since he'd first picked me up. Staring after the receding car, I was startled when a soft, delicate hand slipped into mine. Suzanna was a small woman, and even at my modest height I towered over her. She smiled up at me, and before I could think how to appropriately respond, I realized I was mirroring her happy expression.

Suzanna took hold of Bobby's arm and pulled him close to her other side. From our current angle, it was easy to see the nascent bruise that shadowed the boy's jaw. Her face darkened, and she glanced back at me, her mouth opening to say something about it. I shook my head once to stop her. She took the hint and returned her attention to Bobby, a sunny expression firmly in place.

"You two ready?" she asked excitedly. "Let's go have some fun!"

The price of entry wasn't exorbitant. Even though Bobby was past the age of qualifying for the child's fee, it was only eighteen dollars for the three of us. Suzanna was happy to treat, insisting we save our money for food and games. I didn't know what she meant by "games," but I held my questions, figuring I'd be enlightened soon enough. And I was. I almost couldn't process everything that hit me fast enough as we passed beyond the ticket booth. Bobby tugged at my hand with an impatient "Come on!" and "Zombie Apocalypse coaster!" but I used my superior physical strength to hold him back while I gawked at the spectacle surrounding me.

There were booths and tents of all sizes, some emblazoned with familiar words like "popcorn," "hot dogs," and "shooting gallery." But "bearded lady?" That couldn't possibly be accurate. Some of the tents encompassed such things as a track where children obviously too young to drive were whizzing by in cars, and a thick pole from which sprouted sturdy arms that raised and lowered pods holding screaming people. I was gazing up speechlessly at the gigantic, brightly lit wheel a few hundred yards away when the tugging grew more frantic.

"Tim, let's go!"

I barely heard Bobby's plea over the racket. The blinking, scrolling lights, the smells, the sounds, they threatened to overwhelm my heightened senses. I closed my eyes and struggled to focus through the onslaught, to hear myself think over the cacophony of shouts and ringing bells. When a gentle hand pressed against my bare forearm, I latched on to the sensation with a desperation that surprised me. I opened my eyes to meet Suzanna's concerned gaze.

"Yes, dear," Suzanna added. "We're blocking the path."

I followed her over to the side of the road, dragging Bobby in my wake. I kept my hand clasped firmly around his, unwilling to let go of him in this maelstrom of humanity.

"Are you all right?" Suzanna asked.

I performed a quick but thorough self-assessment. My breathing was slightly elevated, but nothing else seemed outside normal parameters. I concluded that I only needed a little time to acclimate to this new environment.

"I'm fine."

"Okay, then. What do you want to do first?" she asked.

I shook my head. "I don't know. I—"

"You have been to a fair before, haven't you? I know for a fact they have several nice ones over in New Mexico."

"Well...," I replied, stalling. Even Bobby was looking at me with confusion, apparently baffled by the concept of someone my age having never done what was seemingly a common human ritual. I considered lying, telling them that I had, indeed, done so on many occasions. But I knew I wouldn't be able to keep up the deception with so little experience to draw on. "No. My, um, my stepfather wasn't big on them."

Suzanna accepted my stilted explanation with a sympathetic nod, and Bobby's expression radiated understanding, since he was intimately familiar with the notion of having a less than ideal childhood.

"Then it's time to fix that," she said briskly before promptly fastening her hand around my arm and hauling me off, with Bobby eagerly bringing up the rear.

I followed helplessly in their wake, uncertain of our course but trusting that neither of them intended to lead me astray. We hadn't gone more than ten or twenty yards before Bobby made an abrupt detour toward one of the smaller tents. Inside was a man in a white hat and apron worn over clothing I'd seen in archival film footage from the 1950s. He was standing before a large metal drum sitting atop a powerful motor. The tub was coated with a sticky substance of unknown type that the man was gathering up with a long white paper cone. Unable to discern the purpose of the exercise, I watched silently while Bobby bounced up and down beside me in excitement, prompting Suzanna to laugh at his antics.

"Okay, I can take a hint." She smiled at the man and took her wallet from her purse. "How much for three?"

"Six bucks, ma'am."

She surrendered the money, and we waited for the man to finish spooling the odd substance into a large, fluffy mass of pink around the cone.

"Here's one," he announced before reaching behind him for two more already finished cones—one blue and another pink.

"Thanks!" Bobby exclaimed as he claimed the blue one before stuffing a wad of the substance into his mouth.

I appreciated for the first time that it was some sort of food and curiously accepted the one the man handed me.

"Mmmm," Suzanna hummed as she took a bite from her own pink cone. "I haven't had real cotton candy in years. It's as good as I remember!"

I refrained from asking the question resting on the tip of my tongue. *How could candy be made out of cotton, and how was it edible?* Instead I simply joined in and took a bite. "It's sweet!"

Bobby was too lost in the bliss of his treat to respond, but Suzanna paused and blinked up at me. "Well, it is pure sugar. You've never had this before either, have you?"

I shook my head and stuffed some more of the unexpectedly tasty fluff into my mouth in lieu of answering.

She pursed her lips in disgust. "Your stepfather had better hope he and I never meet."

I stared at her, feeling the sticky floss dry on my face from where I'd taken an overly ambitious bite. The odds she would ever come face-to-face with the general were so negligible as to be nonexistent, but I understood her meaning. A sense of warmth blossomed in my chest at her pointless threat, and my throat seized up for no discernible reason. Unable to speak around the mysterious constriction, I smiled at her, the gesture coming naturally to me now. She returned it, and the sensation increased until I felt I might never be cold again.

"Hey, Tim! You ever done the shootin' gallery?"

I followed Bobby's pointing finger to a booth across the roadway. A row of shotguns was tethered to a wooden rail stretching the length of the tent, and along the back wall I could see a moving set of targets. Three people, a man and two children, were braced against the rail, trying to hit the targets with the rifles. Instead of bullets, the weapons shot out small balls which sounded like rubber as they hit the painted sheets of metal fashioned to resemble various barnyard animals. Bobby didn't wait for an answer and ran over to the booth, obliging me and Suzanna to follow. A sign proclaiming "Five Bucks For Five Minutes" explained the cost of playing. I had plenty of money from my wages, since David rarely made me pay for anything other than groceries, and even then, only on those occasions when I insisted.

Bobby grinned at me approvingly as I removed a wad of cash from my back pocket. "Wanna try for the big prize?" He tilted his chin toward a ridiculously gigantic stuffed giraffe sitting at the top of a pyramid of lesser creatures and plastic toys, which were arranged on shelves beneath it. "I came here with my mom last year and almost won it. So I'm warnin' ya, I'm pretty good."

Suzanna somehow managed to look down her nose at the boy even though he was slightly taller than her. "Big words, little man. I'm not such a bad shot myself." She reached into her purse, but I stopped her with a hand on her shoulder.

"My treat."

The smile she gave me was brilliant. "Such a gentleman. Okay, then. Don't say I didn't warn you when I nab that giraffe right out from under you!"

The trio playing ahead of us finally left after a few more minutes, hauling away a couple of stuffed bears for their trouble. The young woman running the booth waved us over and took my money with a smile. She flicked her head, and a tail of long blonde hair fell over her shoulder.

"Step right up and try your luck! Every target is worth a different number of points depending on how difficult it is to hit. You can play for as long as you want, provided you hand over five dollars every five minutes. Take your time, handsome."

The girl winked at me, and I recognized her behavior as flirting. Having successfully determined her motives, I nodded and promptly forgot about her as I took up position behind the centermost rifle. Once Bobby was settled on my left and Suzanna on my right, the girl hit a button and started the game.

It had been a while since I'd fired a gun, but weapons training had once been an almost daily part of my regimen. The rifle felt natural in my hand, and the rhythm of shooting came back to me as easily as breathing. The sounds of the fair dwindled to the background as I focused all of my attention on the targets. They slowly trundled by on five motorized tracks, each successive track slightly above the one in front of it and moving in the opposite direction. The targets popped up randomly, making it difficult to anticipate where to shoot. But even with the artificial difficulty thrown into the game, it presented zero challenge. It took me less than forty-five seconds to knock down every last one of the targets. When the tracks ground to a halt, I straightened and lowered the rifle, resisting the unnecessary instinct to reload.

"Holy shit!"

"Bobby, watch your language."

I glanced first at Bobby and then at Suzanna, only to see that their expressions matched the breathless astonishment in their voices. Then I heard the sound of clapping, and I looked over at the girl working the booth as she slowly applauded.

"Wow, mister. I've never seen anyone clear the targets so fast. You have plenty of time left out of your five minutes. Do you want to go again? Heck, you only need to do that three more times, and the giraffe is yours." She grinned and waved a hand at the wall of toys. "In fact, if you win the giraffe before your time is up, I'll throw in two more gifts for your friends."

"Come on, Tim! Do it!"

I realized I'd made a tactical error in exposing my skill with a weapon. My marksmanship skills were deadly, and even the soldiers I'd trained with had been far beneath me in proficiency. The first rule of infiltration was not to stand out, and I'd just done so in a very big way. Complacency had made me let my guard down, and if the general had been there, I'd be instantly and severely punished for such an inexcusable misstep. I glanced surreptitiously at Suzanna, anxious as I tried to anticipate her reaction. Was she shocked? Or worse, was she afraid? The broad smile on her face caught me completely by surprise.

"Well? Do you think you can?" Her smile grew at my silent nod. "Then get to it! That giraffe would look wonderful in my living room."

Relief. It was easy to identify the sensation that rushed through me, loosening my muscles and relaxing the tension that had knotted my stomach. My lips curved in response to her obvious enjoyment. "No problem," I replied.

Three minutes later the giraffe was mine. The girl fulfilled her promise by also giving me the medium-sized blue elephant Bobby requested and the smaller stuffed pig Suzanna assured me David would appreciate.

"That boy always did love pigs. I have no idea why." Suzanna toyed with the leg of her new giraffe, which I was carrying for her as we made our way farther down the midway. Bobby was once again in the lead, and I didn't even try to guess where we were headed. "So how did you learn to shoot so well?" she asked.

I'd been expecting the question and had come up with a suitable half-truth. "My stepfather likes to hunt. He started taking me with him when I was very young. I quickly learned that the better shot I was, the nicer he would be."

Suzanna was silent as she watched the path in front of us, playing with the giraffe while we walked. We passed by several interesting-looking attractions—a ring toss, a frozen lemonade stand, and a tower topped with a bell beneath which a line of people were waiting to hit a pad and make the bell ring—but neither Suzanna nor Bobby seemed inclined to stop. After a few long minutes, she finally spoke.

"I can't say I approve of young children learning how to shoot a gun, but I certainly have plenty of friends and neighbors who think the younger the better." She shrugged. "Well, at any rate, that was mighty impressive. Your stepfather was a good teacher. In this, at least."

The last was said under her breath, and I didn't let on that I'd heard. Bobby had gotten pretty far ahead of us, and I unconsciously quickened my steps to catch up. When I realized I'd outpaced the woman who'd been walking next to me, I stopped to wait for her to catch up, but she waved me on.

"No, go ahead. Bobby shouldn't be wandering through here on his own."

Fortunately, the boy had stopped four booths down from where we were beneath a sign that indicated what my nose had already told me. My growling stomach prompted a giggle from my companion.

"Growing boys. Nothing but bottomless pits, I swear," Suzanna said, shaking her head in amusement. "Bobby has the right idea. I could go for a polish sausage and fries myself." We walked slowly, our way hampered by the throng of people between us and the line in which Bobby had planted himself. "So what's the story with the bruise on his face?" Suzanna asked, taking advantage of the enforced delay.

I kept my attention on the small figure inching forward toward the booth, both unwilling to let Bobby out of my sight and uncertain of what she might be able to read on my face. "I can't say for sure, but I would guess his father is responsible."

Suzanna uttered an unladylike grunt. "I will never understand how a parent can raise a hand to his own child. I'm not saying I'm against the appropriate swat on the backside now and then, but there is simply no excuse for abusing your own flesh and blood." I could feel her gaze as she looked at me steadily. "Did your stepfather ever hit you?"

The question was blunt, but if I'd learned anything over the past few days it was that Suzanna always spoke her mind. I took my time as I considered how to answer her. The general had never struck me out of anger, but there had been several times during my lessons in hand-to-hand combat, especially when I was younger, when he'd often gotten the upper hand. I had never escaped from those sessions without a bruise or a sprain to show for my failure. Unable to think of a response that wouldn't reveal too much, I settled on a shrug, letting her interpret the silent motion as she would. I knew she'd guessed the worst when I suddenly found my hand captured in a tight grip. She was much weaker than me, so her grasp was far from painful, yet I felt unable to free myself from her hold. Nor, I realized, did I particularly want to.

"You remind me so much of David when he was your age."

I looked over at her in surprise. "His father—"

"No!" she interjected sharply. "That's not what I mean. Hank never laid a hand on David. If he had, I'd have killed him." She sighed. "The two of you are both old souls. I don't know what all you went through growing up, but you and David, your upbringings aged you both far beyond your years." She smiled wistfully, pulling me to a halt in order to keep us out of Bobby's range of hearing. "David knew about himself for a long time before he got the courage to tell his father, and he figured that once he did he would need to be prepared to make his own way in the world without any help. I'm sorry to say his caution was justified." She sighed and shook her head. "My husband isn't a cruel man, but he's very set in his ways. He didn't throw David out, but he made it clear that, after David went off to college, he shouldn't plan on ever living at home again."

"Couldn't you help him?" I asked. I wasn't trying to accuse her, but was genuinely curious. David had told me about his relationship with his father, but it was fascinating to hear the story from her point of view. A flash of pain twisted her features, and I rushed to apologize. "I'm sorry, I didn't mean to imply—"

"No, I know. And you're right. I should have done more for David, but to be honest, I didn't have the means to help him back then. I'd been a homemaker for all of my married life up to that point, and at the time, I didn't have anything my husband hadn't given me. Later, after David had graduated and moved down here, I swore I would never be so dependent again. I started working part time at a fabric store and have for the past ten years or so. I'm on vacation now, but when I get home, I'll go back to work." She looked up at me steadily. "If I can teach you anything, it's that you should always be able to stand on your own two feet. But somehow I think you already know that."

I glanced away, unable to reassure her that I was far more capable of surviving on my own than she could possibly imagine. That is, in all ways but one. My gaze drifted to the menu of the food booth, wondering if I would be able to find the necessary foods at the fair so I wouldn't have to resort to my dwindling supply of blue tablets that evening. I'd been feeling a little tired lately but was determined to ration the pills as much as possible.

"It's a lesson you should teach Bobby too." Following my gaze, Suzanna had wrongly guessed I was thinking about the younger boy. "David told me you've been teaching him martial arts? That's good," she said when I nodded. "A young man should feel like he can take care of himself. But there will be times when he'll need help." Her gaze visibly traced the bruise that had grown even darker over the past hour or so. "I've known Bobby for only a short time, but I can tell he looks up to you like a big brother. I'm glad about that. Bobby needs someone to look out for him."

"I promised to protect him," I said, feeling certain in this, at least. I knew I'd answered correctly when she favored me with a serene smile.

"I'm proud of you." She laughed when I stared at her in surprise. "Oh, I know we haven't been acquainted very long, but since I've already decided you and my son should be together, I've made it my business to learn as much about you as possible. Not that you've made it easy, no siree. You certainly do play things close to the vest, don't you?"

She wanted me and David to be together? I shrugged in response to her question while my heart raced at her shocking announcement.

"When I said I was proud of you, I mean the way you've bonded with Bobby even though you seem far more comfortable just being left to yourself. It's obvious you really care about him, and I think you need that. Someone to care about, that is. It's not healthy to dwell too much on your own problems. Sometimes having someone else to worry about is the very thing you need to put your own life into perspective. Like the song says, everybody needs somebody, no matter how much of a loner he thinks he is." She lurched sideways and knocked me with her shoulder, her grin revealing that the move was meant to be playful. "So do you think you could do the same with my son?"

"Look after him?" I asked, genuinely confused by her request.

She huffed in profound irritation. "No, and don't play dumb with me. You know perfectly well what I'm talking about. I'm asking if you think you can open your heart to David too. Do you think you could fall in love with him?"

Fall in love? It was a phrase I knew only in the abstract. This time I was obtuse on purpose, not wanting to reveal my emotional ignorance. "You want me to fall in love with Bobby and David?" I asked, deliberately twisting her choice of wording. The request for clarification earned me a pointed glare.

"I swear you're as bad as David. Just forget it." Suzanna rolled her eyes. "If you promise me you'll take care of both of them as best you can, I guess I'll have to be satisfied with that. You're clearly a very capable young man." She reached out and snagged the stuffed giraffe out of my arms and headed toward the booth tempting all who passed by with delicious smells and the sound of sizzling meat. She turned to face me, and I could barely see her behind the toy animal, but her voice reached me loud and clear. "As for the rest, you two blockheads are going to have to figure it out for yourselves." She paused and held out her wallet toward me. "Now, go wait in line with Bobby and get us three dogs with the works. Don't forget the fries and drinks!" she called out as I walked away to join Bobby, who had almost made it to the front.

"What kept you? I'm not going to be able to carry everything by myself." Bobby leaned back and looked around me in Suzanna's direction. "She want something too?"

I nodded silently, and his hazel eyes quickly sized me up.

"You're quiet. What's wrong?"

Knowing I wasn't overly talkative at the best of times, I glanced down at him curiously. "What do you mean?"

He shrugged. "I don't know. You look... pensive." Bobby smiled and waggled his eyebrows. "You like that? Pensive. Learned it in school the other day. I'm working on my vocabulary so I can get a good job and take care of Mom when I'm grown."

"A worthy goal."

"So, what's wrong?"

The line had slowed again, as though it was purposely thwarting my desire to change the subject. "Nothing," I replied, hoping he would accept my answer. He leveled a steady gaze at me, warning me the uncomfortable interrogation wasn't over quite yet. "Just something Suzanna said which I found puzzling."

"Oh, you mean about her wanting you and David to get together?"

I froze. An unfamiliar jolt went through me, which I eventually identified as genuine shock. "What are you talking about?"

"Come on, man. Like you two aren't always making goo-goo eyes at each other." Bobby shrugged. "I don't care if you're gay. Fish gotta swim, right? Anyway, I think Suzanna's right. You two might as well hook up. You're already living together, right?"

The feel of David's hands on my body, our lips pressing together with frenzied need. The thrill of exploring David under the pretense of caring for him when he was ill. The casual touches that burned, and the kind gestures that warmed me in turn. These were the memories and impressions that defined what David meant to me. And they were so real, my body responded as if I were reliving them all over again. So this was what Suzanna had been trying to tell me, what even Bobby had guessed. But they were wrong. David might desire me physically, but I doubted it went beyond that. He had never given any indication he felt anything more. Really, it was all for the best. My remaining life span was limited, and the time I had left to spend with David was even shorter. I planned to leave long before my disability exacted its ultimate toll, and once I was gone I was certain David would eventually forget all about my unexpected intrusion into his life.

"Hey, are you sure you're okay? You're looking a little pale."

I nodded and mumbled something I hoped made sense. The smell of grilling meat and fried potatoes threatened to turn my stomach inside out. A second ago the aroma of cooking food had been beyond enticing, so what had changed? Why did I suddenly feel the urge to retch up the little I'd already eaten that day? I subdued my queasiness only by asserting the control I'd gained over my body from years of biofeedback training.

"I'm fine," I said, hoping I sounded convincing. We finally reached the front of the line, and I grabbed at the chance to distract Bobby from his uncomfortable insight. "Why don't you go ahead and order?" Fortunately the rapidly growing thirteen-year-old considered my personal life no match for the promise of greasy food. Bobby turned to the server eagerly and proceeded to request enough to hold us all for the rest of the day, even though it was only eleven in the morning.

Putting the strange nausea down to my acute need to address my vitamin deficiency, I set myself to solving the physics of how the three of us would be able to juggle our stuffed prizes along with the consumable bonanza Bobby was gleefully rounding up.

SIXTEEN

DAVID LOOKED up at the sign for the Tilt-A-Whirl, confirming he was in the right spot. "Yeah, Ma, I'm standing right under it." He stepped farther off the path to avoid the jostling crowd and gripped his phone more securely. When he arrived back at the fair, he'd fully expected his mother and the boys would be ready to leave after being there all day. Clearly he'd underestimated their stamina.

"Okay, I can see the sign now," Suzanna replied, her voice winded from walking. "We'll be there in a jiffy."

His mother disconnected the call, and while he waited he listened to the shrieks of people who apparently thought being spun and whipped around at insane speeds was the height of entertainment. Something on the periphery of his vision caught his attention, and he turned around right in time to see a gigantic stuffed giraffe coming straight at him.

"What the hell—"

"David, language." Suzanna's voice drifted out from somewhere behind the long-necked behemoth.

"Ma? Is that you?" He raised an eyebrow at the three-foot toy. "What is that thing?"

She shifted the creature in her arms and gave him a pursed-lipped glare. "Don't be jealous of Bertie. I'm sure if you ask nicely Tim will win you one of your very own."

"Bertie?" Of course she'd named it. He saw her escorts also had a couple of spoils of carnival war, though not nearly as impressive as the giraffe. "You won these, Tim? On which game?"

The kid's gaze met his briefly before darting away. Was that a blush? Wondering what that was all about, David glanced toward his mother, only to see her looking at Tim with a sly smirk on her lips. Oh God. What in the world had she done now?

"The shooting gallery." Bobby, proudly waving his blue elephant, provided a welcome respite from whatever was going on between Suzanna and Tim. David paid closer attention to the boy than was probably warranted. "You should have seen him. He was awesome!"

"Oh, yeah?"

Tim was staring resolutely at the respectably sized pig he was holding. It was really cute, but not as cute as the color tinting the kid's cheeks.

David cleared his throat. "So," he directed at Bobby, "looks like you guys had fun. What all did you do today?"

"Man, what didn't we do?" The younger teen proceeded to regale him with improbable tales of roller coasters conquered and foodstuffs demolished.

"Really? You finished the quad-cone?" David remembered the towering stack of four different—and usually not complementary—ice cream flavors from his younger fair-going days. Unfortunately, he could also clearly recall the stomachache that had invariably followed the attempt.

"Yeah!" Bobby looked understandably pleased with himself. "Tim did too."

"Except that Tim didn't puke it all up after riding the Gravitron."

Bobby threw Suzanna a dirty glare for ratting him out. David placed a sympathetic hand on the boy's shoulder. "Don't feel bad. That ride always did me in. Man was not meant to be pinned to a wall by centrifugal force alone."

"Especially not after eating ice cream, and two Polish sausages, and an entire platter of fries only an hour beforehand." Suzanna was unapologetic as she aimed a haughty glance at the mortified teen.

David smothered a chuckle, not wanting to wound Bobby's pride any further. Stealing himself, he looked back at the silent figure tightly holding on to the stuffed pig. "What about you, Tim? Any misadventures to report?"

The kid shook his head without looking up. "No. But I have had fun."

"I swear," Suzanna interjected, "nothing fazes this boy. He easily ate as much as Bobby, if not more. But even though he rode the Cyclone right after all that ice cream, he didn't so much as turn green." She shook her head. "I don't know how. I got queasy just watching him."

She waved her hand toward the ride at the back of the park, and David's gaze followed until he was staring up at the enormous roller coaster that was the featured ride of the fair. It was a towering iron structure of twists and loops with an initial drop that was boasted as being over a hundred feet high. He understood his mother's amazement and looked at Tim with new respect.

"Yeah, Tim, that was rad," Bobby concurred. "Even I had enough sense to wait a while before riding the Cyclone."

Tim shrugged. "It was fine. I enjoyed it."

David laughed at the understatement. "Well, kid, you're a better man than me. You'd never get me on that thing. I don't do physical stress well." He shook his head. "Nice and easy, that's more my speed."

"Speaking of which," his mother said as she put her arm through the crook of his, "why don't we grab one last bite to eat and then ride the Ferris wheel." She tilted her head to look up at him. "We were waiting for you to get here, since I know that's your favorite ride."

She wasn't wrong. He'd always enjoyed the slow journey into the sky, even though the Oklahoma landscape hadn't provided much of a view to savor from that height. Texas likely wouldn't be any better, but he didn't let that deter him.

"Sure thing. What do you and Bertie want to eat?" He ducked halfheartedly when a delicate hand delivered a pointed smack to the back of his head.

The group consensus was pizza, and since they all managed to agree on toppings—pepperoni with extra cheese—they settled on one of the picnic benches in an area immediately behind the food booths and gathered around their mutual pie. Bobby was trying to convince Suzanna to let him hold the giraffe for her while she ate, ignoring the fact that his own hands were already covered with grease and cheese. While they squabbled amicably, David watched Tim down his second slice of pizza with an expression that was completely inappropriate in such a public setting.

"Is it good?" David quipped. The kid glanced at him and blinked.

"Very" came the answer, as though it should have been obvious. Slice number two was gone in a flash, and Tim went for a third without missing a beat.

"Whoa, slow down." If he didn't know it was impossible, he would have thought the kid had never eaten pizza before. "There's always more where that came from. You don't want to choke."

Tim paused midchew, his cheeks puffed out like an adorable chipmunk. He set down the surviving piece of the slice and swallowed. "Sorry," he mumbled. "I was hungry."

David smiled, ironically disappointed that the gluttonous display had ended. "So, I know Bobby's favorite ride was the Gravitron, unfortunate food loss and all. But what was yours?"

Tim answered with no hesitation. "The Mega Drop."

David blanched. "You mean the one where you go up and get dropped in free fall several times?" His stomach threatened to rebel at the mere thought. The ride was housed in the 80-foot-high tower situated at the easternmost edge of the fairgrounds. "Why, for Christ's sake?" he asked at Tim's nod.

The kid looked thoughtful for a moment. "It felt like I was flying. Like, if I lifted the harness, I could soar away as far as I wanted to go." He shrugged. "I don't know," he added softly. "It felt like freedom."

Given what he knew of Tim's home life, he could understand the sentiment. Hell, there were plenty of times while he'd been growing up and had begun to understand he wasn't your average Oklahoma boy that he'd wished he could go somewhere far, far away. He nodded and took another bite of his pizza, unsure how to respond without giving his own thoughts away.

"Ugh, I'm stuffed." Suzanna sat back and placed her hands on her gently rounded stomach. Bertie sat beside her, safely away from Bobby's messy hands. She watched for a moment while her menfolk continued to tuck into the pie until nothing was left but crumbs. "David, you're going to regret that, mark my words. You're not a teenager anymore." She shook her head at her son as he ignored her in favor of guzzling a deep swig of his large soft drink. "Anyway, are we ready for the Ferris wheel? It's better at night, but this time of year, sunset is the best we're going to manage, I think."

"Whack-A-Mole first!" Bobby stared at Tim. "You owe me a rematch. Best three out of five. You promised!"

David glanced between the young men curiously. "Sounds like I missed something."

Suzanna laughed. "Bobby and Tim played twice, and Tim crushed him both times. They already got enough points to win prizes, but the barker promised to keep track of their winnings until they finished their 'epic battle.'" Her fingers crooked in air quotes as Bobby continued to stare daggers at Tim's impassive face. "Besides," she added, "we didn't want to have to carry around any more stuff until you got here to help."

Laughing, David heaved himself to his feet, refusing to acknowledge that his mother had been absolutely right. He should never have had that third slice. Surreptitiously adjusting his belt, he stretched and waited for the others to join him. "I used to be quite the hand at Whack-A-Mole myself. Maybe I'll beat both of you."

Bobby held out his hand. "Bring it on, old man!" A handshake sealed the agreement, and they set off to bash plastic moles on the head with plastic mallets.

The barker did indeed remember them. He grinned widely when he saw the foursome approaching. "Hey, you're back, and you brought a new friend!" He reached into his pocket and pulled out a piece of paper. "Okay, so I have you"—he pointed at Bobby—"with 4,344 points, and you"—Tim this time—"with 8,685 points."

David felt his eyes go wide as the man read off the totals. "And you only played twice so far? Wow." He thought about sitting the round out but decided what the heck? He hadn't lied about being good at the game. All he needed was to even the playing field a bit. As usual, his mother was one step ahead of him.

"David, why don't you play two rounds by yourself to make things fair?"

Tim and Bobby were agreeable and stepped back to give him room. David rolled up his shirtsleeves and set to. It had been years since he'd last played the game, but he was pleased to see his reflexes hadn't suffered from the passage of time. He used a trick his first secret boyfriend had taught him back when they'd been freshmen in high school and didn't try to look at each mole individually. Instead he fixed his attention on the center of the field, which allowed him to see more of the playing area at once. He should have felt silly, smacking as hard as he could at the plastic heads as they popped up and retreated, but he couldn't remember the last time he'd had this much fun. After two rounds he stepped back and caught his breath, embarrassed to be so winded but eager to see his score.

"The gentleman has 5,004 points!" the barker announced.

"Aw, man!" Bobby moaned.

David buffed his fingernails on his sleeve. "Read 'em and weep, junior." He knew he'd played well, but his score was nowhere near Tim's. He was suddenly very eager to see the kid play, unable to imagine how he'd racked up such an impressive total in only two rounds.

Bobby shoved his way to the machine first. "No more mister nice guy," he warned. "I've got this!"

"Just look at the middle of the board," David whispered in the boy's ear before the game started. Although he was giving away his secret, he was glad to pass on the knowledge. After all, there was no way he was giving Tim any advice. The kid clearly didn't need any help. Bobby glanced at him in surprise but simply nodded and smiled his thanks.

"And... go!"

It took a few seconds, but David noticed the instant Bobby remembered what he'd said. The boy beat mercilessly at the hapless moles, the bell affixed to the top of the machine dinging cheerfully with each hit. When the minute-long round ended, David glanced up at the scoreboard and smiled proudly at the result.

"And that's 4,123 points for a total of 8,467!"

"Whoo-hoo!" Bobby pumped his fist and met the hand David held up with a resounding smack. He'd nearly matched his two-round total in a single round and had almost matched Tim's per round average. It was an impressive feat, and David was thrilled for the boy even though his own standing was extremely precarious. "Take that, jerk face!" Bobby shouted before sticking out his tongue at Tim.

"Your turn, jerk face," David parroted, struggling not to laugh as Tim tossed him a confused look before taking his place at the game table. Tim obviously wasn't used to being teased, but David was sure he and Bobby could fix that with no problem.

David's smile melted away into slack-jawed awe as he watched Tim apply mallet to mole with a ruthless efficiency he doubted even a robot could match. The kid's gaze was focused at the dead center of the field, and David saw that any advice he could have given would have been completely unnecessary. The plastic bludgeon moved so quickly the effort of trying to follow it with his eyes gave him a headache. The ringing of the bell was almost constant, and he glanced up at the score board, watching in amazement as the numbers shot into the stratosphere.

Everyone was silent when the round ended, and the barker visibly shook himself as he remembered his job. "Um, 9,177 points." The young man glanced at David. "Did you want to go again, sir?"

David shook his head and saw Suzanna push Bobby's jaw closed with a finger. "No," he answered with a wry smile. "Don't suppose there's any point, do you? I guess all those years of martial arts paid off," he said jokingly as he nudged Tim in the shoulder with his arm. The corner of the kid's mouth lifted uncertainly, but the curve became more pronounced when he apparently confirmed that David was, in fact, only teasing.

The barker grinned and turned to the shelf of prizes. "Pick anything you want," he directed at Tim.

Tim looked at Suzanna. "Is there something you would like?"

She shook her head. "Oh, no. I'm quite happy with Bertie here." She hugged her giraffe tightly. "You should get something for you."

David glanced at the pig Suzanna had been holding while Tim played. He'd thought the pig belonged to the kid, but apparently he was mistaken.

"How about the ray gun?" Bobby offered helpfully as he cast a covetous gaze over the sci-fi inspired toy weapon, which sat on one of the higher shelves. "It's pretty sweet."

"No guns," Tim murmured. What teenage boy didn't like guns, David wondered as he watched Tim looking carefully over the assortment of prizes. Finally his gaze settled on something propped up on the lowest shelf, where the cheapest stuff was on display. "I'll take that."

The barker followed Tim's pointing finger and blinked. "This? Are you sure?" He walked over to the display and picked up a plush figure of a bald man wearing a white lab coat and black, thick-rimmed glasses. It looked like a toy for a five-year-old who wanted to play puppet doctor.

"Yes," Tim replied evenly. His face was emotionless as he took the figure from the barker, but when he glanced up at the man with a mumbled "Thanks," David thought the kid's eyes looked brighter than usual. The barker offered them another prize since Tim's score had been the highest in the history of the fair, and Bobby graciously claimed the ray gun for himself when Tim suggested the boy pick whatever he wanted.

They weren't far from the Ferris wheel, and they found the end of the line a few minutes after leaving the abused plastic moles behind. David glanced at Tim furtively while they walked, noticing that the kid never took his gaze off the toy doctor. He wondered at Tim's pensive expression, wanting to ask what it was about the childish-looking figure the kid found so fascinating. *I shouldn't pry*, David told himself. He'd simply have to wait and hope Tim would offer an explanation on his own.

Besides, it wasn't like he was owed an answer. Before David knew it, he'd come to think of Tim as a permanent fixture in his house, at his job, and in his life, as foolish as that may have been. He had no clue if the kid felt the same way. Day by day, he found himself wanting to know more about this unexpected addition to his otherwise mundane existence, but he couldn't assume Tim wanted to share anything more about himself than he already had. For a couple of weeks now, David had realized he would be quite happy if Tim wanted to stay with him forever. Of course, the kid could decide to leave at any moment, and there was nothing he'd be able to do about it. He didn't have any claim on Tim, but that didn't stop him from wanting what he probably shouldn't.

"Oh, good," Suzanna said, interrupting his thoughts. "The line isn't too bad. Bobby, stop trying to shoot that man." Bobby had aimed his ray gun at the back of some frat guy's head and was happily *pew pewing* away. She poked him in the back. "Just for that, you have to ride on the wheel with me."

What? David thought in a panic. *No!* That meant he'd have to ride with Tim, unless the kid wanted to go by himself. The wheel was huge, with dozens of cars, and even though the ride never stopped as people got off and on, it would easily take thirty minutes for them to get all the way around. He looked up at the dangling cars, imagining the two of them trapped in one of them for all that time. Swallowing, he opened his mouth to tell his mother they should ride together, but then he noticed Tim was looking at him, a renewed blush showing clearly beneath his olive complexion. *Fuck it*, he decided, trying to ignore how the pink tint made the kid look even younger than he already was.

Bobby had turned the ray gun on his ride buddy, and Suzanna tossed the stuffed pig at Tim before she gamely tried to save herself from being fake lasered by finding all of the boy's points of ticklish weakness. Tim caught the pink toy deftly by its curly tail and watched with silent intensity as the woman and boy taunted each other. David thought he should probably at least ask the kid if he was all right with Suzanna's imperious assignment of partners, but he was suddenly afraid Tim might say no. He kept his mouth shut as they inched forward in the line, grateful for his mother's and Bobby's antics to distract from the awkward silence between him and Tim.

Before long it was time for the other two to board their slowly moving car. "I'm gonna make it swing the whole time. You're gonna be sooooo scared!"

"Talk is cheap, little man. We'll see who ends up crying for his mommy!"

Despite his trash talking, Bobby solicitously helped Suzanna into the car before getting in behind her. David could hear them happily bickering even after the ride operator shut the car door and they started travelling upward on the long circuit. He tried to remember the last time he'd seen his mother enjoy herself so much, and regretted, not for the first time, that he was her only child. Suzanna had always loved kids, and Bobby could use the influence of a more stable maternal figure in his life. They were good for each other.

Finally it was their turn to board. Since Tim had his hands full, David let him go first, trying to pretend he wasn't staring at the cute, denim-covered ass wiggling its way into the car. It was practically begging him to smack it. *Pervert*. Keeping his hands firmly to himself, he took his place on the seat opposite from the one Tim had claimed. The kid was looking out the window as David got settled, watching the ground fall away as the car began its slow ascent.

"It's pretty up here."

To Be Human

David glanced out and nodded. "Yeah. Too bad we couldn't do this at night. You should see it with all of the lights from the rides and booths. When I was a kid, I would pretend the carnival was really outer space and that everything below me was stars." He smiled as he caught Tim's questioning look. "It was just a silly thing I used to do. Can't pretend it makes any sense," he chuckled. The kid absently fidgeted with the two stuffed figures in his hands, and David latched onto what he considered an innocuous topic. He pointed his chin at the toys. "You really made out well today." He blinked in surprise as the stuffed pig suddenly appeared close to his nose.

"This is for you." Tim continued to push the pig toward him. "Your mother said you liked pigs, so I asked the woman at the shooting gallery to give this to me as my prize."

David had never heard Tim speak so quickly, as if he was nervous about something, but the observation faded before the realization that the kid had gotten him a gift. Hell, had won it for him like they were at the fair on a date or something equally ridiculous. David shut the fantasy down before it could run away with his common sense. He took the pig and studied the overly round body, the smooshed pink nose, the curly tail. Suzanna hadn't lied; he did love pigs. And this one was about the cutest he'd ever seen.

"Thanks," he said, trying for casual, as if the gift meant nothing special. So, of course, the kid ruined it all by favoring him with a bright smile. Though it was becoming more common, the sight of Tim expressing himself never failed to make David's heart beat faster. It was a conspiracy. Tim and his mother were in a conspiracy to make him lose his mind and do something he had no business doing. He deliberately pushed himself back into his seat, trying to put as much distance between him and Tim as he could in the cramped space. Their legs were far too long to be sitting opposite each other, and David cursed his fate as they were forced to play an accidental game of footsy while trying to figure out the best position to accommodate them.

Seemingly ignorant of David's predicament, Tim soon returned his attention to the growing vista of the fairgrounds. They were about a third of the way around, and the sprawl of Lubbock, which was about twenty miles away, was becoming visible in the distance.

"Are we going to do anything besides go around the wheel?"

203

David shook his head. "Nope. That's about it." He shrugged. "It's a nice way to wind down after spending the day on the wilder rides and eating too much food." He tossed the kid a grin, and was both glad and dismayed to see that his teasing had prompted another of those sweet blushes. "But, I admit, it's not very exciting," he continued, hoping Tim didn't notice him shifting in his seat to adjust the fit of his pants.

"So it's not really a ride, then?"

"No, it is. I guess…." David rubbed the back of his neck with the hand not holding his new pig. "I guess it's most popular with couples."

"Couples?"

"Yeah," David added, "because it's slow and takes a long time. And since it's pretty tight in here, it encourages people to sit close together."

"But we're not. You're over there."

David stared at Tim, trying to figure out if he was being provocative on purpose. But, blush aside, the kid's poker face was firmly in place, and David couldn't decipher anything in the slowly fading light. He glanced out the window and noticed the sun was setting quickly. It would probably be mostly gone by the time they got off the ride. The tune for "Some Enchanted Evening" popped into his head, and he wondered what the hell was up with his brain.

"Uh, well…." He scrambled for an innocuous explanation for why he'd chosen the opposite seat when sitting side-by-side would probably have been more comfortable, at least with respect to leg room. "If I sat over there, it might make the car swing. Like that," he added, pointing to the window in the roof of the car. Through it, they could see the pod holding Suzanna and Bobby. It was rocking to and fro in wide arcs, and David figured they were probably trying to make each other throw up.

"Show me."

David's head snapped down, and he frowned at Tim. "Huh?" The kid had moved to one side of his seat, leaving what was obviously meant to be space for him.

"Show me how to make the car swing."

This was not a good idea. David knew that, but he obliged anyway, finding it difficult to refuse one of Tim's exceedingly infrequent requests. As soon as he'd changed positions, the car began to tilt, swaying from the rod connecting the pod to the frame of the giant metal wheel. Tim looked at him expectantly, so David began to shift his weight forward and back ever so slightly.

"Move at the same time I do," he instructed. "The trick is to be in sync."

Tim mirrored him, and their combined motion started the car to swinging, gently at first, but with increasing force as they continued. A creaking sound came from overhead, and the kid looked up through the ceiling window. "Is it safe?"

"Sure." David turned and pointed at the car directly across from them. "See? They're swinging a lot more than we are. It's fine." He turned back and picked up the rhythm again. "Should we see how far we can make it go?"

Tim nodded deliberately, as if he was making a solemn promise, and keeping his gaze fixed on David, he precisely matched his movements. Before they knew it, the car was swaying wildly, going faster and faster as they gained momentum. "Whoa!" David shouted as the car went almost completely horizontal, leaving them flat on their backs. He glanced over at the kid and noted the surprise on his face a second before Tim started laughing uncontrollably.

This was only the second time David had witnessed Tim display such spontaneous, unrestrained joy, and he reveled in it. The kid's eyes were shining, and his full lips were stretched in a wide grin, as though this moment of childish amusement was the most fun he'd ever had. The sudden churning in David's gut baffled him until he identified it as jealousy. He was jealous of this damn Ferris wheel, envious that it was the ride, and not him, that had made Tim so happy. It was the most ridiculous thing he'd ever heard, but he was helpless to fight his sudden desire to own that joy for himself.

The car tilted forward on the backswing, angling them face down. They both braced their legs against the opposite bench, but Tim unexpectedly reached out and grabbed his hand to keep himself from sliding from his seat. The instant the kid touched him, David's remaining shred of control disappeared like melting cotton candy. He hauled Tim close using their joined hands and, clutching his stuffed pig with the other, laid claim to the soft curve of that beautiful smile as the car swung about them.

I STIFFENED in shock as David's lips pressed against mine. It was the first time he had ever initiated any sort of intimate contact between us, and at first I wasn't sure how to respond. Our previous encounter had ended with him pulling away with hastily expressed regret, and I didn't want a repeat of that agonizing rejection. I wanted him to carry on with the amazing kiss. *What should I do*? I pondered, feeling my toes curl in my tennis shoes. My head was beginning to spin, and I thought I might die if he stopped. But was it safe to join in, to show him just how much I wanted this?

Incisively, I took a handful of David's shirt and simply held on without pressing forward or moving away. But when he wrapped his arms around my waist and pulled me even closer, the thinking part of my brain shut down, leaving me with only the need for the kiss to never end. Relinquishing my grip on David's shirt, I thwarted any plans he might have had of escaping by locking my arms around his neck. I heard a moan from somewhere close by. The sound was wanton and needy, and it was only after the thrust of a seeking tongue into my mouth abruptly cut it off that I realized it had come from me.

A frantic rearrangement of limbs and bodies left me half sitting in David's lap, legs gripping his thighs to ensure he would stay put. With my last shred of coherent thought, I thanked the fortuitous turn of events that had left us trapped in the confined space. David couldn't push me away if he wanted to, though he didn't seem to be at all so inclined. Strong hands spread out over my back, holding me in place. But I had no intention of moving anywhere unless it was closer. So when David suddenly broke the kiss, I experienced my first stab of acute panic.

David pulled back far enough to look me in the eye. "Tim, I…."

My imagination rapidly supplied all of the undesirable ways he might finish that sentence. *I'm sorry. I think we should stop. I didn't mean to kiss you.*

"I think we should talk."

Ah. I'd missed that one.

"No. No talking," I murmured, sealing our lips together again before David could object. My tactics were apparently sound, because he relented without further protest. Instead, a hand came up to cup the side of my face, angling my head to deepen the kiss even more. My entire body seemed to sigh with relief as I melted into the embrace. David laid claim to my mouth with an intrepid, searching tongue, and I tasted pizza, soda, and something else that was indescribably… him. An ache grew between my thighs, my hardening flesh beginning to throb as the kiss went on and on. The sound of our breathing filled the car until it echoed from the metal walls. This was what I'd been looking for, what I'd been hoping for ever since making my desperate escape from the Facility. To feel human. To feel alive.

When David once again began to gently push me away, I used my superior strength to hold on. At some point my eyes had drifted shut, and I opened them quickly to fix David with an anxious gaze.

"Easy," David soothed. He exhaled sharply, a crooked smile twisting his lips. "Trust me, I don't want to stop either, but—" David glanced toward the door. "We're almost at the bottom, and unless you want to be the object of a lot of stares and my mother's teasing, we're going to have to put this on hold for now."

Through the window, I could see that our car was indeed nearing the ground. Taking a deep breath, I relinquished my death grip on David's neck and slid backward until I was perched on the opposite seat. "Sorry," I mumbled.

"Don't be." His smile softened as he captured my hand and gave it a squeeze. "But I meant it when I said we need to talk."

Whatever David wanted to say would have to wait. The ride operator opened the door of our car and gestured for us to exit. Since the ride never actually stopped, we were forced to scramble out quickly. I was shocked to note that, for a brief second, my legs didn't quite want to support me. David grabbed my hand to steady me.

"Easy there," David said. "It can feel weird when you first get off. Kind of like when you get off a boat."

I nodded, although I knew the shakiness in my legs wasn't due to the ride. Unwilling to surrender even that small bit of contact, I entwined my fingers with David's and held firm. He smiled at me before leading me through the exit gate and over to where Suzanna and Bobby were waiting. Bobby was still playing with his ray gun, his clean shirt indicating he'd survived the ride with his stomach intact. Suzanna was watching us approach with a quirk to her lips that, for some odd reason, made me unaccountably nervous.

"Oh God. Here we go," David groaned under his breath.

"Guess you really like the pig," Suzanna quipped, her gaze fixed unwaveringly on our joined hands.

"Not now, Ma."

"Whatever you say, dear." She looked quickly in the direction of my lips before her gaze shifted to her son's. "I'm just glad you two had such a... nice time on the Ferris wheel."

I could feel the heat and increased sensitivity in my lips and realized they were probably swollen. A quick glance revealed that David's mouth also displayed unmistakable proof of our recent activities.

Suzanna's smile broadened, her expression a textbook representation of extreme smugness. "That poor couch is going to be so lonely tonight."

"Mother!" David said sharply, cutting his gaze anxiously toward Bobby. Fortunately, Bobby had already started walking away, apparently deciding our reunion meant it was time to leave. David's shoulders slumped in apparent relief that the boy couldn't have heard Suzanna, but that didn't stop him from shooting her an annoyed glare. "Knock it off."

I watched the exchange between them, noting the undercurrent of fondness in their bickering. And, more importantly, while David was obviously uncomfortable with his mother's insinuations, he still hadn't released my hand. I tugged at the grip to test whether David had simply forgotten to let me go, but when I met resistance, I stopped pulling. Gazing down at our joined hands in contentment, I happily trailed behind the two adults as we moved to follow after Bobby.

"Let's go home," I suggested, eager to be alone with David again.

"Good idea." David looked askance at his mother. "I think someone needs a nap."

Suzanna stuck her tongue out at her son at the hint, but she nodded in agreement, her surprisingly youthful features showing her exhaustion. Bobby, on the other hand, was less than thrilled.

"Aww, man! I was going to get another funnel cake," he groused as we headed inexorably toward the exit of the fairgrounds.

"You had one before lunch, and another one afterward." Suzanna placed a hand on the frowning boy's back, softening her rebuke. "I don't think your mom would appreciate it if we took her son away and returned Porky Pig in his place."

David chuckled, and Bobby, accepting that he was fighting a losing battle, merely acknowledged her quip with a semirespectful "Ha-ha."

It took us nearly fifteen minutes to reach the exit gate. The main lane was choked with all the other people who had decided it was a good time to depart. The going was slow, but David, Suzanna, and Bobby passed the time with idle, friendly chatter while I was content to simply soak it all in. I used the opportunity to take one last look around the fair, wondering if I would ever spend another day like this in the limited time I had left.

I knew it was foolish to think about the future. I would need to leave David and Lubbock behind before my medical condition became critical. And the general was almost certainly looking for me. While the inconspicuous life I'd been leading might serve to minimize my chances of being discovered, lingering in one place for too long was dangerous. But it was a risk I was willing to take. I was in no hurry to leave, and I didn't think even the Company had the resources to find me before I ultimately succumbed to my genetic disorder. I probably had several more months before I would seriously need to consider moving on for both my sake and David's.

Glancing down at our clasped hands, I felt that strange warmth fill me once again. Only this time, it was accompanied by the unmistakable desire to continue what David had started on the Ferris wheel. As the exit came within sight, I noticed we were passing by the shooting gallery. I found myself smiling as I looked over at the booth. There were two men playing, both of them tall and well-built. The blond threw his darker-haired companion a grin while he stuffed his mouth with a fresh, hot piece of sugar-coated elephant ear. I could see the man's impressive score from where I stood—he punched his friend playfully in the shoulder, apparently gloating over how well he'd done—and I wondered absently whether the man had had firearms training. The thought was automatic and was gone as quickly as it had come. My next thought was to wonder if the two men were a couple and whether the shooting gallery was doing as much for them as it had for me.

The game had only been the start of what had doubtless been the best day of my life. I noticed one of the men look up and begin to slowly scan the crowd. His gaze seemed almost too intent, but right when he glanced in my direction, Suzanna said something that drew my attention. I was turning toward her when I noticed David swinging the stuffed pig against his thigh. The pig I had won for him. A sense of pride filled me, prompting yet another smile to stretch my lips. The sensation was beginning to feel almost natural. The hand around mine tightened briefly, and I looked up to see my happy expression mirrored on David's face. I returned the squeeze, feeling grateful to have had the chance to experience such unforgettable moments as I had that day at the county fair.

SEVENTEEN

DAVID CHECKED off another item on his list, berating himself as his attention wandered for the umpteenth time to the trio standing near the Customer Service desk. Tim was listening to a woman complaining about the hard-to-remove plastic safety covers on the large first aid kits. David was supposed to be completing the paperwork for the annual OSHA inspection, making sure the store lighting was adequate, testing the smoke detectors and overhead sprinklers, and double-checking the millions of other details that would keep the federal agency from causing him any headaches. Instead, he found himself admiring the slimness of Tim's neck as the kid nodded sedately at the irate customer while she pointed angrily at her young son with one hand and waved the kit emphatically with the other. A month ago, David would have been reluctant to let Tim deal with the situation by himself. His strange awkwardness with people, however, had grown less apparent over the past few weeks. David could thank his mother for much of that. She'd been adamant that everyone treat Tim like any other young man and not one who was on the run from his family. As a result, Tim had begun to act accordingly.

The exchange wasn't worth focusing on, but that wasn't why he was looking. These days, David found he couldn't take his eyes off Tim, no matter what mundane thing the kid was doing. The way he cocked his head, awkwardly trying to telegraph his empathy with the customer, the nonthreatening way he held his hands clasped in front of him, the tiny shifts of his elfin features as he explained that, no, she couldn't make a return nearly a year after purchasing the kit. David thought he could easily study Tim for hours. And this time he couldn't blame Suzanna. Not entirely, at least. While she might have planted the seed that had bloomed so explosively in his mind during the Ferris wheel ride, he was the one who had finally given in to temptation and abandoned the caution he'd tried for so long to inject into his relationship with Tim.

A week and a half had passed since the fair, but he caught himself replaying for the thousandth time the conversation that had taken place between them once they'd returned home and Suzanna had retired to her borrowed room. That night, everything had changed.

For the first time since Tim had been living in the town house, David had consciously invited him into his bedroom. From the expectant look on his face, the kid had clearly been hoping for a continuation of what had occurred on the Ferris wheel, but Tim's expression had slipped into its old default blankness when David carefully kept his distance.

"I don't trust my mother not to eavesdrop," David said, closing the door of his room behind them. Giving the kid a wide berth, he edged around Tim until he reached his bed. During the ride home, he'd had time to think about what he'd done. Tim had been willing and eager, no doubt, but David still couldn't help feeling he'd made a mistake in allowing his attraction to the kid to run away with him. He sat heavily and braced his elbows on his knees, clasping his hands tightly as if to keep them from reaching out and pulling the silent figure standing by the door down onto the bed beside him. "Tim...," he began, faltering as he struggled to figure out what he wanted to say. "Look," he tried again, "about what happened at the fair—"

"I'm not sorry."

David looked up and sighed. Somehow Tim had guessed what he'd settled on in an attempt to restore sanity to their relationship, and he looked none too pleased. Holding up a conciliatory hand, David shook his head. "No," he lied, "that's not what I was going to say. I'm not sorry. Well, not exactly." He felt his jaw clench in frustration. "It's just that... damn, what can I tell you, kid? I do want you," he finally admitted. "A whole hell of a lot."

Tim stood motionless as David's gaze roamed over his face, searching for some indication of his reaction to the confession. His expression remained impassive, offering up nothing David could latch on to to convince himself he was right to put a stop to things before they got even more out of hand. David dropped his gaze toward his clenched hands, girding himself to put up one last fight to appease his conscience.

"Yeah, so, I think we should put this—whatever it is—on ice. My mom will simply have to amuse herself while she's here with something other than trying to matchmake." His smile was short-lived when he saw his attempt at humor had fallen flat.

Tim took a step forward, narrowing the distance between them, as he fixed David with an unwavering gaze. David peered up at Tim warily, his knuckles growing paler as his hands tightened their grip on each other.

"What if I don't want to, how did you say, 'put this on ice'?"

David gaped as Tim fell to his knees in front of him. The kid's slim hands slid up his legs and came to rest on his thighs. Startled, David felt his eyes widen in silent confusion, but Tim held his gaze steadily.

"What if I don't want to?" Tim repeated.

A tremor went through David, as if he was shaking himself out of a trance. He tilted his head back, breaking eye contact, and placed his hands over the ones resting on his thighs, easing them away. Taking the hint, the kid dropped his hands to his own lap. He remained where he was at David's feet, his expression hovering on the edge of wounded.

"Christ." David wasn't sure whether he meant the word as a prayer or a curse. He closed his eyes and shook his head before chuckling dryly. "I'm trying to be a responsible adult here, you know. But, dammit, you're not making it easy." His lips quirked into a crooked smile as he reluctantly met Tim's piercing gaze. "Look, Tim, there are a dozen reasons why this simply can't happen. And, like I said, I'm the adult, so it's up to me to do the right thing and not take advantage of the situation."

Tim's forehead creased in confusion. "Take advantage? I don't understand."

David took a moment to choose his words carefully. "Well, I'm a lot older than you—"

"Twelve years. That's not so much of a difference."

"Well," David hedged, "if you were my age and I was forty-three, then, no, it wouldn't be that big of a deal. But you're only nineteen. You're just a kid."

"I see," Tim murmured.

"Right." David nodded, feeling hopeful that maybe he'd gotten his point across. "And you've been through so much, it wouldn't be right for me to encourage a physical relationship between us, no matter how much you might think you want one," he rushed, heading off any interruption. "You need time to figure things out without worrying about me."

"Then why did you kiss me?"

Why, indeed? David blinked at Tim, having no idea how to respond to the blunt question. It would probably be counterproductive to comment on how Tim's lips looked like soft pink strawberries, just begging to be nibbled. Likewise, mentioning how he dreamed nightly about the way that tight little ass would fit perfectly in his hands would just be rude. And not even on pain of death would he admit how the lost look Tim sometimes wore when he didn't think anyone was looking made David want to hold him close and never let go.

"I...." Really, what could he say? He didn't want to put any feelings of obligation onto Tim. The kid already had enough to deal with, starting with the stepfather who made David want to kill the man every time he thought about him. He opened his mouth to say something appropriately untrue, like that he'd hit his head getting into the Ferris wheel car and had a momentary, but catastrophic, lapse of sanity. But Tim was staring up at him with those big dark eyes which seemed, at times, so innocent, yet, at others, so knowing, and the truth spilled out before he could censor himself.

"I like you, kid. Hell," he swore, "I even think I'm falling in love with you. But I don't want you to feel pressured into offering more than you're ready to give." He glanced away, not wanting to see Tim's reaction to that particular bombshell. He'd tried his best. Now there was nothing left to do except go all in. "What I do know is that I really want you to stay, and not only until you patch things up with your stepfather or whatever else you might decide to do on that front." David leaned forward as he gave up on his good intentions. He finally met

Tim's intent gaze, no longer trying to run away from his feelings. "I mean I want you to stay. Forever if you'd like. Or at least for as long as you think you can put up with me."

"Stop calling me that."

David blinked at Tim, off-balance at the sharp retort. "Calling you what?"

"Kid." Tim watched him steadily, his gaze missing nothing. "I'm not one, no matter what you keep telling yourself."

Mortified at having been seen through so easily, David groaned. "Okay, ki… er, Tim." *Shit*, he thought, embarrassed at almost slipping after being so thoroughly called out. He wasn't sure how Tim had figured out the little trick he'd been using ever since they'd met to prevent his conscious mind from seeing Tim the same way his body so obviously did.

"Thank you."

David wanted to ask Tim what he was thanking him for, but the kid—old habits die hard—reared up and caught him off guard with a kiss that nearly blew his socks off. It was all tongue and heat, and it took all he had to put Tim off. Tim had relented only after being reminded that Suzanna was only a few feet away, separated from them by some very thin drywall.

Tim had gone to his lonely sofa reluctantly that night and every night afterward while Suzanna was there. But she and Bertie had left town a few days ago in a flurry of hugs for him, Tim, and Bobby, and David was running out of excuses. It wasn't that he didn't want to take Tim to his bed. He'd given up that ghost the night after the fair, and to be honest, it was nearly all he could think about. But something was holding him back. He couldn't really explain it, not even to himself. He just felt there was something Tim wasn't telling him about his life in New Mexico with his stepfather, some trauma he was repressing, and David worried taking that final, irrevocable step might trigger something they'd both regret. The kid had been less than pleased with his continued reluctance, trying every night to break his resolve with hot kisses and eager hands, but he refused to be rushed. They had all the time in the world, and if he was going to make love to Tim, he was determined that it would be perfect for both of them.

And if, in the meantime, he had begun resorting to ice-cold showers to cool off after one of Tim's patented attempts to make him cave, and found himself staring after the kid like he was the lovelorn teenager, he had no one but himself to blame.

Deliberately, David turned his back on the scene as Tim deftly handled the now-appeased mother and went back to insuring his store wouldn't run afoul of the agency tasked with insuring the health and safety of his employees.

I SMACKED the bar code labeling machine against yet another box of toddler-appropriate diapers, managing just barely to keep from punching a hole in the merchandise I was tagging. The monotonous task didn't take any concentration, allowing me to wallow in the new but increasingly familiar sensation that had been plaguing me ever since David had finally admitted he wanted more than merely a platonic connection.

Sexual frustration. Night after night of going to bed hard and aching for relief. While I still wasn't exactly sure of my response to the emotional aspect of David's admission, I was perfectly clear what it meant for our physical relationship. Except that, even two weeks on, nothing had happened beyond the kisses I managed to steal before being trundled off to my room like a misbehaving child sent to bed without dessert. While David had promised to stop thinking of me as a kid, or at least to stop referring to me as such, his thoughts were apparently more stubborn. My nightly attacks were intended to accustom David to the concept of physical intimacy between us, but in truth that was only my secondary purpose.

Mainly I was concerned I'd have to leave without ever having crossed that final threshold. So far I'd been able to supplement my constant need for vitamin B12 with food, but my supply of the pills that enabled my altered system to properly absorb the nutrient was dwindling. I had already gone through over a third of the stash Father Paul had given me. If—when—I had to leave, to isolate myself while I succumbed to the inevitable, I didn't want the regret of never having experienced that ultimate closeness with the man who had saved me. I didn't doubt David had done exactly that. If he hadn't found me, I might have physically survived, but I would have failed to achieve Father Paul's ultimate dream for me.

But what about my feelings for David? They remained, as ever, a mystery. David had told me he loved me, but did I love him in return? I still didn't know what the word truly meant. I was aware of the various forms which supposedly existed, such as the love between a parent and a child or between people who consented to cohabitate in a physical partnership. And although I was certain I felt more for David than mere friendship, I had no true reference to accurately categorize my feelings.

Emotions. I paused for a moment, my hand raised above yet another box of diapers. I had never thought in terms of them before, but now I seemed to do little else. This new outlook was certainly a result of David's influence, and not just his. Bobby, Patricia, Suzanna. Each person I had come into contact with since fleeing the Facility had offered me a different perspective on the human condition. Friendship, kindness, even affection—they had all given me something unique and priceless. But David was different. What I felt, yes, *felt*, for the man who had so selflessly taken me in was beyond anything I had the ability to properly conceptualize. Was it love? If not, it was probably the closest I would ever come to experiencing that particular sentiment.

Unfortunately, the insight did nothing to help me figure out a solution to my current predicament. I slapped the labeler against another box and tried not to think about the previous night, when I'd gotten as far as getting David's shirt off before he'd stubbornly put the brakes on my advances. David would likely stand up very well if he were ever captured and tortured for information. As I placed another label, I wondered idly how he would react if I told him that.

I had finished up the current row of diapers and was moving to the next highest shelf when I heard the approach of rapid footsteps. Looking in the direction of the sound, I blinked as Patricia rounded the end of the aisle where I was working and rushed toward me. My muscles tensed at the look of worry imprinted on her normally cheerful features, my body unconsciously readying itself to respond to an unknown threat.

"Tim, have you seen Bobby?" she asked.

"No. He should be due in right about now." I glanced at the large clock which hung on the back wall of the store to confirm what I already knew. It was shortly after 3:00 p.m., the scheduled time of Bobby's arrival.

"Yeah, no, he just came in." Patricia threw a glance over her shoulder like she was checking to make sure we weren't being overheard. "Oh, dear Jesus, I can't imagine who would do something like that to such a sweet boy."

I felt my gut tighten, immediately guessing what had her so upset. "Where is he?"

"He went straight to the break room." She knit her hands together anxiously for lack of anything better to do with them. "He was wearing a jacket, even as hot as it is outside, and had the collar pulled up. But I could still see the—"

Not waiting for her to finish, I handed her the labeling machine and hurried toward the room at the back of the store. I forcibly quieted my mind, deliberately focusing on the matter at hand to keep my newly discovered emotions under control. But I couldn't keep my fingers from curling into fists, my nails digging painfully into my palms as I anticipated what I would find when I finally saw Bobby. The sting helped me stay grounded and was the only thing that prevented me from running the last few yards.

Bobby looked up reflexively from the table where he was sitting as I burst into the room. He quickly turned away, but he hadn't been fast enough to hide the condition of his face from my sharp gaze. I walked slowly over to him, as much as to not frighten him as to give myself time to calm down.

"Did you go to school like this?" I asked as I reached out to take Bobby's chin in my fingers. Asserting gentle pressure, I angled his face toward the overhead light.

Bobby shook his head, the motion pulling against my fingers. "No. It happened after. I went home after school instead of coming straight here because I forgot my snack."

Growing as he was, Bobby had gotten in the habit of eating at the store during his break to hold him over until dinner. I often joined in, as I was no stranger to constant hunger. Patricia jokingly called us "the gluttony twins." I studied the rapidly darkening bruise that stretched from Bobby's left ear to the point of his chin. It was fresh. Clotted blood was crusted in the corner of his mouth. Whoever had hit Bobby had done so at least twice with a fist.

"Who?" My voice was nearly a growl, and I didn't trust myself to form a longer question. I asked only to be completely certain of my target. I had no doubt who was to blame, but information gathering had been one of my primary areas of instruction, and I fell back on it unconsciously. The muscles in my jaw were jumping, and it was a moment before I realized it was because I was clenching my teeth hard enough to shatter them.

Bobby jerked his head away and glared mutinously at the back wall. He was clearly trying to play the tough guy, to hold his troubles close to his chest, but the painful swelling that distorted his face made him look even younger than he normally did. Tears of humiliation welled up in his hazel eyes, further ruining the attempt.

"Bobby," I tried again, struggling to speak in the monotone I'd once found so natural.

"My dad," Bobby confirmed. "He was at home when I got there, yelling at Mom." He shifted in his seat, this time out of obvious discomfort. He winced as he tried to stretch the ache out of his jaw. "He hadn't touched her," Bobby continued, "but she was crying, so I shouted at him to stop. She told me to leave and go to work, but I—" His voice cracked on a sob, and the tears finally won as he squeezed his eyes shut. "I tried to help her. I remembered all the stuff you'd taught me, but I couldn't do anything. When I went to hit him, he got me first, and I just fell down like a little pussy!"

Are you a pussy, boy?

I was kneeling directly in front of the weeping boy before I was aware I'd moved. My arms went around Bobby's narrow shoulders hesitantly, but after a moment of resistance he collapsed against me. It was strange trying to console him when I had so rarely experienced it myself. But I did have one memory on which to draw. Karen, the woman with the auburn hair. Her death had weighed heavily on my young mind. Grief had been as foreign a concept to me as every other emotion, but Father Paul had explained that it was acceptable to feel, that it was okay to mourn. The scientist had pulled me onto his lap and held me for hours, even though I hadn't been able to work up a single tear to express my anguish.

Now, though, I thoroughly understood Bobby's frustration at being unable to help his mother. I felt I was at least partially to blame for his predicament. While I'd only wanted to give him a sense of control, I'd instead given him a false sense of confidence. I was sure Bobby would never have tried to directly interfere in his parents' fight if not for our martial arts lessons. And if this was my fault, then it was my responsibility to fix it.

"It's okay," I said, trying to project sympathy into my voice. I felt awkward as I patted Bobby on the back, but when he wrapped his arms around my waist, I was satisfied I'd expressed myself adequately. I was torn between doing what was best for Bobby right now and figuring out how to permanently remove the danger he faced at home. I decided that my friend's immediate well-being was the most important thing right then. "Come on," I said, moving back so I could see his face. "We need to get you to the hospital."

Bobby shook his head. "No. Really, I'm all right." He tried to move away, but I stopped him, placing insistent hands on his shoulders.

"Let's go. David will take us."

My tone was implacable, and Bobby seemed to recognize I wouldn't be swayed. He acquiesced with only a token display of male teenaged disgust at the prospect of being babied by doctors. David, in fact, was waiting for us right outside the door of the break room, his expression a mask of concern.

"Patricia told me about Bobby," David said, his gaze narrowing into an angry sliver of blue as he took in the condition of the boy's face.

"We should get him to the hospital," I replied, my hand still planted reassuringly on Bobby's shoulder.

David nodded. "We can call his mother when we get there." He turned to Patricia, whose pink face and red eyes revealed that she'd been crying and was on the verge of doing so again. "I probably won't be back. William is out today," he added, referring to his second-shift manager. "Can you close?"

"Sure." Her voice was hoarse, but she favored Bobby with a smile. "You feel better, sweetie, you hear?"

Bobby managed a nod and allowed David and I to hustle him out of the store. I held him close to my side to shield him from prying eyes as we walked through the shopping area and out the front entrance.

David was silent as he went ahead of us to his car, and stayed that way as he unlocked the door. "Covenant is the closest, so we'll go there," he said once we had all settled inside. The terse announcement was all he offered as he pulled out of the lot and sped toward the hospital.

I had installed Bobby in the back while I took the passenger seat next to David and angled myself so I could observe the injured boy. Bobby had propped his legs up and was stretched out the width of the car, the undamaged right side of his face pressed wearily into the headrest. He closed his eyes, and as I watched him carefully, searching for signs that the bruise was progressing abnormally, a plan took root in my mind.

The drive took only a few minutes with David pushing the speed limit wherever he could manage it. He pulled the car up to the curb next to a door which an overhead sign identified as the entrance to the emergency ward.

"Take him inside and notify the triage nurse," David instructed. "I'll join you as soon as I've found a place to park."

I got out of the car, and as I turned to help Bobby, I noticed David remove his cell phone from his pants pocket. Bobby was slightly unsteady once he was on his feet, grimacing as the change in position made the blood rush from his head. "Come on," I said softly, taking his arm in a supporting grip. "I've got you." I heard the car pull away as I shepherded him inside.

"I'm sorry," Bobby said under his breath. "I'm putting you through a lot of trouble."

"It's not your fault." *It's mine.* I kept the thought to myself, instead asking a different question. "Where do you think your father is now? Is he still at home with your mother?"

Bobby shook his head gingerly. "Uh-uh. He always goes to drink after he's smacked one of us around. He usually comes home even worse than when he left."

"Which bar?"

Bobby glanced up at me curiously, though his interest was apparently waylaid by the pounding in his head. He pressed a finger to the vein throbbing at his temple above his bruised jaw as he shrugged.

"I dunno. Probably that bar on Flint that sells shrimp. Um, S-Bar, I think it's called, or something lame like that." He looked toward the seating area, clearly more interested in getting off his feet than in talking about his abusive father. "He told me once that he likes to go there to get shit-faced."

I filed the information away and ushered Bobby toward the nearest molded-plastic chair. "Stay here. I'll let them know you need help." He barely acknowledged me as I walked away, his pain obviously growing worse. I headed quickly to the triage desk and waited impatiently while the nurse on duty finished up with the person in line ahead of me.

"What can I do for you?" the nurse asked when I stepped up to the edge of his desk.

"Male, thirteen, suffering from blunt force trauma to the left side of his face, most likely caused by impact from a fist." The nurse blinked at me, and I realized I probably shouldn't have been so precise. But I was well-versed in first-aid assessments and didn't want to waste time answering unnecessary questions.

"Um, okay." The nurse glanced around me. "That him? The kid in the black T-shirt and blue jeans?"

"Yes."

He peered up at me suspiciously. "You didn't do that to him, did you?"

"No," I answered around a clenched jaw.

The nurse seemed skeptical but didn't press the issue. "Okay, fill this out with his information. Are you over eighteen? Are you his relative?" he pressed when I nodded at the first question.

"No."

"Then you'll have to wait. I can't process him until his legal guardian arrives."

My hand balled into fists at my side, and I pinned the man with a razor-edged stare. "I don't know how long that will take, and he's in pain now."

The nurse blanched and sat back in his seat, but he didn't give in to the death glare being aimed his way. "I'm sorry, sir. His injuries obviously aren't life threatening, so there's nothing I can do. Those are the rules."

A hand pressed firmly against my back before I could threaten the nurse further. I tensed for an instant before recognizing the scent of David's aftershave.

"It's okay, Tim. I reached Bobby's mother. She's on her way." David tossed the man a friendly, if strained, smile. "I'll send her over to you as soon as she arrives."

The nurse nodded, clearly grateful for the interruption. Turning away from the unhelpful man at David's urging, I returned to the boy slumped awkwardly in the uncomfortable seat. David was barely a step behind me, and I stood at Bobby's side as he smiled reassuringly at the injured teen.

"Like I told that guy, your mom will be here shortly." David sat next to Bobby. After determining there was no imminent threat, I took up position on the opposite side. David ran a hand carefully through Bobby's shock of light blond hair. "Does it hurt a lot?" he asked.

Bobby felt at least well enough to roll his eyes at the dumb question. "What do you think?"

David chuckled softly and didn't say anything else as Bobby's eyes slid shut. He simply continued to gently rub the boy's head, and soon Bobby appeared well on his way to being fast asleep. Looking on in what I refused to acknowledge as jealousy, I silently watched David comfort Bobby, perversely wanting to experience the show of affection for myself. Seeing how easy David was with Bobby made me long for something similar, although I wanted far more than David would ever show the dozing boy.

I tracked the passage of time using my own internal measure and had counted just under fourteen minutes when the rotating door leading to the outside began to turn. A disheveled-looking blond woman tumbled into the ward and looked around with frantic hazel eyes the exact same shade as her son's. David stood to catch her attention, and she hurried over to us.

"Mrs. Wood."

"Oh my God," Grace sobbed. "I didn't know it was this bad, or I never would have let him leave the house."

Her eyes were red, and the mascara that wasn't caked on her eyelashes ran in black streaks down her cheeks. I wondered with some malice how she'd managed to see well enough to drive.

David clearly shared my irritation, his shoulders hunching at her explanation. "So he just should have stayed around the man who did this to him?" His voice was rough with barely restrained anger.

Grace's hair flew about as she rapidly shook her head. "No!" she shouted. "Of course not!" She glanced around, apparently worried that she was being disruptive, but the waiting room was virtually empty, save for us. The few other people who were there were too wrapped up in their own problems to pay us much attention. "Don left the house right after...." She looked down at her son, who had woken up at her shout and was peering up at her through his one good eye. The left one was being obstructed by the rapidly swelling tissue of his cheek. Grace immediately burst into tears, and David and I stepped back to give her room as she collapsed in the seat next to her son and drew him to her chest. "Oh, baby, I'm so sorry."

Bobby didn't respond, but he didn't try to pull away as his mother rocked him like he was a little boy.

"Ma'am," David interrupted softly, "you need to fill out the hospital paperwork so he can be seen to."

I watched as David deftly maneuvered the crying woman away from her son and over to the triage desk. I stood guard at Bobby's side, feeling a need to protect him even from his own mother.

"Thanks for bringing me. I guess Mom'll take it from here."

I glanced down Bobby. "Are you sure? We can wait until the doctor comes for you."

Bobby shook his head. "Nah. It might take forever. ERs are always slow as hell."

The swearing was an obvious attempt to project an air of maturity, but Bobby's efforts failed miserably beneath the pathos of his bruised face. I accepted the reasoning at face value, knowing he wouldn't appreciate thinking I was treating him like a little kid. "Okay. I'll tell David we can go." I reached down and tousled Bobby's hair, imitating the gesture David had used on both of us at varying points in time. "If you need anything, anything at all, you can always call me. You know that, right?"

Bobby threw me a lopsided grin, stretching his lips as much as the pain would allow. "Yeah, okay."

I nodded once and went to gather David, who was standing next to Grace. I pulled him aside while she was talking to the triage nurse. "Bobby said we can go. That he'll be okay here with his mother."

David looked over his shoulder toward Bobby and smiled in response when the boy waved. "Sure. Let me tell Grace we're leaving."

I waited for David by the exit and watched in irritation as the woman threw her arms around his neck and hugged him for what seemed to me an inordinate length of time. I turned away right as the embrace was ending and was on the other side of the rotating door before David reached me. I sensed David's presence behind me but didn't look around, worried that my expression—or lack thereof—might give me away.

"Are you all right? You seem a little… agitated." David sighed wearily. "Guess that's not surprising after everything that's happened."

I turned and stared at him, amazed he could read my mood so easily. "Yes, I guess I am." Even to my own ears, I sounded wooden. I consciously relaxed my tense muscles and tried to inject some casualness into my tone. "Do you mind if I walk back to the house?" My face was stiff as I pushed my lips into a smile.

David's expression clouded with concern at the request. "Walk back? It's nearly twenty minutes by car. It will probably take you an hour on foot."

"I'll be okay. I just…." I shrugged. "I want to be alone for a little while, you know, to clear my head."

David looked unconvinced, but after a long moment he nodded. "If you're sure. Here." He reached in his pocket and pulled something out. "Take my cell phone. Call me at the house right away if you need me to pick you up."

I stared at the outstretched hand holding the phone. Then, before I could think better of it, I wrapped my arms around David's waist and hugged him tightly. I let my eyelids drift shut, simply enjoying the feel of his solid frame against me. For a brief moment I thought about simply going home with him and abandoning my plan. If I really were nothing but an average teenager, I wouldn't even consider doing something like this. But I wasn't, and for once I was glad of that fact. I was haunted by Bobby's bruised face, by the humiliation and pain in his eyes, and the memory strengthened my resolve. I forced myself to let David go.

"Thanks," I said, taking the cell. I slipped it into my back pocket. A large hand rested against my cheek, and I looked up to meet David's soft blue gaze.

"I'll see you back at home."

Home. David was right. That's what the town house had come to mean to me. A place I could return to, knowing I would always be welcome. But would it remain open to me after what I was intending to do? I buried the disturbing thought away and nodded, feeling the palm shift against my cheek.

With a parting smile, David turned to leave. I watched until he had found his car in the hospital parking lot and driven off before spinning away in the opposite direction. With my destination firmly in mind, I felt what little humanity I'd gained slowly fall away.

EIGHTEEN

AFTER CONSULTING the map application on David's phone, it didn't take me long to reach the bar where Bobby had indicated his father most likely had gone. I'd run all the way from the hospital, but my heart rate was steady and there was no sweat on my skin to betray my exertion as I stood outside the weathered building that housed the "S-Bar." The front entrance was adorned with a tacky, peeling image of a small crustacean dressed like a tough sailor. A glance at the sign protruding above the roof confirmed that I was, indeed, in the right place, and the second I opened the heavy wooden door, the odor of shrimp assaulted me. I felt a moment of doubt as I hesitated just inside the entrance, realizing I had no idea what Bobby's father looked like. But as I glanced around, a lone figure hunched at the bar caught my eye.

The man pushed back from the counter, the metal leg of his stool making a skin-crawling screech as it scraped across the tiled floor. He looked to be in his late thirties to early forties, his dark brown hair lightly streaked with gray. He wore a dingy plaid shirt over a loose pair of jeans, and his scuffed boots proclaimed his profession as a construction worker or something equally labor intensive. As soon as I saw the man's face, I knew this was how Bobby would look in thirty years. The resemblance between Bobby and his mother was mostly in their coloring, but Bobby was a dead ringer for his father. How did Bobby feel, I wondered, knowing he meant so little to the man whose face he wore?

Although S-Bar wasn't exactly upscale, it seemed a respectable enough place. Other people were ensconced around the bar, but I also noticed a family in the corner, the mother and father chatting quietly as their barely school-aged child struggled to peel the shrimp piled in the bucket on their table. The location was less than ideal for what I was planning. I needed someplace darker and more isolated. It was still fairly early in the afternoon given the time of year, but that didn't seem to affect the amount of alcohol Bobby's father was imbibing. Since he seemed in no hurry to leave, I took a table and ordered a snack so as not to arouse anyone's suspicion.

The hours ticked away, but fortunately S-Bar was apparently the type of place where people were expected to linger. No one gave me a second glance as I nibbled slowly on a platter of ribs and the waitress brought me a steady supply of soft drinks. I began to grow concerned about how long this was taking, knowing that David had likely expected me home hours ago. The fact that he hadn't already called me showed how much he trusted me. I felt even worse at how badly I was planning on abusing that trust. As I considered how best to proceed, Bobby's father suddenly rose from his stool. He slammed back the last of his drink before reaching out to grab the edge of the counter in order to keep from falling to the floor.

Finally. I had already paid my bill, so all I had to do was wait until Bobby's father had exited the bar and then follow behind. The sun had mostly disappeared by that point, and the street lamps cast long shadows that made hiding an easy task. Bobby's father had paused a few feet from the door and stood there for a moment, unaware he was being watched. I waited patiently until he began to walk away before following him, instinctively using the swiftly oncoming darkness to hide my presence.

The man headed away from the main street, turning instead down a quieter side road. The number of people dwindled until no one was about except for me and my target. I could easily take him down right here and now. There would be no witnesses. But, though I longed to make his resemblance to his son complete by inflicting some damage of my own, instinct and training prompted me to gather more information about my quarry first.

Infiltration and data acquisition will be a critical aspect of your missions, TM 05637. Such had been one of the first directives the general had given me when I'd grown old enough to truly understand what I was.

228

You mean spying, Father Paul had countered, and the general hadn't denied it. I had been groomed since childhood to be an assassin, but also a spy, though my instruction in that arena had been far from complete. While both of those skills could be useful to me at present, it was the latter I decided to employ right then. The former could be saved for a more appropriate time.

Stealth came to me as naturally as breathing, and Bobby's father remained oblivious to the fact that he had picked up a tail. Not that I had to try very hard to keep from being seen. The man wobbled unsteadily as he walked, suffering the effects of the many drinks he'd finished before leaving S-Bar. My target followed no discernible path, turning corners seemingly at random as he led me ever farther from the commercial part of town. After nearly thirty aimless minutes, he abruptly veered down an alley with more purposeful steps. I could hear the noise of a crowd, which grew abruptly louder as we emerged into an unexpected bustle of activity.

The street was blocked to traffic, and I paused at the edge of the sidewalk as I looked around to get my bearings. Safe from the intrusion of cars, bodies moved aimlessly in the roadway. The area thronged with people, but there was something off about the atmosphere. The streetlights flickered sporadically, lending only the occasional spot of illumination, but even those rare places were avoided. Attempts to meet the gazes of those around me were put off as everyone looked furtively aside. I quickly grasped that the evasion was purposeful and no one wanted to be observed. Although I couldn't see any faces clearly, I could tell everyone nearby was of the male gender, and in the darkest corners of the crowd, several figures were clandestinely engaged in activity of a sexual nature. Intrigued, I reacquired my target and watched as he disappeared into the building directly across from where I stood. Glancing up, I read the sign above the door.

Club Horus.

This was certainly an unexpected turn of events. Why was Bobby's father going into a place obviously frequented by gay men? The implications were profound. Bobby's father was—what was the term? Right. *Closeted.* He was married and had a child, but he was apparently living an enormous lie. Was this the reason behind his violent behavior toward his family? It was possible, I supposed. Self-loathing and guilt could prompt one to do awful things. I was no stranger to the compulsion, as my very presence there attested. Of course, there was the question of why he felt the need to hide. It was the twenty-first century. Homosexuals had become fairly common fixtures in society, although they weren't necessarily always accepted, and I knew some places were more tolerant than others. Perhaps Lubbock was not one of those places, which might explain the seeming need these men felt to operate under cover of night. The circuitous route we had taken to reach the area suddenly made perfect sense. This was a part of his life Bobby's father clearly wanted to keep firmly under wraps.

I took David's cell phone out of my pocket and snapped a picture of the sign, ignoring the dirty looks thrown my way as the flash glared for a bright instant. Moving quickly, I crossed the street and followed my quarry into the club. The doors had been propped open, leaving my way unobstructed as I stepped inside. It took me only a moment to relocate Bobby's father, having correctly guessed that the bar was the first place he'd go. Loud music washed over me, the floor beneath my feet vibrating from the overwoofered bass. The tang of perspiration hung in the air, nearly overwhelming my heightened senses as I went farther inside.

The dim interior seemed to move like it was a living thing, the play of lights cutting intermittently through the darkness and making it dance. Shadowy figures in varying stages of undress writhed in only the barest acknowledgement of the beat. I briefly wondered what it would be like to be here with David, our bodies pressed together in the dark, pretending to dance as we emulated a more intimate act. As soon as I thought of the man waiting so patiently for me back at the town house, I was flooded with guilt. I had no business being here when I could be at home, spending a quiet evening doing something that didn't involve following strangers to bars in the hopes of finding something incriminating. But this was precisely the type of work I had been trained to do, and for once I wasn't acting on any orders except my own. I was doing this for Bobby, because my friend needed my help. That thought sustained me as I focused my attention on the man who'd led me here.

Watching him order yet another drink, my resolve hardened. This was the man who had hurt Bobby, who had willingly terrorized his own wife and son. And yet, in the face of such a constant threat, Bobby had had the guts to stand up for his mother even at the cost of his own safety. My doubt bled away and was replaced with cold focus. I had a mission to accomplish, and it was of the utmost importance that I succeed. I swiftly considered the most optimal way to make my approach.

Bobby's father remained hunched over his drink, but when his attention wavered from his glass for the briefest instant, I had all the information I required. He glanced blearily at a red-haired kid—only a year or so older than me—who was passing the bar on his way to the dance floor. With clinical precision, I calculated the exact length of time my target's gaze lingered on the young man's ass, and my best avenue of approach became immediately evident. A quick run of my fingers through my hair mussed it out of its combed neatness. I pulled my shirt from my pants and unbuttoned it at the top and bottom until it gaped midway down my chest. Finally, I plastered what I calculated to be a friendly yet lascivious smirk on my face and sauntered up to my unsuspecting prey.

Bobby's father wasn't an unattractive man by any measure. He had passed on his looks to his son, though his own face was creased with weariness. His eyes—dull green, I could see as I got closer—gazed vacantly at nothing. He sat guard over his glass as though it was some precious treasure, seemingly oblivious to the pounding music and the sweaty bodies writhing beneath the distorting flash of strobe lights. He didn't look uncomfortable about being there, however, signifying that he was not unaccustomed to the club or its particular clientele.

Operation Safeguard: Phase One.

"Can you spare one of those for me?"

Bobby's father looked up at me in surprise, obviously unaccustomed to being picked up in a place where looks and youth were everything. I was aware I possessed all of the physical attributes that would make me a primary target for being hit on. He, on the other hand, was past his prime and would likely be caught off guard at being approached by a kid so much younger than himself. I was counting on that fact to keep him as wrong-footed as possible.

Sure enough, he blinked at me in confusion as I stopped beside him, standing unnecessarily close. He followed my gaze and looked down at his drink before glancing back up at me. I favored him with a hooded gaze and what I hoped was a sexy grin.

"You want some of this?" he asked, gesturing with the half-finished drink in his right hand.

"Yeah. What is it?" I leaned over, ostensibly to get a whiff of the drink, taking care to let my bared chest brush against his shoulder.

"Whiskey." His eyes narrowed shrewdly. "What, you can't afford your own? Or did you forget your fake ID at home?"

I allowed my grin to change into a playfully guilty smile, trying to forget the source of the marked improvement in my emotional range. "You got me. So can you buy me one?"

He rolled his eyes but raised his glass in a signal to the bartender and held up two fingers. The bartender threw me a dirty look, but apparently decided he wasn't all that interested in asking for proof of my legality. Given the dull expressions I'd seen on some of the other patrons' faces, I was certain liquor laws were the least of those the club was breaking.

"How old are you?" Bobby's father asked. "Exactly how many years in jail will this buy me?"

"I'm nineteen." I shrugged. "It's so stupid, you know? If this was Louisiana, I could drink no problem."

His forehead creased. "Um, pretty sure the legal age is still twenty-one even over there."

"Not if you pretended to be my dad. Then you could totally buy me a drink."

He grimaced. It was perhaps a tactical error to remind him that he was a father, but I wanted him to feel uncomfortable. "Yeah, well, I'm not." He threw down a couple of bills as the bartender set two glasses in front of him. "Here, enjoy."

"You're not going to let me drink alone, are you?"

Bobby's father glanced at me askance. "Look, kid, why don't you go find someone your own age to party with?"

"Nothing wrong with your age." The conversation bore an awkward resemblance to the one I'd so recently had with David, and I hastily moved it to a different topic. "Besides, there's no harm in sitting here enjoying a drink, is there?" I swallowed the whiskey in one gulp, peripherally aware of the burning sensation as the alcohol passed down my throat. The discomfort I'd been made to endure during my training had been far worse, however, and I didn't even blink as I set the glass back on the countertop. Licking my lips, I winked at Bobby's father, who was staring at me, impressed.

"Damn, kid. You can really hold your liquor."

"So, buy me another…, um, what's your name? I'm Peter."

He laughed and pushed the other full glass over to me. "It's Don. Help yourself, Peter." He watched me with obvious fascination, apparently bemused by the strange kid who perched on the stool next to him and downed the second glass as easily as he had the first. "Another?"

Nodding, I noticed a few subtle clues that informed me I was playing this just right. Don's pupils had dilated, and I could tell by the speeding pace of his pulse that it wasn't merely the alcohol causing the physiological reaction. Under the pretense of reaching for one of the snack bowls arrayed along the bar counter, I leaned forward so my unbuttoned shirt gaped open. Don's gaze tracked my movement keenly as he ordered yet another round of drinks.

"Thanks," I said before palming my third glass. My hand was steady, my body having been designed to withstand most toxins, including alcohol.

"My pleasure." He licked his lips, thoughts clearly turning to the possible outcomes of this unexpected encounter. "Look, kid, is there a reason you're trying to get wasted on my dime?"

Ignoring the twinge in my gut at the familiar moniker, I threw him a sloppy grin. Carefully slurring my words, I bent toward him so my lips were directly against his ear. "I'm trying to work up the courage to ask you to take me out back and fuck me."

Don reared back in shock, but the hopeful gleam in his eyes gave him away. "Why me?" he asked, shaking his head a second later, as though he couldn't believe he was questioning his good fortune.

"Why not you?" I gave him a slow once-over, deliberately lingering over the suspicious bulge at his crotch. "You're hot for a, you know, older guy."

I laughed to cover my gulp as I swallowed the bile that abruptly rose up into the back of my throat. Desperate for a moment to gather myself, I imagined I was having this exchange with David and not a stranger. Though I'd been trained in the art of using seduction to gather information, the thought of such calculated intimacy had always made me uneasy. If this were David I was flirting with, though, I'd do so gladly. It would be amusing to watch him blush and stammer, just like he did whenever we kissed and made out. But doing this with the man who had treated Bobby so terribly was making me nauseous. Still, I was determined to see this through for the sake of my friend. I licked my lips before drawing the bottom one between my teeth in a playful nibble.

"What," I pressed, "you got a better offer waiting for you at home?"

The purposeful dig quickly bore fruit, but the wince that nearly pegged the man as a normal, remorseful human being soon twisted into hateful disgust. "The fuck I do. Ain't got no one at home but a dirty whore and her useless brat."

I stared down at my hand, consciously straightening it to lay flat against the bar instead of balling it into a fist. "So, what," I drawled, "you got an old lady and a kid?" I raised and lowered my shoulders in a boneless shrug. "I don't care if you're bi."

"I ain't no goddamn bisexual," Don grated out. "I was stupid this one fucking time. Now I'm stuck." He slammed back the neglected drink in his hand and glared at the empty glass, squeezing his hand around it like he was trying to make it shatter. "Stuck with that stupid bitch and her stupid kid." Lifting the cold, wet surface to his forehead, he closed his eyes. "I keep thinking, 'Leave. Leave 'em, and live like you want to.' But her daddy told me he'd shoot me in the nuts if I ever abandoned his little girl. His little whore." The sturdy glass dropped to the counter and rolled away intact as Don shot me a dark, blurry glance. "But she ain't here, and the brat ain't here." He pushed back from the bar and stood, the brief sobriety he'd shown earlier nowhere to be found as he clutched at the counter for support. "You said you wanted to fuck. So let's fuck."

I didn't protest as Don grabbed my arm in an overly tight grip and dragged me through the writhing crowd toward the door. Empathy. It wasn't an emotion in which I was well-versed, as it required being able to see and experience the world from another's point of view. I hadn't yet completely figured out how to experience life through my own eyes as opposed to through those who'd controlled me for so long. But I supposed it couldn't be easy for a man to be forced to deny himself in such a way. I remembered David telling me what it was like growing up in his father's house, having to hide the truth about himself for so long before finding the courage to live it. But David had never resorted to violence against his father when he'd felt trapped in his necessary lie. Don could not be excused. Any desire I felt to understand how the man could inflict his vicious frustration so easily on his own family paled in comparison to my need to guarantee Bobby's safety.

Don led me back out into the street, but instead of heading the way we'd first come, he tugged me alongside the front of the building until we reached the narrow alley separating Club Horus from its abandoned, run-down neighbor. I pretended I was having difficulty keeping pace with the taller man, dragging my steps just enough to demonstrate that I was agreeably tipsy. We sloshed through some questionable puddles, the stench of garbage and urine strong in the air. By the time we reached the back of the alley, the sound of the partying crowd was far away. The narrow space was dark and secluded, and it suited me perfectly.

Operation Safeguard: Phase Two.

"Now, then," Don growled, thrusting me against a rough brick wall. I could feel the bass of the music from the club vibrating through the very structure of the building. "I think it's time you put that smart mouth of yours to better use than talking." He reached down and unfastened his pants, taking only long enough to pull his penis through the slit in his boxers and out into the open before he moved forward to pin me in place. The alcohol-fueled confusion on his face remained long after he found himself suddenly slammed against the unfinished brick. Before he could figure out how he had ended up in that position when a moment ago he'd been the one about to do the trapping, I pressed an unnaturally strong arm against his windpipe with deadly force. Soon his only concern was trying desperately to breathe.

"What the—" Don gasped.

"Shut up." My tone was devoid of all emotion. The lessons I'd learned in the past month slipped away all too easily, and I watched dispassionately as he struggled to inhale. Our position was eerily similar to how I'd trapped Bobby when we'd first met, but I didn't let the uncomfortable memory sway me from my purpose. Don attempted to speak again, so I pushed harder, digging my forearm into his throat until his eyes bulged with the need for air. Relenting only enough to keep my target conscious, I stared up into his terrified gaze.

"Does it hurt? Are you afraid?" His petrified green eyes gave me my answer. "Good. Maybe now you'll know how Bobby feels when you choke him." Reaching up with my free hand, I grabbed a fistful of hair and pounded Don's head back against the wall. "Or when you hit him so hard that he's bruised for days."

"Please," Don moaned, barely audible around the crushing pressure against his windpipe. His fingers scrabbled desperately at my arm, but I remained impervious to his feeble struggles.

"Did your son ever beg you like that? Beg you to stop hurting him? How about your wife? The one you claim to hate." I struck his head harder against the wall. "Did you ever tell her how you felt? Or do you just like using her and Bobby as punching bags too much to stop?"

The fear was mixed with confusion. "How do you know them?" He gasped harshly. "Who are you?"

"I'm here to protect your son. That's all you need to know, besides this." I moved closer, until our faces were mere inches apart. "You have two choices: leave them, or swear that you'll never hurt them again. Because if you don't, not only will I tell your wife and son that you enjoy fucking other men in dirty alleys, but I will wreak ten times the pain on you that you've inflicted on them."

It took little effort for me to push up on Don's throat enough so his feet began to leave the ground. Impassively, I watched the terror and agony on his face as he slowly began to choke to death. It was only a few seconds, but I knew from experience it would feel like hours to him. I unhurriedly lowered him to his feet and stepped back until I was no longer supporting his weight. Don fell to his knees, his trousers instantly becoming soiled from the filth slicked over the ground. I stood motionlessly over him as he coughed spastically, alternately sucking in desperate gusts of air down his abused airway.

"Do we have an understanding?"

Don peered up at me through watery green eyes, his expression a mix of humiliation and lingering panic. But his rage made a swift return, and he laughed hoarsely as he ejected the spittle that had formed in his mouth as a reaction to his greedy panting "What are you, some kind of freak?" Shakily, he got his legs beneath him and lurched to his feet. "Some kind of faggot freak?"

I merely raised an eyebrow at the ironic taunt. "I said, do we have an understanding?"

He spat again. "Fuck your understanding. Fuck my wife, fuck my son, and fuck you!" He rose to his full height, which gave him a four-inch advantage. "You think this scared me? Huh, you little punk?" He grinned evilly as he balled his hand into a meaty fist. "All you did was sober me up. Now I'm going to teach your bitch ass a lesson."

The threat was the last thing he managed to say before he found himself slammed against the wall, thrown there by the inhumanely fast punch that landed squarely in his solar plexus. What breath he'd been able to recover fled, and his face twisted at the pain that erupted in his gut.

I waited until Don had regained his senses enough to look up at me in shock before delivering another punch, this time to his left jaw. I watched blankly as his head whipped around, knowing he would soon be sporting a precise match for the bruise currently marring his son's face. He reeled from the brutal right hook, and I took a handful of hair to pull his head around until I could look directly into his face. Don's eyes were stunned, nearly rolling back in his head. I jerked his head back-and-forth by the hair to make sure he was paying attention.

"Do we have an understanding?" I repeated for a third time, speaking slowly to be sure the dazed man comprehended the question.

When I received a weak nod in response, I let go, and Don dropped facedown into a foul-smelling puddle. I stepped back to prevent the murky liquid from splashing onto my shoes, not wanting to ruin the clothes David had bought for me. I started to turn away, but a thought made me pause. Looking back down at the prone figure, I imparted what I hoped would be well-heeded advice.

"As for that choice I gave you, if you're smart, you'll pick the first option." Don might be in pain, he might simply be lashing out against the raw deal life had thrown him, but he had hurt someone I cared about, and I wanted him gone. "And if you're ever tempted to call me a liar…."

I held up David's phone so Don could see the picture I'd taken of the club's sign. It was too bad that I hadn't actually caught him in the shot, but I hoped he was too disoriented to call my bluff. This time I didn't look back as I left him to ponder my ultimatum.

DAVID SHOOK his head as he realized this was the fifth time he'd checked the clock on his DVD player in the last two minutes. He pressed the channel button on the cable remote, flipping through stations mindlessly as he tapped the finger of his free hand on the cordless phone resting next to him on the couch. His gaze traveled from the clock to the silent handset and back to the clock as it had every few minutes since he'd flopped there to watch TV and kill time.

"Come on," he muttered to himself. "Ring already."

He'd been home for hours waiting for Tim to either call for a pick up or to walk through the front door. He hadn't wanted to leave the kid alone outside the hospital, but Tim was a big boy, and heavens knew he could take care of himself, even if he'd decided to take a god-awful long detour somewhere on his way home. David couldn't help but worry, and he was seconds away from breaking the promise he'd made to himself not to act like a mother hen and call Tim first.

David had never seen Tim in the state he'd been in since Bobby had come to the store that afternoon. Tim had never been overly demonstrative, but lately he'd really started to open up and act more, well, normal. When they first met, he'd mentally applied the adjective "robotic" to the kid's behavior more than once. David didn't know why Tim had been so socially awkward, but whatever had been the cause, he'd made a complete U-turn in the past month. The way he interacted with the other employees at the BBW, the way he was with Bobby, no one would know he'd ever been anything other than a regular—if somewhat introverted—nineteen-year-old.

But the way Tim had acted today after seeing Bobby, it was like he'd completely shut down any ability he had to show emotion. Although he'd been a supportive presence for the injured boy, Tim had been distant, his expression never once revealing the anger he must have felt. Hell, David thought, he'd wanted to run out, find Bobby's father, and plant his fist in the man's face himself multiple times, but Tim could have been watching the weather report for all the reaction he'd shown. Frankly, the kid's behavior had scared him a little. He'd been almost relieved when Tim had wanted some time alone to gather his thoughts, proving that he was, in fact, deeply bothered by the whole situation. And the spontaneous hug Tim had given him had gone a long way toward reassuring him that the blankness was the kid's way of dealing with the helplessness he must have been feeling. Still, David really wanted to know where Tim had been for the past five hours and how long it would be until he came home.

David was staring at the phone, lost in thought, when he heard the front door open. He sprang up from the couch and spun toward the sound, breathing a huge sigh of relief when Tim walked in and closed the door behind him. He slumped back against the door, his gaze fixed on the floor like he hadn't noticed David was there. David opened his mouth to speak, but the kid's appearance completely distracted him from whatever he'd been about to say.

Sexy. Disheveled. There were other words he could have thought of to describe the way Tim looked, but they all would have expressed the same thing. The kid looked like he'd either just been fucked or was begging for it. He had on the same clothes he'd been wearing all day, but now the white shirt he'd worn a dozen times to meet the store's employee dress code was unbuttoned halfway down his chest. Smooth olive skin peeked through the gaping fabric, teasing David with the suggestion that the slightest tug would reveal a flat brown nipple. The shirt was also no longer tucked into the waistband of his jeans, and the bottom two buttons were open so every breath revealed a flash of taut stomach. Tim's dark hair was in even more disarray than it usually was, as though someone had run their fingers through it repeatedly. Maybe to hold him still for a kiss. David sucked in a breath and shook himself when he noticed he was both drooling and seeing green.

"Tim, are you okay?" he asked, cringing at the harsh dryness of his voice.

Tim finally glanced up at him, the lack of surprise on his face telling David he'd known he wasn't alone. Tim gazed at him for a long moment, his expression giving nothing away and his eyes showing not even a hint of recognition. It was all David could do to stop himself from going over and giving the kid a hard shake to jolt him out of wherever he'd gone in his head. Instead, he steeled himself against the cold stare warning him to keep away and walked slowly in Tim's direction. As he got closer, he could see the kid's entire body was rigid, like a coiled spring ready to snap at the slightest provocation. Tim looked dangerous, and for the first time, David was actually afraid of him. But he continued to close the distance between them, a reassuring hand outstretched in front of him as if he were approaching a skittish feral cat.

"Tim," he repeated, and the effect was instantaneous, like a switch had been flipped. The kid seemed to collapse in on himself even though he never moved. Thick dark lashes fanned across his cheeks as he closed his eyes, his shoulders rising as he sucked in a deep breath. When Tim looked up again, the dead-eyed stranger was gone, and in his place was the young man David had fallen in love with. Tim shuddered, his face twisting like he was on the verge of tears. The fear vanished in an instant, and David felt his heart ache at Tim's distress. He reached out and pulled the kid toward his chest. "It's okay," he whispered, wrapping Tim in his arms. "I've got you."

"I should have been there." The words were barely audible with Tim's face buried into his shoulder. "I was supposed to protect him. She told me to."

He frowned. "Who told you to?"

"Suzanna."

David sighed and held Tim tighter, resting his chin on Tim's head. He'd known those two had grown close during her visit, but he hadn't fully appreciated how much influence his mother had gained over the kid. "Tim, there was nothing you could have done. We just have to let Bobby know we're here for him if he needs us." He lifted his head when he felt Tim pull away and looked down to meet the kid's gaze. Tim's large eyes were haunted, and he looked unspeakably young.

"Is that all? Is that all I should have done?"

David felt a chill travel down his spine. "Tim, what is it?" He took the kid's face between his hands so he couldn't turn away. "Where did you go after I left you?"

Tim's mouth opened and shut like he desperately wanted to say something but the words wouldn't come. David wanted to tell him it was safe to confide in him, that he could say anything and it would be okay, but he didn't want to push. Tim had apparently been even more bothered by what had happened to Bobby than he'd known. But why? Had it brought something painful up from Tim's past? The kid still hadn't told him everything that had gone down between him and his stepfather. Had Tim been physically abused too? David shuddered to think of the kid being subjected to the sort of damage Bobby's father had inflicted on the young boy. And beyond that, what other horrors might Tim have experienced at his stepfather's hands?

David's imagination threatened to run away with him as he tried to guess what had made the kid so skittish, and he impatiently reined it in. He desperately wanted to know what had happened to the kid after the hospital, but if he wanted Tim's trust he would have to earn it. Subjecting him to an interrogation was definitely the wrong way to go about it. So when Tim merely shook his head in response to his question and leaned into him, he forced himself to accept that he was destined to remain unenlightened. He could feel the weight of the slim body as it rested heavily against him, and David was content to stand there patiently, stroking Tim's back as he held him.

"May I sleep with you?"

David almost missed the question, his mind preoccupied with the effort to bury his disappointment at Tim's reticence. But when he finally caught what Tim had asked, his body froze while his libido instantly went from zero to sixty. He suddenly became painfully aware that he and Tim were pressed close together, their bodies touching from almost head to toe. The layer of clothes between them seemed grossly inadequate, offering no hindrance to the heat radiating between their bodies. David groaned silently as his cock inopportunely decided to sit up and take notice.

"Um...." *Shit*. He wanted to say no. He should say no. This was a very, very bad idea. Tim was simply feeling vulnerable and in need of comfort, which he'd ordinarily be happy to give. But this definitely wasn't the time for anything physical, not with Tim's reluctance to share what was bothering him and David's conflicting desire to figure out what was going on. He tried to move back slowly so as not to make it seem like he was trying to break free of the embrace, but the kid's arms were suddenly a vise around his back, trapping him firmly in place.

"No, not like that," Tim murmured. He titled his head back so David could see his face. While he seemed calmer, he was still raw around the edges. "Just to sleep." He dropped his gaze for a moment before glancing back upward, cheeks pink with a faint blush. "I don't want to be alone tonight."

Weak. That's what he was. David would have berated himself for how quickly he caved at the shy request, but he knew it was pointless. From the moment he'd picked Tim up off the side of the road, he hadn't been able to deny him anything. This time was no different. And, after all, how hard would it be to simply hold the kid while they slept and keep whatever demons were chasing him at bay? David shifted as his burgeoning arousal throbbed, refusing to be ignored. *Damn hard.* He sighed, resigning himself to a sleepless night of self-denial.

"Yeah, okay."

David stood there for a long while after Tim finally let him go and disappeared upstairs, trying to figure out how he'd gotten himself into this crazy situation. The sound of the shower mocked him as he slowly mounted the stairs. Grumbling, he called himself all kinds of idiot. How in the hell did he think he would survive this? Well, procrastinating would get him nowhere. He was usually pretty quick to fall asleep, especially when he was as emotionally tired as he was right then. The roller coaster of anger and helplessness he'd felt by turns that day had left him feeling drained, and dealing with Tim's odd mood swings certainly hadn't helped. He'd already showered, having done so immediately after coming home, so all he had to do was go to bed and hope he passed out before Tim joined him. He went up to his bedroom, and then hastily got himself out of his sweats and into his pajamas, attempting to do precisely that.

Of course, his plan failed miserably as his imagination eagerly supplied him with endless images of the kid in the shower, naked, with water coursing over his bare skin. David lay there, disgusted with himself as he grew harder with every passing second. While Tim would normally be thrilled to find him in such a defenseless state, he was certain sex would be the furthest thing from the kid's mind tonight. Hell, he'd said as much. Turning on his side, David pounded his fist into the pillow, using it as a proxy as he metaphorically beat his gutter thoughts into submission.

The shower finally cut off, and a few minutes later David was faced with the damp, half-clothed reality standing uncertainly in his doorway. Tim had fortunately pulled on a pair of pajama bottoms, apparently serious about just sleeping and nothing else. Ignoring the ache of his neglected arousal, David forced his lips into a reassuring smile and pulled back the bedspread in welcome. Tim returned the smile with a subdued version of his own and slipped beneath the covers. David had expected some awkwardness as they figured out how to share the space without making any unwanted contact, but the kid instantly wrapped his arms and legs around him like he was afraid David would try to get away. The lingering warmth of the shower only enhanced the heat which exuded naturally from him. It penetrated through the thin material of their sleep clothes and seeped into David's skin, filling his senses, just like the scent of soap and something else that was undeniably Tim.

"Good night," Tim whispered.

David felt overheated and overwhelmed. Sweat beaded on his forehead and plastered his pajamas to his skin. He was glad he'd worn a top, the need for self-preservation winning out over habit. The mere thought of the kid's bare skin against his was enough to drive him insane, and was simply one more thing he didn't need right then. He smothered a groan as soft breath wafted like a gentle kiss across the exposed skin at the base of his throat where it peeked above the neckline of his top. For a solid month, he'd gone to sleep every night dreaming about this—Tim in his bed, the young, supple body pressing close as David showed him how very much he wanted him. It was all his for the taking.

David knew the kid wouldn't refuse him if he decided to pursue something more than sleep, but he would never be able to forgive himself. Tim simply needed him to be there. And though he'd finally admitted his feelings to both Tim and himself, he still couldn't shake his reluctance to take things further. David knew he wouldn't feel completely at ease until Tim denied—or God forbid, admitted—that his stepfather had done something unspeakable to him. In the end, putting his own longing aside wasn't as difficult as he'd thought it would be. Being needed was enough. He held Tim to him and closed his eyes, smiling as slim arms around him tightened in a hug.

"Good night, kid," David said gently. An instant later, he was fast asleep.

NINETEEN

"TWELVE." HALF gone.

For the fifth straight morning, I found myself absently counting my supply of blue pills. I'd made them last longer than I'd thought possible. The number wasn't critically low, and at the rate I'd been taking them, I could easily last another three months with the remaining amount. But that's not why I'd recently been obsessing over them. As I stared at the pills, I imagined telling David everything. Everything about being raised in the Facility, the infirmity built into my DNA, the escape that had brought us together on that lonely stretch of highway. How would he react? Would he understand? Could he understand?

More likely he'd be horrified. David was a kind, gentle man. I doubted he'd be able to accept that the person he'd been living with for the past few months was a genetically engineered killer. But I'd been lying to him for so long now, and he deserved better than that. The day would come when I'd have to leave in order to spare David from the awful death I faced when the pills finally ran out, but it wouldn't be right to just disappear with no explanation.

I had no idea how to even begin broaching such an impossible subject. What could I really say, after all? *I broke out of a top secret, quasigovernment compound, and I'm very likely being hunted by the people I escaped from. Did I mention they trained me to be an assassin? Oh, and by the way, I'll be dead in a few months thanks to the trap door built into my genetic code to ensure I can't survive on my own.* Yes, I could imagine that conversation going very well. If

David didn't throw me out in anger for my deception, he would probably run away in horror.

"Hey, Tim!" David's voice carried up the stairs from where he was waiting in the living room. "Are you ready? We need to go now if we want time to grab something to eat before we get to the store."

Courage failing, I closed the box, wishing I could shut away my problems so easily. "Yes, I'll be right there," I answered before hiding the pillbox under my mattress. No matter how hard I tried to ignore it, my dilemma wasn't simply going to go away on its own. Tomorrow morning would probably find me asking the same questions all over again, but I knew I'd come to the same nonanswer as always. I couldn't give this up, not yet. Since the first night David had let me sleep in his bed, it had become a regular occurrence. I looked forward to those moments with an eagerness I wouldn't have even been able to fathom a few weeks ago. Being held night after night in David's arms was better than anything my limited experience could have imagined. For the first time in my life, I could truly say I was happy. If only my burgeoning conscience wasn't so bound and determined to ruin it for me.

The BBW had received a new mass shipment two days before, so most of the staff was involved with the task of cataloguing the merchandise into inventory when we weren't busy helping customers. I was grateful for the routine task. My confrontation with Bobby's father preyed on my thoughts constantly. The mere thought of what I'd done—pretending to seduce the man, threatening his life—was enough to turn my stomach. Plus, it was yet one more secret I had to keep from David. Father Paul had been right; I wasn't the heartless killer the Company and the general had wanted. The general most likely would have ended up ordering my termination, chalking me up as yet another Mobile Termination project failure. I wondered if I'd ever be able to fully appreciate how thoroughly my creator had saved me.

Standing on the wooden beams of a shipping pallet in the stockroom, I was halfway inside the third large container of slow cookers I'd been scanning in when an overly enthusiastic voice rang out behind me. Only my abnormally quick reflexes prevented me from ending up headfirst inside the wooden crate.

"Slow down and try that again," I remarked dryly once I'd righted myself. I threw Bobby an amused smirk, noting with approval the mostly faded bruising along the side of the boy's face.

He looked back at me with a twinkle of excitement in his hazel eyes. "I said, come outside and check out my new ride!"

"Ride?" I repeated, frowning in confusion. As far as I knew, the euphemism referred to motorized vehicles, which Bobby was too young to legally operate. I followed him as he ran toward the front entrance, earning a firm rebuke from Patricia to stop "horsing around." Bobby was waiting for me, impatiently bouncing on the balls of his feet, when I reached the parking lot. He was standing next to a sparkling clean, two-wheeled conveyance, wearing a grin that stretched across his face from ear to ear.

"Check it out, man! My mom bought me a new bike!"

Bobby's euphoria was palpable, and I smiled in reaction. *Bicycle.* The formal name came to me readily. Yet another object I'd only known about from books before working at the BBW. I'd seen the vehicles in the Sports Department, but had never taken the time to study one as closely as I did now. The construction was simple enough: two wheels connected by a rigid aluminum frame, which was painted a bright, metallic, candy apple red. The top of the frame supported a padded seat, and below were a set of pedals attached to a crankset, which was in turn connected by a metal chain to the back wheel. Although the vehicle did not appear overly remarkable when compared to the motorized cycles I had seen on the streets of Lubbock, it was clear that, to Bobby, it was the most amazing thing in the world.

"It looks great," I replied. "Can you ride it?"

He rolled his eyes. "Duh! Of course I can ride it. How do you think I got here?" Usually Bobby walked to the store from his school, which was only a couple of miles away, but today he'd apparently come by different means.

"No," I added, covering up my slip, "I mean, why don't you show me what it can do?" I glanced around the parking lot, but the late afternoon crowd had yet to arrive and traffic was light. "Go on," I prompted, urging the boy on with a nod.

Bobby grinned. "All right!" He hopped onto the seat, which was covered with a material intended to resemble black leather, and braced his feet against the pedals. With a push of his legs, he was off, shooting around the lot at an impressive speed.

"Whoo-hoo!"

I could hear Bobby's shout from where I stood, even though he had already reached the far end of the lot. By the time he made it back to me, a genuine grin had blossomed on my face. After everything Bobby had been through over the last week, I was thrilled at his blatant display of happiness. Although I was reluctant to spoil the mood, I felt compelled to determine the current status of Bobby's domestic situation. I waited until he had come to a halt in front of me, and broached the subject carefully.

"You're pretty good on that thing."

Bobby grinned. "Damn straight! I bet in a few weeks I'll even be able to pop a wheelie."

In lieu of asking what that meant, I nodded in solemn support of the goal. "So, how have things been at home?" I felt bad as the delight vanished from Bobby's face, but I had to know. Fortunately, he seemed more resigned than resentful.

"It's cool." I read the forgiveness in his shrug. "Mom's been really nice to me lately," he elaborated, running an appreciative hand over the handlebars. "But it's actually been kind of nice with just the two of us."

"So your father hasn't come back around?" Bobby shook his head, and I felt relief that the man had apparently decided to heed my warning. "That's good."

"Yeah, I guess." He sounded less than convinced, and I was confused by his ambivalence.

"You want him to come home?" I watched Bobby's face closely, searching for any signs that would give me a clue to his frame of mind. "I would have thought he was the last person you'd want to see."

Bobby toyed with the brake levers as he rocked the bike back and forth on its wheels. He chewed his lip, remaining quiet for a long moment as he stared at the ground.

"I'm sorry," I added, filling the silence. "I didn't mean to pry."

He shook his head. "Nah, that's okay. I mean, we're friends. Friends ask each other stuff like that." Bobby glanced up at me with a muted smile. "It's just… I was trying to figure out how to answer you. Do I want him to come home?" He shrugged. "I guess part of me does. After all, he's my dad. But then again, he's been a real dick to me and my mom. So, no. I'm glad he's stayed away." Bobby's expression changed from introspective to uncertain, making him appear younger than his actual years. "Does that make me a bad person, to hope I never see my dad again?"

My first instinct was to go and find David. His history with his own father would give him some relevant perspective on Bobby's current predicament, and I didn't feel my knowledge of relationships was sufficient to allow me to offer good advice. But I was the only one here, and Bobby needed me.

"It's not wrong to want to feel safe. And you have to think about the best way to protect your mother." I reached out and gripped the handlebars to still Bobby's agitated movements. He met my gaze, his eyes restless as he searched my face for answers. "Sometimes it's simply not possible to be with someone, no matter how much we care about them." I thought about Father Paul and the woman with the pretty red hair, knowing I would never forget their kindly smiles or the incredible sacrifices they had made to protect me. I fully understood now the grief I'd felt at their loss, and while Bobby's father was to blame for his absence from his son's life, I could at least understand how much that separation hurt from Bobby's point of view. "I guess that's part of growing up, learning that who we love and who we can trust aren't always the same."

Sadness darkened Bobby's face, but he nodded. He seemed to age before my eyes, and I felt guilty for suggesting he relinquish even a bit of his childhood innocence. That guilelessness, I'd come to realize, was one of the reasons I enjoyed being around him so much. My own formative years had been as far from normal as could be imagined, and I liked the notion of experiencing a bit of that through him. Perhaps that's why I was so adamant about keeping him safe. It was my way of saving that part of myself.

"Yeah, I guess." Bobby stared down at his new bike, and I waited patiently, leaving him alone with his thoughts. After a while he shook himself and looked up with a cheerful smile, shedding his melancholy as effortlessly as a dog shed water. "So, do you wanna try it?"

The skin between my eyebrows creased as I struggled to keep up with his mercurial shift in mood. "Try what?"

"My bike, doofus." Bracing his feet on the ground, Bobby pulled the handlebars up until the bicycle rested only on its back wheel. "Come on. I'll probably never offer to let you ride it again, so you'd better say yes while you have the chance."

I hesitated, reluctant to admit to what Bobby would likely see as an embarrassing handicap. "I don't know how to ride a bike." Sure enough, he gaped at me in shock. I shrugged. "I've never had reason to try." My training hadn't yet extended to vehicle operation, likely because my handlers were afraid of giving me such a convenient means of escape. In hindsight, their caution was undeniably warranted, but the knowledge didn't help me in my present situation.

"You mean you never had a bike growing up?"

"No." Ruthlessly, I conjured up a fiction that would evoke the most sympathy. "My stepfather didn't like me to play around when I could be helping him work instead." I refused to feel any remorse at the lie when Bobby's expression melted into heartfelt pity.

He hopped off the bike and stepped aside. "Well, no time like the present! Come on, what are you waiting for?" He waved me toward the padded seat. "Get on!"

Not wanting to destroy the return of Bobby's good mood, I obliged. I straddled the aluminum frame and lowered myself onto the seat. My longer legs were bent awkwardly, but I didn't know if that was appropriate or not. "Now what?"

"Now you pedal." Bobby rolled his eyes as he received only a blank stare in return. "Put your foot on this," he said in a mocking tone as he pointed to one of the platforms sticking out from the base of the frame. He waited until I'd complied with the instruction. "Push off with that foot and, once you're going, put your other foot on the other one."

The procedure seemed straightforward enough. I did as ordered and moved forward a few inches. I wobbled slightly when I placed my other foot, but soon grasped that this was a simple application of balance achieved through maintaining sufficient momentum. The concept was not so different to those necessary for various martial arts exercises. In less than a minute, my body had fully adjusted, and I was whizzing through the parking lot, enjoying the feel of the wind blowing through my hair. The sensation of freedom was wonderful and somewhat addictive. I instantly understood why Bobby had been so excited when he'd received the gift.

At the far end of the lot, I angled the bike in a tight left turn by leaning sharply to one side. I noticed the levers on top of the handlebars, and after a few moments of experimentation figured out how to shift the bike into different gears. Dropping it into the highest gear, I pushed hard on one of the pedals while pulling up sharply on the handlebars. I smiled as the bike leapt into the air. Landing on the rear wheel, a subtle shift in my body weight kept the bike in that position for a few yards. I was impressed with the simple efficiency of the design, and attempted a few additional maneuvers before allowing the bike to come down onto its front wheel. Shifting into a lower gear to increase my speed, I took a long swing around the periphery of the lot as I headed back toward the front entrance of the store.

This would provide an excellent way to exercise, something I did not often have time for, given my need to hide the full extent of my physical abilities. Not to mention, having a bicycle would enable me to travel farther once I left, giving me a better chance of evading pursuit and allowing me to put as much distance between myself and Lubbock as possible. I knew I'd need to minimize any temptation I might have to return to the man I would be leaving behind. The store carried a variety of models, and I made a mental note to check the prices once I was back inside. I'd prefer to buy one using my savings, without having to ask David for financial assistance. It would be the ultimate insult to have him pay for the very means I intended to use to someday disappear out of his life.

Lost in thought, I didn't immediately notice the way Bobby was staring at me with his mouth agape when I finally returned to where he was waiting. "That was enjoyable," I said with complete sincerity. "Thank you for letting me try it."

"Try it?"

I raised an eyebrow at the note of high-pitched incredulity in Bobby's voice. "What?" I looked down at the bike, but didn't believe I'd damaged it in any way. "Is there a problem?" Wide eyes stared at me almost unblinking during long seconds of silence, and I was about to ask Bobby if he was all right when he suddenly exploded.

"You jerk, you totally lied to me! You said you'd never ridden a bike before. I knew that had to be complete bullshit. What was that all about?"

It was my turn to blink. "I don't understand. I didn't lie to you. That was my first time."

Bobby's mouth opened and shut but produced no sound. Abruptly his expression changed from indignation to utter confusion. "You're not shitting me?"

"No. I would never lie to you." *Not about anything this trivial*, I clarified silently.

"Then how...?" Bobby shook his head. "It took me weeks to learn how to ride when I first tried, but you figured it out in, like, five seconds!" He peered at me like I was an unknown specimen. "Dude, I swear, sometimes I think you're an alien from outer space."

I didn't comment and was relieved when Bobby merely laughed at his own joke, not appreciating the insightfulness of his observation. "Come on," I said, getting off the bike and handing it back over to its owner. "We've got inventory to catalogue."

"Aw, man," Bobby griped. He always complained that he hated the chore, but it was well-known that he loved using the handheld scanner and pretending it was some sort of high-tech weapon.

I listened with pleasure as Bobby chatted incessantly about any topic that came into his head, veering effortlessly from grousing about his English teacher to making suggestive comments about the girl in his class he apparently liked. Seeing Bobby like this, cheerful and free of injury, was quite enjoyable. Maybe this was what it meant to feel contentment. As we made our way back inside after securing the bike to the rack immediately outside the entrance door, I caught sight of David chatting with Patricia. They were sharing a clipboard, which I suspected held a list of the new merchandise. Patricia didn't trust the computer system and preferred to work with paper when dealing with inventory. David humored her, even though it took her longer to check the incoming stock using the list instead of the computer. He must have seen us come in because he looked up and shot us a quick smile before returning his attention to the chatty manager.

Yes, contentment. It's what I felt when Bobby did something to make me laugh, or whenever one of the other employees at the BBW treated me like a normal teenager. But mostly it defined the moments when I was lying in David's arms at night, waiting to fall asleep and all the while hoping for something more. I would miss the heady sensation once I was back on my own, but at least I would have these memories when the time came to face the inevitable. For now, though, I was determined to savor this priceless sense of tranquility for as long as I could.

TWENTY

DAVID SMOTHERED a chuckle as he watched Tim walk slowly up and down the display of bicycles for the eighth time. He had suspected after seeing the look on the kid's face when he'd come back from taking a spin on Bobby's new bike that he would want one of his very own. He lingered at the end of the row and waited until Tim had made his way back to where he was standing.

"I'll buy you one if you want."

Tim looked over at David and blinked like he was startled to find him there. "Oh, um…." He shook his head. "No. You don't have to do that. I'll save up and buy one myself."

David wasn't sure whether he was proud of Tim's desire for self-sufficiency or disappointed he was being denied an opportunity to spoil him. He was finding that being in love made him want to shower Tim with gifts. "All right," he replied. "Are you ready to go?" They were alone in the store. David wasn't usually the last to leave, but he'd had a few tasks to finish before closing out the log of new inventory. It was getting pretty late, and he wanted to make sure they had plenty of time to eat before hitting the hay.

Tim glanced toward the front of the store. "I wonder if Bobby made it home okay. You've been giving him a ride every day since…."

"The incident," David suggested, for lack of a better word. He tried not to think about the week before, when Bobby had come into the store with his face bearing the marks of his father's abuse. Not wanting to worry about the boy more than he already did, he'd started taking

Bobby home after his shift. While Tim hadn't made a big deal about it in front of Bobby, sparing the boy's pride, he'd adamantly expressed his gratitude for David's thoughtfulness when they were alone in bed. So far the kid had nominally respected his wishes not to take things too far. But he pushed the boundaries at every turn, forcing David to decide whether his stubbornness was really worth all of the cold showers and uncomfortably erotic dreams.

"Yeah," Tim affirmed. He continued to stare out of the store's glass front, as if he could somehow track Bobby's whereabouts from where he stood.

"I'm sure he's fine. Besides, it would have killed him not to have been able to ride his bike home." David laid a reassuring hand on Tim's shoulder. "But you're right. I should have asked him to give me a call once he made it there safely. I'll be sure to tell him to do so tomorrow, okay?"

Tim nodded. "Okay."

David started to turn away, but the hesitation on the kid's face made him pause. "What is it? Are you still worried?" He smiled when Tim dropped his gaze to the floor and shrugged awkwardly. It warmed his heart to see the way Tim doted on Bobby. It was a shame he didn't have any siblings. He would have made a wonderful big brother for some lucky kid. In the absence of any younger sisters or brothers, David supposed it made sense that Bobby had become the fortunate recipient of the fierce desire to protect that seemed so much a part of Tim's makeup. "Do you want to call him and check that he got home all right?"

Tim took a deep breath and shook his head. "No," he said, sounding more like himself. "Like you said, he's probably fine. Otherwise his mother would have called us." His stomach chose that moment to rumble loudly, and David laughed as Tim glared at him with underlying embarrassment.

"Didn't you have a triple-stack from the Ice Cream Emporium a few hours ago for lunch? I swear," David said on a lingering chuckle, "I don't know where you put it all." He reached out and pinched Tim on a denim-covered butt cheek. "If I ate like you, I'd be a blimp."

"My metabolism is faster than yours because I'm younger."

David gaped as he realized Tim had actually made a joke, and at his expense! Thick lashes shielded Tim's eyes as he watched David carefully for a reaction, but they couldn't hide the teasing light that peeked out. The sheer variety of expressions Tim displayed so naturally these days was fascinating to him, all the more for the fact that when they'd first met the kid had shown the emotional range of a turnip. Every smile, every frown, every nuance was worth more to him than gold.

"Oh, is that so?" David couldn't stop laughing, ruining his attempt at feigned anger. But he didn't give up entirely, moving toward Tim with deliberate steps in what he hoped was an intimidating manner. "You calling me old, whippersnapper?"

Tim backed away at the same pace that David moved forward. He cocked his head to the side, his expression curious. "What is a whippersnapper? And, yes, old man." A huge grin crossed his face an instant before he swung around and belted toward the back office with David hard on his heels.

"I'll show you old!" The phone in his pocket rang before David could catch up to Tim, and he had to acknowledge the truth of the kid's taunt when he found himself out of breath once he finally reached his office. He pulled out his cell and held up a finger, asking for a moment to catch his breath and take the call. Tim looked disgustingly unaffected by the chase, and he leaned his hip comfortably against the desk, folding his arms while he waited. "This is Conley," David answered.

"H-help—"

David's blood ran cold as he recognized the voice. He threw Tim a worried glance. "Bobby? Is that you?"

"Please… help." The sound of glass crashing sounded in the background.

David unconsciously gripped the phone tighter, trying not to panic. "Bobby, where are you?"

"He came back." The voice broke into a sob. "He's hurting Mom."

Gritting his teeth, David tried again. "Bobby, tell me where you are," he repeated, barely managing to keep from yelling. The boy was clearly frightened out of his wits, and shouting at him wouldn't help.

"At home."

"Are you in danger?"

"I'm hiding in a closet. But Mom… I left her alone!"

"You did the right thing," he said quickly, not wanting Bobby to put himself in harm's way by trying to help his mother. "We'll be right there." David jerked his chin toward the door, signaling to Tim that they were leaving. The kid had already figured out what was going on, if the growing mix of fury and worry on his face was any indication. He grabbed the keys lying on the desk without a word and followed as David rushed to the front of the store. "Can you get out of the house?" David asked.

"No." There was another crash, and Bobby whined like a frightened puppy. "Please," he cried.

"Just hang on. I'm going to call the police." David headed for his car, trusting that Tim would lock up the store. He had barely reached the vehicle when Tim caught up with him and tossed him the keys.

"No! Don't call them!"

"Bobby." David took a deep breath, trying to keep his voice calm. "I have to call the police."

"They'll hurt him. He'll leave if you come." The boy's voice hitched on another sob. "Just, please. Hurry."

It took David only a few seconds to start the car and slam it into gear. In an instant, he was tearing out of the parking lot, heading north toward Bobby's neighborhood.

"Tell him, 'okay,'" Tim urged, as if he'd heard the boy's plea.

"Okay," David answered. His stomach was churning, but deep down he understood Bobby's reluctance to involve the authorities. The love of a child for his parent was a powerful if often irrational thing, he thought, remembering some of the less pleasant confrontations with his father. Even in those moments when he'd despised his father the most, David would have hated it more if something had happened to him. "We'll be there soon. Here, keep talking to Tim." He passed the phone over. "I need to concentrate on driving," he explained.

Tim stared at him uncertainly as he pressed the microphone to his chest to block his words from reaching the boy on the other end of the line. "What do I say?"

"Anything," David said, distracted as he focused all of his attention on getting to Bobby's house as fast as he could without getting in an accident. "Just stay with him."

Tim nodded, looking nervous but determined. "Bobby? It's me. Everything will be all right."

David only half listened to the one-sided conversation. Bobby lived less than three miles away, and at that late hour the streets were mostly clear. A part of him hoped the police would see him speeding and follow him to the boy's house, taking the decision on whether or not to involve them out of his hands. But there wasn't a single patrol car in sight. Less than ten minutes after he'd first received Bobby's frantic call, they were pulling up in front of his house. David slammed on his brakes, the tires protesting with an unsettling screech as the car lurched to a halt.

"Bobby, we're here." Tim was in the lead as they rushed toward the front door, though his even tone never betrayed the speed at which he was running. "Can you get to the door and let us in?"

Before he could even finish the question, the front door swung open, revealing the terrified boy. Bobby's eyes were wide with fright, and he was clutching a cordless handset to the side of his face that had the least extensive amount of bruising. Not that that was saying much, David thought darkly. This time the damage had been more evenly doled out, and he was amazed Bobby had been able to see out of his swollen eyes well enough to even dial his number.

"Bobby!" Tim yelled, pulling the boy into his arms. The small figure clutched him tightly for a moment, profound relief barely decipherable on his ruined features. But he pushed Tim away an instant later and ran into the house, obliging them to follow.

"Bobby, wait!" David called after him to no effect.

They ended up in the kitchen, where Bobby's father had Grace pinned up against the back door of the house, his hands around her thin neck. Tim moved so quickly all David could make out was a blur. But in the blink of an eye, Grace had been flung out of the way, and Tim and Bobby's father were crashing through the door and out onto the back lawn.

"Don!" Grace shouted in terror, before recognizing who had come to her rescue. Bobby threw himself into her arms, and she held him close, tears falling from identical pairs of hazel eyes down their battered cheeks.

David spared them a momentary glance to satisfy himself that they were out of immediate danger, then ran past the kneeling pair and into the yard. A set of steps led down to a stone path that stretched a few yards from the house. David jumped the stairs in his haste, stumbling as he landed heavily on the path. The sun had recently set, and the sky was rapidly edging toward total darkness. A light on the back of the house cast only a feeble circle of illumination, and he strained his eyes trying to see beyond it.

"Tim!" he called out, searching anxiously for the kid and the man he'd so rashly attacked. From the brief glance David had caught of him, Bobby's father was no lightweight. David spun around at the unmistakable dull thud of a fist hitting flesh, a pained grunt confirming his guess. Images filled his mind of Bobby's father pounding Tim into the ground, and he ran toward the commotion, muscles tightening as he prepared himself to physically wrestle the man off the much-smaller teen. David finally caught sight of two shadowy figures lying on the grass several feet off the path, but his steps faltered when he saw who was on top, dolling out punishing, vicious punches. "Tim?" he whispered in shock as the kid landed another brutal hit to the prone figure's face.

"I told you to leave them alone!"

The shout was filled with a menacing intensity David would have never guessed Tim capable of. Bobby's father moaned, his head whipping to the side at the force of the impact against his jaw. Blood speckled his lips, and one of his eyes had already begun to swell shut. David ran forward and grabbed Tim from behind, barely managing to dodge the elbow the kid aimed in his direction.

"Tim! Calm down!" He held on tightly until Tim realized who was restraining him. The slim figure went deadly still, and only then did David dare let go. He turned Tim around, expecting to see the kid's expression contorted with rage, but was instead caught off guard by the abject fear that had taken control of Tim's beautiful face.

"I'm sorry." The kid's eyes were wild, staring in transfixed horror as David pulled him away from the figure curled on the grass. "I didn't mean to hurt him. I—I warned him to stay away. I warned him!"

David shook his head in confusion. "Warned him?" he echoed. "What are you talking about?"

Tim gasped and pressed his lips shut as though he'd said more than he intended. He bowed his head in an effort to avoid David's gaze.

"Tim, come on. Talk to me."

"Don!"

David looked over his shoulder to see Grace running out of the house, Bobby following hesitantly in her wake. He held up a hand to warn her off. "Just wait there, Mrs. Wood." He glanced quickly at the man on the ground. "He's all right. Why don't you take Bobby back inside? We'll take care of everything out here."

"I…." Grace seemed ready to argue, her gaze darting between her son and her husband.

David recognized the shell-shocked expression on her face, like she didn't know how she should react. He felt sorry for her as he recalled a criminology class he'd taken while studying prelaw. In a chapter on domestic violence, he'd read that victims of domestic abuse often defended their abusers against outsiders, even when the outsider was only trying to help. He was concerned Grace would try to interfere and assist her spouse, but her uncertainty lasted only for a moment. She nodded as she pulled her son close to her side.

"Thank you." Her words were slurred, the gash along the side of her face clearly making it difficult for her to talk. David nodded and was watching them walk back toward the house when a garbled curse rang out behind them.

"You little whore!"

David turned around as Bobby's father rose to his knees and spat bloody spittle onto the grass. The man's breathing was ragged as he pressed a hand against his stomach, the grimace on his battered face hinting at the extent of his pain. David's nose wrinkled as he caught the telltale reek of alcohol that emanated from the swaying figure. He'd assumed the man's—Don's—rancor would be directed toward his wife, so he was stunned when he realized the hooded green eyes were staring daggers at Tim.

"Is that your boyfriend? Huh? Does he know you get your kicks picking up men in bars and then threatening to kill them?"

"Tim," David said in a low voice so only the kid could hear him. "What is he talking about?" Though reluctant to look away from the unhinged man struggling to get up, he risked a quick glance down at the figure standing statue-like beside him. Tim was still facing toward him, his expression dazed. David couldn't tell if the kid's ghostly complexion was the fault of the back porch light or was a result of the dread that seemed permanently etched on his face.

Don bared his teeth in a feral grimace. "How dare you come to my house and attack me? Who the fuck do you think you are?"

Grace had paused in her retreat to the house at her husband's shout, and she stared at him in horror as he pulled a gun from the waistband of his grass-stained pants. The hand not holding on to Bobby flew to cover her mouth. "Don, what on earth are you doing?"

Don swung the gun in his wife's direction. "Shut up, you dumb bitch! I'm sick of hearing your stupid voice!" His eyes were crazed, his voice breaking on a high-pitched shriek. "That's right, I'm gay!" he confessed out of the blue, making David gape at him in shock. "Is that what you wanted to hear? Well, it's true. All of your nagging about where I've been and who I've been seeing. I've been out fucking other men, that's where!"

Whatever Grace had suspected, that particular bombshell clearly wasn't it. Her jaw worked for a moment before she managed to close it enough to speak. "But we're married," she cried. "We have a child!"

"Only because your father forced me to marry you!" The grating sound that burst from Don's throat resembled a laugh in name only. "Hell, I was young and drunk and confused. That's the only reason I even ever touched you that night!"

Afraid the situation was rapidly getting out of control, David forced himself to shake off his surprise at the unexpected twist to this sad drama. "Hey!" he barked sharply, drawing both Don's attention and the aim of the gun back toward him and away from Grace and Bobby. Tim had spun around toward Don at the appearance of the gun, and David tried to maneuver the kid safely behind him. "Look, I of all people understand what it's like to be young and confused about your sexuality, but that doesn't give you any right to act like a complete dick."

"I don't know you," Don growled. "Who the fuck are you?"

"Your son works at my store after school. Tim and I are his friends, and we can't let you keep hurting him and Grace like this. So why don't you put down the gun, and we'll talk—"

"Tim?" Don's grin was ugly. "Another lie, huh, *Peter*?" He spat out more of the blood that welled up from his split lip. "I don't know if I want my son hanging around little punk-ass liars like you."

Tim had gone motionless, his gaze fixed unflinchingly on the gun in Don's hand. David eased forward to stand in front of him, but a hand suddenly gripped his shirt, holding him in place. David didn't know what Don was talking about, but he was willing to wait for answers until after the volatile situation had been defused. He caught the man's deranged stare and struggled to keep his tone as soothing as possible. "Don, look—"

"Shut up!" he yelled, "and get off my property!"

"Not until you put the gun down." David held up a placating hand. "All I want to do is talk. You said that you're gay? Well, so am I. I know what you're going through—"

"No, you fucking well don't!" The tip of the gun flicked back and forth as Don aimed it at the two men blocking his view of his wife and son. "One mistake, and I'm forced to live a lie day in and day out. How is that fair, huh? How is that fucking fair?" Don's eyes blurred as they grew shiny with tears that refused to fall.

Somewhere deep inside, David's soul ached for this tortured man, but that didn't excuse how he'd treated his family. His heart was racing at the sight of the gun waving in his face, but he was determined to make Don listen to him before he made a mistake he could never take back.

"I remember what it was like to have to hide who I was from everyone I cared about. But you're a grown man now, Don. You can decide to live your life however you see fit. No one has to suffer, least of all you."

"Oh, right, like her father would ever let me just walk away from his precious daughter. He promised to kill me if I even tried." Don shook his head, dashing a hand across his eyes to wipe away the incipient tears. "But why am I even talking to you? You have your hot piece of ass, but what do I have? A cunt of a wife and a dumb brat!"

"Stop it!" All of the adults turned toward Bobby as he lurched forward.

"Bobby, no!" Grace shouted as her son pulled free of her protective embrace.

"Tim is my friend. Stop calling him names!"

Don laughed mockingly at the boy's entreaty, his bleary gaze harsh as he caught sight of his son. "Who, him?" he said, gesturing toward Tim with the gun. "Do you know what he did? He promised to let me fuck him in an alley behind a bar." He glared at Bobby's pale face. "He's a slut and a whore, and I can't believe your mother lets you hang around that kind of trash."

"Stop it!" Bobby yelled, his voice cracking, trapped in its transition from adolescence to adulthood.

David acted without thinking, seeing his chance as Bobby drew his father's attention away from him. He yanked free of Tim's grasp and rushed forward, intending to knock the gun from Don's hand, but Tim's hold on him was firmer than he'd anticipated. The extra second it took him to shake Tim loose was enough for Don to recognize what was going on. The gun tracked in his direction, and every cliché about one's life flashing before one's eyes passed through his petrified thoughts in the instant before he saw the man pull the trigger.

"David!"

The report of the gun was deafening, and for a moment the ringing in his ears distracted him from the pain that flared in the upper part of his left arm. David shouted in agony and surprise as he was shoved hard from behind. He gasped at the fire that rushed through his arm as he tried to brace himself before he smashed face-first into the ground. His breath left him in a rush when his arms collapsed beneath him from the pain, and he landed hard. He hadn't yet managed to catch his breath when strong hands rolled him over until he was staring up into panicky eyes.

I'm okay, David tried to say, but all that came out was a wheeze. The impact with the ground had winded him, and the ability to talk temporarily eluded him. He looked up dizzily at Tim, whose gaze raked over him, honing in on his arm at the same instant he realized he'd been shot. The kid was hunched over him protectively, and David instantly knew who had tried to knock him out of the line of fire. He gazed up at Tim in wonder, hoping his eyes would convey what he could not.

"David...." Tim's mouth worked silently but for that one word. The brown of his eyes were nearly swallowed by black pupils as the kid stared down at him in terror, but David knew Tim's fear was for him.

Tim placed a gentle hand against the side of his face, and David reached up with his good hand to cover it with his own. Cautious relief filled the kid's eyes for a moment before a twinge of pain made David groan, his hand slipping away to cradle his injured arm. Alarm replaced the relief, only to be submerged in turn beneath something utterly frightening. David stared in horrified amazement as Tim's eyes narrowed with anger, his pretty features twisting with dark rage. Tim stared up toward a point over David's head, and in a flash he was gone. David managed to roll himself up onto his good arm in time to see the lithe figure cover the several feet between him and Don in a single leap. He stared in awe as Tim's heel connected with the center of the larger man's chest, knocking him hard onto the ground. From where he was lying, he could see only the side of Tim's profile, but when the kid circled the man who was struggling to get back on his feet, David shuddered as he caught a clear glimpse of Tim's face.

"Tim," he whispered, his mind working manically to understand how the shy kid who'd been living with him the past two months had morphed into the cold-eyed stranger who had taken his place.

TWENTY-ONE

ACQUIRE TARGET.

I watched the man struggle to his feet, his hand pressed against the spot where my foot had landed.

Assess target weakness.

The man hissed in pain. Two ribs bruised, likely fractured.

Establish target risk level.

"Goddammit!" The man gasped as he struggled to catch his breath. He glared at me with dazed green eyes.

Target intentions: hostile.

"Ugh, you little bitch." The man saw the weapon he'd dropped after being kicked and scrambled toward it. "I'm gonna kill you!"

Neutralize.

Operating on automatic, I'd instinctively followed the protocol my instructors had drilled into me for efficiently nullifying a threat. But the sight of the weapon suddenly threw me out of the calm place I'd retreated to in my mind. The size of the gun skewed out of proportion, taking on an outside importance as I remembered its significance.

This thing had hurt David.

The image of a bullet streaking toward its target replayed over and over until it was etched indelibly into my brain. I'd thought I understood what anger felt like when I'd seen the results of the abuse this man had inflicted on his son, but it paled in comparison to the terrified fury that had filled me when I'd witnessed the bullet piercing David's arm less than a foot from his heart.

This man had shot David.

From the moment Bobby's father had pulled the gun, I'd had one focus—to keep the man I cared about safe. When I realized David was attempting to shield me, I'd tried to stop him from doing something so foolish and unnecessary. Only one of us had been trained for this type of situation, and it wasn't the Oklahoma-born franchise owner. More importantly, David had no cause to put himself in harm's way in an attempt to protect me. My life was on borrowed time. His stretched out before him, and it was infinitely precious to me.

Mind racing, I'd mentally tested and rejected a dozen ways in which I could defuse the situation without anyone getting hurt. I could have loosened my shoe and flung it in Don's direction to distract him. I could have tried to reason with him until I could get close enough to disarm him. When Bobby had offered the ideal diversion by instigating a verbal altercation with his father, I'd been ready to put any one of a dozen contingencies into action.

It had simply never occurred to me that David would have the same idea. For a critical second, surprise at David's sudden move to rush Don made me freeze in shock. But when I saw the man pull the trigger, my body had reacted without thought, knocking David out of the path of any further shots. Even as we hit the ground, I knew I hadn't been fast enough. The scream of pain that spilled from David's lips as the bullet hit felt like it had been torn from my own throat. My heart lurched to a near standstill when I saw the dark blood spreading from the wound, staining the sleeve of David's shirt and, for an interminable moment, all I could see was Father Paul's blood-covered body as he lay dying in my arms.

This bastard tried to kill David.

David could have died, could have been taken from me in the blink of an eye, and I wouldn't have been able to do anything to stop it. I'd felt utterly helpless as I furiously checked David over to assess the scope of his injuries, trembling in panic at the mere possibility of what I could have lost. And then the fear turned to a rage so hot I thought it might consume me. In desperation, I'd shut my emotions down, falling back on the calming logic I'd been trained to apply to dangerous situations. But I wasn't able hold on to it. I hated this man who had dared to cause David pain, who had dared to threaten his life for no reason other than his own selfishness.

"Eliminate," I murmured, my breath as ragged as the pounding of my heart. I raked my gaze over my enemy, sizing him up in an instant as I eagerly mapped out all of the various ways in which he would die at my hands.

Don recovered the gun and struggled to his feet, teeth gritted against the pain in his ribs. He looked at me, and I could only guess at the expression on my face when I saw his eyes widen in fear. He hid his dread quickly behind bravado, the presence of the weapon in his hand obviously making him believe he had the upper hand.

He couldn't have been more wrong.

"Yeah, that's right. You heard me." Don sneered as he pointed the gun at my face. "And after I kill you, I'm gonna finish off your meddling boyfriend. Then we'll see who has the right to tell me how to treat my own flesh and blood." He didn't even have time to yell before the gun was suddenly flying from his hand. "What the f—" The shock on his face crumpled as a roundhouse kick from the same foot that had knocked away the gun connected with his temple. Don grunted in surprise and pain as he fell hard to the ground. His arm flew up to shield his head from further assault, but the next attack never came. Cautiously, Don peered up dizzily past his arm at me as I stood motionless before him.

"Get up." My voice was guttural, more animal than human. I glared down at Don, my fingers curling into fists as they ached to dole out further punishment. "I said get up!" A voice called my name, but I paid it no mind, refusing to allow my attention to waver from this piece of garbage I was determined to end here and now.

Bolstered by rage and alcohol, Don surged up without warning and rushed at me. I easily sidestepped his clumsy attack and caught him by the shirt as he staggered past. Blocking with one leg, I pivoted on my other foot and used his momentum to throw him over my shoulder and onto his back. He tried to sit up, but another kick to the head collapsed him onto his side.

"Tim...."

"Get up!" I yelled again, but this time Don wasn't responsive. Unsatisfied that my opponent was still breathing, I dropped on top of the prone figure, straddling him. Digging my fingers into his hair, I pulled his head around until I could see his face. Only a ring of green was visible around his dilated pupils, the unfocused gaze an unmistakable sign of a concussion. The image of the bullet burying itself into David's arm overlaid my vision as I stared at down at my enemy.

"Tim, st—"

"Annihilate," I growled.

My fist connected with the soft tissue of Don's cheek, the blow producing a satisfying crunch as his underlying bone gave way to my enhanced strength. Another hit destroyed the blood vessels in his left eye, and red seeped into the white of the sclera. I angled my knee upward to impact his spleen, exacerbating the damage I'd already caused during our first scuffle, and felt the organ soften under the impact. One more blow would likely cause a rupture, but that would end things too quickly. This man deserved to suffer for what he'd done. A backhand delivered to the opposite side of Don's face dislocated his jaw, and I followed it with another blow and then another. The figure beneath me had gone completely still, but I couldn't stop now, not until I was certain David was safe, that this man could never hurt him again. The memory of David's face contorted in agony ripped through me, enraging me all over again. A snarl tore from my throat, and my vision went as red as the blood that had spilled from the man I'd come to care for more than my own life.

"I will destroy you, you fucking son of a bitch!" I grabbed either side of Don's head and lifted it off the ground. One sharp twist, and it would all be over.

"Tim! For the love of God, stop!"

A pair of arms wrapped around me from behind, one holding me less firmly than the other, as if it had been injured.

"David," I whispered. I froze and looked down at the object I held between my hands. Don's face was a mass of bruises and contusions. His broken jaw listed to the side, unable to fight the pull of gravity. He looked half-dead, and if David had been even a moment slower in reaching me…. "He shot you," I croaked, my voice harsh with strain. My chest heaved as I labored for breath. "He shot you."

"I'm okay, kid. Just let him go."

"Oh God," I moaned, unable to properly appreciate my first usage of the irreverent exclamation as I laid Don's head gently on the ground. I didn't understand why it was so hard to breathe. The altercation hadn't taxed me physically. So why couldn't I catch my breath?

"You're hyperventilating. Shhh, relax." David spoke directly against my ear, his voice soft and low. He maneuvered us away from the still body, the slight hitch in his words the only concession to the pain he must have been in. "I've got you."

No one had ever told me that panic could steal the very air from my lungs. I'd never felt it before now, not even when I was running for my life, knowing Father Paul was dead. Sinking to my knees, I dragged David with me as I closed my eyes, desperate to shut out the sight of Don's ruined face. I'd almost killed Bobby's father. What had I been thinking? I hadn't, that was the problem. Nothing had existed for me beyond the primal need to protect David from any and all threats. I'd tried so hard to fit into this new life, to act like a normal human being and not like a genetically engineered freak. But now I'd ruined it all. How could Bobby ever stand to look at me again after I'd tried to beat his father to death? And Grace, she must think me a monster. I could only imagine how they must feel about me after what I'd just done, and the thought of their well-deserved hatred turned my stomach. Yet even their abhorrence was nothing compared to the judgment of the one person I couldn't bear to face.

"Tim, look at me."

"No."

"Tim, please."

"No," I cried. "I can't." I shook my head. "I'm sorry. I only wanted to keep you safe. You were hurt, and I got so angry I couldn't stop myself—"

"It's okay. I understand."

I looked up at that, my gaze meeting David's intense blue eyes. Although he tried to hide it, I could see the wariness hidden beneath the sincerity radiating from his gaze. I shook my head, knowing he was simply trying to make me feel better, but nothing could erase the horror of my actions.

"Liar," I whispered. "How could you possibly understand?" I risked a glance at Don and felt bile rise up into the back of my throat at the enormity of the damage I'd caused with nothing but my bare hands. "If you hadn't stopped me, I would have killed him."

"No, I'm serious." David's smile was sad, but his gaze never wavered. "We do what we have to in order to protect the people we love."

That word again. It was simply one more thing I couldn't wrap my mind around, not on top of everything else I was struggling to cope with.

"Is he…?" a woman's voice asked nervously.

I buried my face in David's uninjured shoulder, leaving him to answer Grace's tremulous question.

"No, but you should go in the house and call 9-1-1 right away," David replied. "Bobby, why don't you go with your mom?"

I pressed further into David as Bobby uttered a muffled reply. The temptation to run so I never had to face Bobby again was overwhelming. The wooden stairs creaked as someone mounted them, the bang of the screen door signaling that Grace had done as David had requested. I'd only heard one set of footsteps, and I braced for the confrontation that was apparently unavoidable.

"I'm okay. How about you?"

A shadow fell over me, and I twitched as my muscles readied themselves for flight. As though guessing my intent, David flexed his arms, keeping me in place. I could have broken free, but I stayed where I was. I didn't speak, as if remaining silent would help shield me from Bobby's condemnation. Not that that I didn't deserve it.

"I think the bullet just grazed me. It's not too bad." David shifted and gathered his legs beneath him to stand. "Why don't we all go into the house and wait for the police?"

"Tim," Bobby said, forestalling David's efforts to separate him from the bloody mess that was his father. "Are you all right? He didn't hurt you, did he?"

I lifted my head from David's shoulder and stared up at Bobby in shock. How could he possibly be concerned about my safety? "I-I almost killed your father. You should hate me."

"You saved us." Bobby darted a quick glance at the motionless figure before losing his nerve. He angled himself so he couldn't see anyone but me and David. "He tried to kill David, and he would have killed you too, if he could have. But you stopped him."

Bobby smiled through the tears that streaked his bruised cheeks, and I watched in mute astonishment as the tears won, shaking his thin body with wrenching sobs. David reached up and put a comforting hand on Bobby's shoulder right before the boy collapsed onto his knees beside us. Bobby wrapped his slim arms around my waist, and it was a moment before I remembered in my bemusement to return the embrace.

"I'm sorry," he mumbled through his tears.

"Why are you apologizing?" I asked, genuinely wanting an answer, but I wasn't disappointed when I didn't receive one. Perhaps it was simply one of those mysteries of human emotions which I might never truly understand. All that mattered was that my friend had forgiven me.

Two police officers arrived on the scene a moment later, an ambulance crew following in their wake as they came out of the house and into the backyard. The paramedics immediately descended on Don, their expressions grave as they assessed the seriousness of his injuries. Grace came out of the house next and hovered just beyond the safety of the porch stairs.

"H-how bad is he?" she stuttered.

The male paramedic glanced at her over his shoulder while his counterpart busied herself with stabilizing Don's neck. "It's hard to tell in this light, but it looks like his jaw—"

"Broken jaw. Fractured left cheekbone. Trauma to the left eye. Cracked sternum and possibly a few ribs. Damaged spleen. Concussion."

Everyone stared at me as I recited the litany of injuries I'd inflicted on the figure lying unmoving on the grass. The officer wearing a sergeant's badge approached me, his eyes narrowed in suspicion.

"And how do you know all that?"

"Tim, don't—"

"Because I did it," I said flatly, interrupting David's attempt to protect me.

Grace rushed toward the officer as he reached for his gun. "He saved our lives, mine and my son's." She stared at the policeman until he gave her his full attention, though he kept his hand resting on the handle of his service revolver.

"I'm listening," he prompted, glancing first at Bobby and then back to her. "And what's all this about?" he asked, his attention fixed on the numerous discolorations indicating her own trauma.

"That's what I'm trying to tell you." Grace pointed her chin vaguely toward where the paramedics were working. "That man is my husband. He's been using me and my son as punching bags for years." She bowed her head, humiliation radiating from her as though she knew how bad that sounded. "My son, Bobby, works with these gentlemen, and he called them for help when Don, my husband, started in on us tonight."

The sergeant turned toward Bobby. "Why didn't you call the police?"

Bobby shrugged, his gaze locked on his knees. "I didn't want to get my dad in trouble. I thought David and Tim could make him leave."

"I see." The officer looked at Bobby, his eyes kind but stern. "I can understand that, son, but you should always call us when you need help. That's what we're here for." His grim expression softened into a brief smile for the cowed boy. "But you," the sergeant continued, his face losing any hint of friendliness as he fixed me with a hard stare. "Why don't you tell me why you tried to beat the man to death?"

I didn't try to deny the assessment. Any attempt would have been a blatant lie. "He had a gun," I said simply. "He shot my boss in the arm, and I was afraid he would kill him and then the rest of us."

The sergeant glanced at the other officer, and the man walked over to where Don was lying before pulling out his flashlight and carefully scanning the area.

"It's true!" Bobby's eyes were wide and earnest as he stared up at the sergeant. "My dad said he was going to kill Tim. He saved us!"

"Found it." The other officer held his flashlight up so the beam illuminated the gun he was holding in a gloved hand.

"Hmmph." The sergeant was studying Bobby's bruised face, his own darkening as he accepted the unfortunate truth of the boy's account. "All right, son," he said, looking from Bobby to me. "I'm not going to take you in, young man. Looks like this was a clear case of self-defense. Though next time, you may want to just knock out your assailant without beating him to a pulp." Surprisingly, the man smiled at the confusion that must have been apparent from my expression. "I'm well aware how being under such an imminent threat can make you overreact. God knows I've been in the line of fire a time or two and have been damned glad I could shoot back. If he presses charges after he wakes up, we may have to have another conversation." The sergeant pursed his lips in disgust as he looked over to where the paramedics were maneuvering Don onto a stretcher. "But I'll see to it that he doesn't."

The sergeant turned away and spoke into his radio. I recognized the codes the man gave as signaling a domestic disturbance, the presence of a gun, and that the situation was all clear.

"I'll stop around tomorrow to take you gentlemen's statements," the sergeant added. "And, ma'am, I'm going to need to call this in to child services. Just to follow procedure, you understand."

Grace nodded, and the sergeant quickly took David's contact information. The other policeman went back into the house, taking Don's gun with him, and the sergeant lingered only long enough for the paramedics to begin the process of moving their patient to the ambulance waiting out front. The female paramedic paused as they neared David.

"Sir, let me take a look at that arm."

"It's only a scratch," David said evasively.

"I insist."

Her no-nonsense tone was not to be argued with, and David sighed as he submitted to her examination. After several minutes of probing, she nodded. "Yeah, it looks pretty minor. You may need a few stitches so you don't end up with a nasty scar, but otherwise it should heal up just fine. Wash it thoroughly as soon as you can, and put a bandage over it. And you," she added, glancing at Grace. "You and the boy should get to the hospital to get those cuts and bruises seen to. I understand if you don't want to ride in the ambulance with your husband." With a final, sympathetic smile, she disappeared after her partner, leaving the four of us alone in the yard.

I stood and helped David to his feet while Bobby scrambled up on his own. "We should go," I said, noticing that David's complexion had paled as the ache in his arm obviously grew worse. Something suddenly fell against me, and I blinked as Grace wrapped me in a tight embrace.

"How can I ever thank you?"

I didn't know how to respond. Though everyone had called my actions reasonable under the circumstances, I couldn't absolve myself so easily. I had been extensively drilled in ways to disarm an attacker, and could have easily removed the threat of the gun without ever laying a hand on Don. But instead I'd hurt the man—hurt him badly—all because I was angry at him for shooting David and for abusing a boy who meant a great deal to me. That I was even capable of such a petty act filled me with self-disgust. It was the first time I'd ever experienced that particular emotion, and I didn't much like it.

I let David run interference with Grace as we made our way back through the house. Several pieces of furniture had been damaged, clear signs of the struggle that had ensued as she'd tried to defend herself and her son. Bobby stuck close to my side until we reached the front door. I was better prepared this time when he gave me a fierce hug, though I didn't feel any more comfortable receiving the gesture than I had before. I hugged him back as hard as I dared before stepping away and turning to open the door.

"Bobby, don't bother coming to the store tomorrow." David's voice was tired, but he mustered a smile. "You can let me know when you're ready, but until then, just worry about taking care of your mom." After receiving a mumbled acknowledgement, David led the way as we walked toward his car.

I glanced back in time to see the front door close before looking back toward David, who was holding his wounded arm against his side. "We should stop by a drugstore on the way home," I suggested as we reached the gray sedan. "I can stitch up your arm, and you should probably take some painkillers."

David glanced at me over the roof with a raised eyebrow. "And where did you learn how to do that?" The pinched look around his mouth ruined the attempt at levity.

"I'll tell you later." I quickly opened the passenger door before he could ask me anything else. David got in immediately after me and steered the car toward downtown, carefully favoring his injured arm.

TWENTY-TWO

DAVID TRIED and failed to repress the hiss of pain that slipped out as the suture needle pierced his skin. He wouldn't have felt so bad about it except that Tim's face went paler every time he reacted to the sting. "Ouch," he muttered, exaggerating his wince in an attempt to inject some humor into the situation.

"Sorry," the kid replied for the umpteenth time.

"No, it's all right."

They were sitting on the couch even though the kitchen provided better light. "I'd rather you be comfortable," Tim had explained.

Tim had suggested they buy a bottle of water along with the suture kit and painkillers so David could take the pills as soon as they left the store. It had been a good idea, and by the time they reached the town house, the analgesic had already begun to kick in. It did nothing, however, to mask the stabbing prick of the needle as Tim expertly sealed up his wound with small, neat stitches.

"So where *did* you learn to do that?" He hadn't really expected to receive an answer, having been put off once already, but he was disappointed anyway when Tim's expression clouded over. The kid shook his head, and David tried to ignore the flare of irritation at the stubborn evasion. "Then, can we at least talk about what happened back there?"

Tim froze for a second, his hands poised midstitch, and he looked like he'd just been punched in the gut. "You said you understood," he said meekly before continuing with his task.

"Yeah, I did. I mean, I do, but…." David waited until Tim had finished with the last stitch before angling his body to face him. "That was pretty brutal. It's like that policeman said, why didn't you stop once you had him down?"

Tim used the scissors provided in the kit to clip off the excess thread. He carefully smeared some antibiotic ointment over the wound before covering it with a piece of sterile gauze. David waited until Tim had finished, but when the kid started to clean up in lieu of answering, his patience began to fray.

"Tim—"

"I was afraid you might die."

Tim's voice was barely above a whisper, but his fear spoke loudly. David sighed and placed a hand on the kid's denim-covered thigh. "He was a lousy shot." Shrugging his injured arm, he smiled. "Look, it's nothing more than a scratch."

"But I didn't know that!" Tim exploded. David reared back as the kid fixed him with a frantic, dark-eyed stare. "I didn't know how badly you were hurt. All I saw was the bullet hit you, and then you were bleeding, and I was afraid… I was afraid…."

"Of what?" David asked gently.

Tim inhaled raggedly, clearly fighting back tears. "That I was going to lose you. I was terrified that I would lose you and be all alone." He sprang up from the couch and began to pace, never straying more than a few feet from where David sat. "Which makes no sense, does it? I mean, that's stupid because I'm the one who has to lea…."

David followed the agitated figure with his gaze, his forehead scrunching in confusion. "Has to what?"

Suddenly Tim jerked to a halt and spun toward him, his eyes wide with shock as his gaze locked on David's face. "I love you."

It was David's turn to look stunned. He sat there motionless, unable for nearly a minute to come up with a coherent response to Tim's earth-shattering revelation. "What?" he breathed stupidly once he regained the ability to speak.

Tim dropped to his knees at David's feet and gripped his thighs with a force that was almost painful. His eyes were bright with

275

amazement and not a little disbelief. "Is that it? Is that why I almost went insane when I thought he'd killed you?"

The kid was talking in a rapid blur, as if he was speaking to himself. David wasn't sure whether he was supposed to respond, not that he could have even if he'd wanted to. Tim loved him? All of those interminable nights with the kid lying next to him, tempting him with his nearness and teasing shows of affection, he'd tortured himself by hoping that, one day, Tim might return his feelings. But now that all of his wishes seemed to be coming true, he wasn't sure if he should trust it.

"Tim," he began, trying desperately to muster his thoughts into something intelligible. "Look, what we went through was intense. I can understand how your feelings might get jumbled up—mmmph!"

David instantly forgot whatever he'd been trying to say as Tim crushed their lips together, stealing away every thought. They had kissed before, but this time was different. It was raw and primitive, as though Tim was trying to pour all of his feelings into that one act. Gone was the shy playfulness Tim usually employed whenever he was trying to get David to break his self-imposed vow of abstinence. The intensity of the kiss was as unnerving as it was unexpected, and David broke away, needing a moment to gather his wits before they were completely scattered to the four winds.

"Hey, kid, wait a sec. Easy, now," he soothed when Tim looked at him with something approaching panic. He traced his hand over Tim's cheek in a reassuring caress. "No, I'm not stopping you, but I want you to be sure about this." He exhaled sharply, forcing his pulse back into something less likely to send him into cardiac arrest. "Look, when I told you that I love you, it was the absolute truth," he rushed to add when Tim opened his mouth to interrupt. "But that doesn't mean I expect you to feel the same way." He smiled, but it felt unnatural and strained. "I know you care about me. You have a big heart." The curve of his lips felt more genuine as Tim jerked in surprise at the assessment. "No, it's true. I didn't realize it at first. Still waters and all that, I guess, but I know it now." He watched his thumb as it followed the curve of Tim's chin. "The way you are with Bobby, I can tell you love him like a little brother. You feel deeply for the people you care about. And I know you're grateful to me for taking you in when you had nowhere else to go, but I…." He paused, praying he sounded wise and not simply pathetic. "I don't want you to mistake that gratitude for something it's not."

"Bobby's father wasn't lying." Tim's dark gaze was unwavering as it captured his. "I did threaten to kill him."

David stuttered to a halt at the unexpected confession. "W-what are you talking about?"

"It's like he said," Tim continued, his tone flat in sharp contrast to his previous urgency. The abrupt shift shook David to the core. "The evening after we left Bobby at the hospital, I tracked his father down and followed him to a gay club. I offered to have sex with him behind the building, and once I had him alone, I threatened to kill him if he didn't disappear from Grace's and Bobby's lives."

It had been so long, David had forgotten how unnerving Tim had seemed at the beginning, with his emotionless stare and mechanical way of speaking. He struggled to voice all the questions slamming through his brain. "Why?" was as far as he got.

"Because he'd hurt Bobby, and I wanted to ensure his safety."

"But you didn't hurt Don."

"No." Tim shook his head, his gaze fixed somewhere around David's chin. "Not badly, anyway. Once I'd extracted his promise, I let him go."

David remembered back to that night after Tim had come home. He'd assumed the kid had merely gone for a long walk, but apparently he'd been gravely mistaken. It made sense now why Tim had seemed so distressed. He'd realized ever since their first encounter with Bobby that Tim's moral code was quite different than his, and could only assume it was a result of his upbringing. It didn't make him comfortable, exactly, but he tried to at least understand where Tim was coming from. "Well, like you said, you didn't do any damage." *Not then, at least*, he finished silently.

Tim finally looked up, and David gasped at the desperation in his gaze, the remoteness gone like he'd only imagined it. "Even though he'd hurt Bobby badly enough to land him in the hospital, all I did was scare him." Tim leaned forward, erasing the distance between them until David could feel the soft whisper of Tim's breath against his face. "But when it was you that he'd hurt, that he tried to kill...." The remaining distance shrunk to nothing, and Tim's next words were spoken directly against his mouth. "I wanted to crush him."

The mobile sweetness of Tim's lips against his was irresistible, and David fell willingly into the kiss, his doubts fading before the undeniable certainty in Tim's voice as he whispered his feelings like a mantra.

"I love you. I love you. I love you," Tim murmured over and over, each renewed declaration followed immediately by another kiss.

David's heart soared, but his body was done with being left out of the conversation. A dull roar sounded in his ears as blood rushed southward of his brain. His hesitation suddenly seemed pointless in the face of Tim's stunning confession. He was tired of being noble, of trying to ignore what his heart had been telling him ever since he'd first looked into those wary brown eyes. Tim needed to learn that not every problem could be solved with violence, but that lesson would have to wait for another time. Right now, there was only one thing David wanted to teach his increasingly enthusiastic pupil.

Tim had crawled into his lap, and David placed his hands on the slim legs straddling his hips, rubbing them soothingly as he began to scoot off the sofa cushions. Tim must have mistaken his maneuver as a renewed attempt to push him away because he whimpered, pulling back only far enough to latch onto his face with a pleading stare.

"No, don't," Tim begged, peppering every part of him he could reach with frantic kisses. "Don't push me away. Not this time. Not now." He placed his hands on either side of David's head, holding him in place. "I promise, I'll tell you anything you want to know about me. But let me have this."

"It's okay," David soothed. He smiled fondly, finding the kid's horny distress as endearing as the rest of him. "I'm just trying to move this to the bedroom. I'm too old to be making out on the couch like I'm still in high school."

Tim stared at him for a long moment before his body relaxed, the tension leaving him in a rush. A corner of his mouth curved shyly, and he pressed his face into the hollow of David's neck in an unspoken display of trust.

David felt ungainly as he half led, half carried Tim up the stairs. They stopped every few steps to indulge in wet, openmouthed kisses, and by the time they reached the door of his room, he was achingly hard, his cock throbbing as brutally as his arm. He dropped Tim onto his bed unceremoniously, grinning in embarrassment as the kid flopped bonelessly on the blanket-covered mattress. "Sorry. Guess my back isn't what it used to be."

"Don't care."

That was all the response David got before he found himself pulled down into a pair of welcoming arms. Once again he was amazed by how much strength was packed into Tim's deceptively slender frame, but his appreciation remained abstract, as he was soon far more pleasantly engaged.

It wasn't the first time they'd been pressed together full length on his bed, but it was the first time David really allowed himself to feel it. Before, he'd always been concerned with keeping things as platonic as possible, with being the adult and taking the high road, but now his mind was firmly in the gutter and had no intention of leaving it. Employing skills he'd thought lost through lack of use, he set about trying to drive Tim out of his mind. He parted his lips and Tim slavishly followed suit, allowing him to slip his tongue inside the kid's unbearably sweet mouth.

Tim dug slim fingers into David's back, clutching the fabric of his shirt. "Mmmm," he moaned as their tongues caressed. As always, he was a quick study, and before long Tim was sucking on his, making David temporarily forget he was trying to take it slow.

"Shhh," David whispered. He pulled back and allowed his lips to drift over Tim's jaw and down the long curve of his neck. "Just relax."

Ignoring him, Tim pushed up with his hips, instinctively signaling what he wanted. He delved impatient hands below the bottom of David's shirt and dragged the fabric up, exposing his bare skin to an eager touch. David groaned as nimble fingers traced down his back and dug into the upper curve of his butt before trailing around his sides to his stomach. Tim scratched blunt nails in teasing lines over David's belly as he trailed them up to his chest, and David felt his cock jump to full attention when Tim flicked lightly over his nipples. He'd never thought of the nubs as being particularly sensitive, but apparently they'd simply been waiting for the right playmate.

"God, kid, you're killing me." He reached down and grabbed Tim's hands, pressing them firmly to either side of his head. Lifting up, he rested his weight on his uninjured arm and gazed into Tim's dazed eyes. "Leave them there, okay?"

"Why? You don't like me touching you?" Confusion was quickly replaced by anxiety. "Did I hurt your arm?"

The gunshot wound did ache, but the kid had done a fabulous job of fixing him up, and David refused to be derailed by something so trivial. He smiled reassuringly. "No, that's not it. Well, the fact that I love you touching me is sort of the problem." Tim's nose scrunched up adorably, and he laughed. "I don't want you making me lose it before I'm good and ready. Got it?"

It was clear from the look on the kid's face that he didn't, but David didn't bother trying to explain any further. He was far more concerned about making certain that Tim's first time—and he had no doubt that it was—would be absolutely perfect. He'd lost his own virginity within his first month of college to a guy he'd only been seeing for a couple of weeks. It was memorable only because it had been so awkward and painful, neither of them really knowing what they were doing. He'd be damned if Tim suffered the same experience.

David moved his hands away from Tim's wrists, gratified when his order was obeyed. Pushing himself up with his good arm, he straddled Tim's hips in a reverse of the position in which they usually ended up. He reached over and flicked on the light switch, illuminating the room and allowing him to fully appreciate his prize. Slowly, he pulled Tim's shirt upward in a less frantic imitation of Tim's early assault on him, gazing appreciatively at each inch of glowing, olive-toned skin as it was revealed. Impatience gripped him before he could finish, and he whisked the shirt up the last few inches and over the kid's head before tossing it blindly to the side. The movement made his wound twinge, but he easily disregarded the discomfort. He wanted nothing to distract him from the sight of Tim willingly stretched out for his pleasure.

"You're so beautiful," David said quietly. He traced his hands downward from Tim's shoulders to the waistband of his jeans, pausing to savor the feel of peaked nipples tickling against his palms. Tim whimpered, and David grinned wickedly as he bent over and licked at the brown nubs with his tongue.

"Ahh!" Tim jerked beneath him, his hips moving erratically as the outline of his erection pressed visibly against the denim of his jeans. "Wait! I'm going to—"

"Hmmm?" David hummed with mock curiosity, knowing full well what the kid had been about to say. His own hardness was trapped just as painfully, but he ignored it, focusing all his attention on the luscious body writhing beneath him. Wrapping his lips around one of the enticing peaks, he sucked gently while his fingers explored the grooves of Tim's defined abs.

"Unngg!" Tim groaned, the teasing fingers dragging the sound out from his throat. "Please!"

After several minutes of nibbling at his new toy, David eventually decided to show mercy. Undoing the button holding Tim's fly together, he pulled the kid's jeans and briefs down far enough that he could take Tim's weeping member into his hand. David moved his mouth lazily across Tim's chest from one nipple to the other, drawing the neglected twin into his mouth as he slowly worked Tim's cock with firm strokes.

Tim didn't last long, crying out incoherently as white, viscous fluid shot over David's hand. His entire body trembled as David drew out the moment for as long as he could, only relenting once Tim calmed down. For once David was glad he was past the point of being able to come with such a minimum of stimulation. His cock was aching, but he wasn't in any danger of things ending before he planned. He'd been waiting a long time for this, and he had no intention of rushing.

"Better now?" he asked, wiping the remnants of the kid's passionate outburst on his pants. He'd worry about doing the laundry later. Much later. David chuckled when Tim's answer came in the form of a groan which seemed to emanate from the bottom of his feet.

"What about you?"

David was somewhat impressed the kid had found the energy to speak at all. "Oh, we're not done." He leaned down and bit gently on the curve of Tim's ear before soothing the hurt with his tongue. "There's no hurry. We have all night." Tim moaned, tensing as his body protested against its reaction to David's teasing. "Whoa!" The room seemed to spin, and David stared up at Tim in surprise when he abruptly found himself on his back with the kid poised over him like a jungle cat ready to pounce. He hissed as his arm protested the manhandling. The kid spared his bandage a swift, apologetic glance, but seemed to have something far more pressing on his mind.

"I don't want to wait," Tim growled.

David felt his cock twitch eagerly within its prison at the animalistic sound. It wasn't trapped for much longer as Tim's determined fingers made short work of his button fly. He winced as he heard the fabric rip, but decided he didn't particularly care if Tim completely ruined his wardrobe. He owned a retail store, for Pete's sake. He'd damned well just buy some new jeans. The thrust of the kid's tongue into his mouth quickly ended all thoughts of clothing. Though his eyes were closed, he could tell by the rustling and wiggling above him that Tim had managed to kick off his jeans and briefs without once relinquishing his assault on David's mouth. His hands landed unerringly on Tim's thighs, a hasty upward slide confirming that the kid was, indeed, completely naked.

"Yeah, okay," David grunted, easily admitting defeat. He worked on taking off his own pants, grateful when Tim helped him, since his hands were suddenly trembling in anticipation. He briefly wondered which one of them was the virgin in this scenario before the kid dropped on top of him, making his breath leave in a rush. "Watch the arm," he cautioned, but all was immediately forgiven as he rejoiced in the novel sensation of skin on skin. "Aww, fuck!" he shouted when a dexterous hand took hold of his arousal and began treating him to a taste of his own medicine.

"Tell me," Tim murmured before slipping his tongue into David's mouth.

Damn, he catches on fast, David thought, his concentration failing as the hand caressed him slowly from root to tip. "Nnngg, tell you what?" he rasped when he finally managed to catch a breath. Tim licked at the shell of his ear, and the limited part of his brain that was still working noticed Tim was copying everything that had been done to him.

"Tell me how it will feel when you're inside me."

"Son of a…" was all David managed as he flung the hand of his uninjured arm out to the side, hissing when it banged against the edge of the nightstand sitting next to the bed. He pulled out the drawer blindly as Tim pillaged his mouth again. After several frantic seconds of groping, he found what he'd been searching for and pulled out the all-important foil packets and squeeze tube. David dropped the items on the bed within easy reach, glad he'd had the foresight to buy them shortly after Tim had started sleeping with him on a regular basis. A song he'd learned in the Boy Scouts drifted in and out of his head as he used his thumb to pop open the lid of the tube.

Caught off guard, Tim reared back as David breached the puckered opening of his ass with a lubed finger. "Ahhh! What are you doing?" He reached behind him and grabbed at David's wrist, making David grunt at the force of his grip.

"Take it easy," David said, trying to calm him. "I only want to make sure I don't hurt you. I need to make you nice and slick for me." He felt mildly ridiculous at using such porny language, but he was reassured when the anxiety on Tim's face cleared and the viselike hold on his wrist disappeared.

"Oh. Okay." The kid visibly tried to make himself relax, and David couldn't help thinking it was cute.

"God, I really am a dirty old man," he grumbled to himself.

"You're not o-old." Tim's breath hitched as another finger was added to the first.

"Well, I'm definitely not too old for this." David lightly grasped Tim's swiftly reawakening member and smiled when the kid started moving his hips in time to the strokes. Each backward shift forced the digits toying at his entrance deeper, and soon Tim was panting, biting at his bottom lip as he whimpered deliciously. "That's it," David urged. "Open up for me."

Tim's mouth was agape, his moist lips shining as he lost himself in the dual sensation of the hand on his cock and the fingers in his ass. David swore he could feel his arousal twitch approvingly with each moan, and he suddenly feared he wouldn't last long enough to take that final, long awaited step. Deciding Tim was as prepared as he was going to be, David cupped his free hand against the kid's cheek to get his attention.

"Hey," he said as unfocused eyes met his gaze. "Are you ready?"

"Mmmm-hmmm," Tim breathed, nodding in response.

Taking him at his word, David pulled his fingers away, smiling at the disgruntled moan he received in response. He fumbled for one of the condom packets, cursing his slick fingers as he tried to open it. Finally he simply ripped it open with his teeth, careful not to tear the latex circle.

"Let me."

David blinked at Tim when he took the condom, and, reaching behind himself, rolled the sheath over David's arousal without looking. *Who in the hell taught him that?* He would have sworn the kid was untouched, but maybe he was wrong. Not that he could find it in himself to care when Tim was at that very moment lowering himself ever so slowly onto his rock-hard cock.

"Holy fuck!" David shouted. Tight and hot. Those were the only two words that managed to coalesce in his brain. He gripped hard at Tim's hips, figuring he could apologize later for any bruises he left behind. Right then he desperately needed something to hold on to. "Easy," he groaned, trying urgently to remember why he wanted to take things slow. "You don't have to rush." Tim's snug passage was squeezing him so tightly it almost hurt, but he was determined to wait until Tim found his pleasure once again before he surrendered to his own needs. "Take your time... aaahhh, fuck it all!" David yelled as Tim pushed down without warning, stopping only when the curve of his ass was resting on top of David's thighs.

"Yes!" Tim moaned. His eyes were squeezed shut, a grimace of discomfort twisting his features for a brief moment before they smoothed into unmistakable ecstasy. "I can feel you," he cried. His body spasmed as it tried to adjust to the intrusion, the pulsing caress making David's eyes roll back in his head. Tim groped until he found the hands clutching his hips and grasped them tightly. "Please, don't go!"

"Never," David groaned. His hips lifted instinctively as he strove to drive himself some further, impossible distance into the intoxicating heat of Tim's body. Tim fell forward until their chests were pressed together, sweat pooling between them.

"Promise?" Tim breathed.

"I promise."

There were no more words as they moved together in a perfect counterpoint. Tim met every upward thrust, their bodies fitting perfectly, as though they'd been purposefully designed precisely for this moment. Tim arched his back, his swollen arousal rubbing in a desperate search for friction against the trail of soft hair that led from David's stomach down to where Tim was riding his cock. The kid was abusing his lip with his teeth, and David drew him down to suck the swollen flesh into his own mouth, soothing the hurt. Tim slammed his hands against the wall above their heads, bracing his arms as he fucked himself on David's cock with wild abandon.

David felt the muscles in his thighs flex, his balls pulling in tight in preparation for releasing the load they'd been holding for far too long. "Jesus, Tim!"

"Say it again," the kid pleaded, sounding like he was on the verge of tears.

"Say what?" he asked, unequal to the task of deciphering the request.

"Nnnngg! Say my name."

"Tim," David obliged, his voice thready as he teetered on the edge of release.

"Again," Tim gasped as he impaled himself over and over with desperate thrusts of his hips. "Please, say it again!"

David placed his hands on either side of Tim's face, his heart full to bursting when those sweet, dazed brown eyes opened and met his adoring gaze. "Tim," he whispered, his voice cracking as he was overcome by the depths of his feelings for this unexpected gift fate had given him.

Tim inhaled on a sob and dropped his face into the crook of David's neck like he could no longer bear the weight of his own feeling. "I love you," he moaned, his body clenching in a timeless rhythm as he came for a second time.

At a loss for words, David let his body speak for him. Light blazed behind his closed eyelids, and he buried himself deep inside Tim's straining body when his release finally claimed him. Tim's passage milked his cock from root to tip, and the intensity of the moment, unequal to anything he'd ever experienced before now, shocked him. Everything he'd thought he knew about love was wrong. He'd never felt like this for anyone else. Tim was his now, and he wouldn't accept anything less than forever. David's arms seemed to move on their own as they encircled the heaving young body lying on top of him, the sting in his arm momentarily forgotten as he tightened his hold in the certain knowledge that he would never let go.

Long minutes passed before their breathing slowed to normal. David smiled lazily as he noticed they were inhaling and exhaling in time with each other. The synchronicity seemed fitting after what they'd shared. He rubbed a hand slowly over the sleek expanse of Tim's back, listening contentedly as the kid's breathing slowed into the cadence of sleep. The wound in his arm began to ache again, scolding him for engaging in such vigorous activity so recently after having been shot, but he relished the discomfort. It was an immediate reminder that he'd experienced something amazing.

"I love you too," he whispered softly into the sleeping figure's ear before allowing the exhaustion of the whirlwind day to claim him.

TWENTY-THREE

I REALIZED I was awake only after my eyes had already opened. I wasn't sure what had disturbed me, but after a lazy scan of my surroundings I detected nothing but the sound of the heart beating steadily next to my ear. I smiled and snuggled further into David's warm chest, relishing the knowledge that there was no place else I wanted to be.

Inhaling deeply, I breathed in the lingering scent of sweat and warm skin. In the time since David had begun letting me sleep in his bed, I thought I'd come to understand the concept of intimacy, but I'd been mistaken. None of the platonic embraces we'd shared in any way equaled the reality of that ultimate joining. I could still feel the imprint of David's lips and hands all over my skin. That part of me that had welcomed him so eagerly ached ever so slightly, providing me with a delicious reminder of how it felt to take David into my body. We'd come together another two times during the night, and each time I experienced that connection I'd only wanted more. Even now, when I was completely sated, my thoughts were consumed with how good David had felt pressed so closely against me that nothing could come between us, not even air. I wanted that again, wanted to feel the warmth and safety of being held in his arms. Maybe I was simply trying to make up for all of the physical affection I'd missed growing up in the cold, sterile environment of the Facility. Or, I thought with a smile, maybe I was just in love.

At last I truly understood exactly what that meant. I wanted to touch David, to kiss him and hold him, and to never let go—everything that amazing word implied. I'd been shocked when I'd realized the truth of my feelings, but I would be forever grateful that I'd had this chance to know the wonder of holding another person so completely in my heart. Unable to express myself in words beyond that one, all-important admission, I'd tried to show David how I felt with my body, begging again and again to know the bliss of his possession. Though he had willingly indulged me, eventually he'd begged for mercy, reminding me that we both had to get up in the morning for work. It was only with great reluctance that I'd finally followed him into sleep, reassured by the knowledge that we could do this all over again tomorrow night.

A sort of giddiness seemed to bubble up from deep inside me, and I couldn't decide whether I wanted to laugh or breach that ultimate barrier of tears. The feelings and emotions that had eluded me for so long were now an indelible part of me, overwhelming me with their power. David had given me this gift of being able to know my own heart, and for that, if nothing else, I owed him everything.

"I love you," I whispered to the man snoring softly next to me, the taste of the words now a familiar sweetness on my tongue. A smile tugged gently at my lips as I watched David sleep.

In the next instant, I was sitting up suddenly, my back ramrod straight with tension. For a moment there was only silence. Then I heard it again—a faint noise coming through the bedroom window. The hair lifted on the back of my neck as my body instinctively registered some form of impending danger. Carefully, I eased out from beneath the covers and reached for my pajama bottoms. They were at the foot of the bed where I'd gotten into the habit of leaving them, and I smiled despite myself at the memory of why I hadn't put them on the night before. I had just pulled them up when a sound from behind me made me pause.

"Mmmm. Where are you going?" David's voice was slurred, and when I glanced back at him, his face was firmly buried in his pillow. I sat down on the edge of the bed and angled myself so he could see me more easily.

"I thought I heard something outside, and it woke me up. It's probably nothing. Go back to sleep."

David flopped his uninjured arm across the space where I had been lying, reaching out until he'd grabbed my wrist. "Not without you."

A goofy smile spread over my lips. Succumbing to the gentle pull, I allowed him to tug me back across the mattress. I knelt beside David and leaned down for a kiss.

"I thought you said you were tired," I teased after several interesting minutes during which David managed to peel me halfway out of my pajamas.

"Took a nap," David replied, sucking at the column of my neck in a way that made my toes curl and my cock stand at attention.

The loud, dissonant screech of brakes sounded like it came from right outside the bedroom window. We sprang apart in surprise, David blinking in confusion as his sleepy and sex-addled brain struggled to process what was going on. My body went ice-cold as I jumped up, leaving David to stare at me as I quickly righted my clothes. I'd picked up the sound of the engines from the vehicles, the timbre instantly betraying their identity to my trained ear. My gut clenched as I realized I'd finally run out of time.

"Get dressed," I ordered, tossing David his pajamas as I rushed around the foot of the bed and toward the bedroom door.

He merely blinked at me, clearly shocked at my commanding tone. "Tim, what—"

"Do it!"

Sparing only a glance at the wounded look on David's face, I flung myself down the stairs and was in the living room in an instant. His hurt feelings would have to wait. My worst nightmares were coming true, and we didn't have a moment to lose. I grabbed our coats from the closet and gathered up the shoes we always left by the door. We'd have to put them on later, once we'd put some distance between us and the town house. Doing so now would take time we didn't have. I hoped David would be able to keep up while barefoot and swiftly calculated the best route that would keep to grassy terrain as much as possible. I was uncertain how long we would have to remain on the run or what conditions we might face.

Never once did the thought of leaving David behind occur to me. He had become a necessary part of my life, and I would do whatever it took to keep him safe. Anything, that is, except not be with him. I could no longer even consider that course as an option. I heard him come into the room behind me and threw him his coat.

David flailed to catch the unexpected projectile hurtling toward his face. "Tim, what the hell is going on?"

"I'll tell you later. Right now, take your shoes." I tried to keep my voice calm as I handed them over. "No, you can put them on later," I said as David grabbed at his shoes and dropped them next to his feet to slide them on. I heard a sound out front and pushed the reluctant man toward the kitchen after stooping to retrieve the shoes a second time. "Come on. Back door. We have to go. Now!" I yelled, fear making me impatient when he merely stood there staring at me like I'd lost my mind.

Before I could say another word, the front door crashed in, and a man wearing a combat uniform and brandishing a high-caliber automatic weapon burst into the room. David cursed in shock, but I didn't respond as my body acted on automatic. Darting forward, I crouched and swung my leg out, catching the intruder across the ankles. The man went down hard, and I rolled toward him in a forward tuck, bashing my elbow into the soldier's nose when he was within range.

I couldn't spare another thought for my incapacitated target, as two more men came in behind him, weapons at the ready. Leaping from my back to my feet, I aimed one of the shoes clutched in my hand at one of the newcomers' heads, taking advantage of the man's resulting distraction to grab hold of the barrel of his gun. Grunting, I pulled hard and swung the soldier into his comrade, taking care to keep the barrel pointed toward the far side of the room and away from David. My knee caught the second of the pair in the groin, and I used the momentum from the ricochet to kick out at the already bloody face of the first intruder, who had begun to climb to his feet. I caught the man again in the face, and the unfortunate soldier went down for a second time with a howl as he slapped a hand over his now broken nose.

Still holding the stock of the assault rifle, I felt myself being jerked forward as its owner tried to pry the weapon free from my grip. A sharp, downward exertion of force relieved the man of his gun, and I whipped it around, unerringly finding the trigger simply by feel as I aimed the weapon at the soldier's midsection. Before I could fire, something barreled through the front window and rolled toward my foot. I gritted my teeth as I saw the black-and-gray cylinder roll across the carpet, but I was already moving before it even came to a halt. I smashed the stock of the rifle into its former owner's face before spinning around toward David, who had been standing back in awe, watching me dispatch the soldiers with professional skill. I covered the distance between us in less than a heartbeat and grabbed David to pull him down to the ground before covering his body with my own.

"Close your eyes!" I shouted before taking my own advice and burying my face in his hair.

The flash-bang went off with a deafening roar. Even through my closed eyelids, the abrupt surge of brightness threatened to shrivel my retinas. The sound of the explosion lingered in my ears, making them ring, but I recovered quickly, as I'd been designed to do. It was only a few seconds before I was able to hear the sound of heavy footsteps treading up the outside stairs.

"Well, well. Isn't this cozy?"

I hugged David tightly as I recognized the familiar drawl, not wanting to confront this particular demon until it was absolutely necessary. "Are you all right?" I asked the man huddled in my arms. I felt something wet against my skin, and grimaced as I saw the spot of red that soiled the gauze covering David's gunshot wound. Some of the sutures must have given way when I'd pushed him down. "Are you okay?" I asked again, the words catching in my throat. David didn't respond except to look up at me with a stunned expression, his senses obviously reeling from the grenade.

"Huh. Like I always told the good doctor, I knew training you in how to impersonate a faggot would come in handy. Looks like I was right."

I could feel the general's ice-blue gaze boring into the back of my head, but I couldn't make myself turn around. I'd tried so hard to forget the sound of that condescending voice. A few more seconds and David and I would have been safely away. On the run, but together. Would David really have gone with me willingly as I forced him to leave his life behind? Now I would never get the chance to find out. My past, it seemed, had finally caught up with me. I saw the rifle lying where I'd dropped it before tackling David, and my hand inched toward it, plans and contingencies forming in my mind.

"Ah, ah. None of that, unless you want me to put a bullet in lover boy's brain."

I turned my head far enough to see the gun in the general's hand and where it was aimed. "How did you find me?" I asked, my plans falling to dust around me. My voice sounded far away as my ears continued to compensate for the damage from the grenade. The general had trained me. Any strategies I might attempt would be useless against this opponent.

"Price. Timmons," Woodard said. "Come on in."

"You're the guys from the coffee shop!"

I looked at David in surprise as he stared over my shoulder. David's dumbfounded expression overcame my reluctance, and I glanced around to see the familiar faces of two men—one blond, the other brunet—as they walked into the house at the general's invitation. I had almost figured them for soldiers at the county fair, but I had let the joy of that day distract me and ruin my instincts. I looked back toward the general, who was looking down at me, his lips twisted in familiar smirk. I hadn't laid eyes on him since I'd seen my beloved Father Paul gunned down before my eyes. He might not have pulled the trigger himself, but that was merely a technicality. It was his fault Father Paul was dead, and the only thing I felt for the man was hatred.

"You've met?" Woodard asked his men, his cold gaze never straying from my face.

"We saw him at a local coffee shop some weeks ago," the brunet answered. "We never suspected he was the one harboring the fugitive."

"Fugitive?" David asked.

I tightened my arm around David's waist, though I didn't know whether it was to keep him safe or to prevent him from shoving me away.

"What, you never told him what you are?" The general chuckled. "Of course you didn't. That would have defeated the purpose of hiding in plain sight, I suppose. Not that it did you any good in the end." Woodard shook his head. "Even with all that garbage Anderson pumped into your head, I never thought you would expose yourself by getting involved in something as trite as a domestic disturbance." He jerked his thumb toward the younger soldiers. "Price and Timmons picked up the call for that mess you were involved in last night and checked it out on a hunch. Imagine my delight when they reported spotting you leaving the scene." Woodard glared at me, his lips curving into a sneer. "All that work we put into finding you, and all it took was listening in on a police scanner." He chuckled humorlessly. "Dumb luck is better than no luck, isn't that what they say? Too bad you've run out of even that, you little piece of shit."

The blood drained from my face as the general taunted me with my carelessness. Showing off at the fair had been one thing, but what I'd done to Bobby's father was sure to have drawn attention. Very unwelcome attention, as it turned out. David chose that moment to stand up, pushing away from my hold. I rose quickly to maintain my position as a shield between him and the general, but David stubbornly tried to put himself out front.

"I asked you a question." David's expression was clouded, likely as much from the disorientation of the flash-bang as with confusion. "Why are you calling Tim a fugitive? And who in the hell are you?"

"Tim?" A gray eyebrow rose incredulously as Woodard glanced from me to David and back. "Is that what he told you his name is? Cute." The general's smile resembled that of a hyena that had scented prey. "Actually, it's not even a 'he.' It's an 'it.' TM 05637 is an escaped lab experiment, a rabid dog that got off its leash. Isn't that right?"

As David turned to me, it was clear from his furrowed brow that he hadn't understood a word of the general's so-called explanation. "Tim, what is he talking about?"

I avoided responding by confronting my tormentor directly. "My name *is* Tim," I declared, staring into Woodard's eyes and daring the man to contradict me. Although I was afraid to meet David's gaze, the sound of my name on his lips gave me confidence. It was the one thing I had ever had for myself, and I wouldn't give it up without a fight.

The general pursed his lips but didn't rise to the bait. "I don't particularly care what you call yourself, though you're obviously in desperate need of mental reconditioning. Something I'll see to as soon as we get you back to the Facility."

"I'm not going back."

"Cut the crap, *Tim*," Woodard hissed. "You're out of options." He pressed a button on the device strapped to his wrist. "Now, you can either come quietly, or I will tie your boyfriend to something sturdy and set this entire place on fire. The very fact that he even knows of your existence should sign his death warrant."

The sound of the back door crashing open shook the house, and I turned toward the kitchen just in time to see four more of the general's men flood into the living room with their weapons drawn. If I had been alone I might have stood a chance, but with David in the picture I knew any further resistance would gain me nothing. My nails dug into my palms as I clenched my fists helplessly. Everything I had worked so hard for was slipping away before my eyes. Grinding my teeth, I struggled to hide my fear as I turned back to face my nemesis.

"I'll go with you if you let this man go free. I swear to you, he won't tell anyone the truth about me."

Woodard looked at me with genuine curiosity. "Why do you even care what happens to him? He's served his purpose in sheltering you, but that's over. What, now you feel guilty about getting him mixed up in this?"

I didn't want to answer. What was between me and David was none of the general's business, but I knew I had to say something. "I—"

"Tim," David growled, "what are you thinking?"

I looked around at the man standing behind me, pausing as I was caught by the angry blue eyes glaring fixedly at Woodard.

"You don't have to go anywhere with these people." David lurched unsteadily toward the general, still suffering the effects of the grenade. "I don't know who you are, you son of a bitch, but you have no right to come into my house and—"

"David!" I rushed forward as the blond soldier, Timmons, moved to block the man threatening his superior, ending the perceived attack with the butt of his handgun. The weapon smashed against the side of David's head, and he fell hard to the floor. I dropped to his side and gathered him into my arms. "David," I whispered, my throat going dry with panic as his head lolled against my chest. In a rush, all of the months of worry about being caught, my grief over losing my mentor, the heady joy of falling in love, everything coalesced in a torrent of emotion that roared up from my chest. I no longer possessed the capacity to isolate myself from my feelings, and I was at their mercy as they poured out of me in an uncontrollable torrent.

"I love him, you bastard!" I shouted, looking up to glare at the general. My voice was hoarse as hot tears scalded my cheeks. "I love him!"

Woodard stared at me, dumbfounded at what he was seeing. "What the fuck is this? Are you actually crying? You were built to be a machine of war, not some pathetic fool that thinks it has feelings," he sneered. "You don't love him. You can't love him. You're an experiment, a genetically engineered machine. Your so-called 'feelings' are nothing but a defect. You're nothing but a goddamn failure." The general shook his head in disgust and leveled his gun at my head. "I should terminate you right here, but," he growled with barely concealed disgust, "the Company has ordered that you be brought back in one piece for reprogramming."

"Uggghh."

I wiped away the tears marring my vision when David stirred in my arms. "Are you all right?" I rasped. Ignoring the general, I looked carefully into David's eyes as he struggled to sit up. I sighed with relief, noting that his pupils were normal and showed no signs of a concussion. "Here," I said gently, "take it easy." I helped him to a sitting position, using my own body to support his back. "I'm begging you," I pleaded when I finally looked toward Woodard. "I'll go with you. Just let David stay here."

The general stared at me for a long moment before nodding sharply. Holstering his weapon, he held up his other hand and circled it twice above his head. Responding to the unspoken signal, his men melted away, leaving the house empty save for the three of us. "Let's go, TM 05637," he ordered.

I winced at the sound of my designation as I forced myself to meet my lover's confused gaze. The sight of those expressive blue eyes making my chest ache at the thought of losing them forever. "David, I have to leave." My breath hitched, my entire body trembling in rebellion against the impending sense of loss. "I'm so sorry."

David blinked at me slowly, trying to make sense of everything despite the recent blow to his head. "I don't understand."

"And I can't explain." He didn't need to know every sordid detail about me. I wanted him to always think of me as I'd pretended to be— simply a normal boy in love. "Please remember that I love you. In spite of everything, I never lied to you about that." I leaned forward and pressed a soft kiss to David's lips as he parted them to speak. "No. No questions," I murmured, pulling back only far enough to hoard one last glimpse of his beloved face. "You have to let me go."

David remained silent as I stood and turned away. Without a word, I walked past the general and out to the line of jeeps that were sitting incongruously in the residential parking lot. Despite the late hour, many lights were on in the windows of the neighboring houses, and several people had ventured out to see what was going on. I had no doubt the general would handle any calls placed to the police with some cleverly spun lies. By morning, it would be like nothing had ever happened.

Two soldiers materialized at my side, herding me in the direction of a nondescript, civilian van. I'd had every intention of merely walking forward, of putting one foot in front of the other, but I couldn't stop myself from turning back for one final look at the life I could have had if things had been different. If I'd been different. The general had stepped outside, and I could see David standing in the doorway immediately behind the imposing figure. Bewilderment and hurt vied for dominance on his face as he watched me walk out of his life. Our gazes met for a brief moment before Woodard pulled something out of his pocket and pressed it against David's neck.

"No!" I screamed as David's limbs twitched uncontrollably from the jolt of electricity the Taser shot through his unsuspecting body before he dropped to lie motionless on the ground. Frozen in shock at the general's betrayal, I was defenseless against the needle one of my escorts suddenly jabbed into my neck. The drug worked fast, numbing my body as it swiftly pulled me into unconsciousness. Unable to fight against the men hustling me into the waiting van, I could only manage one word before I could no longer control my mouth.

"David!" I cried out again, my words already slurred beyond understanding. The general's mocking grin was the last thing I saw before the van door slammed shut behind me.

Coming Soon

The sequel to *To Be Human*

To Be Loved

By Pearl Love

Tim—designation TM 05637—thought he'd escaped his fate as a genetically engineered super-soldier when David Conley offered him a precious chance at a normal life. But General Woodard, Tim's handler, captures them, crushing Tim's short-lived dream. Thrilled at the return of his pet killing machine, Woodard plans to break Tim's resistance by forcing him to virtually kill David.

Fortunately, Dr. Paul Anderson, the scientist who created Tim, offers them a chance at freedom. But a deadly weakness implanted in Tim's DNA threatens his life. Without regular doses of a special medication, Tim faces debilitation and even death. In search of a more permanent solution, Dr. Anderson enlists David's help to infiltrate a base where a cure is kept. But David is unable to fully trust Tim, haunted by seeing Tim killing him in Woodard's brutal training simulations.

Desperate to protect David, both from the general—and himself—Tim struggles to find the strength to leave the man he loves while completing the mission. With Dr. Anderson's help, Tim and David try to stay a step ahead of the general, knowing they must reach the cure before mistrust tears them apart, Woodard catches up with them, or the clock runs out on Tim's life.

http://www.dreamspinnerpress.com

PROLOGUE

INHALE. EXHALE.
> *One.*
> Inhale. Exhale.
> *Two.*
> Inhale. Exhale.
> *Three….*

The unvarying rhythm of air rushing in and out of its lungs allowed it to track the passage of time. The helmet it wore was bolted down to the stiff collar ringing the neck of its suit, muting all external sound. The opaque visor blocked any extraneous visual clues. The lack of stimulus was of no concern. It had no other purpose than to await orders.

It stood completely still, save for the necessary expansion and contraction of its chest. Constantly monitoring its biological systems, it determined that it was running at peak efficiency. And even if it were under stress, the uniform it wore was made of a material that regulated its core temperature, enabling it to continue performing optimally no matter how extreme the conditions. The soft material rested so lightly against its skin, it barely registered the fabric's presence. It wore no body armor that might hamper the speed or agility of its movements.

It had no concept of how long it had been waiting. It had no memory of anything before the present moment. It was aware only of the darkness of the helmet's interior, the caress of the breaths that reflected back toward its face from the curved surface of the shielded polycarbonate, and the rigid feel of the weapon held in its grip. It identified the M16A2 assault rifle in its hands by touch alone, subconsciously aware that it would hit any target it aimed the weapon at without error. It accepted that it knew how to kill.

"TM 05637."

The voice came through the helmet's built-in audio system. Though it did not recognize the speaker, it responded instantly to the inherent authority in the man's tone.

"Sir."

"A terrorist cell has captured one of our diplomats. The group's leader is threatening to execute her unless we release certain prisoners being held by the *local authorities*."

It heard the subtle emphasis, understanding the term as a convenient euphemism for the government of the country in which it was currently stationed.

"If she dies, we will be forced to retaliate. Some of the locals are sympathetic to the cell and don't object to the group operating within their borders. Loyalties might get tested and agreements set aside. The conflict could get ugly. We need to avoid that contingency. Rescue the diplomat. Take any necessary measures."

"Understood," it replied, acknowledging the unspoken command to eliminate all hostile targets.

"We will extract you and your target once you have secured her. Failure is not an option, TM 05637."

Light burst through the visor as the polarization adjusted to transparency. Its heightened visual acuity allowed it to take in the details of its location in an instant. Sand stretched out for endless miles in all directions, broken only by the barren rises of stone that revealed the scoured corpses of long-dead mountains. The rocky outcrop it was currently sheltered behind was situated in a shallow valley between two distant hills. Although the area appeared devoid of life, it could hear the scurrying of small creatures living in the cool, shadowy places beneath the rocks. The wind blew grains of sand into gently whirling columns, though the occasional gust turned the granules into a force that had the power to ground rock to dust over the course of millennia. The sand repelled harmlessly off its helmet while its uniform, sealed airtight at wrists and ankles, did not admit a single grain. Though its feet were protected by heavy boots, its hands were bare, the weapon held securely in its strong fingers.

Detecting a faint sound carried on the wind, it adjusted its hearing to better distinguish the auditory input. It discerned numerous voices—men, women, young, old. Some gruff, some frightened. A detailed map of the area filtered up through the haze of its spotty memory, once carefully studied but somehow forgotten. The terrorists were holed up in a nearby village, obviously intending to use the inhabitants as living shields against any air strikes.

For all the good it would do them.

Judging from the volume of the voices, it determined the village was three klicks due west of its current position. A quick but thorough scan of its immediate surroundings revealed no humans in the vicinity. It rose from behind its shelter and, looking out over the sea of rock and sand, detected the outlines of its destination against the bright glare of the desert sun. The large canvas and cloth structures were well built and sturdy enough to repel the desert's relentless assault. The tent village was the semipermanent residence of a nomadic tribe—families bound together by blood, marriage, and arrangement, clinging to a vanishing tradition.

"Treatment of collateral targets?" it asked.

"Leave them unharmed. We need to keep the locals friendly lest they decide the terrorists are more to their liking."

"Acknowledged."

It set off with a sudden burst of speed. While a more cautious approach may have been desirable, the lack of shelter between the outcrop and the village limited its options. It covered the first mile in slightly less than three minutes, its breathing steady and the rate of its heartbeat remaining unaltered from the exertion. The shapes of the tents soon crystallized, allowing it to distinguish them from the smaller moving figures roaming among them. Several dozen horses and three times as many people were visible within the campsite, which consisted of tents arranged in a series of concentric rings. The humans were all similarly dressed in loose, flowing garments, practical for the harsh environment. But while most of the figures were clothed in overlapping layers of brightly colored cloth, a few wore drab robes of gray and brown.

The crack of flesh against flesh preceded a woman's sharp cry. She wailed a frantic plea, only the sound enduring as her words were blown away by the ever-present wind. A guttural voice answered with obvious displeasure and annoyed frustration. At this distance it could just make them out through the haze of blowing sand. The woman was shielding her head uselessly with her arms as a man loomed over her, gesticulating with the barrel of an ancient, yet still deadly, AK-47 rifle toward her face.

Half a mile out, it aimed the M16A2 at the man's head, its smooth stride keeping the weapon on target. The silencer muzzled the bullet's report, and the terrorist fell without warning, the projectile boring a neat hole through his skull. One of the man's compatriots looked over at his fallen brother, astonishment writ plain on his face as he grasped that the other man was dead. He shouted, raising the alarm, and pointed frantically out into the desert. The figures wearing colored fabric melted away among the maze of tents, leaving the terrorists to face the unknown menace alone. The woman likewise seized the opportunity to flee as the terrorists shouted at each other in confusion, crawling on her hands and knees until she disappeared into the shadows.

The midmorning sun was behind it, blinding its opponents. It was on them before they comprehended the nature of the danger they faced. Three pulls of the trigger, and several more of the extremists joined their fellows in death.

"Where is it coming from? There are no planes!"

"Someone is out there!"

The language was not English, but it understood the words without difficulty. Two more shots took out the speakers. By then, it had reached the outermost ring of tents, and any chance the terrorists had to pick it off in the open had vanished.

Pressing its back against the closest tent, it paused for the reinforcements the dead men had alerted to arrive. It fixed its gaze out onto the shimmering landscape, depending on its ears to warn of approaching hazards. It didn't have to wait long. A boot scuffing against rock from the left prompted it to whirl in that direction, weapon at the ready. A man, his head wrapped in a scarf to shroud against the heat, ran carelessly from behind the tent as he rushed to answer the summons for help. A pair of reflective sunglasses hid the man's eyes, yet surprise was evident in his gaping jaw when he came face-to-face with the barrel of the assault rifle. The man had no time to react and was falling to the ground, shattered glasses covered with blood, even as another terrorist appeared in his wake. Having no time to readjust its aim, it pivoted into a back kick, driving its booted foot into the man's stomach. The newcomer's dun-colored robe blew up, revealing the brown pants he wore underneath as he went flying. A crunch indicated it had broken several of the man's ribs. *Threat neutralized.*

Abandoning its position, it rounded the tent in the direction from which the terrorists had approached, pausing only to gun down another man running recklessly toward him. The circular arrangement of the tents created neat rows and columns that defined the camp's interior layout. The well-worn ruts between the tents indicated the duration of the tribesman's residency, their roaming consistently leading them back to this place. The nomads had likely only recently returned, their absence having unfortunately invited the rogue cell to infiltrate the village.

Cautiously, it eased its way down a passage made narrow by the close press of the tents. It could hear additional voices raised in anger coming from up ahead, the commotion likely originating in the clearing at the center of the camp. It was the most defensible position and was almost certainly where it would find its target.

As it neared the next intersection between the rows of tents, a rifle barrel emerged from around the corner of the canvas wall immediately to its left. It grabbed the barrel and gave a sharp tug, pulling the would-be assailant into a raised elbow. The man's nose spurted blood, breaking implosively against the hard curve of bone. Hearing a shout from the right, it wrenched the dead man's gun from his limp hand and used the newly acquired weapon to take out the attacker. The stolen weapon clicked as it emptied, the chamber spent. Dropping the useless rifle to the ground, it listened closely for signs of new danger. Catching nothing except the blowing wind, it continued onward. Before it could go more than a few steps, the sound of a piteous sob made it whip around. One of the terrorists stood there, using a young boy as a shield. He leveled a handgun, aiming at its unprotected chest, while his other hand held a knife to the boy's throat.

"Drop your weapon, scum, or the boy dies!"

The child was crying, his wails nearly overpowering the snarled order. It took no notice of the distraught boy. The difference in height between the man and his captive left the terrorist's head exposed, and before the echo of his yell had faded away, a bullet was drilling its way out the back of the man's skull. The child screamed as blood splattered down on him from his captor's shattered head.

"Hide," it said in an uninflected monotone. It didn't wait to see if the youth had complied before turning back toward its objective.

The next two minutes saw the death of five more of the dwindling group of terrorists. Their political goals were irrelevant. Nothing mattered but the mission. When it finally reached the center of the camp, it crouched behind one of the sturdy tent walls and peered around the edge. The remaining terrorists had gathered their frightened prisoners into a group to prevent any of them from escaping. The guards numbered slightly over a handful. Taking them all out would not present much difficulty, though it calculated several of the civilians would likely perish in the crossfire.

"If you'll just let me contact the State Department, I promise you, I can get you what you want—"

A loud slap cut off the woman's plea. Identifying her location as the tent immediately ahead and to the right, it backed away from the clearing and moved stealthily toward the gaping opening of the tent. Rescuing the civilians was not its concern. Its task was to secure its target—nothing more.

It found the slit where the fabric parted to grant access to the structure's interior and eased the tip of the M16A2 into the gap. The shifting position of the sun angled a ray of light onto its back, throwing its shadow into sharp relief against the canvas. Knowing it had lost the element of surprise, it burst through the tent opening, hoping to catch its enemy off guard before the terrorist could react.

The interior of the tent was dim, light entering only through an overhead flap designed to provide ventilation for smoke from the currently unlit hearth. Its enhanced vision adjusting swiftly to the poor illumination, it saw that its opponent had dragged his hostage in front of him to act as a barrier between his body and the surprise attacker. The diplomat wore a tailored suit of burnt orange, a choice that went well with her brunette hair and dusky complexion. The shoulder seam of her jacket was torn, as were her stockings, and whatever shoes she'd been wearing were long gone. Her captor, by contrast, was dressed similarly to his compatriots, though the loose material of his desert-appropriate garb was unable to hide the breadth of his shoulders and his impressive height. If the group could claim a leader, this man was clearly it. But whereas the other terrorists had worn scarves and eyeshades to protect them from the sun and sand, the leader wore only a scrap of cloth that hid his face from nose to chin, leaving his uncovered eyes in shadow.

"Oh, thank God!" The diplomat slouched against the terrorist's grip, her posture radiating naked relief. Her expression rapidly morphed into fear when the terrorist pressed a gun against her temple.

"Silence, bitch."

The man's voice was a low growl, soft yet compelling obedience. Tightening its grip on the M16A2, it stepped closer to the incongruous pair. Something about the man's intense stare was unsettling, and an unfamiliar jolt of emotion made its throat suddenly feel uncomfortably tight. It struggled to get a clear view of the man's eyes but was inexplicably unable to penetrate the dimness.

"Hurt her, and you die." An underlying quiver threatened the characteristic flatness of its tone. "Let her go and my superiors will see your demands are met."

"What do you know of my demands?"

"Do not interact with the enemy, TM 05637." The commanding voice spoke through the helmet speakers, pitched so only it could hear. "Neutralize him and secure the package."

The leader wrapped an arm tightly around the diplomat's waist and pulled her firmly against him. For some reason, the sight of them standing so closely together interfered with its ability to breathe. It shook its head slightly to dispel the disquieting anomaly.

"Your comrades. You want them freed." It inched closer, never letting the aim of the rifle stray from the spot between the man's eyes. As it narrowed the distance between them, it could suddenly see the terrorist's eyes. Their color was odd, not the common brown or occasional green of the other men it had eliminated. The leader stared at him with an unwavering gaze of deep, vibrant blue.

"They are not what I want." The man's voice was a low caress.

"TM 05637, eliminate the target."

Swallowing to wet its dry throat, it edged a foot outward, slowly erasing more of the space separating it from the mysterious figure. "Then what do you want?"

Show your face, it willed silently. As though the man had heard the unspoken plea, he reached up and pulled away the concealing piece of cloth, letting it drift toward the ground. The clatter of a round chambering filled the tent, a discordant counterpoint to the keening cry that rose from the terrified woman as the handgun dug into her skull. Though every instinct it possessed screamed at it to rescue the hostage, to complete the mission, it stood there frozen, transfixed by the impossible familiarity of the man's face.

"TM 05637! Kill him!"

"I want you."

The gun's report crashed into the stunned silence. The diplomat's lifeless body dropped bonelessly to the ground.

"No!" I screamed, staring down at the crumpled figure in shock before looking back up at the man who'd killed her. "David?" The whisper was as much a question as a plea, and I soon followed the dead woman into the darkness of oblivion.

ONE

"I LOVE you, David. In spite of everything, I never lied about that."

"Tim, wait." *Despite his pleas, Tim turned around and began to walk away.* "Tim, don't go!" *The slight figure began to blur out of focus, swallowed by an impenetrable mist.* "Tim, please!" *David tried to run after him, but the air around him was so thick he could barely move. His limbs were useless, equally weighed down by the mysterious fog and an internal reluctance he couldn't deny. Tim had lied to him from the moment they'd met, and now, even in the face of his departure, David wasn't sure he wanted to know the truth. But neither was he ready to let the kid he'd grown to love simply walk out of his life without a fight.* "Tim!" *he shouted again.*

"He's not yours. He's mine."

A large menacing shadow rose up in front of David, stopping him in his burdened tracks. The uniform the man wore was vaguely military in design, but the stranger's features were indistinct, save for the burning ice-blue eyes that glared at him. The man lifted his hand, and David's heart clenched in fear as the object the man was holding resolved itself into a deadly looking weapon.

"No, don't!" *he begged.*

The stranger peeled his lips back in a wolfish grin as he pulled the trigger. David screamed, his body jerking helplessly as electricity passed through him in excruciating waves....

"No!"

The terrified cry lingered in the air as David sat up with a gasp, his skin itching with the phantom memory of intense pain. He groaned, pressing a hand to his head as the ache focused into a vicious pounding inside his skull.

"What the hell?"

The question was barely discernible even to his own ears, his voice rusty as though he hadn't spoken in ages. His mouth felt disgusting, like something had crawled inside of it and died. David gave himself a moment before opening his eyes, but when he finally did, he instantly regretted it. A flood of light shriveled his pupils, sending fresh stabs of agony into his head. The sensation was instantly followed by an even sharper pain between his legs. Fear prompted him to open his eyes fully, despite the agonizing brightness of the light. He got the impression of a white room—floor, ceiling, and walls—with nothing to break the blankness except for a small sink and steel toilet sitting in one corner. The only other fixtures included the cot he was lying on, a stand holding an IV bag next to the cot, and the various items attached to his body.

The sight of the IV bag was worrying enough. It was filled with a clear liquid, which was dripping into his arm through the tube taped to his skin. David had been in the hospital before—a case of appendicitis when he was sixteen—so he wasn't wholly unfamiliar with having needles stuck into his veins. But the tube coming from between his legs and out from underneath the hospital gown he was wearing was new to him. Wincing at the twinge in his groin, he peered over the edge of the cot and stared at the bag full of yellow fluid hanging from a hook conveniently attached to the side of the makeshift bed.

"What the hell...?" he repeated queasily.

"Are you all right? You've been unconscious for some time."

David's head whipped up at the unexpected response. He regretted his curiosity when the room immediately started spinning. Grabbing the side of the cot to keep from pitching over onto the floor, he took a deep breath to tamp down the impending nausea. A second, more cautious inspection confirmed that he was, indeed, alone in the room. The voice was male and wavered with advanced age, but otherwise, David was in the dark as to the speaker's identity. "What?" he asked intelligently, unable to marshal his thoughts sufficiently to ask the more salient questions of *where*, *how*, and *why*.

"I said, are you all right?"

"Uh…," David said, trying to figure out the answer to that question himself. He glanced down, flexing his arms and legs as he did. Nothing seemed to be broken, and nothing hurt, save for his head and whatever the heck was coming out of his groin. "I don't know," he replied. "There's, umm, this tube in my… er…."

"It's a catheter," the man replied, his tone calmly reassuring. "You've been here for over two weeks by my reckoning. They've kept you drugged up until now, so the catheter was a necessity."

David rubbed a hand over his face, the full beard that covered his jaw lending credence to the stranger's assertion. He cut his gaze toward the IV stand. "They're injecting me with something." He desperately wanted to know who "they" were, but the IV and the catheter warranted more immediate attention.

"I doubt it's a drug. Otherwise you wouldn't be awake. I'd leave it in," the stranger suggested. "It's probably a glucose drip. You haven't had any real food for a while now. You must be starving."

David's stomach reacted viscerally to the man's words, rumbling in instant agreement. The part of his body the catheter was penetrating once again expressed its disapproval of the invasion. "Okay, but this other thing has got to go. Hey!" he shouted for the benefit of whoever else might be listening. "Come get this thing out of me!"

"Save your breath. They'll come for you when they're good and ready, and not a moment sooner. But don't worry. You simply need to take it out."

"Take it out?" David had figured out the voice was coming from his right, and he looked doubtfully toward the wall in that direction. "I don't know. Shouldn't a doctor do that or something?"

The man chuckled. "I am a doctor. Well, more a scientist these days, but close enough. Trust me, it will be fine. Just ease it out slowly."

David was about to protest, but another spike of pain changed his mind. "Shit," he mumbled before reaching between his legs to take the tube gingerly between his first two fingers and his thumb. Drawing in a deep breath, he began to pull. "Ugh!" The plastic tube burned as it scraped along his urethra. David had no idea what damage he might be causing, but anything was better than leaving the damn thing in. After a long minute of pulling and cursing, the tube came free. Sweating and shaking, David threw it to the floor, ignoring the trickles of urine that dripped from the end of the tube onto white tiles. Unfortunately, his relief was short-lived. It was like the catheter had been holding back the tide, and once the dam had broken, the flood would not be denied. David nearly fell to his knees after he scrambled off the cot, his legs, weak from disuse, struggling to support him. Somehow he managed to drag himself and the IV stand over to the toilet before he could embarrass himself. Sighing with relief, he used the last of his energy to push on the flush handle before sinking to the floor, too exhausted to make it back to the bed.

"Thanks," David said hoarsely as he braced his back against the wall separating him from his mysterious neighbor. "Now, tell me, where the hell am I? Who are you? And where is Tim?" He said the last without any hesitation, having no doubt his erstwhile lover was involved with him being wherever he was. As his mind cleared, David grasped that his dreams of Tim were muddled memories, which were becoming clearer with every passing second. He could still hear Tim shouting his name in the instant before the Taser had rendered him unconscious.

"You're in a place called the Facility. This is where the boy— Tim, you called him? This is where Tim was raised." A smile entered the man's voice. "I like that name. Did you give it to him?"

Hoping further explanations were forthcoming, David forcibly pushed back the myriad of questions the enigmatic response had raised in his mind. "No," he answered. "That's what he told me his name was when we met."

"And when was this?"

David thought back. "A little over three months ago." Had it really been such a short time? David could hardly believe his life had been turned so completely upside down so quickly.

"Ah," the man replied. "Then he wasn't on his own for too long. That's good." A pause. "How much did he tell you about himself?"

It's not a he. It's an it. TM 05637 is an escaped lab experiment, a rabid dog that got off its leash.

David closed his eyes to dispel the memory of the grizzled soldier's taunting revelation. "Not enough, apparently." His arm twinged slightly, and he rubbed a hand over the site where the bullet had grazed him, feeling a dull ache but little pain. He raised the loose arm of the gown and saw only a pinkish scar, the stitches having already been removed. The stranger must have been right about how long he'd been there for him to have healed that much. David remembered how Tim had so expertly stitched up the gunshot wound. It had been one of the many mysteries surrounding the kid, though David realized now that he'd barely scratched the surface.

"Hmm. That's not surprising. The boy was trained from a very early age not to reveal his identity to anyone."

"Who are you?" David repeated more forcefully. He was tired of being kept in the dark and was desperate for any information that might help him make sense of his current predicament.

The man sighed. "A ghost. No, don't mind me," he continued when David scoffed at the odd response. "I'm just being maudlin. The privileges of old age. And heaven knows I carry enough guilt to be doomed to such a hapless eternity." The man took a deep breath, the inhalation audible even through the wall. "I'm Dr. Paul Anderson, Tim's creator."

Father Paul. David remembered the times Tim had talked about the man, and now, out of the blue, here he was. Not that the added qualification shed any light on the situation. "His creator?" David echoed, confused by the strange terminology. "What, are you his father? And aren't you supposed to be dead?"

Anderson chuckled. "Fortunately, I've so far managed to avoid that particular fate, though Tim couldn't have known I survived. And, yes, I am his father in every way that matters. Part of his basic genetic makeup is derived from my own DNA. But more importantly, I designed those parts of Tim no one else on the planet shares. The parts which make him special."

David's head began to throb again, as much from his inability to make sense of Anderson's explanation as from the lack of food and the drug still lingering in his system. "I don't understand," he said flatly, pain lowering his tolerance level for cryptic bullshit.

"Tim is human, but his genetic code was altered to give him enhanced abilities. He can see farther, hear better, and run faster. He is three times as strong as a man his size would normally be, and his rate of healing is five times greater than the average person's. He was trained and drilled in every advanced combat tactic the military could devise nearly from the moment he was born, including hand-to-hand fighting and extensive weaponry. In short, Tim is a genetically enhanced supersoldier possessing superior combat abilities, designed to execute covert infiltration, espionage, and target elimination. He is the perfect weapon, created to feel nothing, want nothing. His only purpose is completing his mission."

David's mind whirled at the startling revelation. Tim wasn't human? No, was more than human. *How could I not have realized it?* David asked himself. In hindsight, it should have been apparent that the strange kid he'd picked up off the side of the highway was simply too perfect to be real. David thought back to all of the incidents and moments with Tim he had found so confusing then, but which now made perfect sense. The way Tim had seemed so awkward when they'd first met. His cold and emotionless demeanor, like he had no clue how regular, everyday interactions worked. Tim's relentless pursuit of Bobby Wood, the young shoplifter who'd eventually become his closest friend, had been startling at the time, but suddenly didn't seem so crazy in light of what Anderson had told him.

And, of course, David couldn't help but remember Tim's thorough and brutally precise dismantling of Bobby's father, Don, the night they'd rescued the boy from his abusive parent. Tim had been merciless, the viciousness of his attack even more disturbing now that David knew for certain Tim had been utterly capable of killing that self-loathing asshole. But neither could he forget how, after they'd gone home, Tim had begged David not to hate him, pleading at first with words and then with his body....

David ruthlessly halted that particular train of thought, shying away from memories he couldn't deal with right then. "So, what?" he forced himself to ask. "You sent him out on some sort of training mission? 'Find some gullible dope and trick him into taking you in'?" His stomach twisted into a knot at the notion that Tim had merely been using him. He swallowed past the lump in his throat, unaware until right then how deep his feeling of betrayal went. "Was that his objective?" He found he couldn't voice his real question. *Had any of it been real?*

"There was no mission, Mister…?"

"Conley." The people who had taken him captive probably already knew who he was, so there was no harm in being honest. "David Conley."

"As I said, Mr. Conley, there was no mission. You asked me if I am Tim's father. Well, I am, and as his father, I wanted my boy to be free. To know the world beyond the walls where he was warped into becoming a killer. What parent wouldn't want a normal life for his son?"

"You're the one who helped him escape from here," David guessed. "That's why they locked you up."

"Yes," Anderson replied bluntly. "The people in charge of this project, perhaps they meant well at the start, but somewhere along the way they forgot they were dealing with a living, breathing human being." He sighed heavily. "No, *we* forgot. I deserve as much of the blame as anyone, if not more. I was in charge of the research side of the project, responsible for manipulating Tim's DNA until he was precisely what we wanted him to be."

"Are there others like him?"

Anderson made a strangled sound. "No. None of the others lived. Tim was the first to be born alive." The scientist stopped speaking for so long, David was beginning to wonder if something had happened to him. When he began again, his voice was weak and tired. "I have committed so many sins I know I can never be forgiven for them. We recruited surrogates, hired young women to gestate the embryos I designed. Several of them died in the process, their bodies unable to cope with the aberrant chemical makeup of the children they carried. But after years of trying, Tim was finally born, and he was as perfect as I'd dreamed he could be. I did what I thought was right letting him go, but, of course, Talbot and the general disagreed," he added with a humorless chuckle.

The latter sparked a memory in David's mind. "The general?"

"General Woodard. I suspect you've met him already. He was in charge of retrieving Tim after I helped the boy escape. I had hoped Tim would be able to permanently avoid detection, to keep a step ahead of the search parties, but it seems I underestimated Woodard's determination."

He got caught because of me. David didn't voice the thought out loud, not sure how much he wanted to share regarding his time with Tim. He couldn't be sure Anderson's openness wasn't part of some plot to get him to reveal details about Tim's life away from the Facility. But if Anderson was telling the truth and Tim's unexpected entry into his life wasn't some ploy, then surely he had something to do with Tim's decision to settle down in Lubbock, at least for a while, rather than remaining on the run. Or so he hoped. The possibility that

Tim's profession of love had been a lie was too painful to contemplate.

"You mentioned another name," David said instead, calling himself a coward but changing the subject all the same. "Talbot. Who is he?"

"She," Anderson corrected. "Coleen Talbot. She is the liaison between the military branch of the operation and the Company, the group which financed the project."

"The Company? The Facility?" David's bark of laugh held no amusement. "God, I feel like I'm in some shitty spy novel."

"You're not wrong." Anderson's smile was evident in his tone. "Talbot is just as dedicated to the success of TM project as the general. Perhaps even more so."

TM project. Tim. Even the name the kid had given him had been nothing more than a clever disguise. David waited for Anderson to elaborate, but after several minutes of silence, he realized the scientist intended to say nothing else about this Talbot woman.

"So, why didn't Woodard simply kill me back at the house?" he asked. It had been bugging him ever since he'd regained his memories of the night the general had barged so dramatically into his life and stolen Tim away. "What does he want with me?" David knocked his head back against the featureless wall in annoyance. "And what the hell is he doing to Tim?" He hadn't forgotten the way the scientist had previously dodged that particular question.

"I have my suspicions about Tim's fate," Anderson answered after a long moment, "and I fear it's nothing good. As for why Woodard kidnapped you instead of eliminating you, I can't say for certain. It's likely you will find out soon enough."

David could hear the concern in Anderson's voice and didn't like the implication. When he'd discovered he was alive, though a prisoner, he'd prayed his ordeal was coming to an end. Apparently that had been a naïve hope. "So, what now?"

"Now, we wait. Tell me, Mr. Conley, what are your feelings for Tim?"

Startled by the blunt question, David hesitated. What did he feel for Tim? Before Woodard had shattered their lives, he would have been able to respond immediately and with complete conviction. But now he wasn't so confident in his answer. Even if Anderson was being truthful and his meeting Tim had merely been a fortunate accident, there was no telling if his creation shared his motivations. Tim may have simply decided to use his freedom to hone his skills by duping some unsuspecting guy into taking care of him. David's lack of certainty began to color his own emotions, and he could only think of one thing to say that would be completely truthful.

"I loved him." David winced at his equivocal usage of the past tense. Yet even his ambivalence failed to completely kill his lingering hope that, somehow, he and Tim could get out of this and go back to the way things had been before. "Is there any chance he could become something other than a soldier?" he asked, pointedly avoiding the other labels Anderson had used. Dozens of images of Tim—nervous, hopeful, shy, beautiful—floated through his mind's eye. How could Tim have faked all of that? David still remembered how amazed and happy he'd been as Tim had slowly opened up. The kid had thoroughly become a part of their lives, his and Bobby's and the other employees of Barry's Bargain Warehouse, the large retail franchise David owned and managed. Not to mention the way his mother, Suzanna, had taken to Tim. He didn't want to believe she could be so easily fooled, even if he had been. "Is there some way to save him?" David asked, the sincerity of the question catching him by surprise. Whatever his feelings for Tim, he couldn't stand the thought of the kid being at the mercy of the cold-eyed bastard who had so cruelly put an end to their quiet life together.

"That depends on him," Anderson replied carefully, "and on how much you care for him. I helped Tim escape from here so he might come to understand there is more to this life than what he was created to do. That he can be his own master if he chooses to be. But so long as Woodard and Talbot have their claws in him...." His voice wavered. "There's nothing either of us can do."

So help me get him out. Before David could voice the thought, he heard coughing through the wall separating them. "Are you okay?"

"My apologies," Anderson managed before his words were disrupted by another harsh bout of coughing. "I'm afraid I've been unwell and need to rest these old bones of mine."

David heard a stifled moan of pain and wondered if Anderson had been injured somehow. Accepting that their conversation was over for the time being, David made his way back to his cot, grimacing in disgust as he stepped over the bag and tube that had been emptying his bladder while he lay unconscious. He still couldn't believe it had been so long, almost two weeks if Anderson's guess was correct. His employees must be worried sick, not to mention his mother if she was aware of his disappearance. Had they called the police? Didn't the Fourth Amendment have something to say about the military simply snatching people out of their homes?

Sighing at his pointlessly spinning thoughts, David tried as best he could to get comfortable. The drugs his captors had used to keep him under hadn't completely left his system, and he realized he was exhausted as well as famished. Deciding sleep was the best way to deal with both problems, he closed his eyes, visions of gorgeous brown eyes and a sweet, bashful smile haunting him as he fell into slumber.

PEARL LOVE has been writing since she was a kid, but it was the pretty boys who frolic around in her head who finally convinced her to pursue it seriously. She's a Midwest transplant who currently thrives in the hustle and bustle of the nation's capital. A jack of many genres, she enjoys just about any type of story, so long as in the end, the boy gets the boy. Pearl is a Marvel fangirl and owns a ridiculously large stash of yarn and knitting needles.

You can contact Pearl at pearllove925@gmail.com.
Visit her website at http://pearllovebooks.com;
Facebook: Pearl Love (pearllove925@gmail.com); and
Twitter: pearllovebooks.

http://www.dreamspinnerpress.com

www.ingramcontent.com/pod-product-compliance
Lightning Source LLC
Chambersburg PA
CBHW070046030726
47506CB00002B/373